A
Little
Murder

Cindy Davis

L & L Dreamspell
Spring, Texas

Cover and Interior Design by L & L Dreamspell

This is a work of fiction, and is produced from the author's imagination. People, places and things mentioned in this novel are used in a fictional manner.

ISBN: 978-1-60318-100-6

Library of Congress Control Number: 2008944383

Visit us on the web at www.lldreamspell.com

Published by L & L Dreamspell
Printed in the United States of America

Acknowledgements:

Mega-thanks to my writers group: Dee, Jen
and Susan for their tireless reading of early
drafts. And to John and Jane for their spot-on
critiques.

This book is for Bob.
He knows why.

One

What was that, a fire alarm? He shot into a sitting position clutching the foam pillow in rigid fingers, sniffed and smelled nothing. He heaved the pillow aside and thumped the other side of the bed with his knuckles. "Fire. The house is on fire!"

He kicked off the tangle of sheets and reached for his pants on the chair beside the bed. The small alarm clock's red LED proclaimed four-thirty. He called out "fire" again then realized the other side of the bed was empty. "Fire!"

The phone rang again, jarring his ears like a right hook to the head. "Damn." With a weighty sigh, he dropped on the bed and picked up the receiver. "Hello."

"Where the hell have you been?"

"Asleep. Sometimes people—"

"I got a job for you."

"I have one already."

Silence pounded the phone line for a ten-count, then, "This is related to the other."

"Not today, okay? Tomorrow."

"The Rottweiler got out of the kennel again."

Damn.

"It needs to be put down before it hurts somebody. He's gone rabid."

"How do you expect me to do it without being seen?" Why argue? It never did any good. Unable to stop himself, he tried again. "There'll be witnesses. I'll be a…"

The line went dead.

"…sitting duck." He slammed down the receiver and raked shaky fingers through his hair. How the hell had he gotten in so deep? How had things gone so wrong?

"Who was that?"

She stood silhouetted in the doorway. How much had she heard? "Nobody. It was nothing. You can go back to sleep."

"It didn't seem like nothing. You sounded angry."

"You should try and get back to sleep."

"Can't. It's time to get up."

Two

"Sometimes a decision comes back to bite you in the ass," Angie Deacon's grandfather used to say. He was full of *isms*. She never understood what most of them meant; she always thought they were things old people said to make kids think they were intelligent. She would listen politely then plant a kiss on his craggy cheek and run off to play with her brother.

Today, the 7th of July, Angie was finally able to put meaning with Granddad's sentiment. A month ago, she'd bought a day on a fishing tour boat for her husband Will's fiftieth birthday. A month ago, it seemed like a great idea. Now, with choppy waves lolling the boat like a pendulum, the idea seemed very bad. Her stomach kept time to the insane rhythm of the water.

Seasickness wasn't the only way her decision had bitten her in the ass—or stomach, if she were to be literal. Lately, Will had grown distant. He claimed it was just their brutal work schedules: her nights as an ER nurse, his days selling real estate. She'd tried everything she knew to get things back on track. The end of the month would be their twenty-sixth anniversary; any relationship could feel stagnant in that length of time. That was another reason for the trip. Maybe a relaxing day on the lake, doing something Will enjoyed, would return the proverbial pep to his step.

Angie leaned back in the plastic bucket chair watching the big bouncer-type Jamaican, Montez Clarke, trying to carry on a conversation with her husband. "Check out this one. Two weeks ago I caught a twenty-pounder on it." He held up a silver fish-shaped lure with a half-dozen barbed hooks dangling from it. Will nodded and reeled in his line. "And this," Montez dangled something red in the air near Will's nose, "won me the fishing derby here last year." Again Will nodded, then checked his bait. What the hell was wrong with him?

Montez gave a one-shoulder shrug and lumbered back to his spot at the stern. He had wide, thick shoulders and nappy hair cut so short scalp showed through.

To cover the awkward moment, Angie asked, "Which lure are you using now?"

He cast the line like a pro; the lure settled in the water—an Olympic diver scoring a perfect 10. He set the bale then dropped the rod in the plastic holder attached to the gunwale of the thirty-seven foot pontoon fishing boat before turning to her. "No lure. Crawlers."

Over coffee on the way to this spot, Montez had introduced himself as a computer repairman from Nashua, which contradicted Angie's introductory image of the man. His delightful Jamaican accent conjured visions of palm trees and tiki bars. Montez smiled a lot, showing big square Chiclet teeth. That wide smile died just once on this trip, when his friend Sonnie asked a simple question: "The boss say what time?" Montez had shot him a vicious scowl and gestured to the pair of black duffel bags they'd carried aboard. One of them had been on the deck near Montez's feet. Big, wide feet. But after Will had shown interest in them, Montez lugged it to the bow and placed it beside Sonnie's.

The bags were about the size of rolled up quilts, and stuffed full, if the bulges were any indication. Angie wondered if she'd brought enough clothes; perhaps it got very cold out on the water. Right now, it was a beautiful day; the sun playing diamonds on the water's surface, and not too much humidity. At least, it would be a nice day if she could get her mind off Will's mood. Better still, if she could get *Will's* mind off his mood. He poked the hook through a worm and cast the line out, careful to stay away from the overhanging branches on Rattlesnake Island. The boat's owner Nolan Little said this was one of the best places to catch lakers—she assumed that meant lake trout—in the whole of Lake Winnipesaukee, New Hampshire.

The roar of a motor brought her attention to the stern. About twenty yards back, a motorboat looking all weighed down by the huge motor on the stern zigged from behind another boat and zoomed toward them at an ungodly speed. Both Montez and Will shouted for the single occupant to pay attention. Angie clutched the chair arms, bracing for the collision. She scrunched her eyes shut when the big horsepower motor revved even louder, closer.

No crash.

She opened her eyes to see the boat disappearing around the far side of the island.

A moment later its wake hit the stern. The boat lurched. Angie's insides swayed and rolled. What had possessed her to come on a boat? What would've been wrong with tickets to a Red Sox game?

Buck up, it's only eight hours.

Yeah, and Gilligan's was only a three-hour tour.

"What happened?" Valerie Little stepped from the cabin, wiping her hands on a towel.

"Some idiot in a motorboat," Montez said.

"Did you get the registration number? I'll call Marine Patrol."

"He was going too fast. Couldn't read it."

"What did he look like? I'll report him anyway."

"Fourteen, maybe sixteen-foot aluminum boat with a big Evinrude. One person wearing a white tee-shirt and a blue baseball cap."

Valerie disappeared into the galley: a room set dead center of the boat, the front, back and left sides were all glass. Valerie faced the right-side wall, running one index finger down what was probably a list of emergency phone numbers. The other hand pulled a cell phone from a back pocket. She dialed, spoke a moment, nodding and gesturing to the end of the island where the boat had vanished.

Angie listened but couldn't hear the growl of the motorboat any more. Perhaps he'd capsized the thing. It would serve him right. Valerie put away the phone and went back to what she'd been doing. A small woman, she stood barely over five feet. Her clothes, jeans and a pink tank top underneath a pink checked blouse with four buttons undone, were inexpensive but clean. Valerie had probably been pretty back in school. Hair the color of café au lait, with eyes the exact same color, as if purposely color coordinated. But she looked tired. As if she'd been—to use another of Angie's grandfather's *isms*—"rode hard and put away wet."

Montez's friend Sonnie Phelps was also big and dark-skinned. But that's where the resemblance stopped. Sonnie had shoulder length dreadlocks and an expression that could send puppies squealing for cover. He stood at the right—which Angie thought was the starboard—side of the bow, bracing a thick leg against the gunwale. "Got one," he announced. He held the rod a second, gauging the motion of the fish.

Valerie came from the galley, again wiping her hands. This time she tucked the towel through a belt loop of her jeans and walked along the narrow aisleway connecting bow to stern. After a minute, the fish was brought over the railing, squirming and wiggling. Like a pro, Valerie removed the hook and carried it to the stern. Sonnie re-baited the hook and cast the line out.

Valerie measured and weighed the trout, calling out the vital statistics so Sonnie could hear: 16", 3.7 pounds. Then she dropped it in the fish well in the deck. With the action of the water, the boat had turned on its anchor line. The sun crested the tops of the trees and shone under the metal canopy directly in Angie's eyes. She lowered her sunglasses from atop her head and set them on her nose.

"Do you need sunscreen?" Valerie asked, wiping her hands on the towel.

"I'm all set, thanks. Do you need help in the kitch—the galley?"

"No thanks. I'm about finished getting lunch ready."

Angie's stomach did a flip-flop. "Gosh, it's not time to eat is it?"

Valerie smiled in a non-patronizing manner. Angie looked away. It wasn't her fault she got seasick.

"In about an hour."

Will turned a bucket chair to face his rod, giving Angie a silhouette view. He had a classic face. Dark hair, always precisely trimmed. Perfect nose. Great lips. Kissable lips. She remembered the times she'd feathered her fingertips around them. He'd purse his lips and suck her finger inside his mouth. Then he'd kiss each finger in turn. The familiar tingle of passion—okay so, it wasn't so familiar the last few months—grew with the frenzied power of a thunderstorm. Angie clenched her eyes shut, willing the sensations to leave her lower body. She opened her eyes, and saw Montez's big brown eyes watching; his wide lips wore an oh-so-knowing smile. He nodded and went back to his fishing. God, she was so humiliated.

She rotated her chair away from both men. She couldn't get in trouble facing the bow of the big boat. A big boat was something Angie double checked before making the reservations. It was most important for Will to have a good time today, but size and the fact that it had pontoons, lent the image of safety and reliability, two things that made seasickness a lot easier to cope with. Along with a container of Dramamine.

Valerie stood in the doorway of the glassed cockpit attached to the front side of the galley. This was her husband Nolan's domain, from where he piloted the boat. Angie could see a bit of the control panel and the back of a vinyl high-backed chair. Nolan sat in the chair, his shoulder leaning against the left-side wall. Valerie had her hands on her hips and was bent slightly toward him.

Angie had seen Nolan just once so far today. As they left the dock, a lean blonde man had come sprinting down the pier shouting for them to wait up. The newcomer had boy-next-door looks, defined but not hard muscles, expensive clothes and a pristine haircut. Angie's grandfather would call him a pansy. The only thing marring the stranger's appearance—the whisper of stubble around his chin. This person hadn't gone home last night.

When he said, "I wonder if you've got room for another customer," it reminded Angie of Thurston Howell the Third, from Gilligan's Island. Two images in one day about the old TV show brought a grin.

At the appearance of the classy intruder, Nolan had marched around the corner of the galley, sandy blond curls bouncing. Lake mist clung to the locks like frost on a margarita glass. Wide muscular shoulders and thick neck—he might have been a football star in another life—but this life had taken his bright blue eyes and nicely shaped lips and mashed them into perpetual scowls, two things not at all sexy or charming. Angie wondered what sort of life events made a person so unhappy to be alive.

Nolan had planted white boatshoes on the stern deck, gave the intruder the once-over and said simply, "No."

"Nolan," Valerie said. "We're licensed to carry six."

"We only take customers with reservations."

"Bet he has a dozen reservations," Sonnie had muttered. "I always do."

Everyone laughed except Nolan who fired a glare at Sonnie that could melt the Arctic. The newcomer reached for his back pocket. On television, that move often produced a gun or a switchblade. "I'll pay cash." He waved three one-hundred dollar bills, twice the usual fare for one person.

Nolan stopped him with, "Money's not the issue."

"I don't mind if he comes along," Montez said.

"Neither do I," Angie had added. Will was the only one who hadn't spoken up.

So, Tyson Goodwell, from Manhattan, climbed aboard, and

was fitted with a rod on the port side of the bow rail. Right now, he sat in one of the white chairs, rod balanced on the rail. Every now and then, if the wind blew just right, Angie heard him whistling. It sounded like the theme from Gilligan's Island. She grinned.

The smile was killed by a shrill scream from Valerie.

Three

Angie ran along the narrow aisleway and shouldered her way into the cockpit doorway beside Valerie. There was little doubt Nolan was dead; deep brown eyes that had squinted at Tyson with contempt were now vacant pools. Cheeks once flush with life now drooped like used teabags. Besides…a six-inch filet knife protruded from his chest. Every sway of the boat threatened to dump him in the ever-widening spill of blood under the tall chair.

Angie avoided stepping in the mess and bent forward, bracing a palm on the doorframe. She touched two fingers to Nolan's carotid. Nothing. She tried the wrist. Still nothing.

Time to call authorities. She backed from the cockpit, into the towering wall of Montez Clarke. He lowered his Foster Grants and frowned over the top of the frame. He looked at Valerie, then Nolan, then Angie and resettled the glasses on the bridge of his wide nose. All he said was, "Shit."

A thick breeze whistled around the island and hit the boat head-on. Somehow Nolan's body shifted an inch to the left. Somehow he didn't topple over. The knife's brass rivets glinted in the sun. A tackle box lay open on the floor under the stool. Blood, puddling in the small orange compartments and coating the lures and assorted tackle in goo, had already begun coagulating. Angie couldn't see a knife in the box.

Montez spared a pokerfaced glance at the tackle box. "What a frigging mess." The blatant Americanism smothered his musical

Jamaican accent. His words carried dual, perhaps triple, meaning. Their lives and perhaps reputations would be turned upside down. Hours of interrogation, days of scrutiny, perhaps weeks of suspicion. Suddenly the air over Lake Winnipesaukee turned claustrophobic. Angie pushed around Montez, and then Sonnie who peered over her head at Nolan and said, "God damn."

Her sentiments exactly.

"Help me, will ya?" Sonnie whispered.

"Sure, what with?"

"Dumpin' him overboard. We'll..."

"Sonnie, don't fool around like that."

"... get the others to swear Valerie took the boat out alone."

"Sonnie!"

"Nolan stayed home sick. When she got back, he was gone. Disappeared without a trace."

"Get serious, will you?"

He removed his sunglasses. The expression issuing from the dark eyes said he *was* serious; that if he were alone, the body would've already done a Houdini. Angie pictured him sauntering up the dock brushing his hands together in a self-congratulatory job-well-done. She turned away.

At the port rail, Tyson was on his feet but had remained in place. Angie met up with Will halfway along the aisle. "What's going on?" he asked.

"Nolan's dead. I need your cell."

His expression as he drew the phone from the leather belt holder mirrored her thoughts—why did this have to happen today of all days?

She dialed 911. "I'd like to report a murder. I'm on the Little Fishing Tour boat. We're anchored off," she looked back toward their port of origin, Alton Bay, "the southeast edge of Rattlesnake Island."

"Get everyone away from the immediate scene," the dispatcher ordered, "help will be there in a few minutes."

Angie handed the phone toward Will, but he wasn't there. He

stood in the cockpit beside a sober-faced Valerie, with a hand on her shoulder. He said something in her ear. She shook her head. He put his other hand on her arm and urged her from cockpit. She fought him a moment and Montez stepped up to help. He took Valerie's other arm. They had to turn sideways to move along the aisle. At one point, she stopped, gathered her arms around herself and hunched over. And started to wail. The sound grew louder as she unfolded and stood up straight. Will encouraged her to move. That's when she lurched against the rail. Angie thought she was the only one who saw the glitter of metal and the flicker of a splash as Valerie threw something in the water.

Will settled Valerie in a chair. Angie dragged hers up on the left of it. She sat and put her arm around the woman's shoulders.

"They said to get everyone away from the scene," Angie told Will. He'd just placed a chair to Valerie's right. He nodded and strode to the bow.

Across from Angie, Montez sat near his rod, stretching his long body out straight. His brown penny loafers had been shined to a high gloss. His jeans bore a crease. He had on a Bob Marley t-shirt. Angie nearly threw up. Dead center of his chest, a three-inch bloodstain stood out like a Rorschach inkblot on white cardboard. To her it looked like a squashed tomato. Or a…her mind scrambled for comparison, and came up with none.

Montez jabbed a thumb at the spot. "From when I punched him in the nose."

Except for her unrelenting queasiness, the confrontation with Nolan was the only thing marring the trip to the island. Valerie had been having trouble with something under the galley sink. Montez went to help out. Nolan had turned on his stool and glowered bullets at him through the cockpit window. Montez finished helping Valerie and marched to the bow. Between the hum of the motor and whoosh of water against the pontoons, Angie could only hear Montez's: "…hell's your problem?" and Nolan's: "…off my wife." Montez had laughed. Nolan poked a finger several times in his chest. Montez took it for a few seconds, then reared back and popped Nolan in the nose. Then Montez strode up front to where Sonnie high-fived him. Montez returned to his fishing and all had been quiet. Till Valerie's scream.

Was that incident enough motivation for Montez to do murder? Angie didn't think so, but she was from a different world than people like Montez. No, it wasn't fair to judge him because his skin was a different color.

Will returned with an angry Sonnie and a red-cheeked Tyson. A smudge of something brown stained the left calf of his tan Dockers. Sonnie flopped into a chair. The plastic creaked and threatened to give way. Tyson glanced around for a place to sit. The only other chair was between Sonnie and Montez. Angie nearly grinned. She'd think twice about being bookended by such ominous-looking men too.

Valerie fell forward, burying her face in her hands, crooning "No no no," in a low voice. Then she began sobbing in great wheezing gasps that seemed to rattle the deck beneath their feet. Angie pulled her close. Valerie's hair smelled like a mixture of pennies and fish.

Just behind them, Will stood with both hands on the rail, his head bowed. She untangled herself from Valerie, went to him and wrapped her arms around him from behind. Startled, he looked up. His left arm came around her. "You all right?" she asked, leaning in.

"Sure." He glanced at Valerie whose shoulders were shaking with her grief. "We'd better go to her." They returned to their seats on either side of Valerie.

Tyson's red cheeks had faded somewhat but he was still obviously distressed. He threw a helpless shrug at Angie. Sonnie, who'd stretched out in the same manner as Montez, checked his watch. He folded forward and leaned across Tyson to frown at Montez. "You know what's gonna happen we don't get back—"

Montez's head tilted back against the rail, his eyes closed. "Chill man," was his only reaction.

"Big trouble."

"Shut up."

"If we're late."

Montez propelled himself upright and shot across a very startled Tyson. "Shut...the fuck...up."

Val stopping crying long enough to see what was going on. She dropped her head back in her hands. Will stretched an arm around her shoulders. Angie gave him a smile, thankful to have such a considerate man for a husband.

Sonnie tried again. "You don't f-ing get it."

"Got it. Can't change it."

Tyson perked to life, eyeing each of the men. "What appointment could be so important—"

"Stay out of this," Sonnie grumbled.

Tyson shook his head. "You can't get off the boat. Deal with it."

This was getting ridiculous. "Sonnie, why don't you just jump over the rail and swim to your stupid appointment?" Angie offered.

Sonnie's hands, spread flat on his wide thighs, bent into fists. Tyson dissolved back in the chair. She didn't flinch, even when Sonnie pulled his feet under him and stabbed a long finger at her. "Enough from you."

"Leave her alone," Will said.

Sonnie's finger swung left. "Stay out of this."

"Leave my husband alone. It's not his fault you—"

Sonnie flew at her. "Not his fault I what?"

"You know what I'm talking about."

"Stop! Just stop it, all of you!" Val shouted.

Everyone did indeed, shut up. Angie patted Val's thigh. "Sorry," was all she could think to say.

Emotions ran high, the only possible explanation for her outburst. Then again, maybe she felt a subconscious desire for everyone to know of Sonnie's offer to throw Nolan overboard.

Why? Wasn't the offer merely a gut reaction to the situation, a way to deal with overwrought nerves?

Still, Valerie didn't deserve this. Angie hugged her close. Suddenly she wondered if she comforted a killer, and stifled the instinctive reaction to get up and jump overboard.

If Valerie hadn't killed Nolan, someone on board had. Perhaps Sonnie Phelps, lounging in the too-small chair, oozing suspicion like sweat. Or Montez, in retaliation for the argument. Any of them could have picked up that filet knife and done the unthinkable.

Question was, who would kill someone when there were so many potential witnesses and no chance of escape? Something to ponder, but something more immediate pressed its question into the atmosphere: what if the killer wasn't finished? What if he planned to do an *And Then There Were None* and slaughter everybody on board?

God, it was hot here.

Regardless of what the following weeks might entail, might do to Will's reputation as a business owner, Angie never felt such relief as when Marine Patrol sirens screamed up the lake. Boats rushed at them from all directions throwing up plumes of water that looked like the approach of a flock of peacocks. Val's sobbing grew louder in proportion to that of the looming authorities. Will stopped moving his hand in a circle on her back long enough to send Angie a sober smile. Her return smile died almost immediately when Sonnie said, "Christ it's frigging ninety-five degrees, why is your husband wearing a jacket?"

Four

Detective Colby Jarvis eyed the unusual collection of people out for a day of fishing on the lake: two bouncer-type black guys, a wuss, and, except for some bloody smudges on the woman's shirt, a couple who looked more suited to shopping than fishing. Tourists! He stifled a grunt. The only time anybody said a kind word to cops was after being rescued from an emergency. Otherwise cops didn't exist.

The couple comforted the dead guy's wife, whose head was bowed, shoulders shaking with grief. People faking sorrow usually cried a while then looked up to see who was paying attention. This one didn't. Her shoulders heaved, just like the damned boat every time a rubbernecker motored past. Now and then she sniffled and coughed. A good actress? He'd soon find out.

If she hadn't killed her husband, one of the others had. As the launch pulled up, Dreadlocks and the wussy one had been arguing. Their discussion stopped as Jarvis stepped foot on the deck. What could those two have to quarrel about: who had the prettiest hairdo? Jarvis tightened his lips against the grin that threatened.

What about the black guys? They only looked marginally more suited to a day of fishing than Wuss. They obviously knew each other, but there was a tension between them, and Jarvis couldn't wait to get to the bottom of it.

God, he loved the hunt.

Where the hell was the blood? Nobody but the dead guy's wife had an appreciable amount on them. Big deal, the killer changed clothes and dumped 'em overboard.

Not easy on a boat like this. Someone was bound to see.

Sure, like somebody witnessed the murder.

He frowned up at the pulsating sun. Probably sunburned his head right through the damned hat. He pulled off the Deerstalker and ran sweaty fingers through sweatier hair. The blonde looked at him and he slapped the hat back on. Had she noticed his bald spot?

Why it mattered he didn't know; she seemed happily married, the look she gave the husband told of a long-time relationship. Jarvis patted the hat tighter to his skull. He should question her first. An observant one, she watched things but pretended not to.

Then again, maybe best to begin with the Jamaican, take that over-confident attitude down a peg or two. Or Dreadlocks—Jarvis would bet that one had a record—he studiously avoided eye contact with anyone in authority. One of the bunch stood out like the proverbial sore thumb: too artificial with his fancy clothes and manicured nails. A wuss. Gay? No, Jarvis didn't think so. But he sure didn't belong on a fishing charter.

Jarvis bypassed them all for now and pointed at the dead guy's wife. "I'll talk with you first."

Everyone's attention shifted toward him, all but the one he wanted. The guy in the windbreaker leaned down and whispered. She looked up, eyes rimmed in red. The blonde handed her a tissue and she blew her nose, crumpled the paper in a fist and rose from the chair. She stood about five-five and wore blue jeans and a pink tank top. Over that, a well-washed cotton shirt with the tails tied at the waist. There was blood matted in her hair and smudges all over her clothes.

When she stood up, so did the blonde, who now had hold of her left hand. "Could I come with her, for moral support?"

"Don't worry, she'll be fine." Jarvis put out a hand; the woman moved but her arm stretched out behind her, reluctant to let go of the blonde. Her first steps were shaky. Both he and the blonde jumped forward to catch her. "I've got her. She'll be fine," he repeated.

Along the gangway he walked tight to her side, blocking her view even though the body had been removed. Forensics people crowded the area. Jarvis stepped around them all, and led her to two chairs set at the bow. He sat in the one facing the scene. The boat had swung around the anchor rope and now settled in shade cast by the oaks on nearby Rattlesnake Island. He flipped open his notebook and leaned ahead. She was nice looking, not glamorous like the blonde, but down-home pretty with shoulder-length brunette hair, sad brown eyes and smooth, tanned skin. "I'm sorry about your husband."

She didn't react.

Afraid words would betray her? Or that she'd lose control? "My name is Detective Jarvis. Tell me your name please."

"Valerie Little."

"Okay Mrs. Little, can you tell me what happened here today?"

Her attention darted to the right, following sounds in the cockpit. "Someone killed him. Someone killed Nolan."

Tell me something I don't know. "Tell me about your day. Start wherever you feel comfortable."

She flashed him a 'you have to be kidding' look and twined her fingers in her lap. A corner of white tissue peeked between her thumbs. "I got up at 4:30 to make muffins and sandwiches for the trip. Nolan got up at 5:30. He had coffee and did some paperwork. I cooked eggs and toast then we went to the marina."

"How were things between you?"

The gaze flashed up and then back to her lap. "Th-the same as usual."

"Which was…."

"I don't know what you've heard, Inspector—"

"Detective."

"Detective. Nolan is gruff and short-tempered, but that's just the way he is—was. He didn't mean any harm. He's under a lot of pressure."

Jarvis scribbled short notes so he could watch her. That's where the best clues came from: gestures and mannerisms. "In what way was he short tempered?"

"I-I'm kind of clumsy and he…corrects me. Things like that." The fingers tore at the tissue. Tiny bits flew off as the breeze whispered past, bringing little respite from the heat.

"How did you feel about his correcting you?"

She shrugged and repeated, "I'm clumsy and not very smart," as if it covered everything.

"Tell me how you…discovered him."

"We were weighing a fish Will caught. I thought Sonnie and Montez—they're the two black men—I thought they might want to see it. They were up front so I went in the galley to knock on the window. At first I thought Nolan was sleeping because he was leaning against the wall. But, something about him just didn't look right, you know what I mean?"

"What did you do then?"

Pink circles formed on the pale cheeks. "I might have screamed." She shook her head. "I don't remember. I know I ran to him."

A thud and a hollow squishing sound emanated from the cockpit area. God, they were fucking up the crime scene. A video of the evening news flashed into his head, a headline scrolled across the bottom of the screen. *Detective Colby Jarvis allows screw-up of forensic evidence in Little murder investigation.* He jumped from the chair. One of the team raised a hand in a gesture intended to indicate that all was okay. Though doubt was his chief emotion, he forced himself to sit and continue questioning. "How well do you know all these people?"

She shrugged. "Montez and Sonnie come on the tour about four times a year. This is the first time for the Deacons. Angie got the trip for Will's birthday. I've never met Tyson before. He didn't have a reservation. He just showed up on the dock this morning."

Another noise from the forensics people and Mrs. Little started crying. The blonde appeared—why hadn't he noticed her approach? He helped Mrs. Little up then handed her off to the blonde. He followed the women to the stern where Dreadlocks and Wuss seemed to be arguing.

"That doesn't give me a motive for murder," Wuss complained.

"Don't need much reason to kill a person. I knew a guy killed for seven freaking bucks. Seven freak—" Dreadlocks spotted Jarvis and slapped his mouth closed.

Jarvis ignored the exchange, for now. The dark-haired man stood up and escorted Mrs. Little back to her chair. Now Jarvis could see the lettering on the jacket: Lakes Region Homes & Land. He gestured to the blonde. "You next."

She handed Mrs. Little a fresh tissue, then glided toward him. A tall woman, probably five-eight or nine, and she had a smudge of blood on the right arm of a blouse made of some slinky fabric. He preceded her along the gangway, but didn't shield the scene as he'd done with Mrs. Little. The consideration wasn't necessary for this one.

As they left the stern, Mrs. Little burst into tears. He didn't have to turn to hear the soft-spoken but very incriminating words: "It's all my fault."

Five

At Sonnie's last words, every eye had turned to Will. Were they accusing him of putting on the jacket to cover up bloodstains? She knew better. Will wasn't a murderer. He probably covered sweat circles or a potato salad stain. He was particular about things like that. Sonnie obviously tried to focus suspicion away from himself.

Angie followed the detective past the cockpit, stepping over blood that had seeped into the aisleway. She sat in the chair facing away from it.

The detective crossed his legs and adjusted his cap. Was he aware of his resemblance to Sherlock Holmes? Perhaps that was the reason for the silly Deerstalker hat in the first place. Otherwise, he looked pretty ordinary, tall and well proportioned. A slight paunch protruded above his belt. A firm set to his mouth told Angie that when he got hold of something, like a hound dog, he wouldn't let go till it was chewed up, no matter what it tasted like. His brows were a funny shape; each came to an upside down vee, making him look like he was always asking a question.

He dragged the chair so his denim-clad legs framed but didn't touch hers. His actions were deliberate as he opened a ring notebook and propped it on his right knee. The brown eyes were serious; a no-nonsense guy. "Your full name and address, please."

"Angelina Nadia Deacon. Bay Hill Road, Alton."

He printed her name at the top of the page in large capital letters. "Where do you work?"

"Lakes Region General. I'm an ER nurse."

"That's where I've seen you." And it explained why she wasn't queasy around the bloody crime scene.

"You were a patient?" she asked.

"I brought in a car accident victim a while ago. Continue. Tell me about today."

Where to begin? The entire day had been off-kilter, like she'd stepped into some bizarre time warp when she got out of bed. Will barely spoke during breakfast at the diner. Usually he bantered with Judy the waitress. Then here, instead of telling Nolan to shut up and leave people alone, he acted like someone sent him to a corner for a time-out. He hadn't mentioned any troubles at the office. So what was wrong?

Maybe he was having trouble dealing with his half-century birthday. The sudden realization of his life plummeting down the other side of the hill might've sent him into an emotional tailspin. When had she first noticed the change? Here on the boat, of course, but had it started before that? At home? Yesterday? Last week? Hard as she thought, nothing about his behavior before this morning seemed abnormal.

"Ms. Deacon," Jarvis encouraged.

"I'm trying to put events in the right order."

Jarvis nodded, but something about the way he nodded told her he didn't believe she had any trouble arranging facts at all. "Tell me anything out of the ordinary that happened today.

"Nothing much happened. Oh, unless you mean Tyson Goodwell. As we were pulling out of the dock, he came running down asking to be taken fishing." She laughed.

"What's wrong?"

"I didn't get the idea he was a fisherman. I mean, Dockers and Brooks Brothers? Anyway, Nolan didn't want Tyson to come."

"But he let him."

"It was probably the three hundred dollars he waved in the air."

"Mrs. Little said you were seasick."

"I'm all right."

"I'm glad to hear it. But you have to see the questions it raises."

"Like what?"

"Like why are you on a boat if you get seasick?"

"It's my husband's birthday." She heaved a sigh that cleared so much of her lungs she got dizzy. "Great gift, a day that's supposed to be relaxing and fun turns us into murder suspects."

"What makes you think you're suspects?"

"You." Seeing the doubtful twitch to his brows, she added, "Besides, isn't everyone?"

"Not necessarily." Jarvis laid the tip of the pen against his lips.

"What's that supposed to mean, that Valerie's the only one who could have done this?"

"You don't agree?"

Angie wanted to cross her legs, but the position of his knees made it impossible. Odd, she was so used to crossing her legs when she sat that she was having trouble thinking straight. Her attention gravitated to his left hand. A bare ring finger. She should've known he was single; his plaid sport shirt was clean but wrinkled, as though he'd taken it directly from the dryer. He wore well-washed Wranglers, definitely not a fashion-phobic guy.

Angie pushed her chair back a foot and crossed her legs. "No, Detective, I don't think Valerie killed her husband."

"Go on, we'll talk about that later."

"She served coffee and muffins." Homemade muffins, something Angie rarely made time to do for Will anymore. Something she'd vowed to do more of starting tomorrow. "We ate en route here." Then she flashed on the bloodstain on Montez's shirt, and the argument between him and Nolan.

"Tell me what you just remembered."

How was he able to read her mind? "Nolan got angry with Montez and accused him of touching Valerie."

"Had he touched her?"

"Not that I noticed. She had a leak or something under the sink. Montez helped her with it and Nolan got upset."

"And Mr. Clarke walloped him in the nose."

"More like a tap. Nolan jabbed him in the chest with his finger. And called Montez the N word."

"Mr. Little bled a lot for just a tap," Jarvis noted.

"Facial wounds tend to bleed a lot."

He nodded, accepting her professional assessment. He spent a considerable time writing in the notebook. "What happened next?" he asked without looking up.

"Montez caught a fish. Then Sonnie caught one. No, that's not right, it happened the other way around." She shook her head, unable to set the correct order of events. Her mind was like a junk drawer and Jarvis' proximity made it necessary to shuffle through the contents to come up with a sensible arrangement.

"The order isn't important right now." He flipped to a fresh page. "How did everyone react to the disagreement between Mr. Little and Mr. Clarke?"

"Tyson and my husband, and even Valerie pretended nothing happened. I don't know how Sonnie reacted; he was fishing up here. I could only see him part of the time."

"How did it make you feel?"

"Personally I hate the word nigger. But what happened between them was there and gone in a flash. Montez went right back to preparing his fishing line."

"What time was this?"

"About seven thirty. We were still en route here."

"Tell me about the wu—the Goodwell fellow. He arrived as the boat was pulling away from the dock?"

"Yes. Nolan was really mad about having to come back. But the rest of us said we didn't mind if he came. I had the idea Tyson was running from something."

"Do you always have such a suspicious nature?"

"No, it's just that he wore evening clothes and...like I said before, he doesn't look like a fishing sort of guy."

Jarvis nodded. "What happened to the money?"

"Nolan crammed it in his shirt pocket."

"What did Tyson do then?"

"He ate, like the rest of us. Then—"

That's when his attention had been caught by the identical pair of duffel bags Sonnie and Montez had brought aboard. He asked what was in them.

"Tell me what you're thinking." Jarvis tipped forward and gave her a look, the once soft brown eyes cutting like daggers. Sweat dripped off the tip of his nose, he swiped at it with the back of the hand holding the pencil.

"It's probably nothing," she said, then told him about the bags. "They were both right here." She pointed to the empty spot near Sonnie's rod holder.

Jarvis called an officer and told him to go look for the bags. Angie and Jarvis waited in silence as the officer sidled along the aisleway, to the stern.

Will had asked Montez what the bags were for and all he said was, "Work." What sort of job required men to carry work around with them? Electrician. Doctor. Lawyer. Diamond smuggler. Drug dealer. Bank robber.

The officer returned, giving a slight shake of his head. No bags.

Where were they?

"Any idea what was inside?" Jarvis asked.

Angie shook her head. The movement allowed air under her hair and cooled the back of her neck a little.

"Who discovered the body?"

"Valerie."

"Did you touch Mr. Little?"

"I checked for a pulse. Twice."

"Twice?"

"I wanted to make sure. I-I've never discovered a body before."

"You must deal with death in the ER all the time."

"Finding someone under these circumstances is different. Besides, nurses aren't usually allowed to pronounce someone dead. That's a doctor's job."

Jarvis gave a slow nod whose meaning Angie couldn't read. "Did anyone else touch Mr. Little?"

"Sonnie offered to push him overboard."

Jarvis' brows sprang up and disappeared under the rim of the hat.

God had she said that out loud? Quickly she added, "He was kidding around. The tension of the moment, you know."

Jarvis scribbled more notes. "How did Mrs. Little act seeing her husband dead?"

With intense surprise right then, Angie realized her feelings for Val went deeper than pity. In a few short hours she'd come to like the quiet woman. She'd bet that underneath the subdued façade beat the heart of a keenly shrewd person. A murderer? Val *could* physically have murdered Nolan, but near as Angie could figure, a motive was missing.

Wait just a minute! When Angie got there, the blood was congealing. That meant, unless Val went up front several minutes earlier—and Angie was almost a hundred percent sure she hadn't—she couldn't have killed Nolan.

"What are you thinking?"

Will often said her thoughts were written on her face. Either that or Detective Colby Jarvis was clairvoyant. She did a mental rehash of events, but right now the whole day, except for Will's quiet detachment, became a jumble in her brain. What was wrong with him anyway?

"Mrs. Deacon?"

Angie physically shook off the reverie. "Upset."

"You think her reaction was genuine?"

Val's emotion had been real, of that Angie felt certain, and she nodded, making sure to look Jarvis straight in the eye.

"What happened next?"

"I dialed 911. Whoever I spoke to said for us to stay away

from the scene. That's what we did. We sat at the stern." Sweat had glued her thighs to the plastic chair again and she shifted to separate everything.

"Tell me about this Montez fellow."

At the mention of Montez Clarke, every hair on her body stood on end. His sexual aura was impossible to deny. All day, he'd concentrated it on her, the square white teeth smiling every time she glanced his way. The big, soft hand, brushed hers at every possible occasion. She'd been unable to stop the sensations rippling through her body. And he'd known.

Thankfully Will didn't seem to notice.

"What do you think he and Dread—Mr. Phelps have in common?"

"I know they work together. I don't know what they do—well, Montez said he was a computer repairman—but when Sonnie realized his afternoon was shot to hell, his words, not mine, he insinuated they'd be in a lot of trouble if they weren't back by a certain time. He kept looking at his watch."

"That doesn't sound computer related. Did either he or Mr. Clarke go to the bow after Mr. Phelps' altercation with Mr. Little?"

Angie had been helping Val get lunch and not really noticing the others. "Montez was fishing right there." She pointed over Jarvis' shoulder. "No, wait a minute. He *was* back with us. He'd caught a fish—a trout I think he said—and brought it to show everyone. They put it in the fish well and he stayed to fish at the stern."

Jarvis wrote. "Okay. Let's get to your theories, tell me why you're so sure Mrs. Little didn't kill her husband."

Angie inhaled as much of the muggy air as her lungs would hold. She told him her thoughts about the blood congealing in the tackle box compartments.

"Besides, she's your friend and you can't imagine her doing such a thing."

"She's not my friend. I never met her before today."

"I recall you saying the tour was for your husband's birthday. Why?"

"Why?"

Jarvis nodded. "Yes. Why a fishing tour? Why this one in particular?"

"Will enjoys fishing, but he's so busy with the agency he never makes time to go. You must know how that is. It must be hard finding time for your hobbies."

Jarvis didn't reply, but she could tell from the set to his jaw that she'd struck a chord.

"Why this tour in particular?"

"Don't laugh. It's because they had a happy looking ad." When Jarvis' mouth didn't even twitch she went on, "I didn't want a regimented tour. I wanted something free and easy." She smoothed hair from her cheek. "Guess I didn't get anything like I wanted."

"Where was your husband during all the commotion?"

"Why do you keep bringing the conversation back to Will? He didn't kill Nolan. He didn't even know him before today."

"But he didn't like the way Nolan treated his wife."

"Neither did I. Neither did Sonnie."

Jarvis slapped the notebook shut. Angie took that as her signal the interview was over and stood.

"Send your husband next."

Six

Angie's return to the stern was met by several pairs of curious eyes. She kept her face noncommittal. A glance under Val's chair confirmed that the duffel bags were indeed missing.

"Lose something?" Sonnie asked.

She met his smirk with an unwavering gaze. He grinned wider.

Tyson's chuckle came out like a squeak, as though he wasn't used to laughing. "You look like you stepped in dog, um... crap."

She took her seat beside Valerie, who gave a crooked smile. "Was it very bad?"

"You aren't done with cops yet, none of us are," Montez offered, peeking at them over the tops of the sunglasses.

"They'll be on us night and day till *somebody* confesses." Sonnie directed the comment to Angie.

"Leave her alone," Montez said. He turned that Chiclet-toothed smile on her. "I don't think you did it."

Will spoke for the first time. "What a comfort."

"Knock it off," an officer broke in.

"The detective wants you next," Angie told Will.

"Go get 'em, killer," Sonnie called.

Just then, the tip of one of the rods flipped violently back and forth. Everybody jumped. Sonnie unwedged himself from the chair and slipped the rod from the tube-shaped holder. He held it a second, then gave it a jerk and began the task of landing a fish. The action provided welcome respite from the tension of the past two hours. Angie expected the cop to tell him to sit down, but he was probably as bored as them. Finally the trout was in the boat.

"Damn thing swallowed the hook," Sonnie said. "He's just about dead already. Anybody got a knife?"

"No knives," said the officer.

"How you expect me to gut the freaking thing? You just wanna watch him suffer? Okay, fine with me."

The mention of a knife made Angie realize that one of these people, with whom she'd spent almost—she checked her watch—seven hours, was a cold-blooded killer. She shivered. And wondered about Tyson Goodwell's unexpected appearance. Maybe he wasn't running *from* something as she first thought. Maybe he was running *toward* something. *Murder.*

She must be cracking up. How could that wimpy-faced guy be a murderer?

The officer retrieved a knife from Will's tackle box and gutted the fish himself.

Why hadn't her inner warning signals gone off when Tyson first appeared? Nothing screeched watch out for this one, he's got murder on his mind. Something must be wrong with her radar. Back in March, didn't she sense her grandmother's death? Didn't she feel it before her friend's husband was fired from his job of twenty-one years? Why didn't she divine that at least one of these people had murderous tendencies? Angie Deacon, a person trained to handle death and injury, should be able to do this.

Sonnie bagged the fish and dropped it in a cooler.

Jarvis strode toward them, a man of action, and prudence. Will had remained near the bow, looking out over the water, his stance straight and solid, his features indistinguishable. A Greek God. Her rock. A wave of love crashed over her.

"Come on," Jarvis called to him.

Will flinched, but came like an obedient puppy. Angie half expected Jarvis to acknowledge him with a pat on the head.

Angie stared at the water, ignoring the others, until Jarvis finished with Will.

The jacket unzipped now, Will's Izod shirt peeked out. Bright white. Clean. Just like she'd taken it from the dryer. Will looked first at his old seat then took the one Sonnie had vacated. "Did it go all right?" Angie whispered across to him. He nodded, his eyes on Sonnie closing the cooler lid.

The sun had dipped behind the trees to the west. There was an occasional glimpse of it when the breeze riffled the treetops one way or another, but at least they'd been exonerated from the temperature.

Jarvis raised that pointing finger.

"Take Momma's boy next." Sonnie's offer resulted in a scathing glower from Tyson.

Jarvis' finger zoomed in on its target. "You."

Sonnie snorted. Slowly, his feet moved. His shuffle was more reminiscent of a walk down Lovers Lane, except no female held his elbow. Funny, Angie couldn't picture a woman on his arm. She didn't envy Jarvis's job. Getting straightforward information from this man would be like hunting for whales in the Mohave.

At the same time, Will and Valerie gave identical ponderous sighs. The sigh was the first sign of life from Valerie in a while. Will glanced at Valerie. They both laughed. That shared intimacy brought Angie to her feet. She shot toward the rail. The guard stepped in front of her. "Sorry, I just can't sit any longer."

He moved back and let her pass. She placed her hands on the rail and leaned on unbent arms. Cool air floated up her short sleeved shirt and wafted across her drenched armpits. Feeling jealous over a shared laugh seemed just plain stupid. What was wrong with her?

No, the real question, what was wrong with Will? His behavior made her paranoid. Were they having money troubles? Guilt punched at her along with the image of her most recent purchase—the navy blue Lexus with all the trimmings. Will had chastised her no end: "We can't afford it." Yet she'd countered with, "It's a great investment." And it was. That car would last forever. Lexus's were better built; they didn't require the repairs other cars needed.

Damn. Was his mood her fault?

The detective appeared again. He smiled. Great, the ordeal was finally over. Sure, there'd be other rounds of questioning, but they'd finally be able to go home, get something to eat. Get some sleep.

But that pointing finger leveled itself again—in her direction. Again she followed him to the bow, and the same chair. At least now it sat completely in the shade. This time he only had one question: were her fingerprints on the knife?

Who would've accused her of murder? Only one person.

On the way back, Angie faced down Sonnie Phelps. His grin said it all. She smiled back, feeling she'd vindicated herself with the cop. No way he'd suspect her of killing Nolan Little. She'd never met the guy before today.

Finally, mercifully, the questioning was over. Like cattle to the slaughter *Little One's* passengers were off-loaded to a Marine Patrol boat, and motored away.

Once again a deck vibrated beneath her feet. This time Angie ignored the unsettled feeling and wished for the thing to go as fast as it could—back to Alton Bay, New Hampshire. Back to her ordinary life where she could figure out what was wrong with her husband.

Seven

Detective Jarvis watched the boatload of suspects whirl and speed back to shore. Soon it would return and haul *Little One* to impound where forensics would dissect it to the frame. Sure be something if he could solve this thing before they got back. How hard could it be? Six suspects. Damn, the Michaelson murder last year had over a hundred and they solved that in four days. He set his hat on a chair and leaned over the stern, bracing himself on a motor housing with one hand and shoveling handfuls of water on his head with the other. He shook off the excess like a dog then retrieved a Coke from his cooler and sucked down half the contents, the carbonation scratching the fatigue from his throat. A breeze pushed past, cooling his wet skin. It smelled like summer and lost childhood.

The galley reminded him of his grandmother's kitchen: too few cabinets, never enough space. Mrs. Little had said she was preparing lunch, noticed Nolan looking a bit strange and went around to check on him. She said he easily got heat stroke so she kept a close eye on him. Though the room smelled like tuna fish, it was immaculate, except for a two-inch spot on the glass over the sink. Looked like a forehead print. He pictured her peering through into the cockpit. She would have seen Nolan on his stool. He'd have his back to her and be tilting to the left. The knife hadn't penetrated to the spine so no blood would show there. But the control panel across both the front and starboard sides, and an issue of Field & Stream were saturated. The front and port side windshields had high velocity spatters that went all the way to the ceiling. Why hadn't she noticed it?

Because she already knew it was there.

She had no motive, his little voice argued.

"That we know of," he said out loud, as though to silence the impatience inside him. By the time he got to shore, his detectives should've turned up someone, possibly the couple's two sons, who could shed some light on their relationship. Guaranteed no trouble between them. Money. Another woman. Another man. He laughed, unable to picture the down-home Valerie Little cheating on her husband.

Why had Tyson Goodwell *needed* to get aboard this boat? As soon as Jarvis had started questioning the twerp, he lawyered up. Damn. There was something behind his appearance on the dock, Jarvis would stake his career on it.

All afternoon, his thoughts followed a meandering and quite confusing path—until he'd questioned Sonnie Phelps. Belligerent and rude, but the man told a credible tale of how he'd come up front to fish and seen the Deacon woman moving away from the body. He swore she'd just taken her hand from the knife. She'd stood up when he accosted her—and run to throw up. Guilt at being discovered? Nerves over discovering a body? Phelps's story sounded plausible enough, except where was the blood? Though certain she'd been moving her hand from the knife, Phelps swore she wasn't wearing gloves. Fingerprinting the knife handle should solve the dilemma.

But what about her motive? Could the dead guy have been porking her? Heaven help Jarvis for forming opinions without proof, but what possible reason could she have to mess with him? Not that he was bad looking, if Jarvis were any judge, but Nolan Little was nothing compared to Willis Deacon. Deacon had looks, personality and money.

Well, blood or no blood, long-term relationship or not, he'd brought Mrs. Deacon up front for a second round of questioning. "Are you sure the only time you touched Mr. Little was to check for a pulse? I won't, for example, find your prints on the knife, will I?"

She'd leaned forward in the chair and, for one moment, looked truly astonished. Then a flush came to her face and spread down her neck. That expression of shock couldn't have been faked.

"The only knife you'll find my prints on, Detective, is a plastic job I used to spread butter on my blueberry muffin."

Fingerprints would show this to be true or not, but one thing Jarvis knew for certain, she knew more than she was telling. Had she seen someone? Heard something? Why keep quiet about it?

Because it related to someone near and dear to her heart.

Whoa, what was that? He strode out of the galley and down the gangway. No door on the four by six cockpit, the port side open to the weather. He tiptoed over the blood and into the room that held only a control panel and an armless stool of white ribbed vinyl. A quarter-inch corner from a piece of white paper protruded from the blood soaked issue of Field & Stream. With two fingernails, he pulled out the paper, moved to the bow and laid it on a chair seat. Triangular in shape, and about eleven inches across one side, it had been torn from a larger sheet—probably 11 x 14. Along the torn side, printed in black was a period and two digits. Unless he missed his guess, this belonged to a spreadsheet, the numbers a final computed dollar tally. A check of the Little's computer should turn up the original. Disappointment struggled to the surface. He'd so wanted it to be a clue.

Jarvis leaned over the rail replaying the act of the murder in his mind: the perp bending down and picking up the filet knife from the tackle box. Stabbing once into the man's heart. Directly into his heart.

Angelina Deacon, the ER nurse. She'd know exactly where to stick the thing.

So would anybody who watches television, argued his little voice.

Jarvis bagged the paper scrap as evidence.

The murder couldn't have been premeditated or the perp

would've brought a weapon. If there had been words, a verbal confrontation would've drawn the attention of five other people. Supposedly not one of them heard a thing.

With that kind of a wound, blood would have doused the killer. Jarvis rubbed his temples. Everyone had *some* blood on them. But no one, not even the wife, had the amount that would occur in this type of killing. So what? The perp changed clothes and dumped the dirty ones overboard. Which didn't make sense. Every witness swore they would've seen anything out of the ordinary. Yes, but if they'd changed clothes and washed shoes before the discovery of the body—a trip to the head—who'd notice?

Unless they were all in this together.

"Shit." He'd seen movies where townspeople banded together to protect a secret. Just last week it had happened on a *Murder She Wrote* rerun. He repeated the curse and crossed back to the cockpit. The floor now a mashed conglomeration of footprints from the techs wrestling the two-hundred pound body from the small compartment, but Jarvis recalled how it looked when he arrived—a coagulating mass spoiled by one thing: half a bloody footprint. From its smooth outline he thought it was probably made by a boat shoe, a thin-soled canvas sneaker, a right one, the exact size hard to determine. Nolan died immediately, which meant he didn't make the print. All but Wuss and Clarke wore some sort of boat shoe.

Where were the blasted duffel bags? For a while, he'd wondered if the Deacon woman made them up just to throw him off track. But their presence was confirmed by everyone else on board, except Clarke and Dreadlocks.

Jarvis plucked the cell-phone from his belt and dialed. "Jarvis here. Find a diver and give him these coordinates. I want him to search under this boat."

"He probably won't be able to do it this afternoon."

"Get him out here."

Clarke and Phelps brought the bags on every trip. A connection between the boat, the Littles, and the bags was a certainty.

The huff huff of the police boat came out of nowhere. It eased alongside. He waved his readiness and moved front and center to accept the towrope thrown by the Marine Patrol officer. Jarvis tied the rope to the mooring ring then hand over hand hauled in the dripping nylon anchor line. It dug into his palms in a way that reminded him how infrequently he worked out, how his only exercise lately was mowing the lawn, an infrequent occurrence in itself. The image of Angelina Deacon popped into his head. She'd sat demurely in her chair then looked at the roll around his middle. Her eyes moved quickly away, but he still could've sworn she stifled a grin. Maybe not. Maybe his vanity just worked overtime.

Little One moved, washing left and right until forging a momentum in the still water. Slowly it picked up speed, heading for the impound marina.

Too many clues pointed toward the Deacon woman.

What might've been her motive to kill? She professed not to know the Littles before today. Time would tell on that too. Sergeant Wilson should already be compiling data. The population of Alton Bay only about 4,000. Chances were good the Deacons and Littles had met prior to today.

Except, knowing someone was not a motive for murder.

Damn his little voice.

What if the women did know each other—were in this together? No. It just didn't fit. As a matter of fact, none of it fit. Yet.

His next thought made him laugh out loud. Wouldn't the suspects be surprised when detectives confiscated their shoes and they all had to go home in stocking feet?

Eight

It took a minute to get the rattletrap Toyota up to speed, but once there, it cruised along Route 28 like a jet. Sounded like one too. Montez contented himself watching the scenery whiz past. Might be the last sunset he'd see. They'd never been late on a delivery. He didn't know what sort of *punishment* was involved, but it sure as hell wouldn't be beer and a game of nine-ball. He hadn't met the man Sonnie called "the boss". In the three years they'd worked together Sonnie never spoke about him, though he made it clear they were "buds", which made Montez low man on the totem pole, a status he'd never questioned. Get the job done and go home alive, that's all he cared about.

From the clench of Sonnie's hands on the wheel, Montez had the idea that being friends with the boss wouldn't make any difference under the circumstances. They covered the ten miles to Wolfeboro in just over nine minutes. Sonnie barely slowed to make the turn into WGs Restaurant. The boss' vehicle wasn't here. Why should it be? They were many hours late.

"Fuck!" Sonnie flung himself from the car and marched toward the building. Montez followed at a more sedate pace. What was the point of hurrying?

Sonnie stood at the bar. The bartender leaned on the polished surface, muscular arms pushed out in front of her. Montez knew if he tried he could look down her blouse, but tonight he had no desire for such distractions. Her brawny face was earnest as she spoke to Sonnie. Montez caught the words, "…spitting fire," as he swung onto a stool. "Gimme a draft."

Sonnie shot him a look he ignored. If he was gonna die to-night he sure as hell deserved a last beer—or four. The bartender pulled herself upright, stuck a glass under the spigot and pulled the handle. She shoved the foamy mug across the counter and went back to leaning on the bar.

Montez polished off half the contents in one swig. If Sonnie was stressed before this, it was nothing to how he looked now. Like a robot he slid onto the stool at Montez's right. The bartender set a brew in front of him without being asked.

Montez drew circles in the spilled foam on the bar. "Did he say anything?"

"Said wait for his call. And don't leave town," the bartender said.

They'd already ignored one order not to leave town, but Montez was sure Sonnie would obey this command.

"Why don't you call him?" Montez suggested. "A show of good faith, you know?"

"He said wait for him to call."

Seemed like he would've called a bunch of times already. Hours ago, the next courier would've tried to retrieve the bags. Found nothing. And reported the fact. To hell with how many successful drops they'd done before, the boss would think they ran off with the goods.

Where the hell would they go? No place on the planet would be safe. Montez didn't bother reminding Sonnie any of that.

"I got an idea, you care to hear about it," he said.

Sonnie drained the contents of his glass onto his tongue. "Can't believe the freaking blonde had to tell the cops about the bags." He banged the glass down on the counter. "Where'd you dump 'em anyway?"

"Me? I didn't dump 'em. Thought you did."

"Where the hell'd they go?" Sonnie asked. "They weren't on the boat. Somebody had to throw them over."

"Well, it wasn't me."

"This just keeps getting better. Man, are we dead fucking meat."

"Why don't we go retrieve the stuff and hand deliver it?"

Sonnie appeared to consider the idea. Then he shook his head. "Probably the fucking cops already been there! You seen the way they were searching the boat. They took the blonde's talk serious. They'll figure out where the bags are."

"I think we should try anyway." Montez lifted one shoulder. "Show of good faith to do it in person. Besides, the boss should've called by now." He finished his beer and wiped the back of a hand across his mouth. "Forget I said anything." He stood, pulled bills from his pocket and pushed them toward the bartender. "C'mon, let's go. I'm beat."

"He said don't leave town."

"He didn't tell me that. If you're not gonna take me, just say so, I'll find a ride."

Sonnie downed the second beer, paid and flung himself off the seat.

Montez followed him outside; the ringing of his own cell phone stopped them both in their tracks. Sonnie actually looked hopeful.

"Not him," Montez said, "He doesn't have my number."

He unclipped the phone, read the screen and flipped open the cover. "Hey punkin'." Sonnie's growl made Montez spin away and lower his voice. "What're you doing up so late?"

"You said you were comin' home early."

"I know, but we had some trouble. Hey listen, I don't think I'm gonna make it home tonight at all." *Might never be home again.* "Will you be all right alone?"

"Y-yeah, I guess. You'll be here in the morning?"

"Early as I can. G'night. Hey, you still there?"

"Uh-huh."

"Love you."

Sonnie was standing by the driver's side door when Montez got there. "Get in."

Sonnie gunned the engine and Montez nearly choked laughing. That motor had seen too many miles to be acting like a teen hotrod. He slid onto the old vinyl seat. He slammed the door because it was the only way to shut it.

Sonnie headed onto Route 28 traveling south, the way they'd come. The same route they would take if traveling back to Nashua so Montez still didn't know where they were going. And didn't bother asking.

Sonnie didn't rev the car up to a hundred this time; he kept the needle hovering near eighty. Montez settled back, ready for whatever the night had in store. Sonnie seemed calmer now. Maybe this was the time to talk to him. To say the words that burned into his tongue during the ride from the boat. The words struggled so hard to escape between his lips that he'd had to clamp his jaws together. At some point he bit a hole in his lower lip. The taste of blood remained there. Truth be told, it had been all day, ever since seeing that tour boat owner slumped like a wet dishrag on his stool.

"Who d'you think killed him?"

The startled way Sonnie glanced at him said his mind had been on a completely different topic. "What the fuck's the matter with you? I told you on the boat, I caught the blonde in the act. When I got there she was just lettin' go a' the knife. Don't know why she's got it in for me."

Yes, Sonnie had mentioned that fact, but Montez had chalked it up to the emotion of the moment. Well, not to emotion because Sonnie didn't have emotions. "She said she was checking his pulse. And anybody would've mentioned the bags."

Sonnie shrugged. "Her life span's getting' shorter by the minute."

Angie Deacon was a convenient scapegoat for Sonnie's anger. All day he and Nolan found things to disagree about, nearly came to blows at least once. Did Sonnie kill the guy? Throwing suspicion on Mrs. Deacon would be just like him. How Sonnie could've killed Nolan, Montez didn't know. Or care. He'd been busy fishing. Really fishing. The weather was prime—the fish biting. For the first time in weeks he relaxed. He hadn't noticed anybody else almost all day. Except for the gorgeous Angie Deacon.

Not that he'd have the slightest chance with her. First off, she was married.

"What the hell you grinnin' about?"

Then the color thing. He didn't know how she'd feel about that.

"I asked what was so funny."

"I don't think the blonde killed the guy."

"Why's that funny?"

"I wasn't—oh, forget it. Why would she kill him, she never met him before today."

Sonnie gave a nasty chuckle. "*You* wouldn't think she did it. You got a hard-on for her so big it was sticking outta your belt. Leave her alone man, she's bad news."

"Listen Sonnie, I gotta say something."

Sonnie swung the car into the Alton Bay marina parking lot and jammed on the brakes, throwing them both against the dash. "What!"

Suddenly words that for weeks had crowded to get out wouldn't leave Montez's mouth. Sonnie removed the key from the ignition and in one motion launched himself across the seat. The key gashed Montez's cheek. He threw up his hands to ward off the attack, but Sonnie had already flung himself out of the car.

Sonnie waited beside the passenger door. This time Montez was ready. If he wanted a fight, then that's what he'd get.

Sonnie pointed the bloody key in Montez's face. "Go get us a boat."

Nine

Will wound the steering wheel left twice and then right, onto Bay Hill Road. "I can't believe they took Valerie in for questioning."

"What I can't believe is they *didn't* take me in," Angie said. "After Sonnie accused me of murder and all."

"Why would Sonnie do that? Besides to get the focus off himself, I mean."

She balled the handful of quick-wipes in her fist and again resisted the urge to strip off the filthy clothes right there in the car. "He proposed throwing the body overboard. I told Jarvis. Sonnie accused me in retaliation."

Will gunned the car up the driveway. "So, why didn't Jarvis take you in?"

"One reason's gotta be that I didn't have blood on me."

"You do have a lot on you."

Will shut off the security system and opened the garage door, then pulled in next to her Lexus. She still considered it brand new; she'd only owned it three months a week and two days. She looked down at her bloody clothes and shuddered. "Most of this I got touching Val. You couldn't hide or wash off the amount of blood you'd get from stabbing someone up close like that." Angie got out and waited for Will. "I still can't believe they took our shoes. Is it legal for them to do that?"

"It was easier than waiting for them to get warrants."

Four stairs led from the garage into the house. She threw

open the kitchen door. Hot, humid air shot out at them. "God Will, we have to get central air."

He slammed the door. "How many times do I have to tell you we can't afford it? Just like that goddamned car."

Angie dropped her purse on the hall table beside the blinking answering machine. She yanked off her blouse and jeans, dropped them down the laundry chute and then raced around opening windows. For a moment she stood breathing in cool night air. She didn't bother turning on lights as she crossed through to the parlor at the back, always cooler because trees lined the yard behind the pool. She flopped in the chintz-covered chair in bra and panties, head back on the soft cushion. Will played the accumulated messages, customers forwarded from the office. She closed her mind to the muted voices. Finally off that boat and safe at home. Nothing else mattered.

The back door opened and slapped shut. Then Will's brother's voice saying, "Where the hell have you guys been?"

She shot upright, jerking the afghan from the back of the adjoining loveseat. She wrapped it around herself. What was he doing here? Will and Wallace were twins, identical in every way except where Will was a hardworking successful businessman, Wallace was lazy, and perpetually in her house. He had a wife and family, yet he chose to hang out here. Of course, it was a lot nicer here, but that wasn't the point.

Their voices approached as Will related the day's events. The men's silhouettes stopped in the doorway, Wallace wearing Will's brown striped thong and dripping on her polished granite floor. She knew not to say anything, Will would say it didn't matter, it was only water.

Will heaved a sigh. "What a day. Can't wait to hit the sack."

"Sure you don't want to stay up and have a brew? I ordered pizza," Wallace said.

"Nah, I'm bushed."

"I wanna hear more about what happened."

Angie went to the bar and, holding the afghan closed with one hand, poured a generous helping of brandy in a snifter, knowing and not caring what it would do on an empty stomach. She took a long drag, put the glass down and refilled it.

"Nice outfit," Wallace said, "I'll have a drink too."

She walked past him and upstairs. She heard the men move into the kitchen and chairs scrape across the floor. Angie stopped in the doorway to the master bedroom, her most treasured decorating creation, an immaculate vision of white on white with touches of peach. She flung open the French door and went onto the long narrow deck. The surrounding oaks provided shelter and privacy. The lounge chair was already moist and chilly with dew. She sipped the brandy, the nighttime sky of black clouds on a blacker background—peaceful and serene—as though the whole horrific day had never happened.

The brilliance of the bedroom light coming on jerked her alert. With an effort, she roused herself and went inside. Will had most of his clothes off and was pulling down the comforter.

"I'm going to take a shower," she said. "Did you eat?"

"I had some of Wally's pizza. I saved you a slice."

She stepped under the spray, leaned against the Italian marble tiles and let the water come at her from all directions, little pinpricks that stung yet soothed.

A while later, body steaming from the hot assault, Angie lifted the covers and eased in beside Will. The Channel 9 News introduction rolled. She cuddled close, putting her hand on his chest and fondling the thick curls there.

He moved her hand away. "Not tonight, it's been a bitch of a day."

"No shit." She heaved herself out of the bed. She put on a robe, about to leave the room when the headline story came on. Angie saw herself climbing off *Little One*. God, she looked terrible, tangled hair, wind-burned cheeks. Will, always dapper, helped Valerie off the boat. Her legs threatened to crumple and his strength held her up. She gave a tight thank-you smile.

The reporter stood near the end of the dock. Behind her, the water looked almost black. "This afternoon the small community of Alton Bay was rocked when one of their own was murdered..." The camera panned the exiting customers. "Nolan Little, resident and owner of *Little Fishing Tours*, was stabbed after an alleged altercation with a member of the charter tour. On the boat were his wife Valerie..." A video of Valerie, taken as she was brought into headquarters flashed across the flat screen. Not in handcuffs, but might as well have been. She looked completely rattled, her cheeks sunken, eyes blank.

The reporter continued, brushing strands of hair from her face without stopping the monologue. "A second Alton Bay couple: Willis and Angelina Deacon. Willis owns Alton Bay Homes & Land, a prominent real estate company." They replayed the video of her and Will stepping off the boat. Next the camera followed Tyson, Montez, and Sonnie. The two dark men went to a decrepit green Toyota. Montez never looked at the camera, but Sonnie spared it a piercing glower. Tyson ducked his head as he climbed into a smoke blue Jaguar.

"Nolan Little was well liked. His death will be a great loss to the community. There have been no arrests as yet." They replayed the scene of Val being shepherded into the police station. The camera swung toward Will, face to face with one of the investigators in an obvious disagreement. After a moment of heated words Will knelt and removed his shoes.

"I still can't believe you argued with them like that," Angie said.

Will made no comment.

The scene switched to the coroner's vehicle: Nolan's body being loaded by white-suited men. The reporter tried several times to get an interview but no one would speak. The picture flashed back to the station steps where one of the detectives from the boat spoke to the press. The officer wiped a wrinkled blue handkerchief across his forehead before speaking. "As you know, Nolan Little, owner of *Little Fishing Tours* died on the lake today. We are compiling witness information and feel certain an arrest will be made soon." The cop stepped away from the microphones, ignoring the bombardment of questions.

The scene zoomed back to the studio and a blonde anchor made her closing statement, "We'll keep you updated on developing news from Alton Bay."

Angie wrapped the robe tighter and went downstairs to find something to eat. Poor Valerie didn't have a prayer.

There was a slice of pizza in the box. Angie tossed the whole thing in the trash, refusing to acknowledge Wallace, even though Will had probably paid for it. She scrambled two eggs and took the plate to the parlor, stopping first to pick up three beer cans from the coffee table and toss them into the trash.

After putting the egg plate in the dishwasher, she went back upstairs. Jay Leno was interviewing Tom Cruise. Angie climbed into bed and lay on her back, this time careful not to touch Will. She tucked the sheet around her breasts; he wouldn't misinterpret her motives again.

"Why wouldn't you give them your shoes?" she asked.

He grunted. "I *did* give them my shoes."

"It's got to be illegal—taking a person's shoes. Isn't it illegal to drive without them?"

"I don't know." His tone said he didn't care.

She opened her mouth to ask why he thought they wanted all their shoes, but the words that came out were far different. "How come you were so quiet all day?"

"God Angie, what do you expect? A man was murdered before our eyes."

"It wasn't before our eyes. And you were like that *before* the murder. You were that way all day."

He sat up and punched the pillows into shape, not speaking till he'd gotten comfortable against them. "All right, I'll say it, I felt guilty. I didn't do anything about the way Nolan treated her. If I'd stopped it right from the start, maybe things wouldn't have gotten so out of control."

"So, you think Valerie did it."

Another sigh, this one long. "I don't want to think that. But who else? Montez and Sonnie, Tyson or us. None of us knew him."

Will punched the remote button, shutting off the laughter and making the ensuing silence all too heavy. He gave her a brotherly kiss on the cheek, turned over and pounded a new dent in the pillow. Angie shaped herself against his back and closed her eyes. How skillfully he'd avoided answering her question about his moodiness. He got a lot of practice in his line of work, knowing which potential buyers' questions to answer right away and which to avoid completely. He'd become so adept she wondered if he even knew he did it.

Ten

The headlamp illuminated the murky depths on the southeastern edge of Rattlesnake Island. Bubbles trickled up, making tiny glug glug sounds. He kicked the rubber fins, forcing himself deeper to give the headlamp better range. Amazing how cold the water got down here.

He moved his head slowly left to right, left to right, the three-foot circle of yellow light tracing an imaginary grid pattern on the lake floor. Where the hell were the bags? This was the spot he'd lowered them overboard. Just to be sure, he swam upward. He surfaced not fifteen feet from the island. He removed the mouthpiece and trod water, turning in several circles, gauging the spot *Little One* had been anchored. Finally he nodded. This was the right place, he just had to open his eyes wider. He rose up, kicked and dove under again. This time he headed straight down and began the grid-search again.

Minutes passed. Anxiety grew as his thirty minutes of air dwindled to six. Time dwindled in another way too. Back at the pier, that diver Carlson Brinks had been loading gear on his boat. He'd bet his television the cops paid him to attempt retrieval of the bags. Brinks had the most up to date equipment, would find the things in a flash.

Suddenly his light picked out something black. Well, everything here was a shade of black. But this one was more solid, less surreal. No growth on it yet. He took hold of the pair of handles and turned in a circle, focusing the light in the same area. He'd dropped them both from the same spot. Even allowing for current, they should be close to one another.

Three precious minutes passed. Damn. He decided to go topside and deposit this one in the canoe, then try and return. If he couldn't find the second, at least he'd have one.

Lifting the unwieldy thing into the boat proved harder than expected. Though the contents were well wrapped, and protected from the water, it was awkward and heavy. After much wrestling the bag dropped in with a great thud.

He popped the rebreather between his lips and prepared to dive. Only three minutes of air; it'd be close. Just then a headlight shone across the water, the sound of a motor followed. He'd been so busy with the stupid bag, he hadn't even heard the approaching craft. Had to be Brinks.

Adrenaline pumped, helped him duck under before the light made a second pass. Probably he hadn't been spotted. They weren't searching for a person, just a landmark on the island. A place to anchor. Time was really of the essence now.

He grasped the rope dangling from the brass ring at the bow of the canoe. He pulled the boat toward the island and hid it under an overhanging shrub. Should've done that in the first place.

The Brinks boat chugged up to the island. Twelve feet out, the motor silenced. So far he hadn't spotted anyone. Whether Brinks himself, or just a crew—well, it didn't really matter.

While the spotlight aimed the other way he dove under. Down down he swam, his actions adrenaline-frantic. It took a moment to get his bearings, but he swam toward the spot where he'd found the first bag. Around and around he went. Where was the blasted thing? Finally, a twinkle at the perimeter of the ring of light. The zipper! How had the bag fallen so far from the other?

Thut thut, the bubbles dribbled to a stop as his oxygen ran out. He spit out the rebreather. He kicked his feet and propelled with his hands, feeling the water rush between his fingers, the rebreather slapping him in the face. Fifteen feet. Could he retrieve the duffel and get to the surface before he drowned?

He had the handle. The coiled vinyl strips felt like gold in his fingers. He jerked it from the suction of the lake floor. Dizzy, his brain felt the effects of the lack of air. Swim!

He kicked—he'd never kicked so hard in his life, even in that swim meet against forty other kids when he was twelve. Up up he went, the bag flopping like limp sausage behind him. All that mattered now was breathing.

His head broke the surface with an audible pop. At least that's how it sounded to him as he gasped for life-giving air. Damn, that was close. He dogpaddled to the canoe and spent quite some time gathering his wits, re-inflating his lungs, watching the Brinks boat.

One head was visible moving about the deck, somehow not hearing the gasping and huffing going on less than twenty feet away. Brinks pulled down the air mask, popped the rebreather into his mouth and flicked on his headlamp. Immediately the beam homed in on him. He jerked back, ducking around the canoe. The light focused on the canoe for a moment before moving away. Hopefully Brinks assumed it was teens smoking dope on the island. And hopefully he wouldn't realize that nobody came to Rattlesnake Island to make out or do drugs. It hadn't gotten its name because there were kittens here. Which galvanized him to action. As soon as Brinks splashed into the water, he boosted the second bag into the canoe then hoisted himself inside. He repositioned the bags, one at each end, picked up the paddle and started for home. Dark, but enough moonlight to show the way. Enough moonlight to show the other boat moving in his direction. Damn this place was busy. He paddled along pretending to be out for a midnight boat ride, waving to the other boat's two male occupants as they passed.

On shore, he unloaded the bags and shoved the stolen canoe onto the sand where he'd found it. He carried both bags up the pier, dumped them in his trunk and sped for home. She was a light sleeper. Hopefully he could sneak in without waking her.

Eleven

Will had already left for the office when Angie woke. He'd prepared coffee; she just had to punch the button. While the machine chugged, she swam her usual twenty laps in the in-ground pool. Wallace hadn't pulled the cover completely shut last night, leaving the water cold. Her limbs tingled for the first five laps.

Afterward, she plopped a sunhat atop wet hair and sipped coffee on the patio, proud that so far she'd been able to pretend it was a normal day. She usually loved morning's peace and serenity. Today she was exhausted. Last night every time she closed her eyes, the day's events played in her mind like a broken phonograph record. She'd gotten up, wandered around the house, dusted, read till her eyes burned, but as soon as she lay back down the images flooded back. For the first time, she envied Will's ability to sleep through anything.

The one time Angie drifted off, she dreamed of her father's death. Though she'd been the one to find him and have the body removed before Mom returned home, her mother's suffering had been acute. Angie's father had been a serious drinker. He'd been rough on her mother. Why had she suffered so badly? Perhaps because of the loneliness she'd face? Perhaps—what? What could a person miss after putting up with an alcoholic? Angie couldn't imagine. Life with Will was easy. He didn't drink. He didn't stay out late. He didn't complain—except when she overspent their limits.

In the wee hours, she'd made a decision. She would seek out Valerie and see what she could do to make the next few days easier.

She went upstairs and spent a fair amount of time repairing yesterday's damage to her skin. Angie clicked on the television. The dark-haired newsman said there was nothing new to report in the Alton Bay murder. They re-ran the same story and videos while Angie stood mesmerized. She'd never admit, not even to Will: a part of her thrilled at being involved in such an affair. Gruesome and gory but a tiny ball of something in the back of her mind had always wondered what it would be like to be involved in a murder investigation. Would people look at her differently? Treat her as a celebrity? After all, how many people get on television? But another part of her, the part sickened by the entire episode, made her punch the OFF button and toss the remote on the dresser.

Angie slipped on a stark white uniform and sleek new sandals. She'd change to nursing shoes at work. Car key in hand, she opened the door. Detective Jarvis, wearing that odd hat, well-creased chinos and a short-sleeved blue plaid shirt, stepped in without waiting to be invited.

"Come in," Angie couldn't help saying. "I was just going to work."

He removed the hat and ran a hand through his hair. "I can see that. Maybe you wouldn't mind waiting a few minutes.

She set her purse on the hall table with just a little more emphasis than necessary. "You look like you've been up all night."

He gave a noncommittal quirk to his mouth.

"To what do I owe this intrusion? Have you come to arrest me?"

"Why would you think that?"

"Look, I know Sonnie says I killed Nolan. I know you're not 100% satisfied that I didn't. Let me ask you this, have you let Valerie go home yet?"

"If you didn't know her before, and she's not your friend,

as you said yesterday, why should you care?" He followed her to the parlor and sat on the pink and green hibiscus-print loveseat. How out of place this Sherlock Holmes looked amongst the bright blooms. She almost asked him to move to the solid green chair.

"Believe it or not, Detective, some people care enough about others to wonder about things like that. Valerie and I aren't friends, not yet anyway. I met her yesterday, and liked her. If the situation were different Will and I would have invited her over for dinner sometime."

"Is that right," he said.

Usually when someone says "is that right" they add inflection to turn it into a question, but Jarvis put a definite period making it into a statement.

"Nolan too?" She must have looked confused, because he clarified with, "When you invited Valerie, would you have included Nolan too?"

"Yes, of course. Are you arresting her?"

"At this time, she's being held on suspicion."

"Can I visit?"

Jarvis shrugged. "Nice outfit, they let you wear those shoes?"

"I can wear any shoes I want. And I have to be leaving soon."

"I have a few questions."

"Interrogation," she corrected.

"I prefer to think of it as fact-finding."

"What facts do you want to find?"

"First, Montez Clarke. I understand there was electricity flying between you two."

"Did you hear that from Sonnie too?" She watched his expression and wasn't surprised to see a twinkle in Jarvis' eyes. "Well, he was wrong."

Jarvis put up a hand and she closed her mouth. "What I want to know is whether electricity is what Mister Little saw sparking between Montez and Valerie."

"I didn't notice anything. Montez acted like a complete gentleman."

"What about between Valerie and Sonnie?"

Angie couldn't help wrinkling her nose. Jarvis' face scrunched into a 'do I look like I'm kidding' expression.

"There were no sexual innuendoes flying around that I noticed. Were you able to locate the duffel bags?"

"Both men deny their existence."

"And since they never existed, Sonnie and Montez couldn't tell you what was in them. And since they never existed, I must've been imagining them." She glanced at the clock on the wall over his shoulder.

"I'll be finished shortly. You said you never saw anyone but Mrs. Little near her husband."

"I didn't say that. Montez went there. They fought."

"We found footprints. Your husband's."

Angie couldn't stop a frown from pinching her mouth.

"Could you try and recall under what circumstances he might have gone there?"

"You want me to incriminate my own husband? Should I be calling a lawyer?"

"I want you to help rule him out."

Angie tried but couldn't picture Will leaving that tiny invisible box he erected around himself at the stern. "The only time I saw him move from his fishing rod was to go to the galley for coffee and muffins, and later a ham sandwich and potato salad. Right after that, he also went to the bathroom."

Jarvis' eyebrows shot up again. This time they remained a trifle longer than before. What could be important about a trip to the bathroom?

"Will you outline your own movements for me, please?"

"Do you want to know if I went to the bathroom too?"

Jarvis was visibly surprised. He gave a small nod.

"No."

"Not the whole day?"

"Not before the murder. I assume that's what you want to know. As for my other movements, I summarized them during our first talk. Nothing's changed." Angie let a hiss escape between her teeth and stood up.

Jarvis got up too. "At the station, ask for Sergeant Wilson."

"Thanks." Angie started to shut the door, then thought of another question. "Has anyone been to visit Valerie?"

"One of her sons. He was wearing a cast on his leg."

Angie nodded, not ready to admit she knew nothing about Valerie's family.

At the station, the dispatcher rolled her chair closer to the tinted bulletproof glass and squinted at Angie.

"I'm supposed to ask for Sergeant Wilson."

The woman rotated on squeaky casters, stood and ambled away. In five minutes, a roundish man—the one who'd answered reporter's questions on television last night—wearing black slacks and white short-sleeved shirt approached. His arms were muscled and tan, the lower half of a tattoo peeked from under the sleeve. She couldn't tell the design except it had long lethal looking toenails.

"I'm Sergeant Wilson," he said in a voice that belonged on the radio, a soothing blend of Burl Ives and Barry White.

"Detective Jarvis said I should ask you about visiting Valerie Little."

"Are you a relative?"

"No."

"Why do you want to see her?"

"I guess, to give moral support."

Wilson gestured for her to meet him at the other end of the brightly lit corridor. Angie couldn't help patting her hair as she passed under the video cameras. Today at least, every strand was in place. The heavy door opened with a buzz given by some unseen button-presser.

"I'm afraid I'll have to search you."

Angie stifled a wisecrack about cakes and hidden files, and endured the examination.

"This way," Wilson said.

She followed, her shoes tip-tapping on the metal stairs. Ahead stretched a long, very narrow corridor made of cinder blocks on the right and heavy black bars on the left. From the change in lighting and mildew-scented air, Angie knew they were in the basement. She felt a momentary hesitation at the wisdom of her decision to visit. Would Valerie want Angie to see her in such surroundings, without her teeth brushed or hair combed?

Her forward motion was abruptly halted when she bumped into the muscular bulk of Sergeant Wilson. He let out a combination of a startled gasp and laugh and grabbed her arm so she wouldn't lose her balance.

"Sorry," she said.

"Fifteen minutes," he said, and clomped back upstairs.

Valerie didn't look like a woman who'd spent a night behind bars. She looked well rested: no red-rimmed eyes or sunken cheeks. The upstairs door shut with a metallic bang.

"Hi Valerie." Angie reached into her purse and handed her a comb and breath mint.

"My friends call me Val."

"My real name is Angelina, but everybody calls me Angie."

Val nodded, then began repairing her bed hair. She popped the mint in her mouth. As though reading Angie's mind, she said in complete seriousness, "Last night was the first time I've slept alone in twenty-four years."

Angie didn't know how to reply. She leaned against the bars, but they had a sticky film from the humidity and she backed away.

"I know it sounds awful after what happened, but did you ever want to just sleep alone? You know, go out on the couch with your pillow and sleep blessedly alone, without the other person draped over you? Without having to yank back the covers a hundred times a night? Without having to push him to his own side of the bed a dozen more times." Val unzipped her jeans and re-tucked her shirt. "When the kids were sick, I sometimes lied to Nolan saying I was afraid they'd throw up or something and wouldn't hear, then I'd go snuggle in bed with them. It's not sleeping alone, I know, but little legs are much easier to push off. I didn't even get to sleep alone when I was a kid, at least not until my sister moved out of the house. Then I got married. That didn't work out and I moved back home. Slept with the kids in my old room. Then Nolan came along."

Angie let Val ramble knowing it was her way of dealing with the anxiety. Eight minutes passed. Finally she stopped for a breath.

"Are they letting you out today?"

"That sergeant questioned me till after ten o'clock. Then that detective from the boat took over. He kept at me till after midnight. He said they could hold me forty-eight hours without charging me. My lawyer got here practically at the crack of dawn. I think he's still somewhere in the building." Val put her hands on the bars. "They told me I wouldn't be able to leave town." She gave a sardonic laugh. "Do you have any idea the last time I went anywhere?"

"1966?" Angie said, joking.

"Just about."

"My life will be very different from now on."

"Not sure what you mean," Angie whispered.

Val sighed and sat on her bunk. "Our marriage wasn't very good."

"Careful who hears you say that."

Val shrugged. "It's not really a secret."

"That's probably why you're still being held."

Val smoothed both hands over her hair.

"How are your sons taking all this?"

"Dale didn't even come see me. You don't have to be a rocket scientist to know what that means. Cal came but barely spoke." She got up, paced a few steps then came and thumped her palms on the bars. "What I don't understand is how they can suspect me of murder. I'm their mother. Nolan's only their stepfather."

The upstairs door whooshed open then thunked closed, the sound followed by heavy footsteps. Sergeant Wilson appeared in increments, shiny boots first, hatless brown crew-cut last. "Time's up, ladies."

Angie reached through the bars to hug Val. "I'll come see you later. Maybe I can help with funeral arrangements."

"Thanks for coming, Angie. Thanks for everything."

Angie followed the officer upstairs. So Dale and Cal were Nolan's stepsons. Interesting.

The humidity blasted outside the station. Almost a relief from the dankness downstairs. How could Val stand it? Angie would go mad. She opened the Lexus' windows then pushed the air conditioner to its coldest. Cool air blasted away the heat.

Angie craved an iced coffee. She stopped at the diner. A few fortifying whiffs of the fresh-brewed coffee and for one moment her sinuses forgot about murder. She unzipped her purse for some cash. The corner of a red envelope caught her eye. Will's birthday card: intended to be given on the boat. Still time before she had to get to work.

Will's office was located on the main thoroughfare. She slipped the car between the florist's little blue hatchback and a purple PT Cruiser. The florist shop window held a cornucopia of color. A huge vase of summer flowers sat among pots of black-centered sunflowers, frilly-edged white asters and delicate baby's breath. Even a spiky bundle of bright yellow goldenrod. What happened to the days when goldenrod was a weed? Angie went inside and bought a summery mixture, then came out and put them on her front seat. The flowers might brighten Val's mood.

Will's office door stood open to the late morning sunshine. Tina Turner's *Proud Mary* blasted onto the sidewalk. Angie stopped a second to look at the listings in the plate glass window. She hadn't known the Bishops' home was on the market. An enormous Georgian Colonial with tennis court and pool.

Listed at $900,000, Angie couldn't suppress her envy. She bet they had central air.

The wind tickled the envelope in her hand. She moved toward the doorway as *Proud Mary* was replaced with *Loving You*. Will stood behind his desk, in silhouette, but there was no mistaking him, she'd been looking at that body for nearly twenty-six years, intimately acquainted with every blemish and pore. What she wasn't acquainted with—seeing his arms wrapped around someone else—a tall shapely blonde. Bright red lacquered nails dug into his back. They broke the embrace and moved apart.

His assistant, Cassie Ferguson.

Like a wad of unchewed meat, Angie choked on the shock and sprinted for the car.

Twelve

Angie didn't remember going home. Suddenly she stood in her kitchen, keys and purse in hand, tears washing away the meticulously applied makeup. She went to the parlor and sat in her chair, then got up and moved out to the patio. The sun shone, oblivious to the turmoil below and she glared at it.

How dare he? With Cassie Ferguson.

Cassie had worked for Will since he'd opened the office ten years ago. Straight out of real estate school she'd been gung-ho selling as many properties as she listed. Friendly and outgoing, small waisted and smooth-skinned. And young. Probably not more than twenty-nine or thirty.

How long had this been going on? Angie marched inside, looking for something to throw. She stood in the small hallway, in the spot where Wallace dripped pool water last night. That's when she heard the television in the living room. She stormed in that direction, snatching up the cordless phone on the way. Wallace lay on the sofa, arms folded under his head. He wore Will's new jeans and the blue Carhartt shirt she'd just bought. Her fingers clenched around the phone. A reporter on CNN said: "...country in civil war. Civilians are using any way necessary to protect themselves." Protection! That's what Wallace was about to need.

She advanced on him. "What are you doing here? Go home!" He sat up, swinging his feet to the floor and eyeing her in confusion. She rarely said anything about his too-frequent appearances in her home. "Get the hell out of here!"

Finally he reacted, standing on the far side of the coffee table, not taking his eyes from her. He left through the front door and walked down the driveway without looking back.

As the door closed, she wanted to shout, "And don't come back," but the words clogged in her throat, just below the gigantic wad of rage. She locked all the doors. The bastard. *How dare he!*

She realized she still held the phone and went to drop it on the charger. Will hadn't followed her from the office. She hadn't spoken or made any sound, maybe he never knew she was there. If he'd known, he would have chased after her before she sped away, wouldn't he? If speeding was what she'd done. Angie   couldn't remember a thing.

None of it mattered. Will had inflicted the ultimate betrayal.

To Angie—and she'd thought, to Will—cheating represented the supreme crime, almost like treason, or murder. How many times had they spoken of it? Not recently of course. After the first ten years recounting beliefs became tedious, one person knew exactly how the other felt, exactly what they'd say or do.

Wasn't tedium the biggest reason for infidelity? A search for the new, the exciting? Escape from encroaching years? A fear of aging? Being with a youthful energetic person had to rejuvenate some of the feelings drowned during long years of marriage.

Angie stepped onto the deck. She'd felt that need for newness too, but hadn't—wouldn't—succumb to such primal urges. Were women stronger? No, women cheated too.

She leaned her elbows on the railing, looking at, but not seeing the surroundings she usually adored. The telephone rang. It rang until the machine picked up. She couldn't hear it from up here, so she didn't try. Maybe it was Will.

So, why didn't he come home?

She'd always thought him a great man. An almost perfect man. He worked hard, provided a nice place to live, rarely complained. When he did, it was usually justified. He didn't drink too much and always came home on time.

Of course that was easy to do when you cheated at work. Sex in the back room between customers wouldn't make you late getting home. Angie slammed a palm on the rail, the sting made her wince. Pain. There were so many kinds. Physical pain caused by external things like railings. Gut pain from things like betrayal. All-over pain from things like murder: the pain Val had to be feeling even though she appeared calm.

How often did suppression of emotions manifest itself in murder? This answer Angie didn't want to know. The compulsion she'd felt to bring the murderer to justice, left as quickly as her so-called invulnerable relationship. Wasn't a long marriage supposed to breed security, an intimacy that made people as one? The unity was supposed to be safe, reliable, comfortable. She pictured Will and Cassie, in one of the homes they'd just listed, trying out the bed and writing on the listing sheet *Spectacular Master Bedroom Suite*. In that room, he told Cassie all Angie's private thoughts and worries, recounted all their discussions, their arguments. Her private thoughts told to another.

Will's betrayal had also been hers.

The front door opened. The alarm didn't sound so she knew it had to be him. 5:12, the exact time he always arrived home. After getting laid in the back room.

Seething, she crossed into the bedroom and listened to his footsteps move through the downstairs, then to the bar to pour himself his usual scotch with a dash of soda. He'd check the kitchen next to see what she'd concocted for dinner. Most nights she left something in the oven for while she was at work. Work! She was supposed to be there hours ago. Why hadn't they called?

Then she remembered; the telephone *had* rung. She'd let the hospital down. Just like she'd let herself down. And in some way, she'd let Will down, caused him to be unfaithful. She knew it in the deepest part of her, it was all her fault. With the back of a hand, she wiped away the vestiges of the afternoon and went downstairs.

Will stood in the kitchen looking out the window a drink in one hand, the other lay on the counter, relaxed—he didn't know she'd been to the office. He didn't know she'd seen. He turned. "Hi, I thought you had to work today."

She strode to the bar and poured herself a drink: scotch without soda, or ice. She sat in the green chair. Will leaned against the counter. Confusion clouded his eyes. With the hesitation borne of a human's built-in reluctance to hear bad news, he came and sat on the loveseat, in the same spot as Jarvis hours before.

Was it only a matter of hours?

In the slight chance Will really did know what she'd witnessed that afternoon, Angie waited. He was, or at least she'd thought he was, an honest person. Guilt should propel him into a confession. What he'd been up to had to be eating away at him. He emptied the glass and went for a refill. Angie sipped. He came back, sat, and stared down at the tinkling ice cubes.

The silence stretched.

When the clock struck the half hour, she spoke, "I know you've been cheating on me."

Six seconds later he nodded. Not the nod of confession, but an 'I was afraid that's what you were going to say' nod.

She waited for a denial, the outright lie: the lie that with other people produced fierce arguments and sometimes even physical violence. Their arguments had never been anything more than shouting matches. So far.

"Sorry."

A single word that could mean anything. Confession. Remorse. Contrition. Conciliation. Mollification.

"Why?" Single word sentences seemed to be in order tonight.

Will opened his mouth the same time Wallace appeared on the patio. Angie handed Will her glass, gathered purse and keys, and left the house through the front door.

"Ange, wait."

As the door closed, Wallace asked, "What the heck's the

matter with her?"

The Lexus was already half way down the driveway when Will appeared on the walk. She saw him in her rear-view mirror, running, yelling. For one mega-second she considered going back. Until Wallace stepped out beside him. She floored the accelerator and squealed onto the road. Let neighbors gawk, she was beyond caring.

She'd been so blind. Too wrapped up in herself. Too worried about tanning beds, new Lexus', and central air. Will had gone to another woman who didn't care about such things—or already had them.

Cassie had made the Millionaire Club several times over the years—an award given to brokers who sold over $4 million in real estate in a given year. Not hard to do with the price of homes in the area. Still, she had to be well off.

Traffic was light, shops closed, tourists tucked safely in their motel rooms. Young people ambled the streets in groups, looking for something new to do.

Why couldn't people remain faithful? Angie pulled off the road, just above the promenade. What made Cassie Ferguson so weak she had to steal someone else's husband? Surely men weren't that scarce. Angie put her forehead on the steering wheel. What to do now? She could go home and hope Wallace had left. Sooner or later she and Will would have to have it out. No way this could hang between them.

Could they get past it and get on with their lives? Did she want to? What were the chances of him cheating again?

A car pulled up in front of her. Angie lifted her head to see a young couple. The male driver smiled at her, then put his arm around his passenger, a blonde with the same hairdo as Cassie.

If Angie stayed with Will, every cute blonde would remind her of Cassie. The wound would always be there, either fading a little with time or festering and growing into distrust and suspicion. Her gaze shifted to the vase of flowers on the seat.

Maybe immersing herself in someone else's problems would

make hers seem less important. She pulled back onto the street. Nothing could make that happen. But maybe the pain wouldn't be so bad. Or possibly she could learn a lesson from Val—how to push the hurt to a spot inside your brain where it could be lived with.

The *Little Fishing Tours* web site had asked payment be sent to an address on Main Street. Angie drove there, confident it was their home address. A middle class neighborhood, the homes in nice shape. The Little's place was a green Contemporary, with fresh paint and a two-car garage. The front porch light illuminated a circle on the front stoop. The flickering blue from a television screen lit up a pair of windows. The shades were pulled and nothing seemed to be moving inside. A green mini-van, the same color as the house, sat in the driveway, in the shadow of a large oak.

Angie carried the flowers to the front door, opened the screen and knocked. A dog barked. Someone shushed it. Footsteps shuffled to the door and it opened a few inches. A tiny nose poked Angie in the shin and barked again. The door opened. Val's somber face appeared then smiled. She picked up the excited, wriggling dog. Val held the dog so he could sniff Angie and he stopped barking. Val put him on the floor and he proceeded to sniff Angie from knee to toe.

She handed Val the vase. "I thought these might cheer you up."

"Thank you." Val set them on an antique-looking sideboard, sniffed the tallest goldenrod and then gave Angie a hug. "That was very nice of you. Have a seat."

Angie chose a chair near the front window because it appeared Val had been using the whole couch. A crumpled pillow bunched against the arm, a blue and white afghan lay balled at the other end. The dog, a terrier mix, poked her shin. Angie reached down and let it sniff the back of her hand. When its tail wagged, she patted its head.

"Beeper, leave the lady alone." Val turned on a lamp at the

end of the sofa and tossed the pillow to the other end. "I can't sleep in the bedroom. I tried sleeping in the boys' old room, but that didn't work either."

Angie nodded. For most couples, their entire intimate relationship was spent in bed. Not just for sex but when there were children in the house, most all discussions took place in the privacy of the bedroom: heart to heart talks, arguments, things kids weren't supposed to hear.

"You doing all right otherwise?"

Val shrugged. "I guess. The boys came. Dale said some comforting things but I could tell his heart wasn't in his words. Cal tried to get me to come stay with them, but the same thing. I know they think I killed Nolan." She swiped at some tears. Beeper hopped on the couch and settled against Val. Absently, she put her hand on its back, kneading his fur.

"You said Nolan's their stepdad?"

"Yeah. We've only been married six years." She gave a wan smile. "He came into town and swept me off my feet." Val groped for the remote and turned off the television. "He changed almost as soon as we were married. All of a sudden he wasn't nice any more. I have no idea what I did wrong."

"Maybe you didn't do anything."

She gave a one-shoulder shrug. "Can I get you something to drink? Coffee, tea? Something stronger?"

"Coffee would be nice."

Val and Beeper went to the kitchen. The dog remained in the doorway, standing guard over his house; a nice home, nothing new or expensive, but neat and clean. Beeper was a small dog, if a burglar attempted to get in Beeper would be kept very busy.

The sounds of cupboards opening and water running came from the kitchen. "Would you care for something to eat?"

Until that moment, Angie hadn't realized how hungry she was. She went to the dimly lit kitchen. Val held out a plate of cookies. Angie's stomach growled. Val laughed. "I guess that answers the question. Wait, I have a better idea. She took a plastic container from the refrigerator, removed the lid and placed it in the microwave.

"Oh goodness, don't go to any trouble."

"It's no trouble, you're helping me out, really. I've been sitting here feeling sorry for myself. I just couldn't make myself get up and cook anything."

Within seconds, the luscious scent of tomato sauce filled the room. Val bustled about getting plates and silverware.

"What were the police doing here?"

"Searching." Val's head disappeared inside the refrigerator. She came out with a chunk of cheese and a grater that she put on the table. "I guess they're looking for evidence to prove I killed Nolan."

"You don't seem worried."

"I didn't kill him. I just have to have faith in the justice system and my lawyer." Val made a palms-up gesture. "What else can I do?"

"Will you keep the business going?"

The microwave beeped three times. Val tested the food then brought it to the table. Angie got her first peek at the contents. Lasagna. If this tasted as good as it smelled...

"We're booked solid the rest of the summer. I can't afford to cancel. Dale's taking vacation time from his job to do the tours with me." Val dished a portion onto Angie's plate, and then her own. "I don't relish it. I can almost hear his unspoken accusations. I can do the tours alone, but they're really too much for one person." She sat and cut off a chunk with the side of her fork. "That's why they let me out, you know. Ties to the community, they called it."

Angie cut a wedge of pasta and touched it with her tongue to make sure it wouldn't burn. They ate in silence for a moment. "This is fantastic."

"Thanks." Val went to retrieve the only bottle of wine from a rack at the end of the counter. She uncorked it, set it on the table to breathe and then took some glasses from the cabinet.

"Nolan had a small insurance policy. It's not enough to retire on or anything like that, but I think it's enough to start my own catering business. I want to call it Prince & Pauper."

"With food like this you'll be an instant hit."

Val gave Angie a grateful look. "I think I can make a go of the food part, but I don't have a clue how to get started."

"Will opened his real estate company. It's mostly a matter of setting up your work space and then doing the proper advertising," Angie said, pushing aside memories that tried to crowd into her brain. "Of course, there are licenses and things like that but that's pretty much dictated by the planning and zoning boards."

Feeling more at ease, Angie poured the wine. "I always wanted to own a neighborhood theater. You know, where we put on plays starring local talent?"

"Sounds like fun. Do you have an acting background?"

"No, I can't act, but in college, I took courses in production and management."

"They offer acting stuff in nursing school?"

Angie laughed. "I got my Bachelor of Science at Rhode Island College and took the other courses nearby."

"Maybe you know the answer to this. What's the proper amount of time for mourning?"

"I'm not sure what you mean."

"I'm worried that if I get a business going, people will either think I killed Nolan for the insurance money, or that I don't care he's dead." Val swallowed. "Either way, I'd have no customers. That sounds cruel and heartless, I know. I just feel like you'll understand. I just know I couldn't sit around the house all the time. I'd go crazy."

Angie crossed to Val, eased her up from the chair and wrapped her in an embrace. Val broke into tears, and so did Angie, realizing suddenly that she, too, needed the release. They cried together for a while then settled back to eat.

"I need to ask you something," Angie said. "And I want you to know I'll keep your answer in the strictest secrecy."

"You don't have to tell me that. What do you want to know?"

"On the boat, after—after...I saw you throw something in the water."

Valerie closed her eyes, bent her head and rubbed her fingertips in her temples. Watching, Angie suddenly knew the answer. "Your wedding ring!"

"I honestly don't know what got into me." Val looked down at the pale white circle around the third finger of her left hand. She smoothed it with her right index finger. "For that one second I almost thought I could fly. God, that sounds so heartless."

"I understand." And she did. Angie gathered the silverware and dropped it in a compartment in the dishwasher. "How did you and Nolan meet?"

Val grinned. "The boys, they were teens at the time, and I were fishing off the dock. Nolan chugged into the marina with *Little One*. The three of them got to talking. Nolan gave them a tour and the rest is history. We were married two months later."

Together they finished clearing the table. They spent some time going over funeral arrangements, Angie making notes in a ring binder.

Valerie put the telephone book away, pushed back her hair and sat opposite Angie. "Can I ask a favor?"

"Of course. Anything."

Val's lips became almost invisible in the set to her mouth. "I'm scared." With those words came a new wave of tears. Angie did her best to comfort her new friend—after all they'd been through, it didn't seem too early to call her a friend—pulling her chair near and wrapping her arms around the small-boned woman.

"It's a frightening time." Then, feeling as though she'd spoken to a small child, she added, "Is there something in particular you're scared of?"

"Being arrested. Being in jail." With great effort, Val lifted her head from Angie's shoulder. Brown eyes looked straight into hers. "I—oh god, Angie, I know they think I killed my husband."

Angie leaned her head against Val's. They sat that way a long time. Val was right. The wife was most always the first suspect, especially when she had such an obvious motive.

"So, will you help me?"

"Of course. What do you need?"

"Will you help me find out who killed him?"

Angie pulled away and shoved the chair backwards.

"They think I killed Nolan. You wouldn't believe the things they asked me."

"It's their job to ask questions."

"Angie, they wanted to know how often we had sex. They wanted to know if anybody ever heard us fighting. I need you to help me. I won't be able to depend on the boys."

"Wouldn't it be better to hire a detective?"

"I can't afford one."

"I'm sure Will and I could give you a loan."

"No!" Val sucked in a raspy breath. "I can't take handouts."

"Well then, why not take out a loan against the insurance?"

Val gave a hesitant nod. "I'd really feel better if you helped me."

"I can't. I would feel devastated if I messed things up worse than they are."

"They can't be worse."

That's when Angie quoted a man she'd once heard speak at school. "Things can always get worse."

"I don't know who else to turn to. Please. Just say you'll think about it."

Angie stood up and slid her chair into place beside the table. "All right, I'll think about it." No danger there. She wasn't committing to anything specific.

"Could we maybe meet for coffee tomorrow sometime? We can talk about how to start looking for Nolan's killer."

"Valerie."

"I know. You're going to think about it. You can give me your decision then."

Angie managed to hold in a sigh. "I'm supposed to work at one, if I still have a job. I don't know what happened, but I totally forgot to go in yesterday."

"What if we meet at the diner around eight a.m., before the tourists jam the place?" Val walked Angie to the door.

She bent to pat Beeper's head and then hugged Val. "Get some sleep."

Angie drove around for more than an hour, alternating between bouts of tears, frustration, worry and all-out rage. One second she was crying so hard she had to pull over, another she was fighting the urge to screech the car home and tear out Will's hair. Part of her wanted to sleep in her own bed. Another had this awful feeling that if she did, she'd find Will and Cassie already there. Deep inside she knew Will would never be that despicable, but the concern lingered.

And then suddenly she couldn't wait to get home.

The porch light was on. A good sign, Will expected her. Or, he'd left it on so Cassie could see on her way out.

Something moved in the shadows a few feet from the car. Will and Wallace stepped into view. Will ran toward her. Wallace strode down the driveway.

Together Angie and Will went inside, he with his hand tightly on her waist, she with her hands clenched around her purse strap. They sat in the dark living room, close but not touching. Will turned sideways on the long couch, one leg on the cushion. Angie, sitting stiffly with both feet on the floor and her fingers still wrapped around her handbag, heard the ticking of the hall clock. Like a dripping faucet. She wanted to speak just to obscure the sounds. But she would not talk first.

After three hundred and twenty two ticks and three hundred and twenty-one tocks, Will opened his mouth. "There's no excuse for what I did. All I can blame, besides my incredible weakness, was our bills and...I guess...I was bored."

Angie didn't answer. If she did, all the anguish might explode all over him.

Then, possibly feeling the need to erase that ticking clock, possibly in a need to cleanse himself, he spoke in a voice laced with sorrow and regret. "She's makes me laugh. Ange, do you realize we never laugh any more?"

Tears tumbled down her cheeks. When he tried to brush them away, she thrust his hand off. He sank deep into the cushions, like a scolded child. She didn't look at him for fear she'd see the same tears she cried.

He went to the bar. He came back with two glasses. "You haven't said anything."

"I'm afraid to," she said, almost whispering. "For the first time, I understand the anger that compels some people to physical violence."

"I've been weak, that's all I can say. I need you. I want you. Us. Together."

She took a large swallow. And another. She got up and climbed the stairs. He followed. Angie slid back the closet door.

"Yes," Will said, coming to stand beside her. "Let's go to bed."

She dug around in the closet. His eyes widened when she came out with a suitcase. She laid it on the bed and stowed clothes inside. At the dressing table she loaded makeup and jewelry into a second case. Job done she picked one bag up in each hand and passed him.

"Angie, no. Please."

"I have to get away. I have to think."

Thirteen

This time Angie didn't drive aimlessly through the streets; she went straight to the nearest place and rented a cabin. The room was small, but clean and comfortable. She unpacked and laid her makeup out on the dresser, the actions of a person planning a long stay. Unable to face getting into bed, she put on a sweater and went for a walk. Well after midnight and the streets were quiet, only the occasional automobile passed. The air was brisk and refreshing, a welcome change from the day's humidity. Stars twinkled in the summer sky. A dog barked somewhere and suddenly Angie wished for something to cuddle, something that loved unconditionally, that trusted without question, who wouldn't betray.

She had no one.

Unlike Val, being alone wasn't a relief. But Angie couldn't stay with a person she couldn't trust. Trust was the mainstay of a relationship. Without it, there was nothing. Angie yawned. She walked back to the cabin, undressed and, naked, got into bed. The pull of sleep deepened and the edges of wakefulness disappeared. She pictured Will in their big white-covered bed; a lump sprawled diagonally on the king-sized mattress, the comforter bunched behind him. The lights off, skinny yellow stripes of moonlight peeped through the vertical blinds to illuminate his nude body, glistening gold and handsome. Angie imagined herself running her hands over the muscles, tracing her fingers in the clefts and indentations, feeling the supple softness of his skin, enjoying the sensations of the tiny, almost invisible hairs against her palms. She turned on her side, imagining the entire length of her body against his. Even their legs and feet melded together.

Angie felt herself rising above this scene, yet still sensing and adoring the feel of their skin touching. From above, she watched her hands move around to his abdomen, fondling, arousing. Will turned over, ready for her.

Something was wrong. Angie couldn't feel his ministrations. The rippling sensations in her abdomen—were absent. From her lofty spot, she peered down at him, so good looking—at herself, anxious beneath his touch, equally ready. The comforter, brilliant white in the moonlight, moved, pushed by a feminine hand. Long manicured nails. Fire engine red nails.

Cassie Ferguson's nails.

The scene dissolved as Angie flew out of the bed, feet tangling in the bedclothes. She landed on her face, the pain of the fall and shock of the revelation sending waves down her spine. She lay on the floor waiting for the initial hurt to subside. The scent of carpet oozed into her senses. Something tickled her nose. She sneezed and sat up, extricating her legs from the sheet, waiting for more pain to replace what had subsided. It didn't. She was unhurt. Physically.

Emotional ache roared back. Visions of Cassie and Will pushed at her from all angles. She pressed her eyes shut with her fingers and laid her head on her knees. She couldn't take this, couldn't be strong like Val.

Dawn's light edged around the heavy drapes, punching at her spirit. Morning had come. Another day. She still sat on the floor. At some point she must have fallen asleep, the sheet tight around her. Angie struggled to her feet, stretching out the kinks of a night on the hard floor.

Don't think about Will. Go on with the day. Meet Val. Go to work.

Work. A dread fear melted her insides. She'd forgotten uniforms at home.

She took a breath. It was all right. Will had to be at work by nine and she wasn't expected at the hospital till one. Plenty of time to get in and out without having to face him. The clock on the bed table said 7:17.

An overcast day , the perfect complement to her mood. Valerie's mini-van was parked in front of the diner. Angie stopped behind it.

"You look like I feel," Val said, bouncing toward her, somewhat the same way Beeper had bounced the previous evening. Angie couldn't help thinking of the saying that people ended up resembling their pets.

"Sorry I'm late. I stopped to get you something." She handed Val a small white paper bag.

"You don't have to buy me something every time we see each other, but thank you." Val peeked inside then took out a tube of hand cream.

"I noticed how much damage you had from your job," Angie offered.

"Thanks." Val tucked the bag under her arm, squeezed some of the cream on her hands and rubbed it in. She sniffed, and "oohed" in appreciation.

"Were your customers upset that you cancelled the trip today?"

"Believe it or not, it's one of our—my—only free days this summer. Which is good because I've got to lease a boat. *Little One* is still in impound. I'm not sure I would have taken the day off anyway. I'm going to need every penny." She lifted her face and inhaled. "I love the smell of fresh air, don't you?"

"Sure." Angie leaned against her car, the metal cool against her backside.

"I'm not sure I can be alone today. You don't by any chance want company at work?"

"Being in an emergency room all day can't be the medicine you need." Angie wasn't sure being at the hospital would be good for her today either.

"Any ideas where we should start the investigation?"

"You're really determined to do this?"

"I'm doing it no matter what. The cops came to the house first thing this morning. Right this minute, they're pawing through all my things."

Angie set her purse on the trunk hood, reached inside and drew out a small white envelope with her bank logo in blue. She pushed it across to Valerie. "It's a thousand dollars. Hire a detective, it's the best way."

"I told you already, I won't take a handout and I can't afford to repay you." Valerie shoved the envelope back. "You'll help me, won't you?"

Angie heaved a sigh that cleared her lungs. "I'm sorry Val, I just can't. It's too dangerous. Whoever killed Nolan might come after us too."

"I kinda thought you'd say that. Thanks for considering it, anyway." Val shrugged. "I guess I'll start by talking to Sonnie and Montez."

Angie couldn't believe the woman's determination. "You're really doing this? Does that detective know?"

"Of course not." Val's keys jingled as she crammed them in her pocket. "Oh, I get it, you thought when you said no, I'd drop the idea and go on with my pitiful life. Sorry, I can't. Not only is my future is at stake, I think...so is my sanity."

"Can't you start with someone besides Sonnie and Montez? Those two give me the willies."

"Don't be silly, they're pussy cats."

Angie couldn't very well mention Sonnie's suggestion for disposing of Nolan's body. "What do you expect to learn from them?"

"They aren't the types to talk to the cops, you know? If they know something, they'll tell me."

Or they'll kill her.

Angie watched a few cars pass on the main road. She slapped

a hand on the trunk hood. "All right. I'm scared what they'll do to you. Will you promise not to go without me?"

Valerie's squeal of delight made passing tourists look in their direction. "You won't be sorry. You'll see. We'll find who did this. And make the cops sorry they suspected me." She stopped bubbling long enough to hug Angie. "Come on, let's go eat. My treat."

Angie started to follow, but the mousy haired woman had stopped. Angie plowed into her backside. Val spun around. "I forgot to tell you, this morning I called a carpenter. He's coming to give an estimate, to tell me whether I should knock out the dining room wall and enlarge the kitchen, or renovate the garage. Angie, I can't tell you how excited I am about this. I went through my recipes and marked all my favorites. I even devised a couple of new ones."

"Don't you think you should slow down a little?"

"Do you have any idea how long I've been thinking about this?"

"You don't want the cops any more suspicious than they already are."

"Shit, I never thought of that. I'll cancel the carpenter. Come on, let's go eat." Again they started for the diner. Again Val stopped. "Angie, is something wrong? Other than not wanting to investigate, I mean. I noticed last night, but didn't want to ask." She tilted her head as though trying to get a better look at Angie. "Sometimes it's good to talk about things."

Did she want to talk about it? Would saying the words make the awfulness all the more real? Any less painful? Before she knew it, the words were out of her mouth. "Will's been cheating on me."

There, she'd said it. A giant pit hadn't swallowed her. The earth hadn't exploded in lava and molten ash. Her insides hadn't dissolved into a vacuum. The green lush landscape was exactly the same. The world hadn't changed one iota since the words left her lips.

Val looked ready to cry. "Oh Angie, I'm so sorry." Tears did indeed well up as she started to pull Angie into a hug. Then she thought better of it and settled for swiping the tears. "So sorry. I can't even tell you."

"I've left him. I'm staying at the cabins near the marina. Next week would've been our twenty-sixth anniversary."

Val drew her keys from her pocket. "You two looked so happy. I thought...I mean I wouldn't have thought... God this is terrible. I'm so sorry. I'll, uh, go."

"You don't have to. I'll be all right."

"You're a nice person. You didn't ask for this." She patted Angie's arm. "I'll leave."

"I'm not the first woman this has happened to."

"I know, but, I guess I tend to forget other people have troubles too."

"Look, I get off at ten tonight, is that too late to come over? We'll talk about how to approach Sonnie and Montez for tomorrow, okay?"

This time Val did hug Angie. "If you're sure you want to do this."

"Just promise you won't go see them alone."

Angie drove home, wondering if she should ask Will to give up the house. The mortgage was low. Could she swing the upkeep and the taxes? She made good money at the hospital but nowadays it took two incomes.

She stopped halfway up the driveway to look at the place. Her house. Hers and Will's. Fresh yellow paint. Neatly trimmed shrubs. Perfectly edged walk. She laid her head on the steering wheel and didn't try to hold back the tears. Accepting one's faults was difficult. The only bone of contention between she and Will was her extravagance. She insisted on top quality everything. Always kept things in pristine condition. She wiped the back of a hand across her face knowing her makeup was beyond repair. No, she couldn't handle things alone.

She'd told Val she'd recover. One way or another, she would.

Whether she went back to Will or didn't, she'd live. Parts of her would be changed forever, but who couldn't say that about any traumatic event in their lives? Look at her parents; they'd survived a breakup. Dad was dead now, of the alcoholism that broke up the marriage. Her mother had turned into a lunatic. But they'd survived and Angie would too.

She got the car moving again. Rounding a slight bend brought the top of the driveway—and vehicles—into view. Two of the three people she least wanted to see were at the house. Wallace for obvious reasons, and Jarvis. What the hell did he want this time?

Fourteen

Jarvis opened the door as if he were the host instead of the intruder. "Good morning Mrs. Deacon, nice to see you."

"What the hell's going on here?" Angie stepped past him.

"Your husband gave us the okay to search the place." Jarvis nodded at Wallace.

Angie's irritation burst. "That's not my husband, you idiot." The pulsing in her temples exploded in an instantaneous migraine. She advanced on the grinning Wallace. "Get out of my house!"

"It's not your house any more."

"Get out!" Angie stormed one more step toward him then turned on the detective. "And stop searching. You most certainly don't have permission." She picked up the phone and punched the first two numbers of the lawyer's office. Things were quickly escalating out of hand. She had to get control, both of herself and the situation.

"Calm down, Mrs. Deacon. Please. We'll get this straightened out." Jarvis's palm in the air should've diffused the situation but only intensified her anger. Even as she fumed, she realized the unreasonableness of her rage both flustered and confused him. He pursed his lips and lowered his hand.

"He has no right in this house let alone giving you permission to search it," Angie said.

Jarvis frowned, the lines like tilled harrows between his eyes. Suddenly Angie knew what was racing through his mind: her anger meant she had something to hide.

"Mrs. Deacon, please. We have permission."

"You idiot, this isn't Will. It's his brother Wallace. He has no right to be in this house, let alone give you permission to search it. I want you both to leave now." She punched a third number.

"You're the one who has no right to be here," Wallace said.

Finally Jarvis understood. He whispered something to one of his men who disappeared upstairs. "Please sit down, Mrs. Deacon."

"Get out of my house. And take him with you."

Wallace went to the patio door. "I'm leaving, but you'd better send her away too."

Jarvis shut the door behind Wallace, waited till he'd disappeared around the corner, then came to her. "Please sit down, Mrs. Deacon."

She said, "Don't patronize me," but obeyed. She took in a breath, let it out. "Now get your men out of my house." She poked the OFF button on the phone.

"Yesterday you indicated your desire to help. I thought you wouldn't mind."

"Would you mind telling me what you're looking for?"

"I'm not at liberty to say right now."

Angie sighed.

"Your husband's brother—what's his name?"

"Wallace."

"Wallace indicated things weren't going well around here." Jarvis sat on the flowered sofa, looking incongruous against the gaiety. "I gather his presence is an issue between you and your husband."

"Wallace has a wife and family whom he chooses not to support to the best of his ability." Wresting her knuckles from their grip of her purse strap, she set the handbag on the floor beside the chair then flexed her fingers in her lap. "He's never held a job for more than a few days. When he loses one, he doesn't want to tell Marty—that's his wife—so he hides out here. Will's always loaning him money because he's worried about Marty and the kids. I keep telling Will it's not his responsibility, if he'd just stop letting Wallace lean on him, he'd have to stand on his own two feet."

"And he might not," Will's voice, from the hallway.

The sight of him brought memories crashing back. Angie blinked away the vision of Cassie in his arms.

"My brother told me what happened."

"His version," Angie said.

"He said the police were searching the house and you were very angry."

"I don't suppose he mentioned he'd impersonated you and gave them permission?"

Will walked around the sofa and stood five feet away; a distance that felt like only centimeters. "What are you looking for?"

Jarvis repeated the stock comment. "I'm not at liberty to say."

Angie and Will's eyes met. They both knew Jarvis was trying to connect their breakup to Nolan's murder. That was ridiculous and her inclination was to tell him so, but an old adage popped into her head: she doth protest too much. Maybe it would be better to wait and see where this headed before volunteering anything.

"I don't have a problem with them searching, do you?" Will asked.

She stood. "I don't care what they do. I have to get to work."

"Ange, can we talk?" Will asked.

"No."

She went upstairs to the bedroom, unsuccessfully trying to squelch the image of Cassie and Will in the bed. She reached in the closet and took out her spare uniforms. Before sentiment could weaken her resolve, she tiptoed downstairs, trying unsuccessfully to sneak out. Both Jarvis and Will met her at the door.

"I need to know where I can reach you," Jarvis said.

"Me too," Will said.

"At work," was all she said. Right now she was in no mood

to make things easy for either of them.

"Ange," Will said.

"I'm not ready to talk yet."

She kept an eye in the rear-view mirror. No one followed, but soon after she'd turned onto Route 11, a nondescript car appeared. She eased to the side of the road and waited for it to pass. It did and she squinted trying to keep it in view around the corner. Sure enough, it slowed onto the shoulder. What the hell, she didn't have anything to hide. She pulled back onto the road.

What were they looking for at her house? Was there some kind of evidence against one of them? Footprints had, after all, been found in the puddle of blood. And Will had given them a hard time when they wanted his shoes. Still, what possible reason could he have to murder Nolan?

Angie poked buttons on her cell-phone and asked for her supervisor.

"Angie, I'm glad to hear from you," said Zoë Pappas. "Yesterday when you didn't show up, I thought I misunderstood something you'd told me."

"No, it was my fault. With the murder and everything, I just plain forgot to come in. I'm so sorry."

"That's okay, hon. As I said, I assumed I'd made the mistake. Got the shift covered just fine."

"Zoë, I need a favor. I need a leave of absence."

Zoë hesitated for only a fleeting second. "Say no more. Any idea how long?"

"A week, maybe two."

The line went quiet while her supervisor processed the information and probably ran a list of replacements through her head. "Is there a problem I should know about? You're not...arrested or anthing?"

"No, everything's okay."

"Keep me posted."

"I will. Thanks." Angie flipped the phone shut and put it in her purse.

The sky had clouded over. The wind picked up, blowing off the bay, rustling treetops and whipping leaves into a frenzy. Rain seemed imminent, the darkening day a perfect complement to her mood. She turned into Val's driveway.

When Val opened the door, Angie smiled and wiggled her hands in the air. "I come bearing no gifts." She bent down and patted Beeper.

They were only seated in the living room for a few seconds when they spoke at the same time. Val saying, "Are you still going to help find who killed Nolan?" And Angie saying, "Will you do me a favor?"

The women laughed, happy to be sharing a moment that didn't include tears or regrets. "I took a leave of absence from work."

Val leaned forward in the chair as if about to deliver important information. "Where will we start the investigation and what's the favor?"

For a mega-second Angie'd been about to ask if she could stay there. Val had an extra room and needed someone to lean on—but she rejected the thought. Unfortunately the first words that came to her lips were, "I've been thinking about those duffel bags. What do you know about them?"

"Just that they always had them. The bags looked alike."

"They brought them aboard. Did they bring them back to shore when the trip was over?"

"I never noticed. I always get right to cleaning up when we dock."

"Did they ever ask you to hide them or indicate you shouldn't touch them?"

"No, not to me. Nolan once asked what was inside. Sonnie shut him up saying, 'My boss.'"

"I can't help thinking they have something to do with Nolan's death."

"I don't see how."

"I don't either right now but they're just too suspicious to let go."

"The police don't think they're important."

"Police have been known to make mistakes," Angie said, thinking about the fiasco at her house. "Do you have access to another boat? Do you know any scuba divers?"

"I've already leased another boat. I have a tour tomorrow. But a diver...that's something Nolan would have known. Wait a second, I know somebody. Let's go for a ride. Do you need a sweater?"

"I have one in the car."

"The guy I know is probably at the marina now." Then, as if reading Angie's seasick thoughts, she added, "Don't worry, we're not going on the water."

Angie watched Val lean back, reveling in the luxurious feel of the leather seat and deep carpet and felt justified in her extravagance. Rain began to spatter on the windshield and she flicked on the wipers. At the bottom of the drive, she turned left.

Just as they turned into the marina parking lot, Val asked, "Wouldn't someone have noticed Sonnie or Montez lowering the bags in the water?"

"Not if we were otherwise occupied."

Angie changed the subject. "Any idea how long *Little One* might be impounded?"

"When I asked, the answer was 'when we're done with it'."

Angie slid the key from the ignition and gazed out at the steadily falling rain. She had neither raincoat nor umbrella.

Val giggled. "My raingear's all on the boat."

"Did they let you transfer things to the new boat?"

"Yeah. That was a chore and a half."

Angie pulled on the door handle. "Ready?"

"As I'll ever be."

The women raced down the tarmac, wind driving the rain in their faces. Val boarded a boat a few slips from hers without waiting to be invited. Angie gripped the moving rail in white knuckles. The storm heaved and tossed everything, including the dock, beneath her feet. She made herself climb aboard reminding herself they weren't sailing anywhere.

The bearded boat owner smiled at the bedraggled women. "Rainin' huh?" The man chuckled and closed the cabin door against the weather. He reached out a scarred hand to Angie. "Carlson Brinks. Friends just call me Brinks." Seeing her notice his hands, he added, "Used to be a deep-sea fisherman. Dangerous work. But there's saltwater running through these veins and I can't give it up completely."

"This is my friend Angie Deacon," Val said.

"Nice to meet you," Angie and Brinks said at the same time.

Rain dribbled down her forehead and nose. She wiped it away but it was hopeless and she gave up, telling herself to be more like Val, who stood dripping as though it were the most natural thing in the world.

Trees along the far banks bent in the wind. Leaves, wrenched from the branches, filled the air like snow. Hollow thuds shook the boat as the waves bucked and lashed at the hull. Tied to the dock or not, Angie couldn't stand much more of this.

On the other side of the bay, the sidewalks were nearly empty. The few brave souls who refused to let a rainstorm mar their vacation were clad in bright blue and yellow plastic and hurried from one place to the next. Angie tensed her stomach muscles, willing everything to remain where it was.

Val and the aged boatman bent over a map spread on the tiny table. Angie bent to look too, as though she understood the blues and greens, and dotted and solid lines. Val's finger indicated a spot in the blue that Angie assumed was lake, about an inch away from the green she assumed was island.

"We anchored here, just off Rattlesnake Island."

Brinks' "waste of time," made both women look up. "Cops had me out there last night. Found nothing."

Angie could hardly contain herself. That meant she was on the right track.

After more condolences about Nolan and best wishes for

their search, they shook hands with the gnarled gentleman and raced up the dock.

"Angie, who do you think killed Nolan?" Val shouted over the sound of the rain.

"If I had to make a guess, I'd say Sonnie and Montez did it together."

Fifteen

At Angie's cabin, Val kicked off her sodden shoes near the doorway. Angie removed all but her undergarments then eyed her reflection in the mirror, trying not to think that she'd just appeared in public looking so bedraggled.

"I don't suppose you have any friends at the DMV," Val asked.

Angie drew the brush through her hair, feeling droplets whisper down her arms. "What for?"

"I want to get Sonnie's address from his license plate number."

"Where'd you get his plate number?"

"He wrote it on the first reservation form he filled out."

Angie flopped on the foot of one bed. "I do know someone. She's a dispatcher for Farmington. She goes to a yoga class with me." Why had she volunteered that information? How easy it would be to say she knew nobody.

"You do yoga?"

Angie shrugged. "Helps keep me in shape. I do a lot of hiking too."

"I envy you. Everything I do is related to the business."

Angie dialed information and soon had the police dispatcher on the line. "Hi Bea, it's Angie, from yoga class. Hey, I hate to bother you but you're the only one I know."

"Wasn't what happened awful? Any idea who did it?"

"No. I have a different problem right now. I was hit and run this morning." Angie spun away from Val's look of surprise. "No serious damage, but I'd like to contact the guy." Angie glanced at the piece of paper where Val had scrawled Sonnie's information. "It's a New Hampshire tag 623-321."

"I'll check it and call you back."

"Thanks, hon." Angie dropped the cell phone beside her on the bed. "She'll call back. Here, I'll get you some dry clothes."

While Angie rummaged for two outfits, Val turned on the clock radio between the beds and classical music filled the room. Val groaned. "Mind if I change this?" She turned the dial and stopped at a rock-and-roll station, then turned up the volume on a trumpet barrage by *Chicago*.

When the crescendo ended in a long single note, Angie said, "I had a whole other image of you when we were on the boat."

Val ceased thumping her fingers to the beat and turned somber. "You thought that mousy little wimp was the real me?"

"I assume everyone did."

"Uh-huh. For one thing, I hate that country stuff Nolan played." She plucked at her sleeve. "And I hate these stuffy clothes. Soon, I'm going shopping. I know I can say this and you'll understand what I mean: I'm so excited to finally be able to live. To just be me. It sounds unfeeling but it's like being able to breathe for the first time."

"I can imagine," Angie said.

"I'm so excited about the catering business idea. I've begun searching the Internet for supplies."

"What if the cops confiscate your computer? I heard that's one of the first things they do."

"Oh God." Then she broke into a smile. "Wait. I might be all right. They took the computer from the office. I've been using the laptop."

"If I were you, I'd find a place to hide it in case they come back."

By the time they'd changed clothes and dried their hair, the dispatcher had phoned back. While Angie recited, Val wrote

Sonnie Phelps' Nashua address on the back of a bank receipt.

"Can we stop at my place first? I have to let Beeper out," Val said.

"You were thinking of going to Nashua now?"

"When did you want to—oh god, I can't go now, I have to meet the carpenter in an hour."

Relief shot through her. Even so, she said, "I thought you were canceling him."

"I was, but it didn't seem like it could hurt anything just to get an estimate."

Angie didn't remind her how word got out, gossip spread. "Okay then, we'll go first thing in the morning." There was still a chance something else could come up to delay this. "Come on, let's get something to eat, I missed lunch."

After lunch, Angie dropped Val off at home, and then drove to headquarters. She was quickly admitted into Detective Jarvis' tiny office with a tiny window, and a tiny desk piled high with empty cardboard coffee containers and crumpled napkins. Definitely Holmes-like.

Making no excuses for the clutter, he folded his hands atop an empty donut bag. "Sit down?"

She sat, crossing the right knee over the left.

"You're not mad at me any more?"

"I realized Wallace duped you. An understandable mistake."

"So, why are you here?"

"I uh, was curious whether there have been any developments in the case."

"Developments?"

"I wondered if you were closing in on anyone."

"Worried?"

"Of course not. I can't stop thinking about those bags."

Jarvis' eyebrows twitched. He looked different without his hat. A little ill-at-ease. Was the hat what 'made the man'? Without it, was he like Samson without his—hair! Suddenly she knew.

His hair was thinning, the hat a way to cover it up.

"What's funny?"

"Why do you always ask me that?"

"Because you always seem like you're listening to your own private comedy routine." He picked up a Styrofoam container and heaved it into the trash. "You've really got a bugger on for those bags, don't you? What's going on between you and your husband?"

"It's not related to this case."

"Prove it."

"Detective, you can't possibly be thinking either Val or I—or Will—are murderers."

He laced his hands together on a donut bag, making it crunch. "Do you have a suspect in mind?"

Angie only wanted details and information, yet she played along. "It's got to be either Sonnie or Montez. Or maybe both."

"What about Mister Goodwell?"

"His appearance on the boat is mysterious, but I can't picture him as a murderer."

"You're still bothered about the bags."

His mouth looked serious, yet playfulness danced in his eyes. He was teasing her. Angie slid forward on the chair. "You aren't?"

"Believe it or not, we are capable of carrying out a murder investigation." He gave an elaborate sigh. "I don't know why I'm telling you this but we can't see how the bags are related to the case. Sure, they might contain contraband, drugs or such, but we cannot in any way, tie Nolan Little to either Phelps or Clarke—or the bags."

Angie slid back on the seat. Maybe he was right. Outside of a severe dislike for the way Nolan treated Val, why would they have wanted him dead?

Someone had.

Who else could it be? She slapped her palms on her thighs. Val. The only logical suspect. Angie rose. Before she could stop them, words sprang from her mouth, "Is there anything I can do to help with the investigation?"

"I just told you, we're capable of investigating by ourselves."

"I wasn't suggesting otherwise. I'd just like to help."

"You can help by staying out of the way."

She opened the door.

"Mrs. Deacon." Angie stopped but didn't turn. "I want you and Mrs. Little to remain at your houses. Cook, clean, gossip, I don't care, just stay out of our way. And, don't leave town."

Jarvis's last words echoed in her head all the way back to the cabin. "Don't leave town."

The phone rang as she stabbed the key in the lock. It had to be Val. Angie answered on the third ring.

"Hi Ange."

The sound of Will's voice melted her bones. She sank onto the bed. That one word echoed with it all the love and loss she had been feeling.

"Ange," he repeated, using the nickname only he used.

Her insides twisted. The compulsion to jump in the car and throw herself into his arms became impossible to ignore. Will waited for her to speak, or maybe, after summoning the courage to call, he couldn't think of anything to say. Or perhaps he'd had nothing planned, and hoped, as soon as they heard each other's voices, the old comradeship would return.

"Are you there?"

She took a breath. "How did you find me?"

"There aren't that many places in town."

"What do you want?"

"I thought you might want to know what the police confiscated from the house."

"Not really." As soon as the words left her lips she knew she did care, very much. And Will knew it. As a couple, they'd been thoroughly in tune to each other. Not that they always agreed about everything—her spending in particular—but each always knew what the other was thinking. Until Cassie came along.

"Will, I don't give a flying shit what they took. They can burn the place to the ground for all I care." She kicked off her shoes, and scuffed her feet on the carpet, the short scratchy fibers an agreeable abrasion on her soles.

Will didn't rise to her attack. "I need to talk to you."

"There's nothing left to say."

"Give me a chance. Don't hang up, please."

"Now's not a good time to talk. I'm still too hurt."

"Look, I made serious mistakes, I don't know what else to do but apologize. I love you."

"You betrayed me."

"How come you can forgive some people, and not me?"

"Because—because other people didn't first try to convince me things were different than I thought." She took a breath and hung up the phone.

Sixteen

Jarvis pushed back the chair so hard it bounced off the windowsill. He paced the narrow space behind his desk, kicking the chair out of the way on the return lap. The day was a total bust starting with the fiasco at the Deacon house and ending with what Wilson overheard between the Little and Deacon women. Just what he needed, two Stephanie Plums screwing up his investigation.

Damned investigation. Eighteen hours and not a solid lead. The household searches were busts. Preliminary results on the computers came back negative. What took so long with the blood samples? And where the hell were the tests from the shoes? Simple request: tell us if there's blood on them. A smirk pushed through the scowl as he thought of the group of suspects traipsing up the marina parking lot in stocking feet. Too bad he hadn't been there to see it.

Wilson rapped and opened the door. "Here are the background checks you wanted. I got the stuff from the dead guy's pocket too." He slapped a stack of pages and a brown envelope on the desk.

Jarvis dropped in the chair and dug his heels in the carpet protector to drag himself up to the desk. About a dozen handwritten pages. Willis Deacon's name at front and center of the topmost one. Below his name, in smaller letters, *Wallace Deacon, twin*. There were photocopies of their drivers' licenses.

Damn, the brothers looked alike! He'd known they were twins, of course, but had never seen them side-by-side. The mix-up at the house hadn't been entirely his fault; Wallace let the cops in as if he owned the place; what should they have done, ask for the man's ID in his own home? Jarvis bent his head and raked chewed fingernails through his hair. If the Deacon woman filed a complaint, Captain Folsom would be all over him for this.

What was up between the Deacons? Yesterday they were a happily married couple, he would've staked his career on it. Today the wife moved out. What could've happened in such a short time? And why would neither of them talk about it?

Jarvis jerked upright, slamming both palms on the desk. One of the Deacons was the killer. They'd argued over it. And the accuser—or the murderer—had moved out of the house. He hadn't figured either of them as legitimate suspects. Murders were committed by either sex, that was a given. Men tended toward the messier crimes, shootings and stabbings. Women usually preferred poison. Usually. Either way, what motive could he or she have?

"Wilson!" The sergeant's face appeared, nonplussed by Jarvis's outburst. "Find out why the Deacons are separated."

"I've been working on it."

Trouble was, it all came back to the blood—nobody had enough on them.

The chair creaked as he settled back to read the stats on Willis Deacon. Born 1956, Lake Placid, New York; graduated LP Central High School 1973. He spun to face the computer—a brand new Mac, compliments of the townsfolk—Googled the school's website, then located the 1973 issue of the yearbook.

Why wasn't he surprised to find Willis Deacon the class Valedictorian, voted most likely to succeed, *and* Prom King? His picture was pasted all over the issue. On the other hand, the only place the twin showed up was the requisite class picture and a photo layout of the varsity swim team squad, in which Will also appeared.

After graduation the charmed twin, Will, took real estate courses at Clinton Community College in Plattsburgh, NY. Married Angelina Nadia Farnsworth in 1980. The couple moved to Alton Bay and bought a house on Bay Hill Road in '84. In large letters at the bottom of Will Deacon's page, it said: NO ARREST RECORD.

Jarvis had heard of the Deacons a number of years ago. There'd been a front-page feature in the Conway Daily Sun when Will opened Alton Bay Homes & Land Real Estate. When was that? Mid 80's, maybe. He couldn't recall hearing anything about them since.

He dug Angelina's stats from the pile and again leaned the chair back. Angelina Marie Farnsworth. Born Yarmouth, Cape Cod, 1954. He didn't try to cover his surprise that she was fifty-five; he'd put her nearer forty. Attended Dennis-Yarmouth Regional High School. No date of graduation but she'd come away from Rhode Island College with her Bachelor of Science in Nursing, in 1976. Nothing to indicate how she and Willis met. Neither did she have a record. Neither of the bios indicated any relationship to the Littles. Just as Angelina said.

Angelina. Nice name. Nice lady. High maintenance. It would take a strong man to keep her happy. To keep her satisfied—in bed. Desire rippled. Before the twinge could swell out of control he lurched to his feet and walked it off; like a charley horse or a foot that had fallen asleep.

The image of Liz pushed into his mind and he went to the window. Darkness outside, just the shadows of things he knew were bushes and cars. Liz's face reflected in the glass. Liz, with the flaming red hair to match her personality. Sadness clutched his throat and for a moment he couldn't pull in a breath. She'd been his reason for living. After she died, he'd holed up in this cave called Alton Bay.

Liz and Angelina, different as peanut butter and jelly, as rain and sunshine. Angelina, the first one who'd moved his emotions in years. He could not get involved with this woman! She was married. She was in an over-emotional state. She was...

A murder suspect.

A tap sounded on the door. Jarvis whirled around. Sergeant Wilson strode in carrying a Styrofoam cup that he set on the desk. "We've got Clarke."

Jarvis stepped away from the window, feeling the guilt of his previous thoughts. As though it were sacrilege to think of something other than the investigation. He jerked the chair into place behind the desk and sat.

Not a good idea to interview the guy before looking at the data sheet. "Gimme a few minutes." He sipped the coffee and made a face. "This stuff's from the Dark Ages." He thumbed through the remainder of the pile. There's nothing here on—" he almost said Wuss. "Goodwell."

"Nothing's come in yet."

"Call Manhattan. Tell 'em to get on the stick. If they think they can jerk us around just because we're in New Hampshire, they've got another think coming."

"Yes sir. I'll make fresh coffee too." Wilson shut the door with just a click.

Jarvis slid Montez Clarke's info page from the pile and skimmed the half page of information. Born Kingston, Jamaica 1982. Moved to Nashua in '84 at the age of two. Graduated Nashua High South in '97. Jarvis punched the intercom button. "Wilson, the sheet on Clarke isn't complete."

"It's coming, sir." Jarvis heard the barely restrained frustration in Wilson's voice. Damn him, he knew better than to submit half-done information.

God, his face hurt, Jarvis rubbed the spot between his eyes, let his hands gravitate to his cheeks then around to the back of his neck. He rubbed hard, head bent low, wondering if he could get the captain to okay a masseuse on his expense account. He jabbed the intercom with a knuckle. "Send Clarke in."

Wilson held the door for the towering black man, who entered looking at ease, as though he were out for a day of...fishing.

Clarke flopped in one of the hard chairs in front of the desk, hands folded over his crotch, feet crossed at the ankles. The two men eyed each other like boxers facing off in the ring.

"Aren't you going to ask why we had you picked up?" Jarvis asked, after letting the silence stretch to almost a minute.

"I figured you'd get around to telling me."

"How many times have you been on one of Little's tours?"

Montez's shrug consisted of a single up and down twitch of one shoulder.

Jarvis tried again, "You hated the way Nolan treated Valerie."

"That's been established."

"You wanted to put a stop to it."

"I wouldn't murder to do it."

"What would you do?"

A slow smile crept across Clarke's face and he sat up in the chair. "Whatever it is, I didn't act on it."

"Did you ever see either of them outside the boundaries of the tour? Supermarket? Golf course?" At the mention of golf, Montez snorted. "Come on Clarke, you know the drill, stop making me drag information out of you."

Montez gave an elaborate sigh. "Sonnie and I went on the tour three or four times a year. When we were in the area. You know? We didn't socialize. I didn't like the guy. Can't understand why she put up with him."

"Maybe she didn't." The shrug came again, this time with two shoulders. Jarvis stifled his irritation. "Do you think she killed him?"

"All I can tell you, it wasn't me."

"I'm asking your opinion."

Montez gave some thought to the question then merely shook his head.

"What about Sonnie?"

"Can't speak for him."

Jarvis' hands wanted to curl into fists. Instead he spread

them flat on the desk and tried a new angle, "Where are the duffel bags?"

The slow smile returned, this time wider. "The blonde was dying to know what was inside. Kicked one." He unfolded his hands and flicked a finger, a digital kicking gesture. "She was pretty disappointed when nobody hollered 'help, I'm being held prisoner!'"

"What *was* inside?"

"Nothing much. Fishing gear, change of clothes."

"Where are the bags now?"

Another two-shoulder shrug and Montez leaned forward laying his forearms along his thighs. "I don't know."

Did this guy think he was a fool? "Where's Phelps?"

"I don't know. I'm not his keeper. I can tell you he doesn't have the bags, either."

"How can you be so sure?"

"Because we looked for them together."

"You trying to say they were stolen?"

Another lop-sided shrug. "The bags have nothing to do with the murder."

"Prove it."

Montez laughed. "That's your job."

"It's your job to keep me from arresting you."

"Why the hell would you arrest me?" Montez rocked onto his feet. "*Are* you arresting me 'cause if you are, do it. If you aren't, I'm outta here."

"Sit down. You'll leave when I say you leave."

Montez eyed him. Jarvis stared back. Finally Montez sat.

"I've got enough to hold you on suspicion."

"Bull shit."

"We got motive: you hated Nolan. We got opportunity: you were up front, ten feet from the cockpit. We got means: the murder weapon was within—"

Montez exploded, "You got the same shit for everybody on that boat!"

"Everyone else isn't avoiding questions. Everyone else isn't impeding an investigation."

"What the hell are you talking about?"

He stabbed a thumb toward his chest. *"I* think the bags are the key to this case. *I* think you're deliberately holding up the investigation by not helping us find them."

"You're on a whole wrong track, I told you the bags aren't related to—"

Jarvis stood up, walked around, plopped his rear on the corner of the desk and leaned into Clarke's face. "Prove it. Or I'll slap your ass in a cell."

"And my lawyer will have me out in an hour. I'm a business owner and a law-abiding citizen."

Jarvis walked back around the desk to cover his shock. A business owner? Damn. Captain Folsom's voice bellowed inside his head, "Cops should never ask questions for which they don't already know answers." Man, the shit was gonna fly.

Then Jarvis spun around, put his palms on the desk, and told a bald-faced lie. "We've got your footprint near the body." Suddenly Montez wasn't meeting his eyes any more; they focused on something over Jarvis' left shoulder.

Clarke was about to crack!

Captain Folsom would ignore the complaints if Jarvis broke the case in—he checked his watch—nineteen hours and seven minutes. Solving a murder in nineteen hours, without a confession. Had to be a record!

Give the man another minute he'll blow wide open. Jarvis brought himself erect and faced the window. And waited.

Whatever he expected to happen, didn't.

"Course you got my footprint, I checked the frigging guy's pulse."

Seventeen

Angie tugged the polyester comforter around herself and snuggled into the pillows. She'd told Will she didn't care what the cops confiscated from their house, but she did. She cared about the case, and about him. A person couldn't turn off twenty-six years of marriage just like that.

His comment that she could forgive some people, and not others, had hit home. He'd been referring to her relationship with her mother; she and her two brothers had a horrific upbringing. Dad's alcoholism generated horrific behaviors from Mom, which trickled down to both defensive and offensive reactions in the kids. Dad died when Angie was fifteen and she'd spent years blaming her mother for everything. Eventually Angie forgave her mother; they'd developed a halfway friendship. Why couldn't she forgive Will?

In time. Maybe.

She moped to the bathroom for a tissue. A glimpse in the mirror brought her mood to a new low. Red-rimmed eyes made her look like a myopic panda: a myopic panda with a case of finger-in-the-light-socket hair. Maybe a shower would help. Angie turned on the tap and let the water run till it turned hot.

The ringing of the cabin's telephone penetrated the sound of water sputtering from the ancient showerhead. She ran to answer it. The dispatcher, Bea, was calling. The hit and run owner's car had been spotted at WG's Restaurant. She thought Angie would want to know. Angie hung up with vociferous thanks. She'd put out a hand to dial Val's number when the phone rang. It would be Will. Finally it stopped. Before she could begin dialing Val's number it rang again. Damn him! She wrenched the phone from the cradle and shouted, "Hello!"

"Whoa, who crapped in your oatmeal?" came Val's voice. "God Angie, I'm sorry. That was something Nolan always said."

"That's all right, I sometimes find myself saying Will-things too." Angie dried herself with the rough terrycloth. "I was in the shower. I planned to call you when I got out. That dispatcher lady called. Sonnie's car was spotted at a restaurant. I thought you might want to go for dinner with me."

"Cool."

"Pick me up in ten minutes." Val arrived in nine.

"We're not supposed to leave town," Val said as Angie shut the passenger door.

Angie snapped the seatbelt in place. "You want to stay home?"

"Nope. Where are we going?"

"WG's Restaurant. By the way, why did you call me earlier?"

It had started raining. Val turned on the wipers and swung the van north on Route 28. "I wanted to tell you about the carpenter."

"Probably it's better not to do that over the phone anyway."

"Gosh, I'm glad you thought of it." Val adjusted the radio station. Heavy rock burst out. Angie leaned forward and turned down the volume.

"Twice you've looked in the mirror. Is somebody following us?" Val asked.

Angie glanced over her shoulder. "I'm not sure. A car just turned in behind us. Take a right turn anywhere as soon as you can."

Val spun the wheel right, launching them into a driveway behind a dark colored pickup. She and Angie ducked their heads.

Angie counted to twenty then inched her head up, laughing.

"I don't think we did that right. I'm pretty sure one of us was supposed to keep looking to see whether the car drove past or not."

Val's laughter grew when someone stepped on the porch. She waved at the unsmiling woman and backed into the street. They drove north, staying around the speed limit. Angie alternated between glances over her shoulder and peeks into the side-view mirror. So far no one seemed to be following.

"Dale was at the house when the carpenter came."

"Oh boy."

Val gave an elaborate sigh. "Now he really thinks I killed his father."

"What did he say?"

"Nothing specific. He just kept giving me this look over the carpenter's shoulder."

"How did it go otherwise?"

"I guess the project is off, the estimate was higher than I expected."

"They usually are."

"Renovations and the purchase of equipment will eat up most of the insurance money. There wouldn't be anything left for inventory or advertising or office supplies."

Angie pointed. "There's WG's on the right. "What about a business loan?"

Val pulled into the lot and stopped. "I hate the idea of owing money. That was one place Nolan and I agreed."

The parking lot was large, paved and surrounded by shrubs and scrub oaks. Angie rolled down the window. The cool night air rushed in. She squinted, trying to locate Sonnie's car. "There it is," she said, indicating the Toyota on the far right hand side, under an overhang of oak trees. Dew encased it, making the windshield glitter in the waning afternoon light. "It's been here a while."

"What do we do now?"

Angie pulled on the door handle.

"What are you doing?" Val's voice held equal measures of curiosity and shock.

"I'm going to look around."

Val shut off the van then almost immediately started it again. "I keep it running right? In case we need to make a getaway."

"You can shut it off. I'm just going to look. We'll go eat in a minute." Angie got out.

"Stay in the shadows. I'll keep my hand on the horn."

"Stop trying to scare me." Angie closed but didn't latch the door and walked as naturally as she could on trembling limbs. The bright green Toyota, backed four feet from the woods, stood out like the proverbial sore thumb amongst the silvers, blacks and even the red cars around it.

No one in the vehicle, neither scrunched in the front seat or dead on the back floor. The thought made the hairs on the back of her neck stand up and she rubbed them down. Through the heavy moisture on the drivers' side window, she noted that the inside of the vehicle was surprisingly neat and clean. Only a pair of extra-large-size McDonalds soda cups sat in the console holder; a crumpled napkin jammed between them. An older automobile so it probably didn't have an alarm that'd bring half the town on the run.

Probably didn't.

Angie tried the door.

All four were locked. Just to make the trip complete, she tried the trunk and wasn't surprised to find it latched tight. Dew dripped off the oak branches and down the back of her sweater making her jump.

Laughter oozed into the parking lot as a door opened and shut. Angie ducked into the shadows behind the car. Customers leaving after a wonderful dinner, she told her thundering heart. A man and woman walked arm in arm, joking and laughing. Obviously they'd had several drinks, but still had their wits about them. It wouldn't pay to have them remember a wild-looking blonde lurking in the shadows. The couple wove between cars, coming closer.

Angie backed until the shrubs wrapped wet arms around her, giving her the willies. The couple stopped at a leisure van in the next row. The woman drew her partner into an embrace. He put his hands on either side of her face and pulled it to his.

Take it home, will you? Angie wanted to shout.

Val wouldn't be able to see the couple in their frenetic sexual embrace. Neither could she see Angie. She must be getting worried.

There was nothing to see in the Toyota, and Angie surely didn't want to hang around watching the lovers. She pushed out the image of Will and Cassie in a clench in her peach-on-white bedroom.

Finally the couple climbed in the vehicle. Angie waited, but the engine didn't start. Another minute went by and she realized they'd taken their passion into the back. She separated the soaked clothing from her back and stepped out of the shrubbery. Just then the restaurant door opened again. More voices came. She kept going at just the right pace, a normal woman walking to her vehicle. The voices grew louder: a lone man stepped outdoors and began walking in her direction. God, were all the cars parked on this side of the lot?

Angie stopped in her tracks. Silhouetted in the white-blue glow of a streetlight was a big-shouldered man, with shoulder length dreadlocks. Sonnie Phelps! He strode purposefully toward his car, and Angie. She raced back to the protection of the bushes.

He passed the leisure van, leaving the spotlighting effect of the streetlamp for a moment. He stopped a second to listen to the couple in the vehicle, gave a small chuckle, then stepped into the circle of a streetlight again. Like a spotlight it showed Angie one thing, he was carrying a dark colored bag, identical to the ones he and Montez brought onto *Little One*! Angie's insides turned to mush.

Sonnie unlocked his door, reached inside and popped the

latch of the trunk that wasn't four feet from where she stood. The light came on. The small bulb seemed to illuminate the fillings in her teeth. She shrank deeper into the bushes, every swoosh and dribble of the dew like wrecking balls against a brick building.

He hoisted the bag onto the trunk edge. She wished he'd grab onto that zipper and yank the thing back; open the bag so she could get a look inside. But the hope was short lived, taken over immediately by the dread for what would happen if he found her there. She pictured the headline: *Angie Deacon performing tonight! Dying before an audience of one.*

She stood on tiptoe as Sonnie jammed the bag into the trunk, wedging it between two others, identical to those on Little One. Then he shut the trunk. And turned around.

Maybe the trickle of water from the branches had caught Sonnie's ear. Or, maybe Angie's sharp intake of breath. Either way, he faced the shrubbery and stared. Angie couldn't see details of his face, couldn't know he was staring, but his stance said he squinted into the shadows. Probably wondering whether he should check things out. What could be there, a skunk or other wild animal taking refuge from the night? Nothing to be concerned about, right?

When he leaned closer, her breath caught in her throat. She stood as still as possible, the urge to inhale developing into a full-fledged necessity. If she didn't breathe soon, she'd pass out.

Sonnie took a step.

Dizziness swept over her. Breathe! her brain shouted.

He took another step, now only three feet from her left arm. A car approached out on the street. Sonnie stopped. He moved only his head to watch the car turn into the parking lot. Angie used the motor's noise as cover and took in a quick breath. God, how good it felt! Two car doors opened. The dome light came on. Suddenly she could see. And Sonnie stared right at her!

Eighteen

That hard chair was like a featherbed to Montez as he watched Jarvis squirm. The cop expected Montez to deny ever being in the cockpit. Montez knew that like he knew his birth date. Instead of a denial, he'd offered up information like a banquet: "Course you got my footprint. I checked the guy's pulse."

Jarvis had opened and closed his mouth no less than three times. Montez came close to telling him he looked like a beached fish, but decided silence was the best way to handle this. Cops hated silence. They liked suspects who chirped like little birds and gave 'em their case on the proverbial silver platter. What would he toss at Montez next? An accusation of murder? Let him just try and make it stick! Five minutes passed.

By now, most people would be feeling mighty uncomfortable. To fill the empty space, they'd talk and talk. That's where they always incriminated themselves. Montez bit back a sarcastic addition to his comment about footprints, stretched out in the chair and waited to see if Jarvis could pry his foot out of his mouth.

As if hearing Montez's thoughts, Jarvis flew out of the chair. It banged off the windowsill behind it, making the glass rattle. He paced a few steps, stopped and eyed Montez, who had a hell of a time keeping a straight face. Jarvis went to the window and leaned his hands on the sill. For three minutes, Montez watched Jarvis looking out the window, at what—scenery? Stars? Wildlife? He was quiet so long Montez began to wonder if a parade of naked ladies marched by.

If Jarvis gazed out there long enough, would he come up with more accusations? That's it! Accusations hung from the tree branches like Christmas ornaments. All a guy had to do was pluck one down and construct a case around it. And the star at the top was the prize—Montez's motive to murder that Little son-of-a-bitch!

Finally Jarvis picked himself off the sill and turned on a heel. He looked tired, almost as tired as Montez felt. Montez did smile then, because he suddenly knew, Jarvis wasn't trying to invent an accusation. He wasn't formulating a motive. He was working on a solution, and enjoying himself immensely. So, why didn't this revelation ease Montez's mind?

Jarvis took hold of the chair back and spun it to face the desk. He settled onto the black cloth and plopped his forearms on the vinyl chair arms, never making eye contact.

"What's your relationship to the Littles?"

"I've told you twice already. There is no relationship. I go on the boat three or four times a year, to go fishing. That's it."

"Tell me about the duffel bags."

"Done already. There's no new information to add."

"Tell me about you and the Deacon woman."

Montez let a slow smile creep onto his face. Let the cop think there was something going on between him and Angie, what was the harm? But when the cop's face pinched together, Montez couldn't help grinning wider. Well, well. So, there was something going on between the cop and the Deacon woman. "Whadya want to know?" Montez asked, hearing the humor in his tone.

"Had you met her before the day of the murder?"

"Nope." Then he couldn't resist adding, "You?"

Montez was disappointed when footsteps sounded in the hall. Things were just getting interesting. The door opened and Sergeant Wilson entered. Jarvis looked relieved at the interruption. Things weren't going at all the way he'd planned. Wilson plopped a manila folder on the desk and retreated to the doorway, watching Montez with a look that bordered on confusion.

He knew he'd interrupted something, but obviously had no idea what it was.

Jarvis knocked a donut bag off the desk with his elbow trying to slide the folder closer. Montez didn't have to squint too hard to see his name printed in magic marker on the tab. The detective didn't bother picking up the donut bag. He transferred his elbows from the chair arms to the desk, put weight on them, and opened the folder. Wordless, he took up three pages. Montez couldn't read anything on them, and didn't hide the fact that he was trying. Three pages? That's all they came up with?

Jarvis' fingers thumped the backside of the sheets as he read. After a long while, he set the papers back in the folder and shut the cover.

"You look like somebody stepped on your puppy," Montez said.

Jarvis tilted the folder aside and scowled at him.

"Can I go now?"

"Wilson!" Jarvis shouted.

The sergeant must've been standing outside the door because it flung open and the uniformed man thundered into the room. He stopped dead seeing there was no emergency. "Take Mr. Clarke downstairs," Jarvis ordered. "We're holding him on suspicion."

Montez leaped to his feet. Both cops jumped to attention. Wilson grabbed Montez's left arm. Jarvis' hand flew to his holster.

Anger rumbled into Montez's throat. "Suspicion of what?"

"Murder." The word spoken with such sincerity that Montez threw back his head and laughed. Wilson's fingers tightened around his arm.

"All you got on me is a footprint. *In* the blood. That means my foot was there *after* the blood."

Jarvis dropped his hand from the gun butt. He said, "I got more than that," without much conviction. He gestured at Montez's file with a tip of his head. "There's enough in there to justify holding you on suspicion."

Shit. "I want my lawyer."

Jarvis' disappointment was evident in the deepening of the lines over his nose. Montez stepped back feeling the momentary exultation of the win; the word *lawyer* always struck fear in the craw of the authorities. The word meant they had to stop their questioning and adhere to all the rules of police conduct.

The win would be short lived, though. Jarvis had the upper hand, and he knew it. He pointed at Montez and said to Wilson, "Take Mr. Clarke to holding."

Wilson tugged Montez's arm. For a moment he considered resisting. But didn't. As he was escorted from the room, he saw Jarvis throw down the trio of pages from his file and pick up a folder lying to the left—one he'd seen had the name Nolan Little written in blue ink on its tab.

The sergeant nudged Montez to the right, down a dark hallway to a telephone on the wall. He handed Montez a quarter and waited for him to dial and tell the lawyer what had transpired. Then he led Montez to a tiny room that smelled like stale cigar smoke. The room contained a table and two chairs, all bolted to the floor.

"Want coffee or something?" Wilson asked.

Montez laughed. "I smelled your coffee. You got Coke?"

A moment later, the sergeant returned carrying two moisture-coated cans and a bag of Doritos that he tossed on the table. "How long before your attorney shows?"

"About an hour," Montez told him and settled back to wait.

Nineteen

He'd waited twenty minutes already at the end of this dank, smelly alley, amongst the cat piss and garbage, and some other aroma he didn't want to think about. Smelled like something dead. The stuff in the trunk grew hotter by the minute. Everybody wanted the stuff. The guys he took it from, the intended receivers, and the cops. Every time he passed a cop on the street it seemed like they were about to stop him. "Sir, we had a call. I'm sure it's nothing, but could we search your car?"

The thoughts germinated in his brain and, as the minutes passed, grew just like Jack's freaking beanstalk, twisting around his neurons and squeezing the sense from his actions.

All in his head though. Nobody could really suspect him. Such a "fine upstanding young man," to quote the *Five Man Electrical Band*. The thought brought a smile to his face. Fine upstanding and young were three things he especially wasn't lately. Even so he couldn't keep from whistling the tune.

The tune cut off abruptly when headlights shone on the end of the alley. They elongated and then shrank as a vehicle turned in, trapping him there. He waited till the other vehicle, fancy with MD plates—probably stolen too—pulled up to his bumper and stopped. He waited till the man got out. A big man. Even if the car didn't trap him in here, he could never make it past such a hulk. Arms the length of yardsticks. Legs like stumps.

Neither spoke. They had only one use for each other.

He reached in the car and pushed the button for the trunk.

The latch released with a thud. Both men peered in. He unzipped one of the still-wet bags and bared the contents. The newcomer did likewise with the second bag and nodded. All in order. They each took a bag and carried them to his trunk.

The hulk pulled a money clip from his belt and counted out the agreed upon number of bills. "Nice doin' business with you," said the hefty voice, slamming the car trunk.

He thought the man intentionally made his voice deeper, but who cared? What the hell was he going to do, turn the guy in? He folded the wad of bills into his wallet and wedged it in his pocket. An unwieldy fit, but satisfying.

"When's the next shipment?"

"This is the end of it."

The hand shot out so fast, it caught him by surprise. It took hold of his windpipe and squeezed, not enough to wound, just enough to send a message. He raised his hands in a gesture of supplication. "Okay, okay," he croaked. "I'll let you know." His throat was released with an extra shove that sent him staggering against the shiny car.

He pulled himself erect and stepped off to the side. That sick-sweet dead smell was stronger here. He didn't want to look. Couldn't stop picturing himself lying behind a dumpster, rotting along with the garbage. The dark figure got into the SUV and drove away.

He remained there until a car came along the main road and startled him to action. He climbed in the car. The motor started immediately. Dawn peeked between the buildings. He eased onto the deserted main street. Only an orange alley cat bore witness to their deal. Their last deal, if he could somehow work it.

Not for the first time, he wondered how he'd gotten in so deep.

He knew how. Greed. But not just his own.

Twenty

She always hoped to die having sex, during that final exultant explosion of passion. Not in a soggy parking lot in Wolfeboro, New Hampshire at the hands of a huge man with dreadlocks. But as the seconds passed, death became a definite possibility as realization dawned on Sonnie Phelps; he'd been caught with the goods—whatever they were.

Angie tried to run. Something gripped her ankle and she tripped. Sonnie seized her arm. Then five fingers bit into her flesh with a vengeance that said he wasn't just keeping her from falling down. He yanked her out of the shadows and flung her against car, shoving her till she lay on the trunk lid. When her body started to slide along the wet metal he jammed his knee in her crotch to hold her in place.

Sonnie rested his whole weight atop her. His face inches away. She smelled alcohol on his breath, saw murder on his face. As he wiggled to conform himself to her body, the pressure on her left arm lessened a bit. She wrenched free and swung a fist at his head. Her knuckles struck his ear with a hollow thump. He grunted. His groping hand found her arm and pinned it down. All his weight rested on her again. Breath came at a premium. Foreheads touched. Not skin on skin but bangs on thick dreadlock. Noses touched. His breath like fire. Lips touched. Hot, moist, filled with an anger she feared would result in…god, no, don't let him rape her.

Suddenly his head jerked violently to the right. His body went limp and he slid the length of her, to the ground. With his knee gone, Angie sank down the wet surface. When her feet touched a soft-solid surface, probably Sonnie's back, they shifted into running mode. She pushed off and sprinted to Val's van hoping the door was open and the engine running.

She made several attempts to pull the door handle, but couldn't make her fingers work. Finally the thing was open. Angie dove inside. The van sat empty. Where the hell was Val?

Angie flew out of the van. A hand clamped down on her shoulder. She made a fist and swung. For the second time in minutes, Angie's fist made contact with human flesh. "Ouch!" She'd swung a second time before the voice registered as familiar. "Angie, stop!"

"Oh my god, I'm sorry, Val."

"Forget it, let's just get out of here." Val ran around the front of the van and leaped into the driver's seat. By the time Angie got back in the vehicle, the engine was running. By the time she had the door shut, the van jerked into motion, squealing tires onto the main road.

"Damn, I thought he planned to kill you!" Val exclaimed.

"I'm sorry I hit you," Angie said between deep breaths, an attempt to control her racing heart. "Why did you sneak up on me like that?"

"Sorry, I was only thinking about getting out of there."

"What the hell happened anyway?" Angie asked.

"I clobbered him."

"With what? He dropped like a truck hit him."

"Does it matter?"

Yes. "No, I guess not."

"I saw Sonnie come out of the restaurant. I hoped you'd seen him too. When I lost him in the shadows, I got out and went over there. I saw him fling you against the car." Val moaned. "I thought he was going to kill you."

He was.

"Maybe you should buckle up."

Angie laughed realizing she perched on the edge of the seat with her hands clenching the dashboard. She settled back and buckled the seatbelt. "What do we do now?"

"Not sure. I don't have much experience with stuff like this."

"I guess I need to change motels."

They drove in silence for several miles. Angie's breathing and heartbeat returned to normal. Val must've felt calmer too; she began tapping the steering wheel to the beat of a Stones song.

"I nearly passed out when he spotted me," Angie said.

After a few seconds, Val said, "The last time I fainted, it turned out I was pregnant."

For some reason the idea struck Angie as ludicrous. She laughed so hard she couldn't stop. Val started too, laughing so hard she kept veering across the double centerline.

"Anybody following is...going to think...we've been...drinking," Angie said between gasps for air.

She found a tissue in her purse and dabbed at the tears running down her un-made-up cheeks. How freeing.

At the cabin and still giggling, Angie began packing. In the bathroom she threw her toiletries in the small leather bag. She took it into the main room and added the few things from the dresser top. Beside her, Val collected things from the top drawer. Angie caught Val's reflection in the mirror. Val's left eye had a full-blown shiner.

"Oh my god." Part of Angie wanted to cry for having hurt her new friend. Another part found it hysterical.

Val leaned into the mirror for a closer inspection. "You did good, girl."

"I'm really sorry. Does it hurt?"

"Only when I breathe."

At another motel, Val set the suitcase on the floor and dropped on the bed near the window. "I don't suppose you have anything to drink."

"No." Angie flopped on the other bed. "I could use a stiff one too."

Val's "Which kind?" rekindled the giggling.

Angie took a breath that said she was ready to act like an adult again. "Let's leave your car at the marina and walk over to Shipley's."

"What about Sonnie?"

"He can pay." Angie gave Val some painkiller then changed into dry clothes. "We'll talk about Sonnie while we get drunk."

They parked the van in the shadows at the marina. Sonnie would have to wonder which way they'd gone, and how. It had stopped raining. Angie took several breaths, thankful that she could.

An hour later, seeing nothing of Sonnie Phelps in or around the restaurant, they returned to the motel. "I would've liked one more drink," Val mumbled.

"Me too, but they said they were closing."

"They were trying to get rid of us."

Angie giggled. "You *were* getting a little rowdy."

"Me!"

"I didn't pull the waiter into my lap." Angie wrapped her sweater tighter and folded her arms around it. "Can I ask you something?"

"Ask me anything." Val tripped but caught herself before landing on her face. "Now I know why they say not to step on the cracks, they're dangerous."

"It's sidewalk cracks you're not supposed to step on."

"So?"

"Val, there's no sidewalk here." More giggling, then silence for a moment. "I'm worried about you."

"Why?"

"You're taking Nolan's death a little too well."

Angie counted fifteen steps and two trips over invisible sidewalk cracks before Val answered. "I'm okay during the day. Nighttime is a bitch."

"That's not what I meant. That kind of behavior makes sense. What doesn't is that wall you put around yourself all those years—so Nolan's meanness wouldn't hurt you. You're using that wall now to protect you from the horror of what happened. One of these days you'll have to knock it down and face everything."

Val stopped walking and steadied herself against a tree trunk. "I'm afraid, Angie. I know it's going to happen. I'm afraid...that when I fall apart...all the shit from the past is going to get caught up with the shit from the present, and I'm scared. I'm scared I'll never come out of it."

At the cabin Angie urged Val to stay the night. Both women removed their shoes at the door but it was all they took off. Like skiers leaving a jump they dropped on individual beds.

Something woke Angie. She thought of the phone, the alarm clock, someone at the door. Then, through her thick cottony brain, she realized somebody was crying. She sat up and blinked to bring the room into focus. Val sat in the center of the other bed, the spread bunched around her, arms wrapped around bent legs, head resting on her knees. Angie wrestled herself out of the tangle of her own sheets and climbed up beside Val, who didn't look up. Angie pulled Val into a bear hug. Val sobbed harder.

Dawn pushed its gray fog between the heavy drapes when she sucked in a gasp of air. She edged her head onto Angie's shoulder. "How do things go so terribly terribly wrong?"

"I don't know," Angie whispered into Val's hair, and thinking as much about her own life as Val's. "I just don't know."

"I was thinking how different my life was just a few days ago, and I started crying and couldn't stop."

"You had to get it out."

"I don't want to go to jail."

"Don't talk like that. Jarvis is smart, he'll figure out who did it."

"Not if he's trying to pin it on me. Did you know they talked to my neighbors and business associates? Everyone we've done business with since day one. They even confiscated our journals and called some of our old clients. Even if I'm found innocent, the business will be gone. Nobody'll want to go on a tour with someone accused of murder."

"Probably they're just trying to find someone else with a grudge against Nolan."

"Do you think Sonnie killed him?"

"He's looking better all the time."

"You gonna tell the cops what he did tonight?"

"Probably not. Jarvis will give us hell for being in Wolfeboro."

"Yes, but what if Sonnie tries something else?"

"We'll be ready. And the heck with the cops, you and I will find who did this. We'll turn over every rock in town if we have to."

"I thought after what happened tonight, you'd back out."

"God, my head hurts. I need a shower." Angie unwound herself from Val's grasp and stood up, unbuttoning her blouse. By the time she dropped the shirt to the floor Val was sound asleep.

The hot needles pounded her back. Why the hell *hadn't* she backed out of this absurd investigation? Sonnie's attack would have been the perfect excuse. She could've concentrated on putting her life back together. With or without Will. Damn! She slapped the shower tiles with an open palm. What was happening? Twice in two days she'd wanted to strike someone.

She'd always abhorred violence, valued human life. She hit the wet wall again. Well, one thing tonight's affair taught her: she *could* defend herself with violence if need be. She wouldn't have hesitated to hurt Sonnie. That was a good thing, right?

And Val—well, she'd proven she could defend herself. Which brought on a whole slew of new worries. Val could be violent.

When Angie walked back into the room, wrapped in a towel, hair dripping down her back, Val was awake, and leaning back against the headboard, the gaudy flowered spread pulled under her chin. She looked like an innocent child. How could she be a murderer?

"Sorry about earlier."

"It's good you got it out." Angie fumbled through her meager wardrobe then laughed. "I have to go home and get more clothes."

Val padded to the bathroom. She turned on the shower. While the water heated up, she stood in the doorway. "Have you and Will talked yet?"

"No."

"You have to, you know."

"Man, have I got a headache."

"Don't change the subject."

"Honestly, right now I'm too angry and too weak to talk to him."

"Are you afraid you'll give in and go back?"

Angie nodded and dropped on the bed. Val turned off the shower and came to kneel in front of Angie. "Would going back be so bad?"

"Things will never be the same."

"Maybe things *shouldn't* be the same. Maybe you both should look for ways to change and improve your relationship. Spice things up." Val stood, rubbing her palms on her knees. "You need to talk to him."

Angie tucked the corner of the towel tighter. "I know. And, we will. It's just too soon."

While Val took her shower, Angie dressed, deliberately not thinking about Will. Events of the previous evening replayed in her head. Where was Sonnie Phelps? Back in Nashua? No such luck.

"Val came from the bathroom all dressed. She sat on the bed to put on her shoes.

"You leaving?"

"I have a tour in an hour and I haven't made sandwiches yet."

Angie walked Val to the door. The air was brisk, but the humidity would return with the sun. The sky glistened in striated shades of red, purple and pink.

"Beautiful."

"Red sky in morning, sailors take warning," Val recited. "What are you doing today?"

"I think I'll visit Tyson. He was either running from something that morning—and if he was, I want to find out what. Or, he came to your boat for a reason."

"You mean he came with the intention of killing Nolan?"

Angie shrugged.

"Take your cell phone."

"Stop trying to scare me."

Val rolled her eyes and started for the van. "How can I do that tour today if I'm worried about you?"

"Don't worry, Tyson's a mouse."

Angie finished her hair and makeup and went out for breakfast. As the door closed, the phone rang. She kept walking.

Twenty-One

At first glance, Nolan Little's folder held nothing out of the ordinary: wallet, keys, Swiss Army knife, and a handful of coins. The black leather tri-fold wallet's left compartment contained a conglomeration of photos: sons and grandsons, and five or six of Valerie; in each she smiled shyly at the camera. One appeared to have been taken recently, in front of *Little One* with the Downings Landing Marina sign in the background. Jarvis had been there the day they erected the sign—three months ago.

The wallet's right compartment held credit cards: Visa, MasterCard, Sears and AAA. The center section had the cash: a twenty, a ten and four one-dollar bills. Jarvis counted it a second time and compared it with the notation on the evidence sheet. Something wasn't right.

He dialed Valerie's cell-phone. She answered on the second ring, not saying hello, but, "Dale, where *are* you?"

"Mrs. Little, it's Detective Jarvis. Is everything all right?" She hesitated so long he began to think they'd lost the signal. "Mrs. Little, are you there? Is there anything wrong?" Even though she proclaimed all was well, doubt budded and blossomed. Like a dandelion the day after mowing the lawn. "Where are you?" He had to accept her answer that she was home. What else could he do but continue the call? "How much money did Mr. Goodwell pay to go on your boat?"

"Three hundred dollars."

"Did he give the money to you or your husband?"

"To Nolan."

"Where is the money now?"

"I'm not sure."

"All right, thanks. Are you sure you're all right?"

"Of course, why wouldn't I be?"

"Call if you need anything." Jarvis hung up but spent a moment staring at the little speaker holes on the receiver. Something about his call made her nervous. He had no idea what. Where was the money now?

He returned to the manila folder. As Clarke said, he owned a business: Affordable Computer Repairs. Jarvis spun the chair toward the computer and typed in the address. A colorful website appeared with a photo of a clean and prosperous looking storefront. The address, 15100 Amherst Street, prominently displayed on the page. Another click produced a map of Nashua. Amherst Street was a major thoroughfare. This guy Clarke seemed legit. Jarvis rubbed fingertips in his throbbing temples.

The second thing in the file—Wuss' background check. Jarvis laid it aside for now.

The third page—the fingerprint report. Lots of prints in the cockpit. All but one set belonged to either Nolan or Valerie. A palm print on the doorframe. And it belonged to Angelina Deacon. Incidental, Jarvis thought. Balancing herself while checking Nolan's pulse. Or before sticking the knife in his chest.

The remaining page, the lab report on the suspect's shoes. Jarvis' adrenaline raced through his veins like a Colorado wildfire. He took a breath to try and slow it, and leaned the chair back against the sill. This might be the best reading he'd done all year.

Nolan Little, negative.

Valerie Little, negative.

Willis Deacon, negative.

Angelina Deacon, positive.

Jarvis thunked the chair forward. His adrenaline throbbed into motion again—till he read the next words—*soles only*. Incidental contact made while checking a pulse. Again he read the fingerprint page. And again he looked at the footprint report. "Wilson!" he shouted, ignoring both phone and intercom. Wilson materialized in the doorway. "Pick up Angelina Deacon."

Jarvis waited till the door shut and went back to the shoe report. Sonnie Phelps, negative. No blood on his shoes. Tyson Goodwell, negative.

What the hell was going on?

Montez Clarke, positive.

Jarvis' adrenaline pressure skyrocketed.

Beside the word *positive,* a notation: Left shoe, one 3.0mm sphere, low velocity, estimated distance 1m. point of origin (POO). Left shoe, one 3.2mm sphere, low velocity, estimated distance 1m. POO.

Jarvis colored the air with a flurry of one-syllable curses. He flung the papers down and stormed to the file cabinets, stopping only because he could go no further. He turned and stomped back to the computer desk. As he paced, the obscenities increased in both syllable and decibel. No one came to check what might be wrong.

His watch showed 2:37 p.m. when he finally sat and read the page again. At the end, he could barely move his hands to lay down the paper. The adrenaline rush vanished. In its wake a smoldering cavernous pit. The blood had slowed its passage through his body; his heartbeats seemed to call out—you got nothing, you got nothing. Over and over the words repeated in his head.

Suddenly words resonated from everywhere, from every corner of the room, every crack and crevice, growing in intensity like the crescendo of a symphony. How blind could he have been?

Jarvis shot to his feet and wrenched open the door. "Wilson!"

The round-shouldered man appeared, unfazed by his boss' outburst. "Is Clarke's attorney here yet?"

"They're in Room B."

Jarvis stomped into his office leaving the door open. He sat and forced himself to a calmness he neither felt nor wanted to feel. Montez Clarke had not murdered Nolan Little. The blood on his shoes had not occurred as high-velocity spatters as when someone jabs a knife into soft flesh. The spots had occurred by dropping from the body. Incidental contact.

Wilson returned. "Clarke and his lawyer want to talk to you."

The two men entered. The lawyer shut the door. He carried a shiny attaché—probably alligator. Clarke took his former seat. The attorney remained standing.

Confusion battered Jarvis' brain as he searched his memory banks for a question to ask. "Where's your partner?"

Clarke glanced at the attorney, who nodded the okay to answer. "Told you already, I haven't seen him since the night of the murder."

"Where are the bags?"

"Don't answer that," the lawyer said but his client ignored him.

"Told you that too. I don't know."

"Where did you last see them?"

"Don't answer that."

"On the boat."

Clarke's gaze shifted over Jarvis's left shoulder. Avoiding eye contact: the man knew more than he was saying. How to get it out of him? Especially now that he'd lawyered up.

Jarvis hit the intercom button. "Wilson, come here, I got a detainee for you."

Clarke jumped to his feet. "No way!" and "You have no grounds to hold my client" came in unison.

Jarvis dealt with the attorney first, telling him exactly what he'd told Clarke earlier. "Means, motive and opportunity," which he outlined in detail. Then he told Clarke, "You don't want to go downstairs, then tell me what I want to know."

"Can I confer with my client a moment?" the lawyer asked.

Jarvis left the room, taking the largest file with him. In the coffee room he poured a cup. The fresh stuff they'd made at his request, thick as mud; just like this case. For distraction, he brewed a new pot, listening to the trickle and gurgle as the water dribbled into the pot.

At the battered table in the middle of the room, he opened Wuss' file and began to read. He'd barely got past the birth date (06/02/80) and date of graduation from business school (05/21/02) when Wilson came to report Clarke's readiness to talk. Wearing a self-satisfied grin, Jarvis returned to the office, making sure to wipe off the smirk before pushing open the door.

Clarke's next words nearly gave Jarvis a coronary. "I have a proposal for you."

Twenty-Two

The only road to HeavenScent, the Goodwell's rented summer home was past Will's office. His Jeep was the only vehicle out front. Of course, he and Cassie didn't need two vehicles. Will probably had her moved into the house by now. Angie's house. Their house. She blinked away the vision of the lovers in her newly decorated bedroom, in the bed where she and Will made so many wonderful memories.

Now Cassie and Will were making memories, and Angie was making herself sick with worry. She headed north on 28A. A couple of miles and a sharp, very steep right turn took her up the winding HeavenScent drive at ten minutes past two. A shiny white Cadillac and a smoke-blue Jaguar sat side-by-side in the driveway.

An elderly woman opened the front door. Angie towered over the petite frame clad in a flowered shirtwaist dress and a triple-strand pearl necklace with matching earrings. Undaunted by the size differential, the woman looked at Angie with a "what the hell do you want" expression.

Angie put up a hand. "Don't worry, I'm not selling anything." The gaze emoted to a suspicious glare. "Is Tyson here?"

The woman's anger snapped like a whip. "You're too old for my son!"

She made a hissing sound between teeth too straight and white for a woman who appeared to be pushing sixty. Yet, Tyson couldn't be more than twenty-five.

"Get out of here and leave my son alone. Do you want me to call the police?"

"Wait, you don't understand."

"I understand your wallet's going to feel the sting of a lawsuit if you come around here again. I won't have floozies hanging around my son."

Angie took a half step forward. "Floozy! Floozy?" Mrs. Goodwell didn't budge. "Tyson and I aren't... As a matter of fact..."

The door opened the rest of the way nudging Mrs. Goodwell aside. Tyson's face appeared. "Angie! Go away, Mother, you're making a fool of yourself."

"Tyson, I will not have you talk to me in that manner."

"Mother!" He waved Angie in. "I'd come out, but I have food on the stove."

The scent of something wonderful oozed out. Angie couldn't help sniffing the air.

Tyson closed the door with an abrupt thud. "Mother, please give us some privacy."

Mrs. Goodwell backed away, scuffing her left shoe down the hallway. Tyson followed her and, feeling very out of place, Angie trailed them both, stifling the urge to run.

The elder Goodwell stopped and gave a laugh that came out more as a snort. "In case my son forgot to tell you, he's been written out of the will."

"Mother!"

She took a left into a dining room, but again stopped to give one more bit of advice. "Maybe you can convince him to get a job."

Tyson didn't yell, "Mother!" again although Angie felt the word screech through the air.

"Sorry about that."

"She reminds me a little of my mom."

"How'd you get her to stop busting your ass?"

"I moved out of state."

The brightly lit kitchen made Angie blink. Gleaming white marble counters and yellow-painted walls reflected the light from the row of windows that opened onto the marvelous panorama of Lake Winnipesaukee. The tumbling whitecaps mesmerized with their beauty and power. Val was out on that lake, swaying and bouncing. Val had said rough water wasn't dangerous in a pontoon boat, but still. Angie let her eyes search for the small dot that might be the leased boat. At least, out there, she'd be safe from Sonnie Phelps.

"So, what are you doing here?" Tyson asked.

Direct and to the point. She liked that.

He strode to the stove, on which bubbled an enormous frying pan of peppers, onions, mushrooms and thinly sliced potatoes.

Angie sniffed. "Wonderful. What is it?"

"Frittata à la Goodwell." He laid the spatula on a cloth and picked up a large bowl of beaten eggs. He swished the contents into a mini yellow whirlpool then poured it atop the vegetables. He expertly tilted the pan and lifted the cooked edges allowing the raw liquid to sift through. The sizzling sounds and luscious aromas almost obliterated the aura Mamma Goodwell had created. Tyson placed the pan in the oven.

"There," he said. "Now I can give you my undivided attention." He pulled out a chair at the table, set with one place setting.

Angie's set her elbow on a thick manuscript. A play. "What's this?"

Tyson took the clipped papers from her hand, not in a gesture of concealment, but of pride. "Promise you won't laugh." He watched her a second. When she didn't appear amused, he continued, "I act. I'm an actor. I tried out at a theater in Manhattan. They're putting on *Death of a Salesman* in two months. They called a while ago to say I got the part."

"How will you do this if you can't leave town?"

Tyson's mother shuffled into the room. She saw the sheaf in Tyson's hand, hurried over and wrenched it away. "I should've known you were behind this," she shouted at Angie.

"Mother." Tyson's fingers groped for the script, but Mrs. Goodwell jerked it out of his reach. He tried once again to get hold of it and she heaved it across the room. "I will not have my son...acting!"

Tyson lurched out of the chair. He grasped his mother's wrists and pushed her backwards out of the room. "Go away. You're making a fool of yourself." She started to say something, but a harsh, deep voice called her name. She closed her mouth, threw Angie a scowl and disappeared down the hall.

Tyson scurried to clean up the papers that had come out of their clip. He set the haphazard mess on the table and began re-ordering the sheets. "I'm sorry," he said. Angie didn't speak. She spotted a page he'd missed near the refrigerator and went to get it. It had a corner torn off. She looked around, even under the fridge, but couldn't find the missing piece. She handed it to Tyson. "This one got torn."

As Angie returned to her seat, she realized that paper wasn't anything like the others. A list of numbers, sort of like a spreadsheet generated from a computer. The last part, where the total would be—gone. Tyson tucked the page on the bottom of the script, put on the metal clip and moved the script to the other end of the table.

"So, why did you come here?"

Direct and to the point, the way to handle him. "I'm helping find Nolan Little's murderer."

Tyson leaned back in the chair and crossed a shiny calfskin loafer across the opposite knee. "Are you working with the cops or freelancing?"

"Val and I are sort of looking into things. Something's been on my mind since the fishing trip. Your appearance on the dock that morning, for one thing."

"So, you don't subscribe to the 'I just felt like fishing' motif?" Tyson got up and flicked the switch on the biggest household coffeemaker Angie had ever seen.

"I can't imagine the cops fell for it either."

"They didn't."

Tyson returned to his chair. He positioned himself on the front of the seat and leaned an elbow on the table. His voice, this time, lowered. "I didn't have the sudden urge to be on a bobbing boat, dangling worms in front of unsuspecting fish with brains the size of pinheads." He grinned. "I'm not saying why I *was* there. I will say—and I know you won't believe me—it had nothing whatsoever to do with the dead man, or Valerie."

"You tell the cops that?"

Tyson nodded.

"What was their reaction?"

"Same as yours. Disbelief."

The appearance of a tall, balding man put a stop to the conversation. Tyson gestured at Angie. "Dad, this is Angie—sorry, I don't know your last name."

"Deacon."

Tyson's father shook her hand with gusto. "William Goodwell. So nice to meet you, my dear."

"Nice to meet you, too, sir."

"Your mother sent me to drag you from the mouth of the dragon." William gave a jovial laugh. "I had to come and see the horrible creature who'd set her sights on my son's inheritance."

Angie opened her mouth, but was stopped by William's laughter. "Agnes thinks all females are after our money." He wrapped an arm around Tyson's shoulder. "What's to eat?"

"Red potato frittata." The buzzer sounded. "Want some?"

Angie wasn't sure to whom the invitation had been offered since Tyson spoke with his head in the oven. He thunked the pan on the stove and bent to examine his handiwork. He tipped his face toward her and gazed at her under his arm.

"I'd love to," she replied.

"Me too," William said, and set two more places.

When they finished the meal and cleared away the mess , Angie reached out to shake hands with William. Instead, he pulled her into a tight bear hug. She'd never smelled aftershave like his before: woodsy and sweet.

After eating, she and Tyson went outdoors. The grass, greened from yesterday's rain, felt soft as velvet under her feet. They walked down the slope, toward the lake.

"You're an excellent cook."

A slow smile spread across his face. "Thanks. Mother says men who cook are sissies. She doesn't seem to notice our cook is a man. Anyway, I've decided to trust you."

"Why?"

"Father likes you."

"I like him too."

"He thinks you're pretty."

Angie laughed. "How do you know that?"

"Because he did this when you weren't looking." Tyson gave an elaborate eye-roll. "So, I've decided to tell you why I ended up at the dock." He fidgeted his hands at his sides. "My mother was right about one thing. Women do chase me for my money."

"How do you know? I mean, do they come right out and tell you?"

He grinned, showing her probably-not-naturally white teeth. "Sometimes."

"So, why were you running?"

"There's this woman I started seeing when we came here a month ago. Just for fun, you know how it is."

"But she got serious?"

"She said she was pregnant and threatened to tell my parents."

"This sounds like a teenage problem. Let me guess, she wasn't pregnant."

He gave a sardonic laugh. "I don't know if she is or isn't. When we got in the car," Tyson continued, "Paula dropped the bomb."

"Paula?"

"Paula Spencer. Lives here in town. I asked her, 'How can you be pregnant?' I'd used protection. She said, 'Nothing's foolproof.

Do you think I'm happy about this?' Anyway, I don't know what got into me." He sighed. "Yes I do. Sometimes I'm an insensitive jerk. Don't look at me that way. I know my faults—some of them anyway. Now and then I get carried away."

"So, what did you do when she used the P word?"

He coughed a little. "I uh...ran."

"Were you planning to, like, dive in the water to escape?"

Tyson kicked at a dandelion head. "No. I'd been at the dock a few times when the Littles came in. When I saw them going out, I got it in my head to try and get aboard."

A light mist blew up from the water, peppering her face.

"Maybe we'd better go back," Tyson suggested.

Going uphill wasn't as fun as down, but was just as pretty. HeavenScent was impeccably landscaped. "Has Paula caught up with you?"

He made a raspy sound in the back of his throat. "She came up here as soon as the boat pulled away from the dock. That's why Mother's angry. Anyone else who comes to the house must be another Paula."

Angie understood this emotion. Mothers spend years protecting their offspring, teaching them how to fend for themselves. When predators show up, Moms must, regardless of their child's age, protect. That's the way of the world.

"Paula told my mother her version of the whole sordid tale. But Mother didn't fall all over the idea of a cuddly pink grand-child. She accused Paula of being a gold-digger and God knows what else. Paula ran out crying. She said she'd sic her husband on us."

"Husband?"

He threw up both hands, palms to the sky. "I swear I didn't know she had one. I know what you're thinking. I'm a lot of things, but I don't chase married women, there are plenty—oh, never mind. As I found out this morning, she and her husband concocted the whole thing so they could sue me for breech of promise or some such crap."

Angie almost laughed. This story wasn't what she'd expected, but on the other hand, she wasn't surprised by it either. Rich people, especially ones like Tyson who wore their hormones on their sleeves, had to be targets for nuts, fruitcakes and con artists.

"What are you going to do?"

"I should do like Mother suggests and get a job. She wants me to go into business with Father. He's a stockbroker. See, I'm unbelievable with numbers." He shrugged. "I have a couple of irons in the fire here in town. I'll see how they play out."

"If you found a job here, you wouldn't have to go back to Manhattan."

"I happen to like New York." Before she could reply, he added, "Dozens of playhouses. I could act somewhere every single night if I wanted to."

A grin spread her lips. "Can I tell you a secret fantasy of mine? I've always wanted—"

"To act?"

"No, to produce a play. I love neighborhood theaters. We have several in New Hampshire."

"What do you er…do? Do you work?"

"I'm a nurse at the hospital."

He peered at her as if seeing her for the first time. He shook his head. "I wouldn't have taken you for a nurse."

"I picture you in real estate," Tyson said. "You're very people oriented." A light rain fell, but with the promise of something more deliberate. "Would you like to come back in the house? Another cup of coffee?"

She didn't want to face Tyson's mother again. "No thanks, I have to be going. Thank you for a wonderful meal. You're a great cook. Did you go to school to learn it…or acting?"

"My degree is in business development. I inherited the talent with numbers from my father. But I hate it—being tied to a desk."

Angie ducked into her car as the rain began falling in earnest. Through the rainbow-curve of the beating wipers, she watched

Tyson hurry away. He ran like a man unencumbered by any problems. Only one o'clock, too early for Val to be back, unless they returned early in inclement weather. Her route took her by the marina. *Little One's* slip remained empty. A familiar figure stood at the end of the pier, rain beating down on him. Will. Angie pulled into the parking lot. What was he doing? He hated being out in the rain. He looked lost in thought, feeling sorry for himself probably. Her twinge of remorse vanished. He'd asked for it.

He turned and walked up the dock. Something about his gait registered in her brain. Not Will. Wallace. He spotted her car and came toward it. She lowered the window an inch.

He bent close to the opening.

"You look like you were thinking of jumping in the lake," she said.

"Bet that would make you happy."

"It's all right, you've got Will all to yourself now." She shut the window and gunned the accelerator, spraying him with dirty water.

Twenty-Three

Could Tyson be a killer? Sure, anyone with enough provocation could be pushed beyond their internal boundaries. Everyone's limits were set at different levels. Tyson had run from the gold-digger. He hadn't slapped her around. Hadn't put her in a frittata. Tyson had run away—so he said.

Who was Paula Spencer? At the motel, Angie dug into the bedside table for a phone book and looked up the name. There were three Spencers: Bruce, Robert and someone with the initial L. She dialed each one and asked anyone who answered if she could speak with Paula.

The third person answered, "This is," in a gravelly smoker's voice.

"Um, this is going to sound a little weird, but I need to ask if you're the Paula who got screwed by Tyson Goodwell."

The unladylike snort said Angie had hit pay dirt. "My name's Angie. I wonder if I could buy you a cup of coffee."

They made a date for an hour from then at the Bay Diner. While waiting, Angie repaired the damage to her hair and makeup. She pawed through her meager belongings, feeling a momentary pang of homesickness for her designer clothes, five minutes away, in a walk-in closet the size of this whole room. She fingered the trio of white uniforms with regret. The rush of excitement she usually got from thinking about her job didn't come. She smoothed her palm down the soft nylon fabric. Nothing.

Tyson's words sounded in her head. "I picture you in real

estate. You're very people oriented."

What made him think of real estate? Maybe he'd seen her wearing the company jacket and his brain processed the information without him knowing it. None of that mattered. What mattered was whether he was involved in Nolan's murder. The short conversation with Paula Spencer proved at least part of Tyson's story true.

At the diner, waitress Judy gave Angie a welcoming wave then wiggled a mug in the air. Angie held up two fingers and zigzagged to a booth at the back.

"How's Valerie holding up?" Judy asked, pouring coffees.

"I'm worried about her. She's still holding everything inside."

"One of these days that dam will burst, and you'll be there for her. Same thing happened to my unc—" Judy turned at the sound of the opening door. "She the one you're waiting for?"

"You know her?"

"Not really. She's been in a couple of times, with two different men."

Paula stood in the doorway, left hand shading her eyes. Exactly the type of woman Angie expected to attract Tyson; tall, shapely, and bottle blonde. Blue eyes peered vacantly about—even though there were only a handful of booths and a line of stools at the counter—most unoccupied. Angie half-stood and waved but Paula continued gazing around. Angie's little voice reminded her that if she didn't look like a nurse, maybe she didn't look like a woman scorned either.

She stood up all the way and waved again. Paula looked startled but strode forward, brows knit over a slightly bulbous nose. "Angie?"

"Yes." Apparently she didn't look like an Angie either. "Sit down," she invited, since the woman didn't seem to be able to think of it on her own. She had after all, been invited for coffee.

Paula dropped a red vinyl purse on the bench and eased it across with her rear end as she sat. She put both forearms on the table and regarded Angie blankly for several seconds.

"Is something wrong?" Angie finally asked.

"No, uh, I guess not." The watery eyes roved from her face, to her blouse, and remained there long enough to make Angie wonder if she'd forgotten to button it. "It's just that you seem a little...old for Tyson."

Great. She didn't look like a nurse. She didn't look like an Angie. She didn't look like a woman scorned. She *did* look too old to be scornable. Angie rebutted with, "I heard love was blind."

Paula laughed at the cliché.

Angie couldn't help adding, "They also say women don't hit their sexual prime till they're forty."

Paula set to sweetening her cup. "Are you seeing Tyson right now?"

"I just left his house."

"His house? Don't you mean his parents' house?"

Angie allowed her eyebrows to lift a half-inch or so.

Paula smiled with superiority, dug inside the vinyl handbag and pulled out a pack of Winston's. "Mind if I smoke?"

Angie shook her head and went in for the kill. With an elaborate smirk she asked, "You mean he doesn't own HeavenScent?"

"Of course not. And, from what his mother told me, he's never going to." As she spoke, Paula's hands moved, sometimes both of them, sometimes just a finger to drive home a point. Right now, it was two fingers. They stabbed the air with each syllable. "If I had a mother like his...bitch through and through..." She shrugged. "But still, it's her house."

"Did he admit that to you? I mean, did you wonder if his mother might be lying just to keep him from getting married and tossing her out on her ear? Maybe Tyson really owns the place and lets her stay there."

"Honey, nobody would let that woman stay with them if she was on her death bed." Paula laughed and added, "Well, maybe if she was on a ventilator with a signed will in her hand and a priest standing over her." Now the hands turned palms up.

Angie chuckled and lowered her voice as though she were about to tell a secret. "So, you don't think Tyson has *any* money at all?"

"Not a penny. His mother told me his behavior's been so abominable lately, she's disinheriting him."

"No."

"Yes."

"Why do they let him continue living there? His mother said he's never even had a job."

Paula's high-pitched laugh made Judy look up from wiping tables. "He works. It's just not the job Momma wants him to have."

"What kind of work is it?"

"One time we were having dinner. He went to the bar to get us a couple more drinks. When he didn't come back, I found him talking business with this guy. In about five minutes, he drew up a financial statement." Paula laughed again. "In less time than it takes for a good screw."

"If he's so useless, why do you want him?"

Paula's mauve-painted lips moved into a wide grin. "Same as you, because he's a firecracker in bed."

Angie tried to look appropriately Tyson-ized, and nodded. Even though she'd come to know him a little better, she still thought him shallow and self-centered. She'd have trouble falling into bed with someone so one-sided. "Did you say something?"

"I asked how long you've been seeing him."

Tyson said he'd been seeing Paula for about a month. If Angie said she'd only been seeing him a short time, Paula would think of Angie as the "other woman." If Angie admitted to seeing him longer than a month, Paula would assume the role of "other woman" and possibly her feeling of superiority would return, and loosen her tongue.

"Five weeks, three days and," Angie gave a wide-eyed glance at her watch, "seventeen hours."

Paula's eyes focused on the watch and Angie tilted it to give

Paula a closer look. She said, "He bought me this," because Tyson seemed the type to buy gifts for women.

Paula's face scrunched and she stood up. "I have to be going."

"I thought we could talk a little longer."

"I'm really quite busy." The hands had stilled and now clutched tightly to the purse strap.

"I thought we might plan some revenge."

Paula's frown smoothed. She sat down.

Gotcha. "Well, I don't know about you but I'm really ticked at him for cheating on me. I think he deserves some payback."

Paula seemed to mull this over. She drained her cup and motioned Judy for a refill. Then she sweetened it, took a sip, and shook her head. "I have a better idea. It may take some time, but I'm going to convince that man to marry me."

"You're kidding."

"And make him realize he doesn't need you or anyone else. I love him, that's all there is to it. He's kind and considerate, a far cry from the guys I've dated in the past."

"What about children?"

"What about them?"

"Don't you want any?"

"No." The word came out sharp and definite.

So, the rumor of her pregnancy was greatly exaggerated. Angie checked the time once more. "Gosh, I forgot an appointment. Are you busy tomorrow morning? Can you meet me here at..." She pretended to count off the hours on her watch face. "Ten thirty?"

Taking Paula's empty stare as assent, Angie tossed some money on the table and ran out. Keeping with her "late for an appointment" lie, she flung open the door and raced headlong into Will. She tried to sidestep him but he got hold of her sleeve. "I thought I saw your car out here."

"I'm really late." She pulled away and started for the car.

"Angie, come on. I've been calling and calling. Why don't

you answer the phone?"

She stopped. "I told you I couldn't talk to you yet."

"Can't you forgive me?"

Over the past twenty-four hours, she'd felt her resolve thawing, the possibility of a reconciliation becoming more concrete—not in her conscious mind—there she remained firm. "Look Will. I just can't get the image of you two out of my head. Now, I really do have to go."

She climbed in the car and shut the door before he could protest further. He stood there staring as she squealed away. She swiped at the tears and gripped the wheel with white knuckles to keep herself from spinning the car in the middle of the road and going back to him.

At the cabin, Angie flung herself on the bed and cried in great heaving gasps of frustration, anger and regret. Did she really want to do this to him? Yes, definitely yes. That human urge for revenge had taken hold. She had to hurt Will as much as he'd hurt her, and the only way she knew how was through total and complete rejection. By the time she'd cried herself out dusk had fallen. The room a study in grays, much like her mood. Someone knocked on the door. She ignored it.

"Angie, are you in there?" Val called.

Go away, her small voice begged. Please, leave me alone.

"Angie, I'm worried about you. Please." Val knocked again, and again, louder. "If you don't open the door, I'll get the manager."

Angie forced herself off the bed and sulked to the door, catching a glimpse of herself in the old dresser mirror. It hardly seemed possible but she looked even worse than she felt.

She twisted the knob and pulled open the door. She didn't acknowledge Val, just went back and buried her face in the pillow.

"You met up with Will, didn't you?"

Angie nodded, not looking up.

Val sat on the bed and put her palm on Angie's back. Angie

turned over and sat up, folding a leg underneath her.

"I'm *so* sorry for all this," Val said.

"I didn't know I could feel so bad."

"It'll get easier."

After several moments of companionable silence, Angie took in a breath and tried to fix a new subject in her brain. She told Val about her journey to HeavenScent. "So, I called Paula."

Val threw off the denim jacket to reveal an all-black outfit—jeans and baggy tee shirt.

"And invited her to meet me."

Val's eyes widened. She sat back on the bed. "Tell me everything."

Angie recounted the meeting, right up to running into Will.

"Do you think Paula said that stuff to get you to back off?"

"Why?" Angie asked. "If what Tyson said was true, the relationship was over."

Val contemplated the situation with a finger to pursed lips. "Maybe-e-e she's got something else."

"Now you're getting morbid."

"I didn't mean anything as drastic as murder, but what if she's planning to blackmail Tyson or something like that?"

"That could be. Should we talk to him?"

"Nah." Val stood up, put on her jacket and tugged Angie's sleeve. "Come on, it's depressing here. Let's go get something to eat."

Val opened the door. There stood a uniformed policeman about to knock. His gaze focused on her. His mouth flattened into a thin line. "Valerie Little, you're under arrest for the murder of Nolan Little. Anything you say..."

Twenty-Four

Montez leaned across the pool table feeling the rail cut into his gut. He could barely see the six-ball through the smoky haze. Could barely breathe either. He pulled back an inch on the cue stick, pushed it an inch forward, then pulled back again, imagining the ball's path: tap the seven-ball, bank off the far cushion and into the corner pocket. No trick to the shot. No big deal. Beat this guy, get the money and go the hell home. Shanda would be waiting up; she always waited up.

"Damn."

Shanda, the reason he couldn't go home. He gave the stick a vicious thrust and immediately regretted the show of emotion. His playing partner, a skinny Puerto Rican with garlic breath, leaped off his stool. The guy's first time here. he'd eaten up the bartender's tease line—"Wanna make a few bucks? See that big black guy over there? He's the worst pool player in town, but won't admit it." That Puerto Rican beelined for Montez, who'd stifled his amusement and beaten the guy two games out of three so far.

In spite of Montez's display of emotion, the six-ball sank neatly in the hole. The Puerto Rican grunted and went back to his stool. As Montez lined up the next shot, he thought of *Little One*. Valerie had mentioned selling the boat. He wondered if Shanda liked the water. Funny, they'd never talked about that. Sure, she liked the pool at the rec center, but that's hardly the same as being on a boat, battling the elements, dealing with customers. If he bought the boat Valerie could pursue opportunities for her future, and he and Shanda could live in the fresh air instead of being buried behind computers all the time.

Shit, what was the use thinking of a future? He lived every minute on the proverbial borrowed time. Where the hell was Sonnie anyway? Not like him to be out of touch. Montez sank the seven-ball. A slow rhythmic clapping began behind him. He figured it was the Puerto Rican trying to rile him. Face it, two more balls and the guy would lose his wad.

When Montez dropped the eight-ball in the corner pocket and the clapping didn't stop, he straightened up and turned around, ready to clap his hands on that dumb ass Puerto Rican. But the PR wasn't on his stool; he'd gone to the bar for a refill. In his place sat that detective from Alton Bay.

What the hell was he doing out here? Montez thought he and his lawyer had gotten the son of a bitch off his back. Montez sank the nine-ball too. By now the Puerto Rican had returned. The guy sent Montez a tight smile, pulled a hundred from a roll in his pants pocket and slapped it in Montez's palm.

Jarvis rose from the stool and strode to an empty booth. He sat then gestured for Montez to sit too. But he remained on his feet. This wouldn't take long enough to justify sitting. Every eye in the place watched. They'd put Jarvis as a cop even though he'd left off the dumb ass hat and wore jeans and a sweatshirt. The look—like a busted leg—impossible to disguise.

"Nice shooting," Jarvis said.

Montez planted his hands on his hips, letting the gawkers know he hadn't invited a cop into their midst. "Cut the small-talk, what do you want? I thought we got our relationship clear this afternoon."

Jarvis stood so they could talk face to face. "Seen Sonnie around?"

"Told you I'd let you know." Montez stifled a grin, even though he'd practically bared his ass to the guy this afternoon, Jarvis didn't trust him. Well, the feeling was mutual.

Montez didn't mention that since getting back in town, he'd

scoured the city of Nashua looking for Sonnie. His landlady thought she'd heard him come home in the wee hours the night of the murder. But, since then, nothing.

Montez also didn't mention his concern. No doubt, shit related to the other night kept Sonnie away. Whether he went into hiding or something worse, Montez didn't know. No rumors floated around either way.

Montez already knew the answer but asked the question anyway. "Put an APB on him?"

"Yeah. Nothing. I thought by now you mighta had some ideas."

Under pressure, Jarvis obviously needed to solve the case. But Montez couldn't help. He went back to the game. For a long time he felt the cop's eyes boring into his spine. When he went for a refill of beer an hour later, Jarvis was gone.

Christ, what a mess. Four games and five hundred richer, he wrenched open the street door and went outside. The mellow tones of a church clock chimed nine times. The sky between the buildings solid black, no clouds, no stars. His eyes burned from the smoke. His neck hurt from leaning over the table. His groin ached with neglect. He thought of Angie Deacon. Jarvis let slip that she and her husband separated just after the murder. Why? In his experience, during stressful times, people came together. The blinking neon of an all-night diner on Claiborn helped get his hormones back on track. He ducked inside the place that smelled of stale grease. Thankful for the dim lighting, Montez slid into a booth and ordered a large Coke with extra ice and two burgers.

He read a copy of the Union Leader somebody'd left in the booth. Nolan's murder still made front-page news. No new information though, just—typical of journalists—a rehash of the same stuff, worded a different way. The meat was greasy and overcooked, the lettuce wilted, but it filled his stomach. He left the diner, folding the paper and tucking it under his arm. As an afterthought he tossed it back on the table.

Seven blocks to the small row house he'd shared with Shanda

since buying it four years ago. Till then they'd lived in a two-room walk-up over a Chinese restaurant. Seven blocks farther than he felt like walking right now, but no cabs around now. Not a surprise in this neighborhood. Even though there was no traffic, no pedestrians, not even a stray cat, he ducked his head against possible recognition and marched along, staying in the shadows of the old brick buildings. Home and sleep looked pretty damn good right now and he walked swiftly.

As he rounded the turn at the second block, he felt more than saw someone step out of a hotel doorway. The person fell into step ten feet behind and three feet to his right, also staying in the shadows. Maybe a coincidence. Somebody couldn't sleep, decided to take a stroll at four in the morning. In any other neighborhood maybe. He clenched his fists in his pockets and picked up the pace.

For two blocks, the person mimicked Montez's pace, not coming closer or lagging back. Abruptly Montez stopped and spun around, and had hold of his stalker's lapels before the guy could change pace.

The follower laughed. Montez flung the guy backward, striking the man's chest with his fists as he did. "You son of a bitch. What the hell you doing, trying to get yourself killed?" Montez shook his fists in Sonnie's face. "Where the hell have you been?"

"Where d'you think, man? Tryin' to get us out of this mess."

Montez flung his arms to his sides and started walking. Sonnie fell into step beside him. "That cop was here looking for you," Montez offered.

"I know."

Had he found a solution to their problem? Managed to somehow atone for losing the duffels? Montez didn't think so. Sonnie seemed too on edge. A door slammed and both men ducked between two brick buildings. When nothing happened except two cats meowing in the dumpster at the end of the alley, they began walking again.

"You think it's smart to go home?" Sonnie asked.

"Prob'ly not. I don't know if it's worse for Shanda if I'm *there* or *not* there."

"Whoa-ho, what's this?"

On the next corner stood a brand new Rite Aid Pharmacy. Closed, of course, but a Jeep sat in the corner of the lot, facing the street, with its engine running. Detective Jarvis had his head back on the headrest, but Montez had no thoughts the man was sleeping. He waited—from here he had an unobstructed view down the length of Montez's street—for him to finally go home. Why his house? And not Sonnie's?

"I'll take the back way home," Montez whispered and started to head out in a different direction.

Sonnie grasped his sleeve and pulled him back. "Wait." He slipped out of the alley.

Montez knew what he planned; he wanted to warn Sonnie off, but the man wouldn't have listened. He operated to the beat of a different set of rules. Montez followed in his wake. Maybe he could waylay his partner before something…unpleasant happened.

He lost sight of Sonnie when he sneaked up behind the vehicle in a low crouch. Something bright reflected off the store's plate glass window. God, Sonnie opened the back seat drivers' side door. Jarvis leaped alert, but Sonnie moved quicker. In a flash, he had his arm around Jarvis' throat. Montez started running.

"Heard you been looking for me," Sonnie said. He'd left the door open and Montez heard Jarvis choking. "What d'you want?"

"I…have…questions." In silhouette, Jarvis's Adam's apple bounced up and then down as he swallowed. Sonnie must've relaxed his grip because Jarvis' next words were clear. "That's how you get to the bottom of these things, Phelps. You ask questions."

"What kinda questions you got for me? I didn't kill the guy."

"Get rid of the knife and climb in front so we can talk like men."

Sonnie gave a low chuckle and pulled his arm away. He didn't get in front, but he did lean between the bucket seats. He laughed. "You're cool man, I gotta give you that. I ask you again, what d'you want with me?"

"I thought the streets woulda made you smarter than that, Phelps. You're involved up to your duffel bag-toting eyeballs and you know it."

Montez didn't think that was the wisest thing Jarvis could've said considering Sonnie still held the knife. He dangled it over the passenger seat. Sonnie gave no denial. No what-the-hell-are-you-talking-about? No reply either.

"Talk to me, Phelps."

"What's in it for me?"

"The satisfaction of seeing a killer brought to justice."

A chuckle.

"We got your footprint near the body."

Funny, that's the exact same thing he'd said to Montez. He smiled. That wise ass.

"Ain't no proof I killed him," Sonnie said.

"It sets you as our leading suspect."

"Let's see you prove it." Sonnie slid across the seat and got out. He waited under a newly planted crabapple tree until Jarvis drove away.

"What the fuck you trying to do, get the whole force on you?" Montez asked.

Sonnie laughed. Montez threw up his hands and started for home. Sonnie would get them both killed, sooner than later.

Twenty-Five

Helpless, Angie watched while the cop escorted the handcuffed, weeping Val to his car.

Angie said the only thing she could think of. "Don't worry."

"Don't leave town," the officer threw back over his shoulder. He helped Val into the back seat of the unmarked patrol car.

As soon as the vehicle drove away, Angie raced inside and searched for Cal's number. She couldn't find the scrap of paper Val had given her, nor was the number in the phone book. Not the end of the world, Val had one phone call, surely she'd call her son.

Angie threw some clean clothes in her suitcase and within minutes headed south on Route 93. The Nashua addresses of Sonnie Phelps and Montez Clarke, scribbled on yellow Post-It notes, lay on the seat beside her.

On the way out of town, she'd had to pass Will's office. Traffic slowed. She had plenty of time to see; there they stood, on the sidewalk. He wore his best suit, the black one with the silk piping on the lapels. She couldn't see the lapels because Cassie was folded in his arms. A tall, slim boy walked up and put his arms around them both. About ten years old with dark curly hair—just like Will!

She suddenly felt dizzy and screeched the car to a stop. Will turned at the sound. He pushed Cassie away and sprinted toward the Lexus. By then Angie had squealed it back onto the road, narrowly missing the front bumper of a school bus. Three horns blared.

She jammed on the brakes to avoid hitting the car ahead. *Get the damned cars moving!* Her eyes darted to the rear view mirror. Will stood on the sidewalk watching her snails-pace escape. And not following. A strangled gurgle escaped her throat. A son? How could Will have hidden a son from her all these years?

Angie skidded to a stop again, this time looking both ways. She turned the car around. Time he faced the music. She drove back to the office. The sidewalk was empty. Will's Jeep was gone, and so were his lover and—son? God, don't let it be true. She turned the vehicle once again and headed on her original journey.

Nearly nine o'clock when she passed the Entering Nashua sign, not remembering most of the trip. Her eyes burned. She longed for a bed and rest but sleep would be an illusive entity for some time. Every time she closed her eyes, all she saw, the tall handsome boy, who looked so much like Will. Try as she would, she couldn't absolve her brain of this newest trouble. It would just have to wait till tomorrow.

Angie located Montez's street on the map she'd bought at a gas station. All the houses were identical boxes, an architect's nightmare, probably housing for factory workers way back when. What little she could see in the circle of her headlights looked clean and well kept. Number forty-two had a Ford Escort, maybe five years old, in the short driveway. No lights on in the house, not even on the stoop, a small cement square, not big enough for one person to stand and open the door at the same time.

What did he do for a living? Was he married? Kids? No toys or bikes dotted the small rectangle of somewhat shaggy lawn. No landscaping, no flower boxes, no woman's touch. Angie drove to the end of the street and turned around. She passed the house slowly for another look. He must be in bed.

She found a decent looking hotel and parked near the back of the lot. For a long time, she stared into space. It probably wasn't smart coming here. What would she gain? Did she think, when confronted, Sonnie and Montez would admit their guilt? More than likely Sonnie would pound her to pulp and park the Lexus in some back alley where her body wouldn't be discovered until summer. She should turn and go back right now, before something bad happened. Angie restarted the car. What was there to go back to? A confrontation with Will, that was all. Nothing much to look forward to.

She shut off the engine and resolutely got out. Brisk air but without the bite of the wind racing down Winnipesaukee. Angie opened the rear door and bent inside to get her suitcase. In one motion she pivoted, set the case on the ground and straightened up. And found herself peering into the muzzle of a gun.

Panic, like a tsunami, numbed her senses. She tried to see beyond the gaping black hole, the gun barrel, but her attacker was cast in silhouette. "Money. Gimme your money," said the faceless voice, a darker shadow in the blackness before her. Her father's warning, "always park under a streetlight," went through her head.

"I—"

The gun wiggled. "Just give me your cash and you won't get hurt."

Angie kept her eyes on the inkiest part of the dark and reached for her purse strap.

"Slowly."

She pulled the bag around to her front and unsnapped the clasp.

In the space of a millisecond, less than the time the eye can focus or the brain can process information, the gun jerked upward. It went off with a bright yellow flash. A bullet shot by her left ear, so close Angie felt the rush of air.

The mugger crumpled and pitched to the ground inches from her feet. Then he rolled, away from whatever or whoever had dumped him. His path drove him into Angie's knees and she went down. He grunted when her elbow caught him in the cheek.

Instinct pressed her into action and she rolled off him and under the car, screaming till her lungs were empty. Grit dug her knees and elbows, tore at her silk blouse, scuffed her new shoes.

The smell of oil. The click click of the engine cooling. The throb of her heartbeat in her head. Adrenaline pushed her to get out and run. Instinct made her stay.

She screamed again as the battle raged. The sound of flesh pounding flesh. One voice, raised in a harsh growl. The other, even meaner, more determined, "This is my strike. Go git your own."

Angie squeezed herself deeper into the shadows, eyes closed, praying for the nightmare to end, promising to go home and be domestic—if she got out of this. Why hadn't anyone answered her screams?

Cell-phone. The word popped into her head like corn in the microwave. Her purse! It must be somewhere on the ground. It couldn't be long before one mugger put the other out of commission and came after her for himself. Would he be happy just to grab the bag and run? Knowing she might have seen him?

Her brain scrambled for a solution. Cell-phone gone. Screeches unanswered. What was left? The gun! She'd never used one, but if small children could kill one another...

She peered out at the pair of feet maneuvering for superiority. The gun lay just a foot away, in the shadows, or one of them would have it by now. Where was the second guy's gun? Didn't all muggers and thieves carry them?

Only a foot away. You can do it.

The problem was the pair of sneakers framing the weapon. They moved first one way, then the other as the owner balanced and thrust at his foe, one moment they were a foot away, the next a quarter inch. Why he didn't step on it, she didn't know.

Reach!

She pushed out her right hand as the feet jockeyed above her.

Angie's fingers closed around the barrel.

Next came the yowl of pain and the thud of a body hitting the ground.

Now, pressure on Angie's hand as someone mashed her knuckles into the tar. She bit her lip to keep from crying out. Fingers reached down and unwound hers from around the gun barrel. "No!" she cried out as her only chance of salvation was wrenched from her grasp.

"Come out."

She didn't move.

Someone knelt. The gun appeared, the black hole waved at her. "Come out."

This time she did. For some unexplainable reason, she didn't want her bullet-riddled body found underneath her car. She wriggled and squirmed, scuffing her thirty dollar manicure. Strong, huge hands grasped her about halfway out, and she screamed again.

"Shh!"

The hands set her on her feet. As soon as they hit solid ground, they made running motions. Giant hands held her back. "Stop. I'm not going to hurt you."

Angie screamed again.

A paw closed over her mouth and a face came into view. A familiar face. Montez Clarke was mugging her!

She flung her arms into his face, and bit into a soft pink palm. Instead of being withdrawn, the grip tightened. His other arm wrapped around her, to keep her still. "Stop screaming, I'm not going to hurt you."

As proof, he let go, pried her fingers open and pressed the gun into her hand. She stood, dumbstruck, gaping from it, dangling stupidly from her index finger, to his face, smiling now.

"You," she said.

He nodded, and pointed at the lump on the ground.

"Saved me."

He nodded again, then took the gun from her and put it in

his jacket pocket. Wordless, he retrieved her suitcase and purse, put a guiding arm around her shoulders and steered her into an all night diner.

Montez nudged her into a booth. He put her things on the other seat, then pushed in against them. "Two coffees," he called to the waitress. He sat silent until Angie had finished a whole cup. "So, tell me what you were doing in front of my house."

"What?"

"You parked out front of my house. You went to the end of the street, turned around and came here."

Emotion flooded back. Confusion. Anger. "You followed me."

"You might be dead if I hadn't."

Reality. Stark naked truth. Angie dropped her head into her hands and began to tremble. An unidentified body found in a parking lot. A statistic. Angie had been millimeters away from becoming a feature story on the Eleven O'clock News. Does anyone know this woman?

Angie wiped her nose on her sleeve and straightened up. Montez's hand poised inches from her face, a napkin hanging from his beefy lifesaving fingers. His face looked serious. Yet behind the concern lurked something else. Mere seconds passed before she realized...that something else, was passion. Fire surged into her face.

Montez smiled. How did he always know her thoughts?

"Thank you," she managed to squeak out, then covered her embarrassment by lifting the cup and draining the last drop. "What now? Do we call the police or something?"

"We go home and forget this ever happened."

"What?"

"This isn't Alton Bay where everybody knows everything that's going on. This is the City where people don't want to know. So long as it doesn't directly affect them, they don't give a shit." He stressed the last three words.

Angie closed her fingers around the cup as a tear escaped

each eye. She swiped at them, then caught a glimpse of the back of her hand, scraped raw from contact with the tar, two artificial nails torn off. She began crying again.

Montez stood up, tossed some cash on the table, then eased her to her feet. He stayed close as they went through the doorway joining the dining room with the hotel. She stood dumbly to one side while he booked a room in his name. Her brain said to run. Run as far and as fast as she could. But she didn't. Couldn't make her feet move.

He helped her into the elevator, opened the door to Room 321, and nudged her inside. She stood while he moved about, putting her suitcase on one bed, then shutting the drapes to the twinkling stars, muggers and killers.

He wore his hair cropped short against his scalp, the beginnings of a bald spot showed near the back. His clean shaven skin looked smooth and silky. His clothes, an entire outfit in black, were clean and neat.

Angie's brain oozed back to life when he went into the bathroom. She heard the tub drain shut and the water turn on—the hollow rushing sound of the water, so far away, yet so close.

Montez returned. "Feeling better yet?"

She hadn't the energy to even nod.

He eased her to a chair and removed her shoes. Angie barely had time to note the toes were scuffed beyond repair before they were tossed into a corner. Montez urged her to stand, knelt before her and undid her jeans. As his hands caressed her hips, Angie realized what was happening. Payback. He'd saved her life and expected compensation.

Could she? Technically she was still married to Will. Being separated didn't negate her responsibilities, though being married didn't hinder his philandering.

This whole thing wasn't right. And it wasn't right for him to exact payment in this manner. She'd tell him. As soon as he made a move. She'd tell him she couldn't do this. What would he do? Would he force her? Would it be better to just let him do it? Safer maybe. Could she live with herself afterward?

The jeans slid down to her knees. She felt herself being lowered back into the chair. Then the jeans were drawn over her feet. Anticipation, fear, worry and at least a dozen other emotions flooded her insides. His touch was featherlight. So tired, she could fall asleep right here in this chair.

She felt herself being helped to her feet, the blouse buttons, of which three were already missing, came undone. Montez stepped behind her and slipped the garment off, his hands dusting the length of her arms, making the little hairs stand on end and her nipples come erect. Terror wrestled with fear and, she had to admit, the tiniest morsel of horniness. What would it be like with a black man who smelled like sandalwood and herbs? Surely no different than with Will. The bra came loose and dropped to the floor.

Angie felt herself being inched toward the bathroom, and the relentless roaring of the water in the tub. Suddenly all she could hear was roaring. It echoed in her head, her ears and her groin.

Her bare feet hit the chilly tile floor and her nipples peaked again. She wanted to rub away the prickly sensation. The door closed and she was trapped here with him. She waited, but he didn't touch her again.

Was he waiting for her to make a move? React in some way? She turned to tell him she couldn't go through with this.

The room was empty.

Twenty-Six

Jarvis cursed Sonnie Phelps. He cursed Montez Clarke. He cursed the case in general. He tipped up the can of root beer and drained the contents. The mound of paperwork on the passenger seat served as a towering reminder of his failure as a detective. The first murder case in Alton Bay in—well, in a damned lot of years—and he couldn't solve it. A freaking closed-room murder had him buffaloed. Well, if Sherlock Holmes could solve them, so could he.

The answer had to be in that pile of folders, the exact order of them etched in his mind. Topmost: copies of Little's insurance policies, fifty thousand Life on each of them, Replacement on the boat, mega Health premiums: typical for the self-employed.

Second in the folder-pile: Dozens of interviews done by detectives, both state and local. It was his job to sift through, to find common denominators between someone—anyone.

Third, Tyson *Wuss* Goodwell's background sheet. On first glance it had yielded nothing unusual. An only child. Parents William Ralph Goodwell (58) and Agnes Smith Goodwell (60). Born in 1980, Wuss must've been a change of life baby. He'd graduated Manhattan's Murry Bergatraum HS 1998. Jarvis was mildly surprised to see a second page stapled at the corner: Tyson Xavier Goodwell's arrest record: from disturbing the peace to possession of marijuana with intent to distribute. Behaviors associated with rebellion. Jarvis would bet this kid spent his time vying for the affection and attention of his parents. Didn't rich folks pay more attention to charity events than to their kids? Let nannies do all the childcare and get pissed as hell when their kid got in any kind of trouble? They were so worried it would ruin their standing in the community they'd do anything to hush up a story.

Question was: did Wuss still crave attention? Would he murder to get it? Try as he might, Jarvis could find no connection to New Hampshire, the Littles, Sonnie or Montez. Could find no reason Tyson Goodwell might want to kill Nolan Little.

Another question that plagued him all night long—had made him less than alert, allowing Phelps to sneak up on him—where the hell was Angelina Deacon? She'd promised she wouldn't leave town, but when he'd driven past her motel on the way out of town, her car had been gone. He'd squealed the Jeep around and gone to see the clerk who said she'd checked out.

Where the hell was she? What prompted their breakup? Was it related to the murder? He'd phoned Wilson and told him to get busy finding her. Chances were good the Little woman was missing too. For some reason Angelina had taken the mousy woman under her wing.

He let his mind revisit Will Deacon's third round of questioning. Will had admitted to the separation from Angelina, though he would not give the reason for it. At Jarvis' suggestion that it had something to do with the murder, Will had launched into serious proclamations of innocence, both his *and* his wife's. Shakespeare's words: he doth protest too much, seemed appropriate. On the other hand, the vehement denial of their involvement in Nolan's death might well be related to guilt over the separation; sometimes guilt manifested itself that way.

As Jarvis eased the car off Route 3 and onto 28, the image of he and Angelina popped into his head. Hand in hand they strolled the Atlantic City's boardwalk with the sun just coming up over the ocean. She had her head on his shoulder. He had a hard-on the size of Everest.

Stop! Even if she and Will divorced and she agreed to go out with him, a relationship couldn't work. Alton was a small town. People would think Jarvis the cause of it. He might lose his job. Then he'd be unable to support her and they'd end up apart too.

His laugh erupted from somewhere deep inside. In less than twenty miles, his subconscious had taken him through an entire relationship—without any sex. Thankfully the fantasy had no sex. Sex wasn't a subject where he and his body agreed lately.

He stopped at McDonalds for a large coffee and was home within five more minutes. He went around to gather the armload of folders from the passenger seat. When he opened the door, Phelps' scent pushed at him—some kind of aftershave and the unmistakable aroma of marijuana. Funny he hadn't noticed it while in the car.

Jarvis' house smelled too, like disuse. What was there to come home to anyway? Since Liz's death, his life was a sham. Until he'd seen Angelina Deacon on that boat. Even with blood on her shirt, disheveled hair, and wind burned cheeks, the most beautiful thing he'd ever seen.

He slammed the front door back against the couch. It made only a thump, which didn't satisfy his craving to throw things. By the time he crossed through the living room and set the folders on the kitchen table, the urge vanished. All he wanted now, a shower to wash Sonnie Phelps's smell out of his clothes.

He stopped at the mirror in the bathroom to examine the spot Phelps's knife made to his throat. A sharp red line, but no break in the skin. Funny how the pricking sensation remained.

He shaved, leaving the mess on his face, and ran hot water in the shower.

Six thirty nine, Jarvis stood in his picture window, a thick towel wrapped around his waist, water dripping down his forehead from the ever-thinning hair. The sun, rising over the east side of the property, emphasized his overgrown lawn. Grass lay in clumps around the mailbox post and the base of the steps. Steam rose off his Jeep, still cooling from the wasted trip to Nashua.

He took off the lid and sipped the still-hot coffee. God, why did they have to make it so damned hot? He stacked the folders and straightened the pile. He flipped the Goodwell folder open and then shut, twice, unable to make himself sit down and read. As the top page fluttered into place, a sentence caught his eye. Adrenaline throbbed. He jerked open the cover and scanned the pages. What the hell had he seen? He tried again, but came up with nothing.

He pushed the cup aside, sat back in the captain's chair and scrubbed his knuckles in his overworked eyes. Probably they were playing tricks on him. A lot of mileage on them the last few days. He read the page again, careful to 'see' every single word. There—near the bottom, in the paragraph listing Father Goodwell's holdings: hidden in the middle of the list, WG's Restaurant.

"Well, well, well." Jarvis could barely contain his elation as he dialed the station. "Wilson, pick up Goodwell. Hold him till I get there."

An elated Jarvis visualized the discussion he'd have with Wuss, cowering in a chair between parents who Jarvis was sure would insist on accompanying him. Should he question Tyson in front of them? Or piss them off by taking him to a private interrogation?

He detoured to the drive-thru for a quick breakfast and more coffee. The stuff at the station at this hour would be leftover from last night. He forgot about the bump leading down to the station. The cup sprang out of his hand. He snatched at it, caught it, but squeezed too hard. The lid popped off. Coffee sloshed down the front of his shirt. Jarvis cursed and brushed it off before it could soak in.

The Jeep passed under a line of overhanging trees and for a moment, the coffee spill looked like blood. The kind of blood the murderer would have by stabbing Nolan Little. High velocity spatters. He slapped his palms on the wheel. Think, you fool. How could someone murder a person and not get HV spatters on them? Just not possible.

Damn, yes it was! How stupid could he have been?

Twenty-Seven

The experience of the evening, not lost on her, yet Angie could think of nothing but the passion in Montez's eyes. And the fact that she might very well have given herself to him. Angie had never been so close to a black man. His scent intoxicated her. The feather-light touch of his hands on her hips sent spasms up and down her spine. She could only imagine the kinky softness of his hair against her breasts.

Had he brought her here intending to seduce her? Or was the whole thing in her mind, a figment of her disheveled brain and nearly-mugged body? Maybe he'd just wanted to calm her, to get her past the horror of the night.

Maybe sex never entered his mind at all. Right.

When she'd turned and found herself alone in the bathroom, she pressed her ear against the door, and heard nothing. Did he stand on the other side wishing she'd open it and call to him? Had he already disappeared down the long hallway? Angie had almost opened the door to find out. But then he might think she wanted him, which she didn't.

She took off her panties and climbed in the tub. The hot water only stirred her fire into deeper emotions and reduced her to tears, bawling both for what had and what hadn't happened.

Finally hours, or maybe minutes, later, after peeking into the room to make sure she remained alone, she climbed under the fresh clean sheets and lay on her back, staring at the patch of yellow moonlight for the rest of the night.

Morning had long since replaced the moonlight on the ceiling. Angie heard the distant, muffled sound of the elevator whirring up the shaft. She didn't hear the doors slide open, but firm footsteps moved along the hall. How she knew it was Montez, she didn't know, but the key card slipped in and the lock disengaged with a tiny click. The tall man entered as though he owned the place, which in a sense he did since he'd paid for the room.

Had he returned expecting her to be recovered and ready for him now?

Montez moved on silent feet, but his presence was as palpable as if he'd arrived with a fanfare of trumpets. He sat on the edge of the bed, softly, as if afraid to wake her. He put a hand on her arm. Angie pretended to startle awake, then peered at him through sleepy eyes.

"Good morning, Sunshine. Get any sleep?"

His lips opened into a smile. She turned over, clutching the sheet to her chin. His hand remained on her arm. Was he playing games? No, the look in his so-dark eyes wasn't playful. Not at all.

"Not much," she managed to answer.

He patted the edge of the mattress. "Get up, I'll take you to breakfast. You got to hurry though, I have to be to work in an hour and a half." He rose and went to the small foyer. "Okay, go ahead, I'm not looking."

After what he'd seen the night before, she didn't think it mattered, but didn't say so. She scrounged in the suitcase, one eye on his big, wide back. Then she took the clothes to the bathroom.

She dressed, and in moments, returned to the room. He sat in one of the chairs near the windows which now gaped open to admit the day. The brightness made her blink.

She donned the only other pair of shoes she'd brought. "I'm ready."

He smiled up from the hotel menu he'd been reading. "You're fast. I'm impressed."

She squelched a comment. "Do I need a jacket?"

"Naah."

He followed her out of the room. "By the way, I really like your hair that way."

In her haste, Angie had left it free, just as it had dried in bed. "Thanks."

They went to the same diner. Thankfully, none of the last night's staff was on duty to recognize her.

"Where do you work?" she asked.

"In a computer shop a few blocks away. I sell, repair, deliver and listen to complaints."

"Sounds like you own the place."

He grinned. "You're quick. I like that."

They ordered. When the waitress left, Angie leaned forward and thanked him for his help.

Montez set the menus in the holder at the back of the table. "Now you owe me." He let a moment pass and then grinned. "You have to tell why you were watching my place last night."

Tears threatened and Angie gulped them down with a half-cup of tea. "Val's been arrested. I'm sure she's innocent."

"Me too," Montez said, then added, "So, you came to ask me who I suspected, right?"

"Ah—no."

An 'I knew it look' crossed his face and remained there, widening his nostrils and dipping his eyebrows. "What made you suspect me?"

"I don't suspect you in particular." She took a breath. "It's got to be someone who was on that boat."

"You check out Momma's boy, or were the big black guys your first suspects?"

"I spent yesterday morning with Tyson."

"And?"

The breakfasts arrived and they waited till the waitress had gone back into the kitchen.

"He had a perfectly valid excuse for being at the dock. His

girlfriend told him she was pregnant. He was running away."

Montez forked a wedge of pancakes into his mouth. "You believed him?"

"It sounded like something that'd happen to someone like him. Then I called the woman and talked to her. Their stories jibed, sort of."

"And then you thought you'd come to Nashua."

Angie could feel the playfulness of his words and relaxed. "Have the police been all over you?"

"Four times so far. You been to see Sonnie yet, or you couldn't wait to see me again?"

Angie smiled away the innuendo. "I haven't seen him yet. What brings you and Sonnie to Alton Bay so often?"

Montez took another bite of pancake, then folded a strip of bacon between his teeth. He told her to eat before her eggs got cold. She obeyed.

"My girlfriend's parents are in California," he said, "on top of the San Andreas fault line. I don't admit this to many people and if you tell anybody, your ass is grass—I'm scared shitless of earthquakes."

"Sounds rational to me. So, while your girlfriend goes to California, you and Sonnie go fishing?"

"Yep."

"Where does Sonnie work?"

"Sonnie ah, sort of freelances. Sells this, hauls that, repairs the other. You know."

"So, what's in the duffel bags?"

"Still stuck on them, are you?" Montez smiled widely.

Angie shrugged. "Just curious."

"You know what they say about curiosity."

"I do, but as you saw last night, I seem to have nine lives."

"You're not careful, you might use them all up here in Nashua." He pushed the plate, still containing a whole pancake, aside. He drank the remaining half glass of orange juice in one gulp and set it firmly on the table. He pulled up his sleeve and looked at his watch. "I have to go. Promise you won't go wandering around any more dark parking lots."

She made the Scouts' honor sign.

"I get off at two today. Will you have lunch with me?"

"I don't know. I might have gone home by then."

"Good. Nashua's no place for you." His words said one thing, his tone said, "someone like you."

Maybe he was right. He started to leave but stopped and re-traced his steps. He withdrew a rectangular blue card from his shirt pocket and handed it to her. His business card.

Sonnie's neighborhood consisted of older four- and six-family tenements. His building was a brown-shingled affair. She entered the tall double doors, whose paint peeled in long sad strips of brown over blue over green. The place smelled musty, like the door stayed shut all the time. The muted sound of a trumpet spouting jazz music oozed down from the second floor. The only thing in the hallway was an elderly ten-speed bicycle leaning against the wall.

His apartment was 1A, first on the right. The door stood open about an inch, the way it might if Sonnie just went outside for the mail and didn't want to lock himself out. Angie tapped near the hinged side, trying not to make the door open further.

No one answered. "Sonnie?" She knocked a little harder and called again.

A door opened on the second floor. The jazz music blared now, and a frizzy gray head appeared in the stairwell. "Knock harder, he's in there."

"Okay, thanks." Under the intensity of Angie's knock, the door moved. Still no answer, but it stood open more than a foot now. She peered inside. A dim place; shades covering the windows blocked out all but the merest of the morning's light.

She waited till her eyes accustomed to the dimness. "Sonnie? It's Angie."

The silence loomed at her like some childhood monster. Then

came the smell. Just like on *Little One*. With perspiring fingers and a guilty heart—this wasn't how nurses should act—she pulled the door shut and backed into the hallway.

The woman called down, "He's probably in the can. Go on in, he won't mind."

"If he's busy, I don't want to bother him."

"Bull crap." Pouffy pink slippers shushed down the bare wooden stairs. The blue striped housedress looked new, but stretched tight across an ample bosom. An equally ample bra was visible between the second and third buttons. "I know he's here. He dropped something a while ago. Sounded heavy." She edged past Angie and flung open the door. "Sonnie! Hey, get the hell out here. You got company."

Angie stifled the urge to escape, and stepped into the room as a throaty gurgle gushed from the woman. Angie followed her gaze to the couch where, sprawled in death, lay Sonnie Phelps.

"What the hell has he gone and done now?" the woman said, taking two steps closer.

Beside the couch sat an orange crate that had seen better days. On the crate, a ceramic lamp with no shade. Careful to touch only the knob, Angie turned it on. A low-watt bulb, but still enough to illuminate Sonnie, his left leg and arm dangling toward the bare wood floor. The lopsided posture brought to mind Nolan Little, whom Angie had feared would slip off his tall stool at any second. Sonnie hadn't been stabbed with a filet knife though; he'd been shot in the temple. The wound wasn't immediately obvious because it was on his right side. Angie had to walk around the sofa to get a look at it. She had no experience with guns but the hole didn't look too big. With the black marks all around it, she guessed he'd been shot up close. The blood was still wet, which meant the murder had happened recently. The woman from upstairs said she'd heard Sonnie drop something. Over the rhythm of the loud music, that's probably how it would sound.

Sonnie's dark eyes, that looked even more ominous in this light, stared at the yellowed, chipped ceiling. Angie bent toward him, prepared to check his carotid and nearly bumped heads with the woman who gave an irritated curse. "Damn. Don't this just beat all? Two tenants in one week."

"Someone else died too?"

"Yeah, guy from 3B keeled over in the laundry room. He was 90 if he was a day."

Angie took out her cell phone and dialed the number from Montez's business card. He answered on the first ring. Seeing things were "in hand" the landlady shuffled back upstairs.

As Angie bent for a closer look, her foot struck something on the floor. Something heavy slid under the couch. She didn't have to look—but did anyway—to know she kicked a gun. A revolver maybe. Weren't they the kind where the bullets got fed into the little holes? She left the gun where it lay. Let the cops figure out how it got so far under the sofa.

Sonnie's apartment consisted of a kitchen/living room combination, a tiny bedroom and an aged bathroom complete with pocked claw-foot tub. The place was sparsely furnished and almost hygienically clean. Besides the flower-patterned sofa and orange crate, the room contained a battered wood kitchen table and two chairs. Bare windows and floor . Between the street-side windows hung a framed picture of Jesus hanging on the cross. The only other decoration sat on the kitchen table: an 8"x10" photograph in a cheap wood frame. The photo showed a blond man in his twenties, with his arm around a young black boy of about twelve. The boy held a basketball and grinned at the camera. She didn't know why, but she slipped the picture in her purse.

Footsteps sounded in the hall. Angie anchored the handbag on her shoulder as Montez entered the apartment. He gazed at Sonnie without emotion. Then he looked at Angie. "Didn't expect you to be calling *this* soon." He put out a hand. "Come on."

She crossed the room while drawing the cell phone from her bag. He shook his head. "Put it away. Let's go."

"What! You've got to be kidding."

"Not kidding." He put a hand on her shoulder and tried to

steer her out of the room. She resisted and he dropped the hand. "You are one stubborn woman. This is a drug killing, don't get involved."

"How do you know?"

"Just trust me, okay. Get out now."

"You can really walk away?" How could he ignore this? Murder was different than mugging. Murder needed to be reported, avenged. Just like Nolan's.

Sirens sounded from close by.

"Nothing we can do," Montez said. "We're into this deep enough already."

"A second ago you said it was drug related. Now you're insinuating it's related to Nolan's murder."

He heaved a sigh. "I'm out of it, that's it." Tires squealed out front, he threw up his hands. "Don't say I didn't warn you."

He marched out the door, turned right and disappeared down the hall as the cops swarmed in the front.

Twenty-Eight

Bleary-eyed and starving, Angie headed for home after one o'clock. For two hours, Nashua police questioned her, badgered her and even did a paraffin test—she hadn't fired a gun. No shit. Finally, they'd let her go.

She pulled into the first fast food joint. Taking the food to a lone table, she sat to eat. The events of the day were all too vivid. Sonnie sprawled across the sofa, the massive amount of blood being absorbed by the stuffing. She'd been surprised at his neatness and felt bad for stereotyping the big dreadlocked man. Then she remembered the photo she'd taken from Sonnie's kitchen table, and withdrew it from her purse. Though the apartment had been very clean, she noted no other mementos, no personal items—except this picture. There must be some strong sentiment involved with it.

The shot had been taken at a basketball court; a hoop towered on a metal pole above the young boy. The child was obviously Sonnie. No dreadlocks here, just a short natural style. He wore newish blue jeans and an emerald green sweatshirt with the Celtics logo in the center. His sneakers looked old—comfortable. He smiled up at the man, who gazed down on him with undisguised pride. Something about him seemed familiar. She stared hard, but couldn't place the wide-set nostrils and dark eyes.

The frame had probably been purchased at a chain store. Just four pieces of wood, beveled together. The edges didn't meet in smooth joints. She turned it over. A triangular wedge of cardboard for a stand. Cheap cardboard backing; little metal tabs, bent over to hold it in place. Angie used the edge of her plastic fork to pry them up. She removed the cardboard and set it on her food tray beside the unopened containers, her rumbling stomach momentarily forgotten. There was writing on the back of the photo. She spun the frame to read it upright. *Sonnie and Vic. Summer 1994.* Who was this Vic? She flipped the thing around and gazed into the face. Still, that nudge of familiarity. It had been taken twelve or more years ago. People changed a lot in the amount of time.

She took out her cell phone and dialed Montez. He didn't say hello. His smooth as mercury voice said, "I hope you're home sitting in a hot bubble bath."

She ignored his suggestive tone. "Hi Montez. Hey, do you know where Sonnie grew up?"

"Nashua."

"Where in Nashua?" She hung up the phone and laid it on the table. Some people got suspicious so easily. That's when she noticed she had a message. She punched the appropriate buttons. The display showed a number she didn't recognize. But the voice was familiar. Carlson Brinks, the elderly diver who moored his boat near *Little One.*

"Miss Deacon? I-I'm not sure it's anything, but I *might* have some information for you regarding the night of Nolan's death. Call me at 555-4456 when you get in." Angie tried the number, but there was no answer.

She picked up two French fries, eyeing the picture again. Where could this have been taken? On a public basketball court, that was obvious. She squinted and bent closer. Edged with maples and oaks, a single birch tree overhung a battered chain link fence along the court. A sidewalk directly on the other side of the fence bordered a wide street, with a lot of traffic and cars parked densely along either side. Okay, so it was a main road. Most of the landmarks on the other side of the street were obliterated by the trees and cars, but it looked like an Asian super-

market and maybe a Laundromat. She could make out the words
WASH & DRY in ONE HOUR.

Angie slapped the picture down on the table. The sound made
a guy in a nearby table turn and look. She shrugged.

What was the use? So what if Sonnie grew up in Nashua? Who
cared where the park was? It had probably been torn down for a
high-rise by now anyway. Angie just couldn't shake the feeling
she'd seen the man in the photo somewhere before.

Was it possible Sonnie committed suicide? He didn't seem
the type to her, but could you ever really know what went on inside someone?

She finished her lunch, most of it anyway. An hour later, she
moped into Detective Jarvis' office. She sat, not missing the fact
that the vee-shaped eyebrows were flat; he was angry and not
trying to hide it. And she didn't have to ask why.

He planted his elbows on the desk, which she noticed had
been cleared of debris, and made a tent with his fingers. "Nashua
police tell me you've been having quite the little adventure."

Adventure?

"You were asked not to leave town." He stabbed a finger at
her. "When we make these requests it's not just because we've
gone power mad. Sometimes—just sometimes—it's because we
fear for your safety."

"Aw shucks, I didn't know you cared." Angie stifled the
twinge of guilt.

He got up and started pacing behind his desk. She resisted
the urge to see if he'd worn a path in the tan tiled floor. "Tell me
about Sonnie Phelps," he said without stopping.

For a moment, she watched him pace, then dizzy, she gazed
out the window. Nothing there but sky and a single maple tree.
Breaking into goose bumps, she told him the same story she'd
told the Nashua authorities. Again not mentioning how Montez
suggested she run away.

"Don't say I didn't warn you," Montez had said.

He'd been right, of course. "The ordeal with the police had

begun as a simple Q&A, but when she'd explained the reason for her presence at Sonnie's place, things turned more serious: "What makes you think Phelps is involved?" "How did you come to find him?" "Sarge, call Alton Bay and see what they got."

Sonnie's time of death was set around four a.m. Angie had been sleeping soundly in her hotel—alone. They'd been satisfied until learning Montez had paid for the room. That brought another round of questions. One cop had the audacity to suggest she'd probably come here to buy drugs from Sonnie.

"I wondered if it was suicide," Angie said.

"They put it as a drug deal gone bad," Jarvis said, stopping the infernal pacing finally.

Most of Angie's body relaxed; one thing they'd never associate with her, anything related to drugs. The story must've jived with what the Nashua authorities told him because, although his expression remained stern, he nodded.

"Why did you search my house?"

He slid his butt on the corner of his desk. "I already told you, I'm not—"

"—at liberty to discuss it. Yes, I know. But you confiscated things. I deserve to know what they were."

"Why not ask your husband?"

Jarvis knew they were separated. Did that change her suspect status? Definitely. A couple becoming separated the night after a horrific murder didn't bode well for either of them.

"Want to tell me why you two aren't together?"

"Take my word, it's got nothing to do with Nolan's murder."

He shook his head.

Angie blew out a sigh and wished she could erase the last seventy-two hours from her memory—from her life. "I found out he's been cheating on me." She swallowed the sensation of loss that always accompanied the thought. "See? Nothing to do with the Littles."

Jarvis climbed off the desk. "I have a murder investigation to work on." He waited till she rose, then nudged her toward the door. "Go home, make up with your husband and let us do our jobs."

Was he kidding? "Did you find out why Tyson Goodwell had a sudden urge to go fishing?"

He didn't answer.

"I did. I'll tell you, if you tell me something."

Jarvis sighed and went back to his chair. "You first."

She almost asked, *how do I know I can trust you* but didn't think he'd see the humor in it. "Tyson told me he was running from a woman and got on the boat to avoid her."

No reaction.

"The girlfriend told me a different story."

"You spoke to her?"

"Yes. Didn't you?"

Again, no reaction.

"They've been seeing each other since he came to town in May. She says she's going to marry him."

Jarvis wrote on a notepad. "Mr. Goodwell doesn't seem the marrying type to me," he said without looking up.

"I didn't say he *agreed* to marry her. Just that she's working on him." Jarvis looked at her strangely now. She almost asked what was wrong, then it struck her. "You don't know her name!"

No reaction.

Angie handed over the address she'd gotten from the phone book. "It's Paula Spencer."

"What else you got?"

"Your turn."

He leaned back in his chair and laced his fingers behind his head. "Both Phelps and Clarke have records."

Angie wasn't really surprised about Sonnie, but Montez seemed to have both feet firmly planted in his computer business. "What for?"

"Phelps for GTA. Clarke, for being in the company of a known felon."

"So, Sonnie got arrested for stealing a car, and Montez got tagged for being with him?"

"The two incidents weren't related."

"To each other or the murder?"

"Both."

"Do you think Sonnie and Nolan's deaths are related?"

"Let's just say there's more coincidence than I'm comfortable with. Another thing that makes me uncomfortable is your presence at both situations."

"Give me a break. You can't possibly think I'm involved in either thing."

"Someone near and dear to you might be."

"Val?"

Jarvis shook his head.

"I'm too tired to play games, detective." Then she knew. "Will? You're crazy if you think he's involved."

"He was out of town too. They went to Hudson."

They?

"Our officer lost them in Nashua for thirteen minutes. Just long enough for him to have stopped off to do a little murder."

"Why would he, for heaven sakes?" *And what the hell is in Hudson?*

"Your turn."

"Val and I went to Wolfeboro. Don't make that face, I know you think I'm obsessed with those bags, but listen." She told about seeing Sonnie put the bag in his trunk.

"Where did he go from there?"

"We um…left him lying on the—Um, Val clobbered him. He attacked me."

The word "shit"…whispered, but unmistakable in its intensity.

"Your turn, detective."

"Nothing much else. Forensic tests proved everyone on board

was somewhere around that cockpit, at some point during the day. Did you know people drop evidence everywhere they go? Turn around in the chair. I'd bet my next paycheck at least one of your hairs has stuck to the back of it."

Sure enough, two stray auburn strands were lodged in the crack where the wooden upright and crosspieces met. She jerked them loose and crumpled them in her palm. She began to shake her head, then realized where the conversation led: fingerprints.

"We have your palm print in the cockpit."

She opened her mouth. She'd put her hand on the doorframe to steady herself when the boat rocked.

"We also have your footprint."

Angie took a breath. She let it out. "In light of what you said a minute ago, about dropping evidence everywhere we go, I'd be surprised if you didn't find evidence like that. I told you I was in the cockpit. I checked Nolan's pulse." The last four words she emphasized, then leaned back in the chair. Recalling the trapped hairs, she moved forward, all the way to the edge. And ignored Jarvis' self-satisfied smirk.

"One more thing. When I was at Tyson's house." Jarvis rolled his eyes but made no comment. "I saw an interesting piece of paper. It looked like a spreadsheet. You know, something that lays out expenditures and income? A lot of people use them for—"

"I know what they are Ms. Deacon."

"Well, there was one tucked inside a script. A play in Manhattan."

The phone on the corner of the desk jangled, startling them both. Jarvis kept his eyes on her while he answered it. "Yeah?" He listened for a long time.

She grew bored watching him watching her. A photo perched on top of the file cabinets of a plain woman whose smile lit up her face, making her almost pretty. She had brilliant red hair that looked natural. Either that or she paid a fortune to a hairdresser. The photo's background was blue—like something a professional photographer would use. Angie wondered if it was Jarvis' girl-friend, or wife. The only personal item in the place, it brought to mind Sonnie's apartment and his lone photograph.

A pile of manila folders covered the left corner of the desk. Familiar names decorated their tabs. A folder, about a half-inch thick, lay open in front of him. His elbows anchored the corners of the pages inside. All but one. A triangular piece, obviously torn from something larger. And exactly the shape of the piece missing from the spreadsheet in Tyson's kitchen! Suddenly the folder slammed shut. Jarvis glared at her. When his vee-shaped brows flattened and then knit together in a single vee, she knew she was in trouble. What this time?

"All right, call me back." Jarvis set the phone in the cradle with barely a sound. He stood up and walked around the desk.

"Is that your girlfriend?" Angie asked, nodding toward the photo on the file cabinet, trying to lighten the moment. His gaze settled on the picture briefly, and returned to her. He gestured for her to rise, but she wasn't ready to leave yet. She had to get permission to visit Valerie.

"That torn paper." She pointed to the folder. "Where did you find it?"

He sighed and settled on the corner of the desk. "In a magazine in the boat's cockpit."

She felt elation light up her face. "That ties Tyson to the murder!"

He let out another breath of air, reached back and slid the phone toward him. It rang making him jump. He listened for four seconds, then put it down. He stood up. "Let's go."

"What's happening?"

"That diver down at the marina, he's been murdered."

"Oh my god, I was going to stop and see him on the way back to the motel." She took out her cell phone and let Jarvis listen to the message. "I returned the call but there was no answer."

"Why would he call you?"

Angie told him about she and Val trying to hire him to find

the bags. Jarvis took her elbow and turned her toward the door. His fingers dug hard into her flesh.

"One more thing," Angie said. "Would it be all right to visit Val? Night before last, one of your men re-arrested her."

"Re-arrest?" His forehead wrinkled into a trio of lines.

"I don't know cop terminology, but a policeman took her away in handcuffs."

The trio of lines turned into four, then five.

Angie didn't feel very well at all.

Twenty-Nine

Kidnapped! The word screamed through Angie's head like a train into a railway station. Someone took Val. Horror was quickly replaced with guilt. Why hadn't she asked the officer for identification? She'd stood there dumbstruck while he hauled her friend away. In broad daylight. In handcuffs. In an unmarked car.

Jarvis' voice broke through her recriminations. "Describe the kidnapper."

"Six feet, olive skin, dark hair and eyes. Hollow cheeks."

"I assume you've never seen him before."

Angie shook her head. "He flashed a badge."

"You read it?"

No. She hadn't even tried.

"If I get an artist up here, can you help with a drawing?"

"Sure."

He finished taking notes then led her out of the office. "Just so you know, we never send *one* officer to pick up a suspect. It's always at least two. What kind of vehicle was it?"

"Uh, plain, dark-brown. Like the kind you all drive."

"That's only on television. We drive police vehicles with distinct writing that even five-year-olds can read. Was there anything unusual about the car?"

Angie closed her eyes and visualized the vehicle. "No." They stopped at the dispatcher's station. "Put out an APB on Valerie Little."

Jarvis held the outer the door. "I can have that artist here in the morning, where can we find you?"

She told him and he hurried off toward the marina.

Why would someone kidnap Val? Because they thought she knew something? Or maybe to stop her investigating. Angie's guilt roiled in her gut. Why hadn't she and Val just left well enough alone? Their questions had probably gotten Val killed, just like her spending money had driven Will to Cassie.

Suddenly she needed to talk to him. To apologize. Now just after 5:30 p.m., Will should be at home. What if Cassie was there? Angie's fingers strangled the steering wheel. Cassie could just go to hell.

The driveway was empty, which didn't mean a lot since Will often put his car in the garage. So too did Wallace. He was really taking over. She'd put a stop to that too. With a resolve she hadn't felt since deciding to put her mother in therapy, Angie sped up the driveway.

The alarm not armed; someone must be home. She flung open the door prepared to see Cassie standing in the hallway wearing Angie's best negligee. The *Price is Right* blared from the living room. Just Cassie's speed, Angie thought, and headed for the noise. Wallace stretched out on the couch, newspapers and trash piled high around him, asleep. Her determination to oust Cassie out transferred easily to her brother-in-law, and she advanced on him, purse raised as a potential weapon.

Wallace awoke and leaped to his feet, eyes wide.

Anger welled up in her fists. "Get out of my house," she shouted over the TV.

"Shut the hell up. It's no wonder Will cheats on you. Always complaining."

"Me complaining? How many years have you been mooching off us and I never said a word?"

"You're fucking useless." He pointed a finger at her. "People like you, always treating others like shit."

She picked up a brass candlestick from the end table and pointed it like a dagger. "You're drunk. Go home and sleep it off."

Wallace took a step forward. "What're you gonna do?"

"If I can handle a mugger, I can surely take care of a useless son of a bitch like you. Now, get the hell out of my house."

He took another step.

She sounded as melodramatic as a soap opera but the words slipped out anyway, "Take one more step."

He did. She brought the candlestick down just above his left ear.

He staggered but didn't fall. He touched the wound that already seeped blood. He screamed, "You bitch!" and made two fists.

"Go ahead." She shook the candlestick. "I'm in the mood to hurt someone."

Wallace's inebriated brain absorbed her threat. He eyed the blood on his hand and raced for the bathroom, palm clamped to the side of his head. She kept the candleholder in case he returned. The parlor was in shambles just like the living room. Rubbish, dirt and newspapers lay everywhere. Dirty dishes and Styrofoam containers decorated the kitchen. Well, it wasn't her responsibility any more. Maybe once Will got home and they made up, they could clean up the place together. The thought calmed her and she took a breath.

Where was he anyway? Upstairs? Surely the yelling would have brought him running. A half-empty brandy glass rested on the table beside the green chair. Next to the glass lay a photo album, the one with the blue cover—their wedding pictures. She turned the pages, reliving the same things Will must have: the wedding, her mother getting drunk and asking her father to screw her on the dance floor, Wallace and Marty dancing.

On the cushion lay two other albums. The one with the green leather cover held photos from Will and Wallace's childhood. The pink album held her and Will's first year of marriage; that first year they'd carried the camera everywhere. Not a single thing they hadn't photographed, not a single thing.

The front door opened and footsteps sounded in the hall. In a second Will appeared carrying two brown paper bags. He spotted her and shoved the bags onto the counter, dislodging some trash that clattered to the floor. He ignored it and hurried to her. For a moment, she could tell he considered hugging her, then thought better of it and pushed the albums to one side so he could sit.

"Sorry about the mess. Where's Wallace? I'll get him to clean up."

"I've seen enough of him for today. I came to tell you, Val's missing."

"Do the police know?"

Angie nodded, suddenly so weary she could barely move, and told him the story.

"Who would do this?"

"Whoever killed Nolan, I guess. They must think she knows something, or they want her to stop investigating."

"Who? The black guys?"

"Can't be. Sonnie's dead. Shot in the head." *And Montez almost coerced me into bed.*

"Goddamn." He put his head down and raked his fingers through his hair.

"I guess I'd better tell you the rest." He looked up, then toward the living room where the television had just said, *And now, breaking news out of Quebec.* "Where's Wallace?"

"In the bathroom. I clobbered him." She gestured to the candlestick holder lying in her lap.

Will didn't ask why she'd hit him. "The police confiscated all our bank and phone records, and the computer," he said.

What next? How could their bank records be related to Nolan's murder?

Will's next words sent her mind into a renewed tailspin. "Wallace was arrested. He drained our accounts. They caught him on his way out of town."

Fury sizzled in her intestines. "Why isn't he in jail?"

"He posted bail. And before you get mad…madder, I didn't do it. I don't know who did. Maybe Marty came up with the money somehow."

"One question, why is the bastard here in our house?"

"Marty threw him out."

"That doesn't explain why he's here."

"He didn't have anywhere else to go. The cops were going to take him back to jail."

"It's where he belongs, Will!"

He nodded. "I know, but I couldn't do it to him. He's my brother. He's sick."

"He's not sick! He's a lazy piece of trash you insist on babying. If only you'd stop it and make him stand on his own two feet."

"You don't understand. Ange. Our whole lives, he was always in my shadow. I don't know how it happened. It just did." He went silent and for a minute started out the glass doors to the patio. "I never told you this." He sucked in a breath. "I'm not proud of what I did. You know how I was always an A student and Wallace barely pulled in D's. Well, we both applied to Dartmouth. Our father told Wallace not to bother, but he did anyway. None of us could believe when he was accepted and I wasn't."

"But you went to Dartmouth."

"Wallace went to Dartmouth. When he was accepted, I was green with envy and decided to take a year off. Anyway, he came home just before Christmas. He confided in me that he wanted to drop out and wanted my advice."

"Your father would've been livid."

"Exactly. So we devised a scheme where I'd go to school in his place."

"All the grades you made, you said were Wallace's."

Will nodded wearily. "It seemed like a good plan. I'd get the education I wanted and he'd save face with Dad. Anyway, in some ways it made the situation worse. It accentuated Wallace's feelings of inadequacy around me."

"You're not responsible for how he felt."

He said "He's my brother" as if it answered everything.

Angie got up; the candleholder thudded to the carpet. "This

isn't my problem any more." She started for the door.

"Ange, wait."

She turned, realizing she still clutched the photo album to her chest.

"Do you want to try and find Valerie?"

One thing she didn't want was to be around either of the Deacon men, but Valerie needed all the help she could get. She nodded. Two cars were in the yard, her Lexus and his Jeep. The Jeep's roof and doors had been removed. She rarely rode in it, hating the way the wind ruined her hair and makeup. Angie beelined for the Jeep and got in. Will didn't say anything, but she knew he noticed by the double-take he gave her car.

He climbed in and buckled his seatbelt. "Where should we start?"

"Why not try her house?"

Will drove down the steep grade of Bay Hill Road, turned left and left again onto Main Street. Moonlight illuminated the field by the river, lighting up the daisies and buttercups that waved in the evening breeze that rippled the blooms like tiny whitecaps.

"That detective said your DNA was found in the boat's cockpit," Angie said.

"What! How?" Will's hands tightened around the steering wheel. His loafer pressed on the accelerator and the Jeep lurched. He said something but the wind whisked away his words.

He pulled into Valerie's empty driveway. "Where's her car?"

"At my motel."

They went up the walk, past pink petunias, a little bedraggled in cool night air. A frantic barking began inside, very close to the door. "I forgot about the dog." Angie twisted the knob. Unlocked, so she pushed it open a couple of inches. She put her hand in the way to prevent Beeper from rushing out. Angie scooped him into her arms and went inside. The place looked as neat and clean as she remembered. A frying pan, plate, fork and glass soaked in the sink; otherwise nothing seemed out of place.

Will put a hand on her shoulder. "Don't worry, we'll find her. Come on."

Angie opened the back door and let Beeper out to do his business. The small yard, butted up to another home at the back. Where toys dotted the other yard, Val's was pristine and with a row of red and white snapdragons against the back fence.

Angie walked down the hallway off the living room, and opened the first door on the right. She had no idea what to look for. She just hoped, if she found a clue to who'd taken Val, she'd be astute enough to recognize it.

This must have been the boys' room at one time. Sports figures dotted the wallpaper, neutral tan carpet with two blue stains just inside the doorway. Trophies and memorabilia overloaded a wall shelf in the far corner. The only disparate thing in the room was the frilly white spread and blue and white throw pillows on one twin bed, telling her this must be where Val had been sleeping. If Will died, Angie didn't think she could face that big empty bed either. A stuffed beagle posed in front of the pillows, one black plastic eye missing. Angie picked him up. Beeper hopped on the bed and tried to take it away. She ruffled Beeper's ears, then hugged the stuffed dog to her chest, trying to absorb an aura, get a visceral idea of where Val might be. It smelled like Val's strawberry shampoo, but yielded no clue as to the whereabouts of its owner.

In the middle of a short table between the beds sat Val and Nolan's wedding picture. Actually a collage, more than a dozen pictures trimmed and fitted into a frame too big for the table. It must've hung somewhere else and Val had brought here for comfort. The centermost shot was the largest. Taken on the church steps, the couple had their arms around each other. Both wore broad grins. It was the first time she'd seen Nolan smile. It puckered his cheeks like a child. The wide but well-shaped nose and nice teeth complemented the face. For the first time, Angie understood Val's attraction to him. She turned away from the picture.

On the big dresser, she found a hairbrush and matching comb, a spray bottle of Jean Naté and a container of Peony Pink nail polish. No makeup or jewelry.

Angie went to the back door and called the dog who bounded inside. Will filled the water bowl. Beeper bounced behind them along the hallway, to the second door on the right, which opened to a green and white bathroom smelling like Pinesol. A green and white striped towel bunched on the rack near the tub. Angie took it down and deposited it in the hamper.

On the little shelf below the mirror, there stood a bottle of aspirin and one of those circular Pill dispensers. The last one taken had been Saturday, two days after Nolan's death. Angie found herself frowning over this, then shrugged. Taking the pill was a habit. The third day, Val probably realized she didn't need them any more.

Angie sucked in her breath before opening the door on the opposite side of the hallway, knowing it had to be the master bedroom. The door swung open on silent hinges. The aroma reminded her of her grandmother's nursing home room. Angie breathed through her mouth. The shades were down, casting the place in dark shadows. The dark wasn't a place she felt comfortable in right now and groped for the wall light switch. She flicked it, but nothing happened. She tried again, nothing.

Saying a little prayer that she didn't trip on the bouncy little dog, Angie took a step.

"What's taking you so long?"

Will's voice nearly made her jump out of her shoes. "God Will, don't sneak up on me like that."

"I didn't sneak, I walked in the back door and down the hall. What's the matter?"

"The light switch doesn't work."

"Then just open the curtains." He strode to the window. The vinyl shade flew up with a rattle as it wound round and round on the spindle. He opened a second, and third shade too. "There."

Like the rest of the house, the furniture here looked

inexpensive, but in good condition. Someone had sat on the bed and not straightened the spread, a book lay open on the night table. Nothing out of the ordinary.

"I just thought of something. The police confiscated Val's computer after Nolan died."

"They must have a hell of a collection by now," Will said, getting a grin from Angie.

"She has a laptop they didn't get." Angie went back into the room and put a finger to her chin, turning in a circle, trying to figure where Val might have put the narrow sliver of computer.

"There won't be anything on it to tell us where she is."

"No, but it might give us a clue to Nolan's murderer. You never know what's in someone's e-mail."

They searched the house again, this time opening drawers and poking into narrow places. She sent Will out to search the garage and miniscule shed in the back yard while she re-searched both bedrooms.

Will strolled into Val's bedroom, followed by the little dog. Angie sat on the bed, gazing about. "I see you didn't find anything."

She gave the room once last glance, then went out. Will held Beeper so Angie could step outdoors. The little dog barked for them to return. Angie gave a regretful look back but kept walking, telling herself one of the boys would be there soon to take care of him. It wasn't till halfway down the walk that Angie realized she still held the stuffed one-eyed beagle. She carried it to the Jeep and set it on the seat, on top of the green-covered photo album.

Will got in. "Where to now?"

"God, I don't know. What about the marina?"

The trip to the pier was done in silence. Will parked as close to the dock as he could.

They walked down the pier, side by side, arms touching with every other step. A deep-down part of Angie wished he'd reach out and take her hand, as he had that fateful day. How was she to know that trip would change both their lives forever?

"Remember how much my parents loved this place? We came here every summer. My dad loved the water so much we used to call him Jacques Cousteau. He's the reason we spent so much time on the water."

"I know you miss him."

"And I miss you." He reached for her hand. She didn't pull away.

"Part of me misses you too."

"And the other part wants to shoot me."

An understatement if she ever heard one. She heard her mouth saying, "Will, I'm going to file for divorce."

He dropped her hand and faced her, the dock rocked gently underneath them, like a giant porch swing.

"It's time I took care of myself for a while. I've never depended on me for anything."

"You could do that with me."

"I assumed you and your new family had pretty well mapped out the future."

Will's bewilderment was evident in the pursing of his lips. "What the hell are you talking about?"

"Don't play me for a fool. I saw you and Cassie right there on the street." Angie couldn't stop the tears. "And I know about your son."

Will grasped her upper arms and waited till she looked him in the eye. "I have no son. Cassie and I aren't seeing each other."

She clenched her fists at her sides, trying to stem the explosion that had been building for several days. Softly she said, "I'm not blind."

He let go of her. "Believe me. Please."

"Shit." Angie stepped away, rubbing her arms where his fingers had dug her flesh. Ten spots seared pain up her arms and into her heart. What a fool she'd been. She stepped away, but he grabbed her again and turned her around. Angie stood firm, her eyes glued to the front of his shirt.

"Look at me. I value our marriage so much. More than you can imagine. I admire your strength and conviction." He dropped his hands. "You don't know how much I wish I could be more like you. I think that's part of what drove me away, that feeling of inadequacy every time I looked at you."

"That's ridiculous."

"Maybe to you. This whole thing has become such a mess. I wish I could take so many things back."

"Me too."

"You have no idea."

She did though.

"Maybe that laptop is here," he said. "Let's check out the boat and then go home to talk this through."

Home. What home? Angie no longer had her precious home on the hill, nor did she have the camaraderie she'd once felt with Will. Standing there, with him holding her, she'd realized the sensation was gone. The one thing she'd valued over all their friends' relationships, she and Will had had friendship.

Things changed too fast for her to absorb. She wanted to go someplace and pull a blanket over her head. Maybe in winter when she exited the hibernation, all this would be over.

The small gate in the leased boat's railing was locked but Will climbed over and held out a hand for her. Suddenly she didn't want his touch. Didn't want to feel the softness of the hand that always made her feel so safe and protected. Didn't want to let go of the anger or pain right now. She just wanted to wallow in it. A strong drink would help.

Turn and leave now. Let him handle this alone. He was strong, stronger than he knew. This would prove it to him.

"I'll check up front," he said, "you look in the galley."

She didn't move. Couldn't.

How sad was that? Will was seriously mistaken thinking of her as the strong one. But Val was her friend. She owed it to Val to try and find her. She shuffled her feet from where they'd rooted to the fiberglass deck and headed obediently to the galley.

A spotless room, every utensil in the holder, every surface shining. Val would make an excellent caterer—if she were alive. Angie turned her mind from the sadness by picturing Val's bubbling enthusiasm over her new venture.

The bathroom door would only open a couple of inches. Angie peeked inside. A diffused light oozed through the opaque glass strips around the ceiling area and she could see clearly. Her frantic shout brought Will running.

Thirty

Like a bundle of laundry, Val lay crumpled in the small bathroom, not more than four feet square, with most of the space taken up by the toilet and sink. Angie recognized the denim jacket she'd been wearing when the fake officer carted her away.

"Val?" Angie called, bumping the door against Val's rear end. No response. Angie rattled the door again, trying to shake Val awake.

From behind, Will pushed up against Angie. "What is it?" He put his hands on her shoulders. She ducked out and let him take her place.

"Val? Val, honey, can you hear me?" He called louder, "Val?" Then he backed from the door. "Ange, come here. You're smaller than me, squeeze through there and move her away from the door so we can open it."

Angie knelt and stretched her arm around the door, trying to feel for Val's carotid artery. But she couldn't reach. "Call an ambulance."

While Will dialed his cell-phone, Angie took off her sweater and tossed it on the galley counter. She mashed her right side into the narrow opening Will created by pushing his foot against the door. She squeezed the leg through, knee first, wedging her shoe into the space between Val's calf and thigh, nice because it provided some leverage. Angie put pressure on the door with her hip. Then she inched her right breast through, wincing as her nipple flicked past the edge of the door.

Little by little Angie oozed herself into the room. To keep balance, she had to move her right foot from the little crevice at Val's leg to the narrow space between the toilet and wall. The left foot fit into the spot the right foot had just vacated.

Finally inside, leaning at an uncomfortable and precarious angle, Angie braced her hands on the wall and peered down at Val. She had probably been seated on the toilet when she lost consciousness. It looked like she'd slid to the floor, landing almost in the fetal position, but with her upper body wedged into the space on the farthest side of the toilet. The folds of her jacket hid her face.

While Angie slid herself into the room, Will called Val's name. So far there had been no sign of life.

Angie eyed Val's back, trying to discern the rise and fall of breathing. She bent, put a hand on Val's shoulder and nudged. "Val?" She put two fingers to Val's throat. That infinitesimal second between the touch and actual pulse seemed like eons. Angie heaved a sigh when she felt the gentle throb of blood pulsing through Val's carotid artery. "She's alive."

"Thank God. Get her up so I can fit in there."

"You're joking." The woman had to weigh 125 pounds. Angie couldn't possibly lift that much. In the hospital she always had help in these situations.

Angie found a foothold behind Val's back and grabbed fistfuls of the jacket. Bracing her rear end on the sink and tensing her knees, she wiggled Val into a sitting position. At least now she could see Val's face. Pale but pink, not blue or bloated. She put her cheek to Val's nose and mouth, and waited to feel the warmth of her breath. Yes, there it was, shallow but unmistakable.

Still not enough room to open the door. Somehow Angie had to get Val on her feet. She put her hands under Val's arms, braced her own feet against the wall and toilet and lifted the limp woman. An unfeminine grunt escaped Angie's lips and she almost laughed. But at least Val was up, leaning awkwardly against the wall, head sagged down on her chest, arms limp at her sides, but wonderfully, marvelously alive.

Will squeezed into the room that had been intended for one person instead of three, and held Val up so Angie could squash herself out. From the kitchen area, she watched their reflections in the tiny mirror. Will wrapped his arms around Val, drag/carried her out to the galley and laid her on the floor. Angie rolled up her sweater and put it under Val's head as sirens screamed into the parking lot.

"I'll go get them," Will said.

Angie did a cursory examination finding no obvious wounds, gunshots or otherwise. She lifted Val's left eyelid as the ambulance attendants burst inside.

"She's been drugged." Angie stepped aside, pulse pounding in her ears. The attendants measured Val's vital signs and attached an IV while asking questions. After Val had been loaded into the ambulance and sped off to the hospital, Angie asked Will, "What now?" The wind had picked up, rippling the lake's surface and banging the boats off the dock pilings. She put her sweater back on.

"I think we should go to the hospital. Val shouldn't wake up alone."

She and Will trudged to the Jeep and waited for traffic to get moving after gawkers stopped to watch the ambulance. Just as Will was about to turn onto Route 11, a smoky purple Jaguar sidled past, going the opposite direction.

"That's Tyson. Follow him, I want to see where he's going."

"What about Val?" Will asked, spinning the wheel right instead of left.

"They'll be working on her a while."

"Okay, but if Tyson heads out of town, we're turning back."

It wasn't hard to follow the Jag, it stood out like the proverbial sore thumb. The trick was to make sure Tyson didn't know he was being followed. Just near the Crab Shack, he slowed, then slipped the car between a Mustang and a rusty Cavalier with a yellow rubber raft bungeed to the roof. Will went slowly past.

Angie kept her face averted in case Tyson looked their way.

"Stop. Let me out," Angie said.

Will eased to a stop in the driving lane. "I'll find a place to park. Don't do anything stupid."

"Who me?" Angie hopped out and ducked behind a couple with cameras around their necks.

Tyson had crossed to one of the benches overlooking Alton Bay. There were several situated along the promenade, most shaded by towering maples and oaks. The one Tyson selected sat in the bright sunshine facing the bay. Boats sailed, motored and paddled past on the calm water.

He crossed his legs and made himself look like just another tourist, which, in reality he was. It wasn't long before a blonde woman stepped off the sidewalk onto the grass. She wore a striped mini-skirt and matching tank top, and carried a shiny red handbag. She put a hand to her forehead, shading the sun, peering around. Paula, the one Tyson professed to be avoiding at all costs.

She spotted him and went to sit beside him, close, like a lover. Tyson glanced around, nervous. Afraid Momma would see? Afraid of Paula's husband?

Angie stepped behind the enormous trunk of a maple. She gripped the rough bark and peeked around it as though playing hide and seek. Paula did the talking, as usual most of it with her hands. Once in a while Tyson nodded, or shook his head in response.

The conversation seemed to be going well enough. No further nervousness on his part. No peering around on hers. She had something to say and said it.

Where had Will gone? Maybe he'd had to drive all the way to Gunstock Mountain before finding a place to turn around or park. She peered through the colorful and energetic crowd, and when she looked back at the bench, it was empty.

Anxious, she stepped from her hiding place, and right into Tyson Goodwell. "Oomph," he said, then recognized Angie.

"Well, well, what a surprise."

Angie nodded, letting her glance slip past his shoulder. Where did Paula go? Wearing that striped outfit she stood out like an Art Deco sofa in a Colonial living room. She stopped at a compact car and looked back once before getting in.

"What are you doing down here? Slumming?"

"What makes you think I don't come here every day?" Angie asked as Paula made a u-turn in a narrow break in the traffic.

Tyson's blue eyes weren't watching Paula's retreat, they focused on her. And they weren't happy.

"I thought you broke up with her."

"She called and threatened me."

Angie grasped Tyson's sleeve and edged him off the sidewalk, out of the path of an oncoming skateboarder.

"What about?"

"What isn't she doing to me?"

"Tyson, I'm not stupid. Paula's body language didn't say, I'm angry and threatening you. It said, I'm your girlfriend and telling you about my day."

Tyson reacted with just a slight shrug of one shoulder. After a lull, during which they both watched tourists—Angie spotted Will lounging against a cement post.

Tyson said, "She told me you two met."

"Did she tell you what we talked about?"

"She said you wanted revenge because I'd cheated on you."

"I was—"

"You were checking to see if what I told you was true. What could my relationship with Paula have to do with Nolan?"

An elderly couple passed. The woman flashed a pitying smile at Angie. "It has nothing to do with me. And might have everything to do with him."

"You still think I'm involved in the murder?"

"Maybe three. Sonnie and that old diver are dead."

Tyson's legs seemed to give out. He leaned against the big rough tree.

"Where were you Saturday?"

Tyson frowned. "What?"

"Saturday night. Where were you?"

His eyes narrowed to tiny slits.

"Tyson, if you have nothing to hide, you won't mind answering."

He sighed. "What time?"

"From noontime on."

"Paula and I went for lunch at George's in Meredith. Then we walked along the waterfront for a while. We hit a few yard sales, then ate dinner at Abondante's."

"What time did you bring her home?"

There were several second's hesitation before he said, "I didn't."

Why wasn't she surprised? "Where did you stay?"

"HeavenScent. My parents were in the City, at the theater. Now tell me why you want to know all that."

"Because Valerie was kidnapped around lunchtime."

His immediate reaction—surprise. If he had anything to do with Val's disappearance, he hid it well.

"I didn't know Sonnie or Nolan or that diver."

"Don't get your Jockeys in a bunch, I'm just eliminating possibilities."

"Isn't it enough the cops are all over me?"

"Stop feeling sorry for yourself, the cops have been questioning everyone. They'll do it till they arrest someone."

"I don't like what you're implying."

"Well, Val didn't kidnap herself. Chances are good that the person who murdered Nolan tried to silence her, or at least stop her from investigating. Therefore, we can assume Valerie didn't kill her husband. Which leads to the next logical conclusion: someone else did. And that someone had to be on *Little One*. Who else was there? You, Montez, me and my husband. Use your head, who's left? And don't forget about that poor diver. Some-body must've thought he knew something."

Tyson spun on a shiny-clad heel and stalked to his car, not even noticing Will, who'd brought himself erect and started toward them. Tyson climbed into the Jaguar, squealed the tires and headed in the direction of HeavenScent.

"Come on," Angie said to Will, who also watched Tyson's ignominious departure. "Let's go."

On the way to the hospital, Angie related what had gone on with Tyson. In between sentences her mind raced with thoughts and contradictions about the whole episode. He and Paula. Not broken up as Tyson said. Not filing lawsuits. Not flaunting unproven pregnancies. Two people dating.

Had they really been together while Sonnie and Mr. Brinks were murdered? Angie could follow the chain of evidence, go to Meredith to see if he and Paula had left a mark anywhere there. She could spend a whole day on the road, chasing down this stuff, or she could talk to Paula again. The thought brought a smile and a renewed level of self-preservation because she just might need it on their next encounter.

Which brought another question. Paula supposedly considered Angie a rival. In the coffee shop, Paula had vowed to get rid of her. So, why had she run away when Angie appeared? If Angie had been with her man and the 'other woman' came along, she certainly wouldn't run away. She'd either confront the bitch or pound her into the ground.

Bah! said Angie's little voice. What did you do when you saw Will and Cassie? You turned your ass and ran.

That's different.

How? Just how was it different?

Thirty-One

At the hospital, Angie's supervisor rushed to her. "Whee girl, it's nice to see you. I've been wondering how things were going. I called your house yesterday but nobody answered."

Angie hugged Zoë. "It's nice to see you too, Zo. A friend was brought in about an hour ago. Valerie Little?" Zoë aimed a thumb over her shoulder. "She's in Two." Zoë lowered her voice. "She the one whose husband was murdered?"

"Yes." Angie stepped in the direction of Exam Room 2. "They find what drug it was yet?"

"Not yet. She's awake though. Maybe she can tell you."

"Thanks." Angie pulled the curtain aside and stepped into the cubicle. Val reclined on a gurney, a sheet spread width-wise leaving shoulders and feet bare. Her face still pale, yet a light in her eyes brightened when she saw Angie and Will.

"How are you?" she kissed Val's cheek, then lifted her wrist and took her pulse.

"Ange, leave the nursing to the staff," Will said. The look Angie threw made him snap his lips together. "Okay, sorry."

Angie pulled up one of Val's eyelids and looked at the pupil. "My head is throbbing like my brain's trying to get out." Val's voice sounded like that of someone with a huge hangover.

Angie let go of the eyelid and straightened up. "But you're alive."

"I'm alive."

"Where's Dale?" Angie asked.

"Talking to the doctor."

"Tell us what happened." Will spoke for the first time. "I don't mean to rush you but I have to meet someone in twenty minutes, and I don't want to leave without knowing."

"Detective Jarvis was already here." Val said the name as if she'd just swallowed a mouthful of chicken liver. "He made me describe the guy right down to the number of hairs in his monobrow: white, 5'9", a permanent scowl. Anyway, he shoved me in a car with the back seat door-handles off. We drove around in circles for a long time. He wouldn't speak or answer any of my questions. The first night he took me to some shack in the woods. He locked me in the bathroom. The next day, after it got dark we went to the boat." Val winced and rubbed her knuckles in her eyes.

Angie had never been drugged but knew that as the brain returns to normal function, the blood surges, creating the most terrible pressure. Val closed her eyes and put a finger to each temple, waiting for the worst of the pulsing to ease. "He put something over my mouth. The only time he spoke during the two days was when he warned us to stop looking for Nolan's murderer or next time I'd be dead." Even though Val didn't put any particular stress on the word, Angie didn't miss when she said us.

And neither did Will. "You'll both stop now, and let the police do their jobs, right?"

Angie nodded. Val made an OK sign with her thumb and forefinger.

Will kissed Angie on the temple. "I've got to go to that appointment. Behave both of you." He put a warm hand on Angie's shoulder. "I really want you to stop. Just go home and wait for me."

He pushed back the curtain and left. In a second they heard he and Dale talking. "How's Mom?"

"She'll be all right, I think. Angie's with her."

"Good, I'll leave them alone for now." He poked his head through the curtain. "I'll come back in a while."

"Okay," Val winced again.

Angie dragged a chair from the corner. "I'm glad you're all right."

"They told me you and Will found me. I don't know how to thank you." Val took Angie's hand. Warm and clammy grip, but as comforting as a mother's hug.

"You were so brave. I don't think I could've taken it."

"I wasn't brave. The whole time I pleaded for him to let me go. Begging him not to kill me."

Angie grinned. "I wouldn't have been even *that* composed. I'd never seen him before, had you?"

"No."

"Any idea who sent him?"

"No. How'd you know he wasn't a real cop?"

"I didn't. Not until I was in Jarvis' office this morning and asked to see you."

Val pulled the sheet up to her chin, exposing her legs all the way to the knee. Angie picked up the sheet and turned it the long way. "Whoever killed Nolan must have hired him to scare us off."

"I've decided I don't care who killed Nolan. I'm just going to learn to live with not knowing. They want to keep an eye on me overnight."

"Call me in the morning and I'll pick you up."

Val gave Angie's hand a squeeze. "I couldn't believe my eyes when you two came in together. Does this mean what I hope it means?"

"No. I went to the house to tell him the news about you and Sonnie. I thought he deserved to know."

"Something happened to Sonnie?"

Angie put a palm against her forehead. "Sorry, I forgot you didn't know." Feeling trepidation creep back into her, Angie told Val all that had transpired over the past thirty-six hours.

"Mister Brinks is dead too? Such a nice old man. I sometimes gave him leftovers from our trips. Do you think the same person killed all three?"

"Jarvis thinks Montez did it."

The sound of Montez's name brought a flush to her cheeks. Val saw the change and mistakenly assumed it was due to fear. "I can't believe it. I mean, I always thought there was something about him. Something scary, but…"

Definitely something fishy about Montez, but Angie felt it as more of a passion, a deep-down sexual compulsion he somehow kept under control.

"I'm sure Sonnie's murder had something to do with the duffel bag he never brought back from your boat. Maybe they killed him because it was valuable and he lost it."

Val put her hands to the sides of her head and gave a breathy moan. "So why didn't they kill Montez too?"

Angie stood up. "Maybe they can't find him."

"Or maybe he's the murderer."

She squeezed Val's arm. "I'll see you in the morning."

"Thanks for everything, Angie."

Northern New England weather was as changeable as a chameleon, scudding from the nip of April rain to the oppression of August summer heat and humidity, then just as quickly to the raw chill of the autumn wind off the lake.

"Everything all right?"

Angie turned to see Dale behind her. "Just thinking how nice it is to be alive."

"Mom's been realizing that too. I hope it makes you both think hard. Can I give you a ride home?"

Angie nodded. "I'd appreciate it."

Will's car sat in the driveway.

"Thanks for the ride."

Will must have been watching for her. He came out and stood on the front porch. Angie wiggled two fingers in the air. She pushed the button to release her car alarm and unlock the doors.

Will ran down the walk. "How's Valerie?"

"She'll be all right. They're keeping her overnight." Angie opened the door. "I'll see you. Thanks for helping find her."

"Wait." He went to his Jeep and returned with the photo album and Val's stuffed dog.

"Thanks." She got in the car and opened the window.

He opened his mouth, then shut it again. Then she did one of the hardest things she'd ever done—she drove away.

Back at the motel, Angie sat in the car a moment, gripping it with the fingers that had begun trembling when Will handed her the album. She laid her head on her hands and once again wept—for everything lost and everything yet to come.

Angie got out of the car. Things were becoming too complicated. She should just get back in and drive, till she became totally and completely lost. Till she knew no one , and had no place else to go. She bent back inside to retrieve her things.

"Your friend was warned, no more investigating!" growled a voice, as a blinding pain in the back of her neck dropped her to the pavement.

Angie came to, sitting in her front seat, feet on the ground, right arm through the steering wheel. A gray cloud obscured her vision. An ocean of pain shot through her head. She blinked several times and the cloud emoted into the concerned face of Detective Colby Jarvis. She blinked again. Still there. "Are you all right?"

Angie palpated the painful spot. Pain. No blood. "Yes. Did you catch him?"

She looked up, squinting at him kneeling beside her. The truth became clear. He hadn't chased after the guy. He'd stayed to make sure she was all right.

"Go. Don't let him get away." The exertion made her flinch.

"Sit quiet, an ambulance is on the way."

"No hospital."

"Yes hospital." He fingered the brim of his hat.

Haltingly and through clenched teeth, she repeated what she'd said that morning, "Aw shucks, I didn't know you cared."

"Well, I do. What happened?"

"I was getting my things from the car when a voice said to stop investigating. That's all. What were you doing here?"

"I came to see if you remembered anything else about Val's abductor, or his car."

"He's the same one who took Val."

"Did you recognize him?"

She tried to shake her head, but the pain played like a tom-tom. "No, I bent to get something from the backseat and was struck on the back of the head. He s-said he'd already warned my friend to stop investigating."

The sound of a powerful motor turned into the yard and roared toward them. The ambulance emitted a tiny squeal when it stopped beside her car. The same attendants who'd rescued Val helped Angie aboard. Jarvis climbed in also. While the EMTs performed an examination, he sat on the other gurney.

"What's on your mind?" she asked, seeing the deep vee between his eyes. When he didn't respond, she said, "Until a few minutes ago, I was convinced Montez was our man."

"Uh-uh."

What did that mean, that he'd thought so too? He understood English?

Finally he said, "We don't think Mr. Clarke had a strong enough motive to kill Nolan." Then he changed tacks. "Clarke tell you what he and Phelps were doing in town?"

"Montez told me his girlfriend goes to California a couple times a year to visit her parents. He takes that time to go fishing."

"He say what else they do while they're here?"

"No. You think they've got ties to Nolan other than fishing, don't you?" Angie's head jerked backward as the ambulance braked at the hospital. She flinched at the sudden rush of pain down her spine. He didn't reply.

At the same time they both said, "I'm not at liberty to say."

"Really, I don't need hospitalization. I'm fine. Aren't I?" she asked the attendant. A silent communication transpired between he and Jarvis before he said, "I think you should stay overnight for observation."

The staff gave Angie a bed beside Val. Jarvis posted a guard at the door. "No one gets in or out without authorization from me."

Angie sighed and said to Val, "I guess I won't be picking you up in the morning."

Thirty-Two

"Jarvis can't keep us prisoner here," Angie said, pacing the room. The introduction of Motrin 800 an hour before, muted the pain in her head. Morning had entered the hospital. The sounds of hospital staff distributing breakfast trays squeezed through the walls.

"I think he can do anything he wants," Val replied. She stood beside the locker-sized closet in the corner. "I think that detective likes you." She returned to her bed, smiling. "Really, I bet he asks you out."

Angie stopped pacing and rolled her eyes. "I have enough problems right now." She spotted the small rectangular object clutched in Val's left hand.

"Will you sit a minute?" Val said. "There's something I have to show you."

Angie obeyed, alighting beside her. Val handed her a cell phone. Small, gray, unremarkable. She reached over Angie's arm, punched a couple of buttons and the voice mail played. The first two messages were from people wanting to arrange a tour. As the time stamp played for the third call—July 13, 10:07 pm—Val said, "Tell me whose voice this is."

A male voice, soft-spoken and yet self-assured. She'd talked with its owner just yesterday.

"You missed our appointment. I promise you, my suggestions to improve the business' financial outlook are significant.

Call me on my cell in the morning, 555-9474, so we can set up a meeting."

"Where did you find this?"

"Nolan kept it on the boat—for emergencies."

That explained why the call had come in at 10 p.m. and Val hadn't known about it.

A knock sounded on the room's door. Angie and Val jerked their heads around to see the door open a crack. "You ladies decent?" called Detective Jarvis.

In unison they shouted, "No!"

Angie stood up, pushing the phone into the folds of her hospital gown. She spun around and sat on her own bed as he stepped inside, waving an arm at a pair of wheelchairs in the hall. "Ladies, your chariots await."

"In case you haven't noticed, we aren't dressed," Angie told him.

A half-hour later the women settled in the wheelchairs; Val's pushed by Jarvis, Angie's by a chubby round-faced nurse. Jarvis flung open the cruiser doors and the women climbed in the back seat. It was Angie's first time in a cruiser. It smelled like popcorn. She made a face at Val, who grinned. Angie leaned her head against the window and watched the scenery fly past. She realized they were in town when Jarvis slammed on the brakes and she pitched forward against the seatbelt.

"Where did you get your license?"

"Sorry, there's an idiot tourist in front of me. Jarvis turned in Val's driveway and stopped. "You're both under protective custody."

Val's fingers tightened around the seatbelt strap. Angie started to complain. Jarvis stopped her with a hand in the air.

"The guy only tried to warn us. He won't bother us again as long as we behave."

"You watch too much television."

"I don't watch any television."

Val laughed. "Cut it out you two, you sound like my boys."

Jarvis turned on the seat. "You were mugged, both here and in Nashua. Alton Bay's last mugging happened in 1987 and—" The rest of the sentence trailed off as he raced around the car opening doors.

Angie followed Jarvis and Val into the house. They stood in the living room while he checked the place for intruders. Beeper pranced along on his heels. Jarvis returned and pointed a long finger at Val. "You will stay home. Indoors. Don't even go outside to pick posies."

"Posies?" Both women laughed.

"I have a business to run," Val said.

"Cancel the trips. Or let your sons do 'em till we get this cleared up."

"That could take weeks. Months."

He laid a palm on Val's shoulder. "We're closing in on him. Trust me."

"You're looking for Montez, aren't you?" Angie asked. When he didn't reply, she added, "He's not the one who mugged me in Nashua."

"You were mugged?"

"Tell you later."

"Why would he mug me and then pretend to save me?"

"To gain your trust. So you'd tell what you knew about the murder."

"Or," Val interrupted, saying "about the bags," looking proud that she'd gotten the gist of the conversation.

Angie pursed her lips. "I don't know anything about the bags."

"They don't know that," Val said.

A cruiser slid up behind Jarvis' car and Sergeant Wilson climbed out. "He'll stay here with you." His words left no room for protest. He turned to Angie. "Are you staying here or going home?"

She didn't want to do either thing. She wanted to talk to the voice from Val's cell phone.

"What'll it be?" Jarvis asked. "You staying or not?"

"I have things to do."

"Oh no. You're under guard too." He flung open the front passenger door and waved her back inside. "Don't make me have to lock you up."

"Talk to you later," she told Val and climbed in the front seat. The way Jarvis looked at her as he slid behind the wheel made her cringe and nearly jump over the seat and into the back.

"Will you take me to my house? I need to get my car."

"You aren't going to need your car for anything for a while."

"I'm not leaving it where my useless brother-in-law can get his hands on it. He knows where the spare key is."

He gunned the car up the road and into her driveway. Surprisingly the Lexus sat where she'd left it. Neither of the brothers' cars were in sight. Jarvis waited while she got into her car, then gestured for her to lead the way to the motel where she was staying. There, he went inside and made the same check he made on Val's house, but on a smaller scale.

Just then his radio crackled. "We got a 10-27, fender bender on 28 near McDonalds."

"Damn," he said before pressing the button on the microphone attached to his collar. "10-4."

"First responder says it looks bad," the radio replied.

"I'll be back," he said to Angie. "Stay put. I'll bring food." And he left.

She watched his car pull onto the highway and then went inside and threw all her things into suitcases. She had the room vacated inside three minutes. Adrenaline pushed into her limbs making them tingle in anticipation, yet she somehow contained the urge to speed out of the parking lot.

Angie drove to a motel and registered under the name of Brenda Starr. She dropped everything on the bed, including the photo album and the beagle, drove to the nearest car rental, left her precious Lexus in the back lot, and left driving a white Ford Escort. Ignoring the cramped feeling of the unfamiliar vehicle, and keeping an eye out for the detective and his cronies, she stopped at the first hairdresser. An hour and a half later, sporting a new cut and color, mended fingernails, and a large pepperoni pizza, Brenda Starr stepped inside her motel room.

Angie unpacked. Breathe. Relax, she told herself and sat at the small two-seater table to eat. The new room was dark with the drapes drawn across the picture window. The place smelled like antiseptic and carpet shampoo.

Cuddling Val's stuffed beagle, she picked up the photo album and thumbed through Will and Wallace's childhood photos. Whoever took the snapshots hadn't known a thing about photography, most were off-center and many were blurry. For someone who knew them, the twins were easy to tell apart. She smiled at a shot of the boys in their side-by-side bassinets— Wallace the scowling one, Will sleeping. Another picture, taken during toilet training. Once again, there was Wallace racing butt naked away from the bathroom, while Will sat sedately on the tiny potty chair. Their first day of school, dressed alike: Will crying, Wallace being held back from rushing headlong for the bus. The boys in their Cub Scout uniforms. In swimsuits and snorkels on the boat with Dad. On the baseball team. At the piano. Always, Will serious and Wallace either fooling around or acting rebellious.

Talk about rebellion. What alien had taken possession of her body in the past few hours? Angie's head ached. She squeezed her eyes shut and rubbed her knuckles in them. Jarvis would be furious. And worried. Those thoughts didn't make her happy but she couldn't be penned up, not now when things were coming to a head.

Thirty-Three

"Angie, are you nuts?" Val hissed when Angie told her what she'd done.

"You won't even recognize me. Any chance you can sneak away, too?"

Val gave a nervous, though whispered, laugh. "That sergeant is watching me like…like he thinks I'm guilty."

"Come on, you can do it. You're a renegade now—heavy metal music and all that."

"Changing clothes and music is one thing. Changing your identity and hiding from the cops is something else."

"Don't you want to find Nolan's killer?"

"You're forgetting, *he* found us!"

"That means we're getting close."

"Close to getting killed." After a second's hesitation, Val said, "Count me in. That bastard's not getting away with what he did to us. Or Nolan."

"What's the cop doing?"

Val giggled. "Watching *Cops*. Okay, meet me on the dock at nine o'clock. Two can play the 'change your identity' game."

Angie ate another slice of pizza and gazed at herself in the mirror. The woman who looked back had dark auburn hair cut in a just-below-the-ears bob. She now had bangs that met newly plucked brows, in a shape that made it look like she was always wondering about something. Kind of like Detective Jarvis. This made her laugh out loud.

Angie applied makeup to her cheeks, making them appear higher and fuller. She dabbed blue eye shadow at the inner corners of her lids to accent the what's up expression. It had been several days since she'd been to the gym. Several days of eating junk food and sleeping erratic hours. She'd have a lot of making up to do when this ended. If it ever ended. Angie dressed in clothes as nondescript as her car, and drove downtown. Angie hit the grocery store; a few fruits and vegetables, juice, and some trail mix.

Her head ached; the Motrin was wearing off. She closed her eyes. That's when she felt someone watching. Keeping her face averted and certain she looked every bit the criminal, she hurriedly paid for and carried her things outside.

"Wait up," came a familiar voice saying a familiar nickname. "Ange, stop."

Run, her little voice ordered. He's seen you, her logical side said.

Run anyway!

On the narrow walk in front of the store, she stopped and put down her bags. Will approached, and set his purchases beside hers. "What the hell happened to you? Jarvis has been all over me to find you."

"He put me under protective custody."

"Then what the hell are you doing here?"

"I was hungry."

"You need to go back and let them do their job."

She shook her head, the short hairdo feeling odd and lightweight. "No. I have to find out who's been terrorizing me and Val."

"You brought it on yourselves. Look, if you don't want Jarvis watching you, come home with me. Let me protect you, Jarvis won't care either way."

"Like you protected me from Nolan's murderer?" What had she just said? "I'm sorry, that was uncalled for."

Will frowned. "What happened to your neck?"

"What do you mean?"

He touched the nape of her neck, making her wince. "Ange, what happened?"

"I bumped into something. It's nothing."

He slapped a palm to the side of his head. "Jeez, what am I going to do with you?" He took hold of her arm.

"I said I'm all right." She pulled her sleeve from his grasp.

"Look. I did something really asinine. It doesn't mean I've stopped loving you. If anything, it's made me realize how special you are. How much I want you in my life."

The little voice in the back of her head started again: see, told you, he's a good guy. Even good guys screw up sometimes. Go with him. Just go.

"Shut up!" Angie hollered, putting her hands to her ears.

"All right. All right, but I'm not letting this drop. You and I will have things out. Soon." Will grabbed her hand. "Come on, I'm taking you back to Jarvis."

Angie gave an exaggerated sigh. "All right. Wait a second." Angie bent and twined her fingers through the plastic handles of her bags.

Will picked up his bags. "By the way, love your new look."

She straightened up, hefting the bags to better balance the contents, and took off. She ran along the sidewalk that fronted the market, peering wildly for her car. What did the darned thing look like? As she crouched between a pair of compact cars that provided nowhere to hide at all, Angie realized that even if she found hers, she couldn't let Will see it. Bad enough he'd so easily seen through her disguise. Why the hell wouldn't he after so many years?

What was she doing? Running from him was stupid.

Call to him. Let him take care of you.

She raced across the parking lot, the hard hot pavement slapping under her thin-soled shoes. Angie ducked behind a mini-van, a pickup reeking of manure, then one of those new cars that look like it should belong to a gangster. Find people. Go back into the supermarket.

Too late for that. She was already half-way down the parking lot. Half-way to the street.

Will was thirty or so feet behind, and closing fast. "Angie, come on, I'm sorry."

On the street, a bus moved along, stopping and starting in the light traffic. She ran toward it, the plastic bags bumping and twisting against her thighs. She should drop them, to gain that small amount of freedom. But she didn't. The sign over the bus windshield said Boston. That meant it was full of tourists with an agenda. Roll had been taken, Angie wouldn't be allowed on. As it roared past, accelerating, she raced off the sidewalk, right into its path.

"Angie!" Will screamed.

The driver slammed on his brakes. But she made it past, the front bumper grazing her sleeve. The driver shook his fist and cursed out the side window. She remained on the double white line, tucked against the big vehicle, the knuckles of her left hand brushing against the gritty bus wall as it moved. There was a traffic light up ahead, Angie prayed it would be red.

But it was green. Inside the bus, the gears shifted and it accelerated, throwing up clouds of black, smelly smoke. Soon it would be gone, leaving her standing in the middle of the road, like the proverbial sitting duck. Angie's eyes darted one way and then another. As the bus passed, she dove in front of a big black car whose driver hollered, "Get out of the road you drunken idiot!"

Angie's feet suddenly had wings. She pushed across, aiming for the Secondhand Shop, the nearest thing with people and, just possibly, a place to hide. Twenty-five feet away—it seemed like a mile.

Where was Will? He'd stopped calling. Had he given up? More likely, he was trying to sneak up on her. She gave a wild-eyed look around, but saw no one. At least no one who seemed to be chasing the crazy woman carrying handfuls of shopping bags. A woman and small boy blocked the sidewalk. Angie sidestepped them the same time the toddler fell down. Angie tripped over him, staggering several steps before regaining her balance and forging on. The child's mother hollered obscenities. Angie wanted to call back that it wasn't her fault the child fell, but she felt Will closing.

She spotted him darting back and forth on the sidewalk, ducking and weaving like a linebacker. She raced behind the shop, then around the furthest corner where there was a pair of cedar trees, relics of some long-ago landscaping. Angie tucked herself between the trees and the vinyl-clad wall. Her breath coming in gasps, the result of adrenaline and anxiety, had to be brought under control. Angie clenched her jaw and sucked in her gut, trying to still her racing heart and heaving lungs.

Where was Will? She peered between the branches, wanting to lean against the wall, but needing to be upright and ready to take flight again. Cars whizzed by on the small side street, the drivers oblivious to the angst in the bushes just feet away. Angie stopped breathing as Will's head appeared atop a bush at the other corner of the shop. She moved further under cover of the wispy branches as he looked one way and the other. How he missed her, she didn't know, he passed so close she could hear the hitch in his breath and the soft curse when he couldn't locate her. He stopped near the corner and dug his cell-phone from his pocket. He punched in some numbers and waited, holding an index finger in the other ear.

Angie became aware of the bags dangling at her sides. The handles, stretched tight, cut into her joints. Her fingers were numb. Throbbing, palpitating blood pounded up her arms and into her head, overshadowing all other senses, almost erasing Will's words. "Can I speak to Detective Jarvis?"

The bags became an obsession, even more than the need to avoid Will or hear what he said to Jarvis. Like the time as a child— at prim and proper Auntie Joan's needing to go to the bathroom, too shy to ask where it was, that one urge had consumed her every thought. Just like that, more than anything, Angie needed to put down those bags, flex her fingers, get the blood flowing again.

"Could you ask him to call Will Deacon? It's an emergency." He left his cell number. The phone clicked shut and disappeared into the pocket.

Angie opened, then closed the fingers of each hand, praying the plastic wouldn't rustle.

She let out the breath she'd been holding, saying a quick prayer he couldn't hear the gentle hiss of air over the sound of the traffic. He moved away, scanning the supermarket parking lot for her Lexus. She'd originally bought the car because it stood out in a crowd. Thank goodness for that rental.

A car passed, screening Will for a moment. Ever so slowly, Angie slid down the wall until she was on her haunches. She released the bags to the ground, the handles were ready to snap. She rubbed her hands together, wringing and massaging, urging the feeling to return.

The car moved into traffic and Will came into sight again. He slapped a palm against his thigh, a gesture that meant he was frustrated. He often did that when dealing with his brother. What would become of Wallace? Would he receive a jail term or would Will find a way to get him out of that too? Hopefully, cashing checks from someone else's account was a federal crime for which Will's influence would be useless.

Angie had no idea what compelled Will's responsibility toward Wallace. But it might just be exorcised if his brother went to prison. Then again, losing Wallace might be Will's downfall. Without his brother or wife to protect, what would happen to him? She suddenly felt sorry for him, and very concerned.

Will walked up and down the rows of cars in the lot, looking into each one, perhaps somehow knowing she had a different vehicle.

There it was! The little, white Ford. Will peeked into the front seat. Had she left anything incriminating there? The stuffed dog? The album? Angie's brain scrambled, searching for the image that would tell her where she'd left them. Will backed away, still looking at the car. Did something about it scream rental? Probably. She had no experience with these things. Probably, had a sticker somewhere on it: Rented to Angelina Deacon in place of her expensive Lexus.

Angie took a breath, the first one in quite some time, when Will moved to the next car. He leaped away when a dog lunged at the window, yipping. Finally he went to his Jeep and climbed in. Still, he didn't drive away. He cruised up and down the rows, looking in all directions.

Twenty minutes later, after going round the lot four more times, he pulled onto the side street and disappeared. Angie waited, counted three minutes on her watch, then picked up the bags and her purse, and ducked out of her green haven. She climbed into the Ford and drove out the back of the lot, one street over from the one Will had used.

She circumvented all the main streets, knowing that even though it would be easier to hide in traffic, she couldn't escape should he spot her. And as soon as he got hold of Jarvis, he'd give a complete description of her new look.

Thirty-Four

Since it was early in the week, the town was nearly deserted; just a few teens skateboarding or walking in pairs along the promenade. A woman with short blonde hair and a baggy sweatshirt sat alone at the end of the Downings Landing dock, with her feet dangling over the edge. Had to be Val. She didn't turn around, but Angie could tell she knew someone approached because her legs stopped swinging.

Angie sat beside her. "Blonde looks good on you. How'd you get out of the house?"

"Told the officer I was taking a shower."

"You climbed out the bathroom window?"

"No, I figured that's what he'd expect. I hid in the cellar till he went looking for me."

"Smart girl. I have to change my hair again tonight. I went to the grocery store and guess who I bumped into?"

"Not Jarvis."

"No, he would have cuffed me to the car. I met Will. I almost got run over in traffic trying to dodge him. I ducked into some bushes and waited till he left."

Val giggled. "Sorry, I just can't picture you diving into bushes."

"I can't believe I ran away like that. Running isn't like me at all." She gave a nervous laugh. "Then again, maybe it is. I'm not sure what the real me is any more. Come on, let's walk."

They moved up the parking lot and along the promenade

overlooking the bay, dark and peaceful now. Trees overhung the area, shielding it from passing vehicles.

"So, I take it you and Will didn't kiss and make up?"

"One minute I'm sure leaving him is the right thing to do, the next minute I want to rush back home."

"Would it be so bad to go back?"

"Once all this is cleared up, I'll take a few days to go away. To think."

"What's to think about? Don't you think he's still seeing her?"

"No. There's more going on than you know."

"For what it's worth, I think Will's a nice guy who really loves you, and you should run back as fast as you can. Losing Nolan made me realize some things about life and love. What we had was crap, pure and simple. But you and Will, you're soul mates. It's not often in life people find theirs. You should do whatever you can to keep it."

"Thanks." Angie pulled Val into a quick hug. They walked along the narrow paved promenade strip, back toward the cars.

Angie unlocked the passenger door. Val ducked inside. "Nice car. So, what do we do next?"

"We find Tyson. He's got some explaining to do."

"About what?" Val asked.

"It was his voice on your cell phone."

"I thought I recognized it." She pulled out the phone and played the message. "What do you think it means?"

Angie told Val about the torn spreadsheet. Val's nose wrinkled. "I didn't know we were in financial trouble."

"The message doesn't say you are, it just says he can improve things."

"I guess. Where do we find Tyson?"

"Let's try HeavenScent first."

They headed north on Route 28A, soft drinks from McDonalds in the holder between them.

"I got online this afternoon and found some restaurant

equipment," Val said. "I explained the situation to the guy and he's agreed to hold the stuff for a couple of weeks without a deposit. Oh Angie, I'm so excited about this. I've never in my life done anything on my own. Oh, I forgot to tell you, I have a client already. I was at the gas station this afternoon and met up with Carl Rosenstein—do you know him?"

"Isn't he head of the planning board? How did he act? Did he mention Nolan?"

"Yeah. He said he was sorry for my loss and hoped they found the killer soon."

"I was wondering if people would automatically blame you."

"Probably they will. He's the first I've met up with since Nolan died. Except old man Smith next door. He went inside without saying good morning." She shrugged. "He'll find out the truth sooner or later."

"What did Rosenstein say?"

"I mentioned I was thinking about starting a catering business. I said I couldn't bear running the tour without Nolan. He got all excited saying the board had been looking all over for someone to cater their meetings. It's a small job compared to things like weddings, but it's a start. How long do you think I need to wait before really going for this?"

"People have short memories but I don't think you should do anything before Nolan's murderer has been found and this whole thing's calmed down. What you can do is, as soon as the boat's out of impound, put the business up for sale. Keep running it, of course. No one will be suspicious of you selling out; you're grieving, can't stand the sight of the boat, etc."

"Where do I advertise something like a tour business?"

"Why not call Will and ask him? He knows things like that."

There was another length of silence during which Angie lost herself in reminiscences of her marriage: their first vacation abroad in Italy, where it rained every day; the day Will slipped on their icy walk and broke his arm, what a baby he'd been; the first time they'd made love, on the banks of the Ammonoosuc, with cars whizzing past on Route 3 just yards away. Angie wiped away a tear and wondered what he was doing right now. Almost ten p.m. Most nights he'd have been asleep for an hour already. Did he have trouble sleeping these days, too? Did he lie awake remembering, loving, regretting?

"There is some news on the home front." Val roused herself from whatever thoughts she'd been having and slid her left knee on the seat, to half-turn toward Angie. "It's part of the reason I don't feel comfortable going back to Will," Angie explained. "His brother Wallace was arrested the other day—for passing bad checks. Trouble is, the checks he wrote came from our bank accounts. He drained every penny. I don't know if they'll be able to get the money back."

"Oh my God, Angie. I can't believe you've been going through all this and all I've done is whine about my own troubles."

"You had no way of knowing."

"What's that got to do with going back to Will?"

"Because after Wallace got bailed out of jail—"

"Will didn't bail him out, did he?"

"He swears he didn't. But he *did* let the thieving slime move into our house." Angie heaved out a breath. "He told me this sob story about how Wallace is his brother and he owes him for some crap he did to him years ago."

"Will did something to Wallace? Seems like it would be the other way around."

Angie slowed for the turn into the HeavenScent driveway. Not a car in sight. Most likely Tyson wasn't here. Angie got out and went to the door, hoping to avoid Tyson's mother. A strange woman pulled open the door and after a minute admitted Tyson wasn't home, and that she had no idea where he was.

"Now what Ms. Sherlock?" Val asked, when Angie got back in the car.

"Dinner. I'm starving and don't dare be seen in Alton."

The headlights illuminated the sign *Entering Meredith*. "We're going to WG's aren't we?" Val asked.

"Yup."

"Woo wee, you are brave, girl! They must be busy, the parking lot's jammed."

Angie found a spot just a few feet from where Sonnie parked a few nights previous. They got out, locking the doors. They'd gone four steps from the car when Angie spun around and went back to unlock them.

"What's the matter?"

"We might have to make a quick getaway."

Val groaned and slung her purse over her shoulder.

"Recognize any cars?"

"No."

The place was dimly lit, conducive to romance, bad for seeking out unsavory Duffel Bag Gang members.

The place wasn't too full; a few tables had parties of two or four. Two men sat mid-way along the bar, one stool separating them. Both had half-drunk beers before them.

Angie and Val slipped onto stools at the far end of the bar, a perfect place from which to watch the goings-on. Soft music played in the background, definitely a place for a romantic rendezvous.

A female bartender, who looked more like a bouncer, approached. "What'll you have, ladies?"

"White wine," Angie said.

"A Scarlett O'Hara."

Val's request put a grin on the bartender's lips. The expression gave her a little more feminine look. "Coming right up."

"How much you want to bet she's got to look up what goes in a Scarlett O'Hara?" Val said.

Angie laughed and watched, but the woman didn't pull a book from a secret place under the counter. Neither did she begin making Val's drink. She did disappear down a hallway as the other end of the bar and, upon returning, set right to work on the drink.

"You win," Angie said.

Val giggled.

"Do you notice anything unusual in here?"

"Beside the fact that I'm at a bar with another woman, waiting for God knows who to come out and kill us?"

"I mean…" Angie said, "that the parking lot is full of cars and there's hardly anyone in the place."

"There are plenty of people in here."

"But think how many cars are out there."

"Well, maybe they have one of those sports rooms. You know, where guys go to watch football games."

"I'm thinking something like that. But I don't think their room is the kind of place you can talk about in public."

Val groaned.

"Try and look like you're on the make."

Val groaned again.

"Look friendly but unapproachable."

"How the heck do I do that? Oh, never mind."

The bartender slapped a pair of Budweiser coasters on the counter, then topped them with the drinks. "Out for a night away from the hubbies?"

"Something like that," Angie replied. "Anything going on around here?"

"Nah. It's Tuesday and it's Wolfeboro," she said as though that explained everything.

Val thanked her, removed the wedge of lime from the rim and took a long swig. She set the glass down and put the lime in her mouth. For a moment she had a wide green smile as she sucked out the juice. They sipped in comfortable camaraderie. Trying to remain anonymous, they peered into the mirrored wall behind the bar looking for anyone they might know.

"You getting a table or want to eat here?" the bartender asked.

Just then a pudgy balding man strode from the same hallway

the bartender had used. He wore a white dress shirt, open at the neck, charcoal gray dress slacks, cordovan loafers, and an expression of utter disbelief, as though he'd found the men's room full of naked women. He went straight to the exit.

Angie pretended not to notice the man, and said to Val, "Why don't we get a couple of appetizers for now." They ordered stuffed mushrooms.

Four minutes later, another man made the same journey as the first. This one wasn't dressed for business; he wore blue jeans with a sharp crease pressed into the legs, and a short-sleeved pullover. Angie couldn't see his face.

She slid off the stool. "Keep an eye on things. I'm going to the ladies."

"Be careful," Val whispered.

Angie headed down for the hallway. Dark, except for the light coming from a low-watt bulb in a wall sconce at the other end—yet there was enough light for her to know the restrooms weren't here. A single door at the back was the only opening in the fifteen-foot corridor. As Angie got about halfway, strong fingers clamped on her shoulder.

"The ladies room isn't down here."

Angie gawked into the sulking eyes of the bartender.

Just then, the door opened. Light flooded the hall making Angie blink. Two men came out. Both tall: one bearded, one pony-tailed.

The bartender spun Angie around and gave her a nudge back the way she'd come. "The restrooms are that way."

The men walked quickly, separating to pass the women. The one with the ponytail looked Angie up and down. She smiled even though the fingers squeezed tighter into her shoulder. Neither of the men acknowledged the bartender. Angie hurried to her stool, keeping an eye on the men—but pretending she wasn't—in the long mirror behind the bar. They dressed alike in jeans and white t-shirts, but the two were as different as green and red. The pony-tailed one had a decided limp while the bearded one walked hunched over, as if he had a bad back. As the double doors shut behind them, Angie almost fell off her stool. How had she missed it? There was one other strikingly similar thing about them: they both carried duffel bags.

She pulled a few bills from her purse and threw them on the bar.

"I thought you had to go to the bathroom," the bartender called.

"It's dirty, I'll go at home. Come on, Val."

Val gave the bartender a one-shoulder shrug and followed Angie. Once the doors shut, she poked Angie in the back. "What's going on?"

"Where are those two men who came out?"

"There!" Val pointed to the other side of the parking lot.

The bearded guy had gotten into a red pickup; the engine running. The pony-tailed man jammed his bag onto the passenger side floor and squeezed himself in. The headlights came on.

"Let's follow them," Angie said, blinking against the glare.

"I don't think so," came a voice from behind. Fingers closed around Angie's wrist. "Back inside."

"Run!" Angie screamed.

Val, who'd stopped at the sound of the bartender's voice, sprinted toward the car.

"Get back here or your friend dies!"

"Go, Val!"

Val ran. This confused the bartender, who obviously wasn't used to being ignored. Maybe she wasn't used to being punched either. Angie drove her fist into the woman's nose. The woman howled and dropped to her knees. Angie hit her again in the right ear.

The pickup's headlights shone on them as it began to pull away. A male shouted, "Cat fight! Go girl!"

Angie did. She rammed her knuckles into the bartender's nose again and dashed for the car, hearing more cheers from the men. Val sat in the passenger seat, and left the drivers' side door open. Angie slid inside and popped the key in the ignition. The little engine started and it surprised Angie when the tires actually squealed on the pavement.

They traveled a mile out of town when Val said, "I think we're being followed."

Angie peeked in the rear view mirror. A vehicle definitely closed on them. She jabbed her foot on the accelerator and the little car crept to 60 mph. She edged the vehicle around a sharp corner.

Val groped for the door handle. Angie wrapped sweaty hands around the steering wheel and leaned forward, heartbeat pounding in her ears. She squinted at the unlit road, trying to recall the twists and turns—and turnoffs. It rapidly became clear that, in lieu of speed, she'd need some fancy driving. Where was Jeff Gordon when you needed him?

"How far back are they?"

Val knelt half-turned to see both forward and back. "About two hundred feet."

Angie maneuvered around the next bend, the compact car seeming to take it on two wheels. Suddenly the radio blared over the throbbing of her heart. The Beach Boys' *Little GTO*.

"They're gaining on us. There're two people inside."

"No way we can outrun them in this car. We're going to have to outmaneuver them. I think there's a long straightaway up ahead. They'll gain a lot on us then. Just after that, there's a sharp right-hand bend, and then an intersection. The obvious thing would be to take a right—"

"Let me guess, we're going left?"

The road straightened out, the long stretch loomed, Angie pushed the car to 65. "Right. I mean left. I'll shut off the headlights and try to make the turn. Be ready."

"They're about a hundred fifty feet back now."

"We should be out of their sight for a fraction of a second after rounding that corner."

"I sure hope you know what you're doing," Val said, not for the first time.

So did she. "Okay, get ready." Angie let off the gas, the car slowed. She slammed on the brakes. Their speed plummeted to 30. She let off the brakes, flipped off the headlights and wrenched the wheel hard left. Tires squealed. Angie's seatbelt locked. The car obeyed, and made the corner.

At 30 mph, and even with Angie's death grip on the wheel, the little car couldn't right itself. It slid sideways, bumping off the pavement and into soft gravel shoulder.

Val screamed. Angie held her breath as the car continued its breakneck slide into hell. Val's fingernails locked on Angie's arm. Her sweaty fingers lost their grip and the steering wheel spun hard to the right. The car lurched onto two wheels and rolled.

Twin female screams pierced the small cab as over and over they went.

Thirty-Five

For the first time in days Jarvis had something to laugh at. Real grab-the-belly laughter. The Goodwells were a bigger joke than the Munsters. No wonder Wuss had been in and out of trouble his whole life. The man in question sat straight in the hard chair before him, hands on his thighs.

"Why did you want to get aboard *Little One* so bad?"

"I didn't want to *so bad*."

"What were you doing out at the crack of dawn? You don't impress me as the kind of person who's up before noon."

Goodwell's fingers clenched and unclenched the meat of his thigh. He opened his mouth.

"Never mind, just tell me about your father's restaurant."

Goodwell blanched visibly and began stuttering, swearing he had no connection to the place. None whatsoever. "It's just one of Father's holdings. Investments. You know?"

Jarvis leaned on his elbows and fed Goodwell his sternest expression, one he probably got often from his father. He held up his fingers and counted things off for the wuss. "One—the restaurant is tied to Nolan Little's murder. Two—you are tied to the murder. Three—you're tied to the restaurant. If you were me, what would you be thinking now?"

Jarvis hadn't thought it possible, but wuss turned even paler. Too bad Jarvis hadn't invited the parents here too. Would be nice to see the father's face right about now. Suddenly Jarvis couldn't wait to talk to them.

And where the hell was the three hundred bucks wuss paid to get aboard *Little One*?

He shouted at dispatch on the intercom. "Call Goodwell's parents. Get them down here."

The Goodwell kid nearly fell off the seat. "I'm twenty-five years old, can't you keep my parents out of this?"

Jarvis arrested a self-satisfied grin. "Okay, you don't want Mommy and Daddy involved, tell me what I want to know."

Tyson gave Jarvis a palms up. "I know it looks bad. But I assure you I didn't kill anyone."

"Tell me about that spreadsheet. We found a torn sheet of paper near Little's body. It had numbers on it." Jarvis added a blatant lie: "And your prints."

"I—"

"You what?" Come on, spit it out. Let's get this shit over with."

"I-I want my lawyer."

Damn, not another one.

After Goodwell was taken to holding Jarvis began wearing out the tiles in front of his desk. Wuss had means and opportunity. Jarvis had been certain the information about the spreadsheet would force the guys' motive into the open. But he'd clammed up. Just like Montez Clarke.

God, maybe his interrogation tactics had gone south for the season.

He'd gotten a glimpse of the guy as he ran away from striking Mrs. Deacon. Didn't look like any of the suspects. Just what he needed, a hired kidnapper. Probably the same one who'd kidnapped Mrs. Little.

Who'd hire someone to do their dirty work? Someone who feared recognition. Or was a sissy about blood. Again, it came back to Goodwell.

He made out the paperwork to request a search warrant for WGs Restaurant.

A half hour later, reading the address Goodwell had provided,

Jarvis drove to Paula Spencer's house. She stepped back to let him in the back door. What a piece of work. Everything about her was fake, from the double D boobs down to the dagger-like acrylic fingernails. Orange and green plaid polyester. She slid skin-tight polyester pants onto the brown vinyl loveseat and motioned him to the matching chair.

"Want some tea, or a beer?"

"No thanks. I won't take up much of your time. Were you and Tyson Goodwell together Friday night?"

"This about that guy who got murdered on the boat?"

"What makes you think that?"

"I'm not stupid, Detective. I know Tyson went on that tour. I know a guy got killed."

"You think he did it?"

She shrugged. "Tyson's a lot of things, but I can't see him as a killer."

"Does he enjoy fishing?"

Her smile, which hadn't faded, widened. "Fishing? I doubt it. Fact of the matter is, I told him I was pregnant. He was doing the guy-thing, running away."

"When are you due?"

"I ah, lost it."

It? "You weren't pregnant, were you?"

Like he'd actually slapped it off her face, the smile passed away. "I just wanted him to marry me."

"His mother thinks you're after the family fortune."

Instead of the expected denial, she exclaimed, "I wasn't the only one!"

Jarvis drove from the Spencer residence, laughing. He had to agree with the bimbo about one thing: Tyson Goodwell did not seem like the murdering type.

That's why he was the biggest suspect.

What about that damned Phelps? In his car the other night, Jarvis had accused Phelps: "You're involved up to your duffel bag-toting eyeballs." There had been no denial. Did the lack of reaction signify guilt? Not from a street-smart guy like Phelps; he was born with a poker face. And he'd challenged Jarvis to prove his guilt.

That's just what he'd do. Phelps looked like the best suspect. He had all the important criteria—in spades. Trouble was, he *could* have kidnapped Valerie, but he *couldn't* have attacked Angelina, because he was dead by then. Which landed Jarvis back at square one because he was convinced the same person perpetrated both crimes.

Another consideration, the kidnapper hadn't harmed either Valerie or Angelina—they'd been content to issue warnings, which spoke volumes. Jarvis nodded. Anyone who didn't really know Valerie Little would think a warning would frighten the mousy woman. They hadn't seen the true lady—the one who was strong and determined—like a cockroach. He laughed. She and Angelina made a great pair. He just hoped they didn't make a dead pair.

His cell-phone rang. A frown puckered the skin between his eyes seeing it was the office. He absently rubbed at the wrinkles as he wrote the number the dispatcher gave. He pushed Off, then On and dialed Will Deacon's number. Six rings and a mechanical voice replied, "Thank you for using Verizon, the subscriber you've called is either—"

He hung up. What sort of emergency could Will Deacon have? Was he too an attack victim, with just a moment to call for help? No, he wouldn't have asked for Jarvis in particular. What other emergency could the man have? Before the thought was complete, Jarvis knew. It was something to do with Wallace, who faced years in prison. He had taken every cent of Will and Angelina's money and was headed out of town when nabbed on a traffic violation. Most brothers would be rip-shit at a relative who committed forgery, larceny, credit card fraud and identity theft. But apparently not Will.

Wallace had used his one phone call to call him. What frosted Jarvis was that Will not only accepted the call, but had gone running to the jail to give him a ride home! What was up with that? Was the bond between twins different than average siblings? Was backstabbing and treachery moot if you shared identical genetic makeup? If *his* brother perpetrated such monstrous deeds, he'd let him rot in jail.

Funny Wallace should take this particular time to run off with their cash. Could this have anything to do with, 1-Nolan's murder, 2-Will and Angelina's separation, 3-Valerie Little's abduction? 4-Angelina's attack? 5-Sonnie's murder?

On first learning that Wallace had been bailed out, his reaction was to slap something on him too: let the boys be together, in jail. Accessory. Aiding and Abetting. Jarvis was unable to find a charge that could stick. Then he'd learned it was Wallace's wife who bailed him out.

Thirsty, he spun the car into the fast-food parking lot. At the order box, he remembered he'd promised to bring Angelina something to eat. Before the notion—did someone like her eat here—fully materialized he'd placed the order. While idling at the window, he tried Will's number again.

The phone rang unanswered. A chilling thought struck. Will was calling about Angelina. Something happened to her! He jammed money into the surprised clerk's fingers, dropped the bags on the passenger seat and skidded out of the lot. Heart swelling like an oil gusher, he pulled onto the highway, bags of food teetering on top of Wallace Deacon's folder. Fast food, great way to impress a lady, but there may be no time to waste. He raced to the motel, the scent of French fries making his stomach growl.

Jarvis realized he was chewing. The fries went down like a drain clog. He tried washing it down with a mouthful of Coke, but the blockage barely moved. He could actually feel it sitting in his gullet. Burning like lava. When had he last eaten? During investigations—even though few and far between in northern New Hampshire—he didn't think about sustenance. Every thought was consumed with details of the case.

Bailing Wallace out was like giving him permission to rob

them blind. Maybe that's what broke up Will and his wife. She found out about the theft, gave Will an ultimatum. Anger that anyone could choose scum like Wallace over a treasure like Angelina pushed the fry-clog back into his throat. He swallowed it down with another mouthful of Coke as he pulled up in front of Angelina's cabin. The lights were out, including the one on the tiny porch. Now after ten o'clock, she must be in bed. Where was her car?

He got out and knocked on her door so hard a man from the next cabin poked his head outside. "You seen the lady from this cabin?" Jarvis asked.

The man stared at him, the question *who the hell are you* playing on his features. Jarvis flashed his badge. "Where's the woman who's staying here?"

"I, er…She went out."

"When?"

The man ducked inside. There was a muffled exchange and he reappeared. "My wife said she left late this afternoon. She had a suitcase."

Damn! He stormed to the office and slammed his palm on the counter, making the sleepy-eyed clerk jump. "What time did the lady from Cabin 4 check out?"

The clerk leaned toward the file box, but stopped with the lid half way up. "She didn't check out. Nobody checked out today."

"Gimme the key!"

The man fumbled in a drawer. Jarvis nearly flew over the counter to help. Finally the clerk came up with a large yellow-tagged key bearing a magic marker 4, which Jarvis jerked from befuddled fingers. He ran to the cabin and erupted into her room. A single glance said she'd gone. No sign of foul play. Nothing left behind, not even an earring. No open phone book. No indentation on the notepad. Angelina Deacon had left nothing but the scent of lavender from a recent shower. She'd definitely moved out of her own free will—he hoped.

He heaved the key on the dresser and went to Cabin 5, but

didn't have to knock, the door opened. A woman looking like a Martian in pink spongy curlers eyed him. "The lady from that cabin. Did she leave alone?"

The curlers nodded. "Did you see which way she went?" An arm raised and pointed north. Jarvis mumbled thanks and got in his car, berating himself for not following his instincts. When she showed interest in working on the case he should've given her some busy job interviewing long-lost relatives or something to keep her out of his hair. His thinning hair.

Why couldn't they stay put and do female-things like cooking and cleaning?

He punched numbers in his cell-phone. "Wilson, the Little woman behaving herself all right?"

"Yep. No problem. She's in the shower." There was a hesitation, then he added, "Come to think of it, she's been in there a while."

Jarvis heard the television go mute, then the sound of rustling as though Wilson had risen from a sofa. Jarvis leaned his forehead on the steering wheel, that sensation of dread returning. A moment passed. Then two. In the distance Wilson cursed. Jarvis didn't have to hear the man's next words. "Damn, she's gone. Bathroom window's open, she probably went out that way."

Jarvis hit the mike button and told dispatch, "Put out an APB for a dark blue Lexus. Check with DMV for the plate. The owner is Angelina Deacon, Bay Hill Road. Put out another APB on a green Dodge Caravan registered to Valerie or Nolan Little."

Jarvis cursed and sped to the Deacon residence, not expecting to find either woman there, but not knowing where else to check. Then he drove down the hill and turned left to go past Valerie's house. Neither vehicle was there either.

Wilson stood in the Little's driveway, looking lost. Jarvis didn't want to, but he stopped. He brushed away words of apology with, "Looks like they're both gone," and finished it with the thought, *The Captain's going to crucify me.*

"Where the hell would they go?"

Wilson didn't answer. Jarvis didn't expect one, but it would have been nice. "You might as well go home." The aroma of the fries reminded him about the food he'd bought for Angelina. "You hungry?"

"No. She made beef stew. The best stuff I ever ate." Wilson jingled his keys. "Oh yeah, one more thing. There's a mess in the bathroom wastebasket. Looks like she's cut her hair."

Thirty-Six

The Escort stopped rolling, and landed miraculously on its wheels. The final chords of *Little GTO* were fading. The motor was running. Headlights picked out tall grass and scrub pines. For a moment, Angie's only goal was taking in the next breath. In out, in out.

"Val? Val, are you all right?" There was no answer, but try as she might, Angie couldn't unclasp her fingers from around the steering wheel. "Val!"

Finally, a rustle of fabric and a "What?"

"Are you okay?"

"Compared to what?"

"God, I'm glad you're okay. Can you help me?"

Val sat up. "What's wrong? Are you hurt?" She undid the seatbelt and slid across to her. "Angie, what's the matter?"

"I can't move."

"Please God. No!" Val unhooked Angie's belt, then shut off the motor, silencing the voice of the announcer telling everyone what a beautiful night it was for lovers. "Where does it hurt?"

Angie gave a small laugh. "It doesn't hurt anywhere. I just can't move."

Val opened her door and got out. Moonlight and headlights illuminated her stumbling in the tall grass, her face a grim mask. She made her way around and opened Angie's door. One at a time, she unclasped Angie's fingers from the wheel, then lifted Angie's feet and set them flat on the ground.

"Can you stand?" Val asked. "Come on, I'll help you."

Little by little sensation returned to her limbs and Angie found she could move. She wiggled her arms, shook her legs, and rotated her head, flexing rigid neck muscles. "That's better, thanks."

"What happened?"

"Shock paralysis." Angie leaned against the car and gave several deep breaths. "I didn't know air could smell so good."

"Where do you think they are?"

"You mean you weren't watching for them to go past?"

They both laughed. Angie moved away from the car, stretching her legs a little more. "You ready to head home?"

"I'll drive."

"No need."

"I can crash at least as good as you."

"Yeah, maybe you should. Drive, not crash."

Suddenly, lights on the trees cast an elongated, moving shadow. Val dove to her left, yanking Angie with her. They dropped to the ground, Angie's startled oof and the rustle of undergrowth the only sounds. She lay there a second, the long grass scratching wrists and ankles. She didn't know how far off the road the Escort had gone, but as other vehicle's lights neared, she realized it wasn't far enough. If that car turned onto this road, they'd surely spot the Ford. The skid marks were long gouges, like fingernail scratches; unmistakable with headlights shining on them.

The shadow stretched and then narrowed as the car approached. The motor slowed to make the turn. They crept Army-style into the woods just as the car turned onto the side road.

Fear stabbed at Angie from both front and rear now. She'd never liked deep, dark places. "I wish we had a flashlight."

The car stopped. Angie heard voices, most likely teenaged boys.

"That's not them."

Two car doors opened. The dome light came on.

"What do we do!" Val wanted to know.

"I don't know. I wish we knew if the car still worked."

The light illuminated a pair of tall, lithe silhouettes—definitely not the men from the restaurant.

"I'll check if anyone's inside," one of the silhouettes said, plowing through the tall grass and flinging open the drivers' side door.

"Nobody here."

"Check the area, maybe he was thrown clear."

"Couldn't be, the door's shut."

"Let's check anyway. Somebody might be hurt."

"No blood in the grass."

"Stay here," Angie whispered. "Be ready to run for help." She got to her feet and stepped out of the shadows, calling, "I'm right here. I'm not hurt."

They came toward her, non-threatening and yet still her knees nearly gave way. One teen took Angie's arm and leaned her against the Ford's fender. "I'm all right, really. Just a little shaken up." She gave a nervous laugh. "Guess that'll teach me to take corners on two wheels."

One of the teens laughed too. "You gonna play race car driver, you ought to get something with a bigger motor. Like our Camaro. It has a 350 V-8."

Angie clamped her lips tight so she wouldn't blurt out about the nice big motor in her Lexus—the Lexus she'd probably have to give up when the divorce was final.

One of the kids took her sigh to mean there really was something wrong. "Come on, we'll take you to the hospital."

"Really, I'm all right. Takes a few minutes for the adrenaline to stop pumping, that's all."

Just then, another set of headlights appeared out on the main road. The car slowed and began the turn for the side road. Angie somehow kept herself from diving back in the woods. If it was the pursuers, hopefully the presence of the two boys would keep them from killing her. Somehow that didn't inspire confidence.

The second car was a pickup. Angie's blood raced as the vehicle pulled up in front of the Camaro—with the 350 V-8—a great escape car. It was so dark she couldn't tell if it was the men from the restaurant. Things that hadn't already been drenched with sweat, now were.

"Need help there?" shouted a baritone voice.

The boys walked to the pickup. "Car went off the road. We got things under control."

The passenger got out anyway. A big man, hulking like a monster. He could be the one!

Angie tiptoed away and plunged back into the woods. Some deep-rooted intuition sent a message to her feet and she couldn't disobey. She ducked behind a large tree, trembling fingers accepting the security of the rough bark.

"Need an ambulance?" The monster started toward the Ford.

"No. The driver's shaken up, but okay."

Is this the truck from the restaurant? Too dark to tell.

From behind, fingers took hold of her arm. A tiny peep of surprise squeezed between her lips.

"What was that?" the monster asked.

"Sounded like she's hurt after all," said the teen.

"Come on, let's check." The driver got out of the pickup. Eight shoes tromped in long grass. They were coming!

Angie tugged Val's hand. Thankful the recent rain had made the leaves soft and nearly crunchless, they crept toward the street.

"Where'd she go?"

"I dunno, she was right here."

"Just one lady?"

"Yeah."

Stepping from the tree cover, yet remaining in shadows, Angie and Val moved toward the road. Angie still held Val's hand, which was good, because when she sneaked to the door of the Camaro, Val tried to pull away. The passenger door was still open and the dome light shone like a beacon. Angie put a hand in the small of Val's back and gave a little shove, then rushed to the drivers' side.

Inside, in a single movement she shifted, gunned and twisted. Two tires spun in the gravel, but two tried to grip pavement. The powerful motor the boys bragged about obeyed, squealing in an abrupt circle and onto Route 28.

Val knelt on the seat, fists gripping the back like a kid on a circus ride. "I don't see them yet. Oh, yes I do. Here they come."

Angie turned off the headlights. Val screeched.

With one streetlight for guidance, Angie raced a few hundred feet south, took her foot off the gas and wrenched the car right, praying this car handled sharp corners better than the Ford. She jammed her foot on the gas. They sped along the narrow bumpy road. She let go of the steering wheel one hand at a time, to dry her palms on her slacks.

"Hurry, they should be passing any second."

Angie pressed the car for more speed. "Those kids didn't lie about the motor."

"There they are." A second later, "They went past. I didn't see any brake lights."

"Hold on." Angie slowed the car so quickly they were both thrown at the windshield.

Val caught herself just before sliding backwards to the floor. "Whoa Nellie."

Angie pulled onto a two-rut logging road. "Tell me when you can't see the road any more."

"I haven't seen it for a long time."

"Well, open your eyes and keep watch."

The car bounced and jolted, bottoming out twice in the deep ruts made by huge log trucks.

"You go any further, you'll shake the teeth right out of my head."

The car rolled to a stop.

"What's the plan now, Nancy Drew?"

Angie didn't have a plan. Something told her Val already knew that.

"Do you think it was the guys from the restaurant?"

"I couldn't tell."

"You mean we might have run from *two* pairs of do-gooders?"

Angie sighed and wiped her palms. "Maybe."

"You realize we're guilty of Grand Theft Auto now, right?"

"I didn't know what else to do. I have an idea if you want to hear it."

"Gee, your ideas have worked great so far," Val said.

"I think we should walk back to the Ford and see if it'll go."

"Can't we drive back?" Val asked then answered her own question. "Of course we can't. How far is it?"

"Maybe a half mile. Wipe off your fingerprints."

"Shit."

It was after 2 a.m. when they arrived at the rented car. "It doesn't look like they came back," Val noted.

"Go to the corner and keep watch while I see if the car runs."

"You are picking me up, aren't you?"

"If you can dive through the window as I go past."

Angie trotted through the tangled grass and got in, then rolled down the window to hear Val. Angie said a quick prayer for the car to be all right. She turned the key.

The little engine came to life as if it were just as anxious to be out of this mess. With only a little slippage in the grass, she eased back on the road, and to the corner where Val got in.

"Feels nice to use headlights again." Her voice sounded a lot more confident than she felt.

"Just get us back to Alton Bay," was all Val said during the entire ride, which she spent perched on the edge of the seat, hands on the dashboard, eyeing the road ahead.

No other cars either passed or came toward them. Still Angie didn't allow herself a sustaining breath until they arrived at her room. They sat side by side on the bed with the lights off, letting the stress flow out of their bodies. On the table near the window, illuminated in the moonlight, sat the photo album and stuffed dog. Val went to get the beagle. She wiggled it in the air. "Where'd you get Pooky?"

"Pooky?"

Val shrugged. "I've had him since I was six." She hugged him to her chest.

"We went to your house trying to find some clue to where they might have taken you." Angie shrugged. "I don't know why I took him. I guess he helped me believe you were still alive. By the way, where did you hide your laptop? We couldn't find it."

"In the file cabinet in a brown envelope marked, INCOME TAX 1976."

Val removed her shoes and placed them neatly by the door. "I just hope those guys didn't have time to get the plate number off our car."

Thirty-Seven

Damn those women! Why couldn't they stay put and mind their own business?

Jarvis repeated the words all the way back to the station after leaving Wilson open-mouthed in Little's driveway. He slammed his office door. Jawed down the cold hamburgers and opened the folder containing detective's interviews. He ground his knuckles in his burning eyes. There had to be something here. Detective Stevens had questioned the Goodwells and—Goodwells! They were supposed to be here hours ago. He stomped from the office, to dispatch. "Did Goodwells show up?"

"Yes. They stayed an hour. Mr. Goodwell said you know where to find him."

"Call them. Get them here."

"Sir, it's three in the morning."

So it was. He turned on a heel, returned to his office and took a nap in his chair.

A sound woke him at eight a.m. Jarvis ran a hand through his hair and shook off the sleep-woozies.

Wilson stepped in the room. "Sir, the Goodwells are here."

"Gimme a minute."

Wilson nodded, but the door was shoved into his shoulder, jolting him aside. Agnes Goodwell burst into the room, if bursting could be done while using a cane. She gave a disdainful look at the hard wooden chair before sitting on the edge. She wore a two-tone green striped dress that belonged on a much younger woman. Her hair was piled on her head and fastened with a fancy diamond thing that looked like a brooch his grandmother used to have.

William Goodwell was the antithesis of his wife. Tall and lean, and at ease; he'd been through this before. He nodded to Wilson who, like a proper butler, backed out and let the door click shut. William reached across and shook hands with Jarvis, then took the chair beside his wife.

Mrs. Goodwell leaned the cane against her left knee and turned penetrating green eyes on him. "Officer, I want to know why you've dragged us all the way here."

Jarvis wanted to laugh. The station was exactly two and a half miles from HeavenScent. He set his elbows on a pile of manila folders and leaned forward in his you'd-better-take-this-seriously pose. He thought about informing her about his rank of detective, not an officer. Bah! She wouldn't give a damn about rank. To her, they were all underlings, even the distinguished man seated beside her.

Jarvis said, "Madam, your son in a suspect in a murder investigation."

"My son hasn't murdered anyone and you know it. He doesn't *know* anyone in this town." She said the word town as though it carried some dread plague she might catch if she remained here too long. As far as Jarvis was concerned, she'd already outstayed her welcome.

"Where was your son last Friday night?"

She fixed him with a piercing glance. "At HeavenScent with us, of course."

William interrupted with a sharp, "Agnes!"

"We played three-handed bridge until well after midnight."

Jarvis brought his fingers together in the shape of a tent. He pretended to study them for a moment then he peered over the top. "Your son's testimony disputes what you said." When she opened her mouth to speak, he put up a hand. "He admits to spending the night with a Mrs. Paula Spencer."

"Mrs?"

"In the morning she told him she was pregnant and he took off."

"Pregnant? My son would never get anyone like her pregnant." She slapped the cane tip on the floor. "Money! That's what they all want! Even that blonde hussy in the Lexus."

Jarvis' eruption of laughter brought Mrs. Goodwell's protests to a halt. "Madam, Mrs. Deacon isn't after your money. She's helping out with the case." Why had he said that? Angelina Deacon had been nothing but a concern: a fly in the ointment.

He continued, "Let's get back to the subject of your visit. Then you can be on your way. Your son says he was driving Mrs. Spencer to her car at six Saturday morning. They'd left it in the Downings Landing parking lot. As she exited his car, that's when she broke the news of her pregnancy, which was a lie, by the way."

"Of course." Mrs. Goodwell ran the palms of whisper-thin-skinned hands down her thighs.

"Your son flew into a panic and ran away."

"Never! Tyson always faces his obligations."

"Agnes," William said.

"He spotted the Little's tour boat leaving the dock. Waving cash he raced down there and asked to be let aboard."

"So? He wanted to go fishing."

"Agnes!"

"Has your son ever been fishing before?"

"Of course, he's been fishing. Dozens of times."

"Agnes." William Goodwell turned to Jarvis. "Tyson's never been fishing in his life."

"William!" Agnes said. "This officer is—"

"Detective," corrected William. "This man is a detective. It's his job to figure out who killed that boat owner." He took a breath. "Detective, our son has been a constant source of concern, for which I take full responsibility. I worked long hours and left his upbringing to his mother. She's turned him into a...a sissy."

"William!"

"A pansy. He has no social skills. No drive. No ambition. He's been in trouble since his first day of school. Yet I still didn't take charge. Not till it came time for him to go to college, I tried then, but…" He took a breath. "By then it was too late. The truth is, we don't know where he was or what he was doing that night. We rarely do. Still and all, I can't see my son involved in murder. But if it turns out…"

Jarvis waited, but William didn't finish the thought. Jarvis spared a glance at Mama Goodwell. She looked like she'd been stabbed with a pin. She started to get to her feet.

"Sit down, Agnes," William said.

It surprised Jarvis when she obeyed. "Tell me about WG's Restaurant."

William's eyebrows twitched, but quickly returned to normal. "Seven years ago, I think it was the second year we summered here, I bought a floundering restaurant and two gift shops in the Wolfeboro area. I have numerous holdings in New Hampshire, Detective. Can you tell me, does the restaurant have something to do with the murder?"

"Who runs WG's? I assume that stands for William Goodwell."

"Yes. The manager's name is Alphonse Delgado. I brought him here from the City. He's an excellent chef and manager. I can't believe he'd be involved in anything nefarious."

"He's done an exemplary job," said Mrs. Goodwell. Jarvis let his eyes roll toward her. He'd almost forgot she was there. She continued, "Tell me how in the world an upstanding restaurant in Wolfeboro could possibly be involved in a *fisherman's* death in Alton Bay."

Wilson entered, this time without knocking, and placed a sheaf of papers in front of Jarvis. He waved a page at Mamma Goodwell. "I have search warrants for your home and WG's." He ignored Mamma's sputtering protest, "Sergeant Wilson and a team of officers will proceed to those locations immediately.

You can accompany them if you like."

"What do you expect to find?" Mr. Goodwell asked.

"I'm not at liberty to say right now."

Mamma crossed her arms, or at least attempted to get them around that sizeable bosom. "We aren't leaving until you tell us, Detective."

"I'll have food and blankets sent to you then," Jarvis rose and strode to the door.

William Goodwell stood and helped his wife to her feet. "If there's anything I can do to help, please let me know."

Jarvis watched out the window as the Goodwells got into their Cadillac. For the first time, he felt sorry for Tyson. He crossed the hall for fresh coffee and returned to the pile of paperwork. Half way through the stack of interviews, he got up to pace again. Nothing useful here, many of the people questioned hadn't seen Nolan or Valerie in ten years. Most had never been on *Little One*. The consensus was unanimous though: everyone loved Valerie and disliked Nolan.

Jarvis thought about something Angelina said on the boat, something about Nolan being a totally different person away from the boat. Jarvis could tell by the way her eyes looked at something over his left shoulder that she hadn't believed it any more than he had.

Damn her! Why couldn't she sit home and act like other women? A laugh burst from Jarvis' tight lips. Because she wasn't like other women. She was outrageous and adventurous. Life with her had to be one wild roller coaster ride.

Was that what he wanted? Was he ready for roller coasters at his age? Definitely. Lately, life was too damned tame. Jarvis threw himself in the chair, tilted it back against the sill, kicked his feet onto the desk and closed his eyes. A scene immediately began playing in his mind: he and Angelina on a beach, palm trees swaying gently in a tropical breeze, sweating pina colada glasses teetering in the sand. She lay on a pink beach towel, and wore a blue and white stripe string bikini; he was in denim cutoffs and that stupid hat. He flew upright, raking his fingers through the thinning hair and wondered if she'd noticed his hair. Of course she had, she didn't miss anything.

Fool! Dreaming of vacations with her and he hadn't even asked her out yet.

A vacation, that's what he needed. How long had it been anyway? He couldn't recall. Not a good sign. Wouldn't be long before the captain would force him to take some time off. Probably right after this case. It was taking too freaking long to solve.

Intensive questioning had failed to turn up someone who'd either gone up front, or seen anyone go up front. Jarvis had never known so many people who claimed to be minding their own business. It wasn't human nature. It *was* human nature to look, listen and/or get involved.

He leaned the chair back again. This time another scene appeared in his minds' eye, *Little One* and the back of Nolan Little seated in his cockpit chair. Jarvis tried to blink the vision away, to make Angelina and the beach scene reappear, but Nolan remained. He leaned against the starboard wall reading a magazine. There was a glimmer of white, like a door opening and closing. Or maybe a person wearing a lot of white. Or a flash of lightning. Jarvis erased the frown of annoyance and waited for the scene to continue. A man, cast in silhouette, stepped through the port-side opening. Nolan looked up. Jarvis couldn't read his face since he stood behind, but Nolan's manner suggested irritation at being disturbed. The intruder didn't speak. His right arm, which had been hidden till now by the galley window frame, moved upward. A long-bladed knife glinted against the electric blue sky, then disappeared as it was plunged into Nolan's chest. The figure moved away. Jarvis lost sight of him as he went around the starboard side of the galley. He released a curse of frustration.

Obviously his brain tried to tell him he'd missed a clue somewhere. What? Jarvis paced three routes around the room then flung himself back in the chair and leaned back to see if the image would replay. When it did he didn't censor a single image.

Moments later he launched himself to the office door and flung it open. "Wilson, get in here!" he shouted just about the time he remembered Wilson was out executing search warrants.

Thirty-Eight

Morning arrived too quickly. Angie pulled the pillow over her head to block out the encroaching sunlight. Who chased them last night? It wasn't Montez, the silhouette was wrong. As far as she knew Tyson didn't have a pickup truck. Who else?

It all went back to that restaurant, she was sure. Whoever saw her in that hallway thought she'd seen something and chased her to—keep her quiet. The idea made her tremble. What exactly was going on there? When the door to that room had opened, she had a fleeting glimpse inside. But the flash of light had been too brief, her fear too overwhelming.

In the tangle of bedding, she realized she still wore yesterday's clothes. She wrestled herself loose from the sheet and padded to the bathroom. What she saw in the mirror nearly made her faint. "Oh my god."

Val was instantly awake and beside her. Angie held up her hands so Val could see the crusted blood caking her sleeves, hands and face. Creepy! She'd spent the entire night wearing someone else's blood. Before Val could speak, Angie was out of her clothes and in the shower, letting the hottest water beat away the previous evening.

Blood.

That's what had been missing on *Little One*!

Someone on the boat murdered Nolan. Why didn't anyone have blood on them? She thought back to what everyone was wearing when they got on the boat. Far as she could remember, they all wore the same thing when they left. Except Will who'd put his jacket back on. Angie still hadn't found out why. She reached around the curtain for a towel. It was scratchy but absorbent. God no! It couldn't be!

She stopped drying herself and let the images on the boat play back. First thing in the morning, serving coffee and muffins. In the galley, cleaning up the lunch mess. On the deck, stowing fish in the box under the deck. At all times, Valerie had a hand-towel stuck through her belt loop.

But when the police arrived, the towel wasn't there. Then she thought of the three one-hundred dollar bills Tyson paid to be let aboard *Little One*. She'd told Detective Jarvis that Tyson gave the money to Nolan. But he hadn't. He'd given it to Valerie. Yet, Valerie had told Jarvis she couldn't remember who'd taken the money. And then she'd paid for their lunch with a hundred-dollar bill!

It couldn't be. It just couldn't be.

Angie slipped into her robe, started to open the door and halted. She dug through the zippered makeup bag and pocketed a metal nail file. It was all she could find. She went into the main room.

Sit cross-legged, look at ease. Smile. Not too much, it'll make her suspicious.

Val sat Indian-style on the bed. "You okay? That was a lot of blood."

Ask her. Angie undid the towel draped around her hair. The strangeness of the hair's length made her look in the mirror. Nerves had made her very pale. *Ask her.* She took a breath.

"Something's wrong."

"No." *Yes.*

"Just tell me what it is."

Angie put her hand in her pocket, feeling the dubious safety of the file. "On the boat...On the boat..."

Val's eyes narrowed. This wasn't a conversation she'd expected.

"Tyson paid Nolan three hundred dollars. You told Jarvis you didn't know where it was."

Val's eyes narrowed further, becoming tight, straight lines.

"But you bought me breakfast the day after Nolan died and you paid with a hundred dollar bill."

Val looked away. "I knew if I said I had it, they'd take it as evidence. Angie, you won't believe this, but that was the first cash—cash that didn't *have* to go in a joint bank account—that I've had in years. I just couldn't give it to them." She took a breath. "I know how it looks. Do you think they've realized it?"

Angie shrugged. "I wouldn't put it past Jarvis. He's pretty shrewd. There's another thing. You always had a towel through the belt loop of your jeans."

"Uh-huh." The implication was crystal clear yet it didn't anger Val. "I always keep one there to wipe my hands. Food. Fish guts."

"It wasn't there when we got back to shore."

"I use about a dozen every trip. As soon as one's dirty I drop it in a bag in the galley. Dirty ones give me the willies."

A simple explanation. Surely the cops found, and tested the towels for human blood. Angie finally managed to relax. Things were okay. Weren't they?

Val stood up. She seemed utterly at ease. "Do you feel better now?"

Angie felt a blush creep up her neck. She avoided Val's eyes and nodded.

"Good. So, what's on the agenda? Where do we look for Nolan's killer?"

"You still want to after what happened last night?"

"We're getting close, I can feel it. Come on, we can talk about it over breakfast."

"What about Jarvis?" Angie asked.

"If he shows up, he can pay."

"What about your work?"

"Since Jarvis put me under protective custody, I had the boys take over. It's the least they could do as payment for suspecting their mother as a murderer."

In the parking lot, the sight of the rental car stopped them in their tracks. It looked like it had been through a demolition derby; crusted with mud, grass clumped in every nook and cranny, a long scrape on the roof. Angie burst into laughter. She laughed so hard she had to grip the door handle to keep from falling down.

"What's so funny?"

Angie managed to blurt out between gulps for air, "I just pictured us explaining to the agency what happened to their car."

Val still didn't laugh. "Let's just get it back to them and see if they'll trust you with another one."

"Trust *me* with one?"

"I wasn't driving."

A man dressed in a three-piece suit and carrying an overstuffed briefcase passed. He looked from the women to the car, and back, then shook his head and hurried to his shiny black Cadillac.

Now Val laughed.

At the rental agency, Angie explained how they'd run off the road trying to avoid hitting a moose.

"Where was the thing, in a mud bog?"

"Is this the sympathy we get for nearly being killed?"

"You have a police report?"

"How were we supposed to call the cops while we're sitting upside down in the car at two o'clock in the morning?"

"How did you get it back on its wheels?"

"You see it was like this..." Angie started to say. Val gave an unladylike snort, put a hand to her mouth and ran outside.

"She all right?"

"I hope so, she's been sick all morning. Shock, I guess. Or maybe she's pregnant. Yeah, that's it, she's having a baby."

"What were you saying about the car?"

"Fortunately we were on a bit of a hill after we rolled up this embankment. All we had to do was nudge it and poof! It rolled right back over, slick as a bean." Angie waved her hands with a flourish.

The man pushed a stack of papers toward her and handed her a pen. The expression on his face was overloaded with doubt. "Fill this out."

"What is it?"

"Damage report." When Angie put her signature on the bottom line and handed the paperwork to the agent, he wiggled a key in the air and handed it to her. "I hope your friend's all right."

"She'll be fine."

He pointed Angie toward a puke green Ford Focus. She gave him an eye roll that only made him grin. Obviously they'd abused his good nature once too often. She accepted the keys, saying to Val, "Should we get something to eat?"

"Yes, I'm starving. But one thing…would you mind if we took my van? This thing feels like a tuna can."

Angie drove to the marina, left the Ford and hiked to Val's house where they made sure no cops staked out the place, watching for them, before taking the van. Because it was out of the way, a place they'd be unlikely to be spotted, Val drove to Meredith for breakfast at a diner frequented by tourists. A booth near the back was vacant.

"Oh God," Angie pulled up short, recognizing the inhabitant of the booth behind the empty one—Tyson, nursing a cup of coffee as though it were the world's most expensive brandy.

He didn't notice them until they were standing a foot from his table. First his face registered surprise. Then a frown twitched the corners of his mouth and he leaned left to look past them. Then shrugged and smiled up at them. "You two on some kind of makeover program or something?"

"We needed a change," Val offered.

"I assume this is related to your search for the murderer. You didn't find him yet?"

"We're closing in on him," Angie said.

"Man, I wish you'd hurry, I'd really like to get back to the City."

"Running isn't the answer," Val said.

"I'm not running. Tryouts for The Man of LaMancha are in two days."

Angie didn't want to hear about plays. She wanted to hear about murderers. She wanted to know where he'd been last night; if he'd chased them from WG's. Unfortunately, now wasn't the time to find out. It was clear Tyson waited for someone and their appearance had upset those plans.

Tyson dropped his fork. She blinked a couple of times. She'd lost track of the conversation.

Val was speaking. "...to be $35,000 in renovations and equipment alone. Then there's outlay for permits, outfitting the van, printing business cards, advertising."

"I assumed the tour business was a gold mine."

"I guess it was." Val sighed. "Is. I just don't think I—It was Nolan's thing, not mine. I always wanted to have a catering business."

Val's fits and starts of dialogue belied her turmoil. It wouldn't be easy to leave the old life behind. But change wasn't just something she'd dreamt of, she needed it.

"We had a $50,000 insurance policy. It'll help, but it won't be enough. I'll probably re-mortgage the house. And I should have something once the boat sells."

Tyson nodded, threw another glance toward the door and said, "Well, it's been nice seeing you, how about we meet for lunch at WG's?"

Why did he want to meet there? To finish what he started last night? Val's brain must've take the same route because she asked, "Why there?"

Tyson shrugged. "Why not?" When neither of them answered, he added, "Noonish?"

"I can't. I have to be somewhere," Val said.

"I'll be there," Angie said.

They strode to the register and ordered coffees. All the while, Tyson tried not to look anxious. Outside, the women ducked around the corner of the building, out of the bright sunshine and Tyson's line of sight.

"He's waiting for somebody, right?" Val asked. "And you knew they wouldn't come with us there."

"Right. And unless I miss my guess, she just got here."

A blue car pulled in and parked next to Val's van. The woman who got out had bright red hair and a vinyl handbag.

"Who's that?" Val asked.

"The woman Tyson said he was running from when he asked to get on the boat."

Paula walked with a determined step as she passed into the diner.

"Sure wish we could go back inside and listen," Val said.

"I've got to go to the ladies room."

"I'll go cool off in the car," Val said.

Angie ran inside and ducked behind a dividing wall. Once they were seated, and a captive audience, she'd confront them: find out what was going on, once and for all. She peeked out expecting to see Tyson's face in his previous seat and the back of Paula's head. But things weren't going the way she expected. Tyson was on his feet in the aisle. Paula covered the last two steps and practically leaped on him, flinging her arms around his neck. His face appeared in the crook between her shoulder and neck. He looked both surprised and baffled. He spotted Angie then pushed Paula away, threw some bills on the table and hurried her along the aisle ahead of him.

Angie wondered what the problem was, but then realized—he hadn't expected Paula any more than he expected Angie and Val to show up. He waited for someone else entirely!

The couple stepped outside. Angie ducked from her hiding spot. Tyson, with his hand on Paula's lower back, nudged her toward her vehicle. They spoke a moment. He seemed to be trying to coax her into the car; she kept shaking her head. Finally she got in and drove away. Tyson spun on his heel and marched toward the diner. His appointment must be mighty serious for him to venture back inside knowing Angie and Val still lingered.

Angie scooted to the ladies room. Maybe he'd think she left. She waited three minutes then inched open the door. Tyson sat in his booth; she could see the back of his expensive haircut. Angie opened the door a little more searching for another possible exit. The only way was through the kitchen.

The clammy atmosphere smelled of fried food. Homefries sizzled on the grill. The cook looked up seeing a stranger in his domain. Angie gave a helpless palms-up gesture. "Please don't tell him you saw me." She left him standing open-mouthed and shot out the back door that stood open to the cooler morning air.

They parked the van halfway down the lot. Angie couldn't see Val inside. She probably got worried when Angie hadn't come out, and went back in looking for her. Angie decided to wait a few minutes or they might end up doing this all day long.

Fifteen feet away, a deep voice came from the opposite side of the van. "Well if she's not out here, then she must be inside with Tyson."

Then Val's voice. "I told you, she isn't even with me." A slapping sound preceded Val's exclamation, "Hey!"

Angie launched herself around the bumper and heaved herself on Paula's back just as she took steps to strike Valerie again. Feeling Angie's weight on her, she slithered from underneath. Angie dropped to her knees on the pavement. Bolts of pain shot up her legs. Hands clutched her shoulders and Angie felt herself being propelled backward. Her head thumped on the tar. Then Paula stood above, straddling her. She leaned down. "I guess you're too stupid to take the hint. When I said I was going to fight for him, I meant it. Now, are you going to take whatever dignity you still have and get the hell outta town?"

Paula suddenly pitched sideways. Her head struck the side of the van and sounded like a ripe melon. Angie scuttled to her feet. "Run Angie!" Val shouted as she climbed into the vehicle. Angie ran too, and jumped in just as Paula got to her feet. Angie held on while Val swerved the van onto the main road. Through the back window, Angie watched Paula shaking a fist at them. Tyson stood in the diner doorway. He was shaking hands with a tallish man with dark hair.

"Val, go back. Tyson's appointment is there."

"Go back? You're kidding, right?"

"He looks a little familiar. I want to see him up close."

Thirty-Nine

Angie settled back in the seat, willing her thumping heart to normalcy. "Val, we've got to go back and see who Tyson's meeting."

"We're not going back." Val's tone left no room for argument.

So, what was up with Tyson? If all on the up and up, he wouldn't have tried to hurry them away from the diner. Who was the man he'd met? Had Angie been mistaken thinking he looked familiar? It had been just too far for her to get a good look. She wondered if Paula had gone back inside, confronted Tyson—knew the man's identity. Regardless, Paula sure wouldn't tell her!

"What's so funny?"

Angie told her and finished with "What do we do next?"

"I promised to go to the grandkids' ball game at the rec center. After the game why don't we meet at your place to figure out what to do next. I should be through about three."

"I'm surprised Dale lets you near the kids."

"Probably wouldn't if he thought we'd be alone together." Val swiped at a tear, then clenched the steering wheel with determination. Angie reached across and patted Val's arm.

Val left Angie at the marina to pick up the puke green car. "See you around three." She dug in her purse for the Ford keys, got in and locked the door.

There had to be more to learn from Tyson, specifically, the purpose of that spreadsheet and the indentity of the man he'd met. She would find out at lunch. She'd go back to the motel right now and formulate questions that he'd think were mere womanly curiosity, but would be so wily, so devious, this case would burst wide open.

Angie suddenly had a boulder in her throat. It blocked her ability to swallow. Nothing to be nervous about. She'd go see Jarvis and explain everything going on. He'd be happy to sit at the next table and listen. Witnesses were important when it came to evidence. Maybe there were even some specific questions he'd want her to ask. Then she remembered: he was trying to capture her. Protective custody, he called it.

Well, he'd just have to suck it up. She'd offer herself up as a guinea pig, over the phone, of course. He couldn't turn down a chance to solve Nolan's murder.

She got the boulder past her esophagus and managed to croak out, "So, Mrs. Deacon, why are you so sure the duffel bags are related to Nolan's death?" The next sentence contained one word, "Shit." What made her think she could pull this off?

What was there to be worried about? Jarvis wouldn't let anything happen. Besides, it was a public place.

Yeah, full of men carrying black bags full of—cash, drugs, jewels, pornography, bank records. Body Parts. Angie cursed again.

Was Tyson dangerous? Part of her couldn't imagine him doing bodily damage, especially to a woman, but there were no guarantees with anything these days. Angie laid her head on the steering wheel, eyes closed against the sting of her nerves. Where the hell were those bags? They must've been dumped overboard. Somebody had retrieved them. That was clear because Jarvis had sent Mr. Brinks out to get them, but they were already gone. She ignored the voice that reminded her of Brinks' death. She couldn't bring him back, but she could avenge the innocent man's murder.

Since Brinks hadn't found the bags mere hours after they turned up missing that meant someone had gotten them. Angie drew the keys from the ignition, got out and walked across the street.

Above the renovated two-car garage a hand painted sign read: Triangle Diving • Skin and Scuba Diving Equipment. Rentals. One garage door stood open. A tall, spare man aligned air tanks along one wall. Angie cleared her throat and the man straightened up. A smile brightened the craggy face. He came forward, hand outstretched. Angie shook it, feeling the calluses and sinewy fingers on her palm.

"My name is Angie Deacon, I'm investigating a homicide that took place last week."

"Nolan Little, right?"

"Did you know him?"

"Sure, everybody knew him."

"Sometime the day he was killed, did you see two large dark-skinned men? Did you possibly rent equipment to them?"

He didn't think more than a second. "Nope. Didn't rent any equipment that day. We were closed. My partner's mother-in-law died. We went to the funeral. Only rented one unit all week."

"Is that unusual?"

"Hell yes. Oh, sorry. Most weeks it's about eighteen units. That's why this one guy sticks in the mind, you know? Wasn't the kind of guy you'd expect to be diving. He was more the walk-in-the-park type."

Angie stopped dead. "Was he well dressed? Kind of pris-sy?"

The man's blue eyes lit up. "Yeah. Fancy car too."

Angie's heart started thumping.

"Antique T-Bird. Electric blue."

Her elation fizzled like three-day old Coke. "Was he blond?"

"Nah. Dark curly hair, with a—"

She didn't hear any more. Angie thanked the man and left. First thing she did from home was phone Jarvis. He wasn't in his office. The dispatcher didn't know where he was, but if

Angie would leave a number...

She hung up, fingers trembling. The hell with him, she could handle this alone.

At WG's, Tyson was just getting out of his car. He didn't notice the Ford when she pulled in and parked two spots away. When he went to open his trunk, Angie nearly gunned the car back into traffic.

Tyson carried a black duffel bag.

Forty

Tyson put his hand on the trunk lid, about to slam it shut.
Angie gave a friendly "Hey!" and leaped out. In one step, she
stood beside him, jabbering about the weather, anything to distract him from shutting the evidence out of sight.

He started, then smiled, as he recognized her. The trunk
shut with a woof. She wanted to scream. He put the keychain in
the pocket of his Dockers. "Are you all right? You look a little
green."

"I'm fine."

Tyson's brows knit slightly, he took her elbow. No hostess
on duty this early so a waitress waved them to seat themselves.
Tyson ordered a draft beer and a burger, Angie asked for iced tea
and a Caesar salad.

"You look like you could use something stronger." He took
a sip of his beer and wiped the foam from his lip with the back
of his hand. "Why?"

"Why what?"

"Why are you so determined to find the killer? Excuse me
for asking, but could it be because you suspect someone you're
close to?"

"What!" When nearby customers turned to look, she lowered
her voice. "What are you saying?"

Tyson drew circles in the beads of moisture on his glass
with an index finger. "Yesterday you told me I was one of the
only suspects left." He pointed the damp finger at her. "I think

you're worried your husband had something to do with it." Tyson lowered the finger with an air of a person having done a good day's work.

The memory of Will putting on his jacket suffused into her head. She gave a violent shake to her head. "I can't believe you said that. What possible reason could Will have to kill Nolan?"

"What possible reason could I have?"

The conversation moved close to out of control. "It's just that I know Will inside and out. He didn't even know Nolan Little before that tour. He's not a murderer."

"You didn't think he was an adulterer either."

Ouch.

Was it possible she overlooked Will as a suspect because of her emotional attachment? Because she thought he didn't know Nolan? Alton Bay was a small town, people tended to know each other. Possible they'd met at some point. But seeing each other at a town meeting or bumping into each other at the grocery checkout didn't give motives for murder.

"I can see those little wheels turning," Tyson said. "All your fears about your husband have leaped to the surface. You're wondering if he's the one."

"You're wrong."

Lunch arrived. Angie speared a piece of lettuce. "So, were you born in Manhattan?"

Tyson stopped mid-move of burger to mouth. "Yeah, right in the heart of the activity. I love it. Mom loves it."

"If you love the city so much, why come to New Hampshire?"

He laughed. "It's Dad. He loves it here."

"Your mother doesn't?"

He laughed again, this one full of mirth. "She hates it."

Why would Agnes Goodwell agree to spend every summer in a place she hated? As if reading her thoughts, Tyson said, "It's a compromise. For years, Mom dictated where we'd eat, what shows we'd see. About eight years ago, Dad put his foot down.

'I've had it, Agnes,' he said, 'We're spending summers in New Hampshire.' You should've seen her face! She didn't argue with him, though."

"So what happened?"

"Obviously we came to New Hampshire." Tyson said this proudly, as though his father's rebellion had somehow been liberating for him too. "Almost first thing, Dad went out and bought some real estate in the area."

"So he'd have an excuse to come back."

"I'm sure. It made a turning point in their marriage too. After that, Dad had a different attitude. Like he'd finally taken his first step as a man."

"Why do you come too? You must have friends, things to do in the city."

"I don't have my father's courage." His expression said this was the first time he'd admitted this out loud.

"So, what did your father buy that would tie him to the area?"

"A couple of gift shops, some land, and a restaurant."

Angie's adrenaline bubbled like water in a spaghetti pot. It was suddenly crystal clear. WG's. WG stood for William Goodwell. Why hadn't Tyson mentioned this before? When she and Val said they'd rather eat someplace besides WG's, it would have been a logical time. It made sense to want to eat here. Free food. Good food.

If he was on the up and up.

The vision of him putting the duffel bag in his trunk overlapped the one of Sonnie exiting the restaurant carrying an identical one. Tyson had to know about the restaurant being a front for—something.

Why? He only came here a few weeks of the year. If the managers were running something illegal, they'd surely hide it from the owners. What if the owners were the ringleaders? And the boat trip, some sort of business meeting. Angie's knuckles hurt. She realized she had a death-grip on the fork.

Of eveyone, Sonnie and Montez were the only ones who seemed to know each other. She hadn't overheard a single whispered word, seen any heads bent together that would indicate otherwise. Hadn't noticed anyone near the bags. Even if the trip was a business meeting, why was Nolan killed? What relation, if any, could he have? Or was he just an innocent bystander who overheard or saw something he shouldn't have?

She felt a tap on the back of her hand. Tyson leaned forward, peering into her eyes. "Earth to Angie."

She managed a grin. "So, what kind of questions did Jarvis ask you? He literally badgered me. I almost started to feel like Nolan's killer."

"Usual stuff, I guess. Mostly he wanted to know what happened on the boat. Did I see anything, things like that."

"Did you see anything?"

"Sure." He let the statement lie while chewing and swallowing a mouthful of sandwich. "Nothing to do with the murder."

"How do you know?"

"Because I didn't see anyone but you and the big black guy go up front."

"You don't think either of us did it?"

"Not really." He shrugged and took another bite.

"Who do you suspect?"

"Valerie. Who else?"

They finished the rest of their meal in relative silence. Angie's thoughts went back to Tyson's duffel bag. Maybe he belonged to a club, like the Red Hat Society or the Boy Scouts. The Black Duffel Bag Gang. Instead of red hats or badges, each member had a black vinyl bag.

"Will you stop that scratching!" Tyson said, "People will think you've got lice."

"I've never worn a wig before. Darned thing itches like crazy."

Tyson pushed away his empty plate. "Dessert?"

"No, thanks."

"Come on, live dangerously."

Living dangerously was exactly what she'd been doing—was about to do. She said, "All right" for one reason only: to buy time.

Tyson ordered two slices of cheesecake and strawberries.

Angie got up. "Do you know where the ladies room is? Never mind, I see it. Be right back."

She went down a different hallway from the other night, walked past the restroom door and ducked into the shining kitchen, creeping along so the cook wouldn't spot her. Angie slipped out the back door and ran to Tyson's car. The side window of the Jag was part way down. She wedged her arm through the very narrow opening. With some effort, she got her fingers around the tiny lock button. As soon as she pulled up on the thing, the car alarm sounded nearly jolting her out of her shoes. Beep beep beep.

Now everyone and their brother would come running. Angie would not be thwarted. Not when she was so close. She opened the door, hit the trunk button and flew around back. She wrenched open the lid, the insistent beeping ringing in her ears. Any second someone would come.

She grabbed the bag and flung it into the bushes at the edge of the lot. It landed with a whoosh and a thud about five feet in. No branches broke. No open space marked the location. She slammed the trunk and sprinted back into the kitchen.

In the hallway, Angie took a second to get her breath. She could barely hear the alarm. Several people made their way out the restaurant's front door, including Tyson.

He spotted her walking down the hallway and raised a finger. "Be right back. Someone's car alarm is going off."

On quaking legs, she went back to the table. The hands that gripped the glass trembled too. She put down the tea, sucked in a breath and held it, waiting for her heartbeat to slow, her breathing to return to normal. Where had this brazen behavior come from?

Where? What a dumb question. That bag left no doubt of Tyson's involvement with Sonnie and Montez, and maybe Nolan too. Tyson was a potential murderer. And she was having lunch with him. Big deal. They weren't alone. No way he could do anything with people around.

When he realized the bag was missing, would he realize she took it? She'd made no secret of her obsession with the damned things. She drained her glass, thinking as she put it on the table about all that caffeine, not good when she needed to remain calm.

Tyson and the other patrons returned. He had his cell phone to his ear. Angie focused her ears in his direction, trying to hear, but all she got was, "Okay, talk to you later." Tyson slid onto his chair and put the phone on the table just as the waitress brought two gigantic desserts.

"Good grief," Angie remarked to the waitress, "why didn't you say they were so big?"

The waitress gave a sly grin, and left.

"Who were you talking to on the phone?"

"My mother. She called the house a bunch of times and I didn't answer. Finally lowered herself to call my cell. She hates modern technology."

Angie dug into her dessert. Cheesecake, the last thing she wanted, but she had to do something to keep Tyson's suspicions at bay. "Find out what the alarm was all about?"

He nodded and finished chewing before answering. "It was my car. Someone must've bumped it or something. Those alarms are really sensitive."

"I assume everything was all right."

"I'd left the window down a little." He shrugged. "The stereo is still there. And the phone." He tapped the phone in front of him. "I'd left it on the seat. Oh well, no harm done. Except to my adrenaline."

"Well, relax and eat your dessert. Goodness, this thing is big."

A half hour later, Tyson and Angie stood between their cars. Angie couldn't help glancing at the shrubbery where she'd tossed the bag. Things looked undisturbed.

"How can you stand this humidity?" Tyson asked, wiping his forehead with a handkerchief.

Angie laughed. "I've been to Manhattan, the humidity's worse there."

"I know."

"Where do you hang out when you're there?"

"The theater mostly." Then he added, "We have homes in Virginia Beach and Paris, too."

"Figures."

"I guess," was all he said. He put a hand on her arm. "Are you all right? All afternoon you've looked like you were about to pass out or something."

Angie forced a laugh. "I haven't been sleeping much."

"Probably not eating either."

She jingled her keys in the air. "I think I'll go back to the motel and get some rest." She unlocked her puke green car door. "Well, thanks for lunch. It was delicious. I'm stuffed like a holiday turkey."

"You're welcome. Climb in, I'll follow you back to town."

"That's not necessary. I've got to pick up a couple of things at the supermarket."

"You can do that back in town."

"I can't be seen in Alton Bay."

"No one's going to recognize you in that get-up."

"Will recognized me in the last one."

"All right then," Tyson said. "I'll go to the store with you, then follow you home."

Angie climbed in the car wondering how to get rid of him so she could retrieve the bag from the bushes. All she needed was a few seconds, a few miserable seconds. Was that so much to ask?

Tyson turned off the alarm and opened the door of the Jag.

"Are you coming?"

"It's not really necessary."

He gave her a look that made her think he would force her in if she didn't move. So she did. Angie put the rental in gear. Tyson eased onto the street, hanging right on her bumper.

Why was he acting so gallant? Maybe he really was worried about her wellbeing. Then again, maybe he wanted her around in case she uncovered a juicy clue. Or maybe he wanted to keep an eye on her.

Did Tyson think she was a member of the Black Bag Gang? Could be this group was so elite that, except for their partners, the members didn't know each other.

Which brought her back to wondering what was in the bags. She'd been so close to knowing, and would know, providing no one found the thing and took it before she returned. Once Tyson got to his destination and realized the bag went missing, would he immediately think of his car alarm and—wait a minute—if that bag was so valuable, why hadn't he checked the trunk when he went outdoors?

Maybe he had. Of course, he couldn't let on to her. What would he say? I had this bag of contraband in my trunk, and it's gone. That could explain the phone call. He'd called reinforcements to come look for it.

Angie maneuvered through the sparse traffic toward the supermarket. That had to be the answer. Tyson had wanted her off the restaurant premises. With that in mind, should she try and ditch him or just wait till his cohorts searched near the restaurant? That couldn't take very long. They'd be sure to find the bag in the bushes.

Angie steered into the parking lot and wiped her suddenly-sweaty palms on the upholstery one at a time while trying to find a parking place that didn't have an empty one next to it. If Tyson couldn't park next to her, maybe she'd have a better chance for a getaway when they came out of the store.

They went into the store together, like a happy couple out to pick up a few things. Angie took a basket and piled fruit into it, two apples, three bananas and an orange. In the juice section, she laid a quart of orange juice on top of the fruit.

Tyson took the basket from her and rearranged things. "You're going to squash the fruit."

Angie continued on to the deli where she asked the man for a quarter pound of smoked turkey.

"I'll have the same," came a familiar voice from her right.

Forty-One

Angie peeked around Tyson to see Wallace gazing into the glassed case. He didn't act like he'd recognized her.

Tyson dragged her into the bread aisle. "What's your husband doing here?"

"That's not Will." The deli man interrupted by calling, "Ma'am, you forgot your meat."

Angie nudged Tyson to go get it. This left a perfect opportunity for a getaway. She spun around and ran smack into a woman with a cart full of groceries. Its unyielding weight rammed Angie in the stomach. "Gosh, I'm sorry," said the pudgy young woman. "Tom's always telling me to look where I'm going."

"Not your fault." Angie stepped around the cart, this time bumping into something tall, and male.

Tyson grasped her elbow and hurried her toward the quick checkout line. "What the hell's Will doing here?"

"That's not Will, it's his brother. Do you think he recognized me?"

"I don't think so. What difference does it make?"

"None, I guess. Let's get out of here."

Outdoors, the sky had clouded over, a slight wind erased some of the intense July heat. Tyson put her groceries in her back seat. "Thanks for—"

"Don't turn around. He's standing out front of the building."

Angie stole a peek over her shoulder anyway. Wallace, with

a twelve-pack of beer dangling from his right hand, stood under the supermarket overhang. He scanned the parking lot.

"He's looking for me."

"Maybe he just forgot where he left his car."

She climbed into the Ford. While Tyson sprinted to his Jag, she watched her brother-in-law in the rear view mirror. He stepped away from the store and walked down the center lane of the parking lot, in Angie's general direction. Not moving fast, just a regular step, but what made her fingers develop instant frostbite—he stared straight at her. She clenched her hands into fists to thwart the terrible cold and swiveled on the seat for a better view. Beyond the red Subaru parked behind her, she could see that Wallace definitely approached. And he most definitely glared right at her. Damn, last thing she wanted was a confrontation with him.

Angie started the car. She slipped the shift lever into Drive and pushed on the gas pedal. Then jammed on the brakes. A woman in a LandRover stopped in front of her waiting for another car to pull out. Angie put a stranglehold on the steering wheel and readied her leg muscles for movement to the accelerator.

Wallace stood behind the Subaru. He stepped between the vehicles. She had an unobstructed view of Will's blue plaid shirt in the rear view mirror. Why couldn't that ass wear his own clothes?

Then he stood right behind her car. His mouth pinched into scowl; his eyes squinted almost shut with undisguised hatred. Hatred? What was his problem?

Then she knew. He'd seen Tyson, thought they were together. Of course, in Wallace's eyes it would be okay for Will to cheat, but not for her to do likewise. Then again, it couldn't have anything to do with her clobbering him with a candlestick.

"Move!" she shouted at the LandRover. Frantically Angie waved at the lady and mouthed *move!* The woman smiled and shrugged, and inched—inched—the vehicle ahead.

No room to get past.

Wallace vanished out of the rear view's line of sight. Angie ducked her head to look in the side mirror. But she didn't need the mirror any more; he towered beside her door. She punched down the lock button. Adrenaline felt like lava gushing through her veins. Lay on the horn, get Tyson's attention. Not yet, you have to escape from them both.

Wallace's face appeared in the window. "Open! I want to talk to you."

Every hair on her body stood up. She shook her head no.

His face was obliterated by his big palm slamming on the glass. "Open the door." The hand disappeared. He stepped back. In the mirror she saw him take hold of the rear door handle. God, it was unlocked. And opening!

Angie gunned the car forward and cut the wheel hard to the right. Metal ground on metal as her bumper slammed into the rear quarter of the LandRover. Angie kept her foot on the gas, the momentum shoving the obstruction out of the way. The Ford lurched free, taking part of the white car with it. Wallace howled as the door wrenched out of his hand. The last thing Angie saw in the mirror was a gusher of beer as cans bounced like beach balls on the pavement.

The Ford bounded into traffic, the open-door sound pinging insistently. Tyson pulled up behind, tapping the steering wheel to a rapid-fire music beat. She put the car in Park, got out and made sure the back doors were both shut and locked. Tyson stopped tapping his fingers long enough to wiggle them at her. She waved back as she glanced everywhere for Wallace. No doubt he was here somewhere because the hairs on her body still stood at attention. God, she hated this.

Traffic finally got moving. Looked like she'd disposed of Wallace, but what about Tyson? WG's was only three blocks away. How to ditch the man in that short distance? A light rain dotted the windshield. The sky had turned a somber slate gray that matched her mood exactly. Wind beat the surrounding trees. Like a crowd at a ball game doing the wave, the maples flipped up their pale green undersides and then flapped them back down. Then came the downpour.

A half-block from the restaurant, the rain became so heavy that, at top speed, her wipers couldn't clear a space for her to see. Even at a crawl, Angie couldn't see more than shadows. And if she thought seeing forward was a problem, seeing behind was even more hopeless. She should turn off and wait for the torrent to stop; it was ludicrous to take a chance of crashing. Then she'd be at both their mercies.

She didn't bother signaling before turning into the restaurant lot and stopping not far from where she and Tyson had parked less than an hour ago. Rain hammered the roof, sounding like a tunnel. Surely any second Tyson would pull up beside her and… what would he do? They were at a place he felt comfortable, would be protected. Perhaps she should try and head back to Alton Bay; come back for the bag another time. Angie eased the car closer to the woods. Maybe Tyson's cohorts found it already. If they had, they'd know she'd be back. Probably waiting.

How much worse could it be? They could only torture and kill her once. Angie shivered, took a steadying breath, got out and ran to where she'd seen the bag land. Bullets of rain beat her. Two feet from the car she was drenched. She used her forearms to move the branches and push into the overgrowth. She had to double over to see through the shadows. Wet leaves, soggy trash, an old boot.

Gone! Damn!

Angie thrust aside more branches just in case she'd mistaken the exact spot. Nothing. Nothing but wet leaves, wet branches and wet Angie. She kicked at a lump of something wrapped in black plastic and her fingers twitched. For only a moment. It wasn't a duffel bag. Her sodden brain envisioned body parts—hers.

She turned back to the car.

Soaking wet upholstery, just one more thing to explain to the car rental agent. Not to mention the crunched bumper. Angie had no idea how bad it was, but since part of the LandRover tore off, the damage to her car must be considerable. She wondered if the rental place had a black list. For some reason, this notion struck her as funny. She couldn't stop laughing. Angie laughed so hard rain dribbled in her mouth. The sensation felt cool and clean.

She took a step. And fell flat on her face, air driven out of her lungs by the impact. She got to her knees, mentally examining body parts for injury as the rain pounded her backside. Nothing hurt but her pride. She peeked through the branches. No sign of Tyson or Wallace. Sure, Tyson had received a phone call saying they'd found it. There was no more need for him to baby-sit her.

Angie stood up and tested her limbs for injury. Everything okay, she started back to the car. That's when she realized what she'd tripped over. Not an old tire. Not rubbish. The bag. Clear as day. Lit up like a full-moon sky. Not really, but it seemed that way. Providence had finally shone on her.

Even in her rush to get back to the car, she couldn't help testing the bag's heft, trying to ascertain the contents. She opened the door and pushed the bag onto the passenger floor, wedging it between seat and dash. No jacket, nothing to throw over it, to hide it from prying eyes.

The rain still beat an interminable cadence. The damned wig weighed a hundred pounds. The long hair tangled under her arms; every time she turned the steering wheel she felt a tug on the wig. No matter. The only one likely to see her now was Tyson and he'd only be concerned with the bag. She heaved the wig atop the duffel bag.

At five miles an hour, the drive back to Alton Bay seemed endless, but the simple fact she moved closer improved her mood. The more distance she put between herself and that restaurant, the better. It didn't do any good to look for a tail, the rain still pounded with a ferocity she'd felt too often of late. The rear window an ethereal sheet through which everything appeared ghostlike and spooky. The wick-wick of the wipers overrode even the music on the radio that Angie realized remained tuned to

Val's favorite heavy metal station.

The sign for Alton Bay loomed ahead. Instead of a blur of black on white, she could actually read it; the rain abated. Too bad really, the storm had lent a measure of invisibility. The comforting thought whooshed like dishwater down a drain when Wallace's Saab appeared in her side window. He traveled well over the speed limit. How could he go so fast in this weather? Maybe with the downpour, he hadn't seen her, just in a hurry to get home.

As if in response, the Saab swerved toward her. Angie slammed on her brakes and veered right. Too late. His passenger door struck the front fender of the Ford. Angie's head rammed into the window as the car swung in a circle. Then it stopped. Fear shoved off dizziness and she twisted the key. Start damn car, won't you start! Please? Wallace's car had stopped in front of hers. He wasn't inside.

Her window exploded, the shards tumbled on her. Start car. Please! A hand clamped on her shoulder. Fingers gouged her flesh. "I'll teach you to cheat on my brother!"

The Ford's motor sputtered and then caught. She slammed the shift lever into Reverse and stomped the accelerator. The car backed up. The Saab came too, stuck somehow to hers. She stomped harder, the tires spun in the sopping gravel. With a crunch and thud the Saab popped loose. She was moving! Wallace let out a sound like an angry dog.

Angie forced the car up to 60. With poor visibility, she leaned forward squinting for glimpses of the yellow centerline. A hundred feet from the motel, she pulled into a driveway. Within ten seconds, Wallace flew past. She waited to be sure he hadn't seen her, then pulled out and headed straight to the rental agent and dropped off the car. Back in her precious Lexus, she laughed all the way back to the motel. That poor agent. She knew without a doubt, he never wanted to lay eyes on her again. She parked under some ancient pines between the motel owners' vehicles, took the wig, shopping bags and duffel bag from the trunk and ran.

She reached around the doorframe and flicked on the lights.

Nobody in sight. That didn't mean nobody hid in the closet or the bathroom. Stop being so melodramatic and go in, she ordered herself.

Angie stepped inside, she put down her things and did a thorough check, leaving all the lights on as she went. She slid the chain in the slot on the doorframe, made sure to yank the drapes shut tight and somehow kept herself from going outside to double check that no light or shadows showed through.

A hulking object on the low-pile carpet the black bag seemed to grow bigger by the second. Suddenly afraid to know its contents, she used every delay tactic she could think of. She kicked off her shoes and put them in the bathroom; water actually ran out when she turned them upside down in the sink. She picked up the grocery bags and laid them on the dresser. She unpacked them. She set her purse on the table, hung the wig in the bathroom, removed all her clothes and took the hottest shower her flesh could stand.

After toweling off, Angie walked naked into the bedroom, and stopped. The bag had grown eyes. All of a sudden she felt more naked than the time a group of boys had burst into the high school locker room.

She seized clothes from the drawer and ran in the bathroom to dress. Pulling up the sweat pants, Angie began to feel ridiculous. What was there to be frightened of?

Because knowing the contents would get her killed.

So what? Nobody would believe she hadn't already looked inside.

Angie peeked around the doorframe. The bag still squatted there, mocking her.

With a shout of confidence, she stalked to the bag. She stood over it, bare feet just inches to either side, daring the contents to taunt her while standing so close. As if in response, the air grew heavy with challenge.

"I'll show you," she said, but didn't move for several more seconds.

Forcing thoughts of death and dismemberment from her mind, Angie bent and touched sweaty fingers to the handles. No shock waves. No colorful emanations. No—

She picked up the bag; the contents felt more soft than solid, although there was a heft to it—maybe ten or twelve pounds. She put it on the spare bed.

Black. Zipper closure. Vinyl handles. Plastic clips where a shoulder strap could be attached. She parted the handles, baring the wide plastic zipper, grabbed the pull-tab and slid it back.

Forty-Two

The only sound, the gentle wick wick as the zipper edges separated. Angie's knees had turned to jelly but, acknowledging the possible need to spring away quickly, she didn't sit. Thumbs and index fingers pried the zipper apart. Dark inside.

Very dark.

The seconds crawled past as a visible entity—like sheep over an insomniac's fence—while her eyes adjusted to the dimness. Enough to see a piece of dark colored cloth—black or navy blue. The whole thing was about the size of a rolled up bathrobe.

No amount of wiping would dry her palms, so she gave up. And reached in.

She heard the sound of the explosion. Felt the pressure both inside her head and as her brains burst against the walls. Sensed the fingers disintegrate inside the bag which, in her imagination, was undamaged by the blast. It sat on the bed, as it did this moment, a gaping ravine of mystery. A vast cavity of intrigue. Her nemesis.

An imagined nemesis.

She waited till her breathing returned to relative normalcy, and gave a slight squeeze of the material, compressing a mere inch or so. The fabric felt soft and malleable, and thick. Angie took hold with both hands. And eased the bulk between the zipper edges using gentle pressure first on one side, then the other, keeping movements to the barest minimum and her eyes squinted almost shut. Not that it would help if the thing exploded in her face.

She laid the object on the bed and stepped back. Navy blue cloth. Sweatshirt-type material. About fourteen inches long, ten inches wide and ten inches thick.

She poked a finger into it. Soft. No resistance. Curiosity killed the cat. And the Angie.

She inhaled, then exhaled till her lungs emptied. With two fingertips, she lifted a corner. And pulled back another corner, then another. The room was so quiet she thought she heard the ticking of her watch on the dresser. At last, the material was spread wide. Bewilderment radiated as she stared down at white block lettering: Property of Notre Dame. Angie gave a sigh of exasperation, and held the thing in the air: a sweatshirt, long sleeved, hooded, good condition.

The sweatshirt hadn't been wrapped around a kilo of heroine or a bundle of forged credit cards. It didn't contain severed body parts. Stupid. Dumb ass. Fool. She lay the shirt down and shook her head as the self-chastisement emoted to logic.

Decoy. The sweatshirt was a decoy. If she were moving contraband, she'd surely hide it from prying eyes using an everyday item as a decoy. Determination pushed out a small bit of trepidation. She reached in again. The zipper scratched her forearms, an agreeable abrasion in a disagreeable situation.

If something moved, how quickly could she pull back? Groping fingertips grazed another piece of cloth; soft and cottony, like the sweatshirt. Another decoy. She started to remove it, had actually raised it an inch or so when she let go.

There was something different about this bundle. It was more solid. Not brick-solid. More like ground-meat solid; too large to remove with one hand. If she had any hands left by the time this was over.

The phone on the table between the beds rang. Angie jumped, dropping the package. She scrunched her eyes shut and tensed. Nothing happened. Nothing but the insistent jangle of the phone. Who could be calling, not using her cell? The cell! She'd shut it off so it wouldn't interfere while she sneaked around WG's. She'd

forgot to turn it back on. Angie took a breath before answering.
At the sound of Val's frantic voice, the nerves she'd been
keeping at bay over the last three hours, surfaced. She shivered.
Not a cold-weather sort of shiver. This started deep inside and
rumbled to the surface, spreading down her limbs and into finger-
and toe-nails. "Val, what's wrong?"

"Where have you been? I've been calling forever."

"I'm sorry, hon, I had to shut my phone off. Forgot to turn
it back on. Listen, there's—" Angie cut herself off. She'd been
about to invite Val over to watch the unveiling, but if something
happened, it was best it happened to just one of them. "I had a
very revealing lunch with Tyson. Look Val, can I call you back in
a few minutes? I'm sort of in the middle of something."

"You're not doing anything stupid, are you? Anything
dangerous."

"Would I do anything dangerous? I'll call you right back."
She set the receiver into the cradle then turned on the cell phone.
The whole time, she hadn't taken her eyes from Tyson's bag. Just
do it. No more delays.

She reached in, took a breath, lifted the bundle. It weighed
about two pounds. She laid it on the bed. More cloth. Navy blue
and white in color. The blue, a heavy material, the same as the
sweatshirt. The white, lighter in weight, and shocking in its
whiteness. She palpated the material, firm on the side nearest
her, a bit more solid on the side facing the wall. She pried back
the folds one at a time.

As expected, the blue fabric was sweatpants, the mate to the
shirt. The white, a t-shirt—white. They'd been rolled around a
package that was itself wrapped in something that looked like
a towel.

Angie took three steadying breaths and unfolded the
terrycloth. She blinked in anticipation, then again in astonishment,
and sank into the nearest chair.

"You idiot!" she shouted at the bundle. "You frigging, stupid idiot." This time she waved her arms like flags in a hurricane. "You moron, you suspicious fool."

Angie's arm motions nearly knocked the telephone on the floor. She caught it and replaced it, then fell on the opposite bed, unable to take her eyes from the bag's contents. Contraband. Cash. Drugs. Jewels. Pornography. Securities. Credit cards. Computer programs. Bank records. Body Parts. All the things she'd imagined inside.

None of them.

Suddenly Angie laughed; arms wrapped around herself and rocking back and forth on the edge of the bed. Tears ran down her cheeks and she swiped them away with the back of her hand.

Tyson's duffel bag, which he'd put in his trunk as though it held the secret to breaking into Fort Knox, held nothing more than gym clothes, and a worn pair of Converse running shoes.

She'd spent the entire day chasing after Tyson's laundry. How ridiculous was that?

The next thought sobered her completely. Tyson's cohorts were figments of her imagination. Tyson's participation in the Black Bag Gang, imagined. His devoted attention had been out of concern for her welfare.

Something didn't feel right. The exact cause an illusive entity. But something definitely was wrong. She slid off the bed, and dropped to her knees before Tyson's belongings, each item separate and lying flat on the spread. The bag tipped on its side, its mouth gaping at her like a cave.

What if it wasn't the bag's contents that were important?

She drew the bag near, and tilted her head to peer inside. Too dark. She took it to the other bed, bracing the black vinyl between her knees. She eased her hands inside, then sneaked her fingers across seams and over the smooth, flat interior. No bumps, lumps or other obstructions. Nothing glued inside. Maybe something attached to the seams? If she transported something illegal she'd damn sure make it undetectable.

Angie could just about hear Jarvis' voice. "Lady, you watch too much television."

She laid the bag aside, went to the bathroom and dug her manicure scissors from her makeup bag. The blades were only two inches long and not very sharp. Nonetheless, it was all she had.

Angie proceeded to cut along one side seam, through the zipper and one handle-anchor. By the time she got to the end, she had three blisters, one on her right forefinger and two on her thumb. The scissors had been intended to cut things like hair and fingernails, not tough, thick vinyl.

It took almost an hour, but at last the thing lay open in one flat rectangular piece on the bedspread. Angie put the scissors down, digging them out of the grooves they'd made in her fingers.

The cell phone chirped. She jumped and flipped open the phone and said, "Hello" hoping it wasn't Will. "Sorry, Val, I got involved in something. If you're not doing anything, come over."

"Now?"

"Yeah."

Angie put down the phone. She moved the bag onto the side table and turned on the light. Parts of the vinyl flopped over the edge, but the innards remained visible. Nothing appeared out of the ordinary. She leaned in close, eyes and fingers probing every centimeter.

Careful as she was, she couldn't find a single thing out of place. Outside the door, a car pulled up, shut off. A door closed. A knock sounded. "Angie, it's me."

She admitted Val, then without a word dug a bottle of brandy from the suitcase, retrieved the plastic drinking cups from the bathroom and filled them to the top with the aromatic amber liquid. Val took one, her eyes roving between Angie and the mess around the room. Angie sat on the bed, sipping and relating the day's events to the wide-eyed Valerie. All the while, she couldn't stop thinking how she'd made a complete fool of herself.

Or was there something she'd missed? She picked up the

clothes again and squeezed the fabric, inch by inch, being most careful along the seams. The clothes smelled like a combination of Tyson's aftershave and sweat. No lumps, no bumps, no bloodstains, nothing but a wad of gray lint in one pants pocket.

"It's got to be here somewhere," Angie said.

Val, who'd perched on the edge of the chair nearest the door, came and sat gingerly on the bed as Angie began examining the left sneaker. "You have no idea what the it is though, right?"

"Right. At this point, what's left? I know it sounds stupid, but I guess there could be microfilm."

"Or, what do they call 'em, microdots?"

"What size are those anyway?"

"Why you asking me? I take people fishing for a living."

The shoe looked normal. The sole evenly worn. Tyson obviously didn't have any foot problems. No cracks in the heel where something might have been stored. She undid the laces and removed them, then pulled the tongues out as far as they'd go. Holding each one under the lamp, Angie held her breath and peered inside. Reluctance to put her hand inside someone else's shoe only fleeting; the desire to get to the bottom of the situation propelled her on.

"Another question," Val said. "What makes you think Tyson's involved? Just because he put a bag in his trunk?"

After the first shoe, Angie's drive abated, and began to feel more like a wild goose chase. She wondered where that saying had originated. Who'd want to chase a wild goose anyway? Why not just shoot it?

"I guess I forgot to tell you a piece of news he volunteered over lunch. His father owns WG's."

Val's high-pitched "Woo wee" made Angie grin. Feeling mildly revived, she jabbed her hand inside the second shoe, using her fingers to probe every centimeter. As with the bag, clothes and first shoe, nothing where it shouldn't be.

She heaved the shoe beside the other. The day had been a total waste. "Damn."

"So, tell me how you got in Tyson's car. I'd think he'd have an alarm."

For the first time in a while, Angie had reason to laugh. "He does. It went off as I opened the door to reach the trunk button."

But Val didn't laugh. "You did that even after you knew Tyson's dad owned the place? Shit, you could have been killed."

"Sure, by the imaginary Black Bag Gang."

"I believe they exist."

"I'm not so sure now."

"There's no way Montez and Sonnie brought their laundry fishing. You went overboard with Tyson's stuff, that's all. Or maybe it was a decoy."

"Or maybe we're imagining everything."

"Maybe not. How much would you say Tyson's bag weighed?"

"About ten pounds."

"Well, that's just about the weight of Montez's."

"You've held it?"

"Last year, I moved one out of the way when we were landing a forty-pound salmon. I'm sure his bag weighed that much."

Forty-Three

At Val's declaration, Angie shut her eyes and leaned back on the pillow. For the longest time there was absolute silence; no automobiles whooshed past, not even the tick of a clock or the drip of a faucet was heard. She must've fallen asleep because she suddenly jerked awake. Val had turned on the television. Seeing Angie she apologized. "Sorry, I got bored watching you sleep."

For a moment Angie felt disoriented, but the sight of Tyson's belongings heaped on the table, brought it all back. She pulled a pillow over her head, and forced thoughts of murder and mayhem from her brain. Empty of all Val's problems there was nothing to prevent thoughts of Will and marriage and infidelity from squeaking in, and she jerked fully awake. She sat up, clutching the bedclothes to her chin, feeling barren and morose, and scrunching her eyes to keep the tears at bay.

"What's the matter?"

"Today's my twenty-sixth wedding anniversary."

"Should I say congratulations?"

"No." Was it still an anniversary if the parties separated? Maybe if they weren't together it didn't count. If they got back together, they could start counting all over again, delete the previous week from the calendar and begin again.

If they got back together.

So far, Will had shown plenty of willingness to let the past be the past. She was the holdout, unsure about trust and fidelity, and life in general. Had her life been a waste? Don't go there.

Just don't go there.

She turned, stretching her neck and back muscles to check the digital clock on the table between the beds—8:22. The protesting muscles reminded her of how lax she'd been in getting to the gym. She hadn't even brought gym clothes. Thoughts of sweat pants brought her mind to Tyson's gym things. Wouldn't he be surprised when he found them missing from his trunk! Maybe she should report it to Jarvis. They could laugh about her escapades.

Angie really needed to talk to him. Maybe there was a break in the case. Without Jarvis, how else could she get information? So far she'd made a damned bad detective, managing to get Val kidnapped, and uncovering no useful information. Why not give up? Go back to work. Go back to Will. Resume the routine life.

Routine. That was what had been bothering her. Angie had been bored silly with her life, and bet it had been the same with Will. That's why he'd cheated. Not because of anything specific she'd done, or not done. In twenty-six years of marriage, routine had taken over. The flash and glitz they'd had in the early years had dissolved into what a lot of folks called life. Was it possible to recreate the early passion, resurrect what was in shambles? She supposed it was, and maybe she would think more about it—later.

Right now, she had to clear Val, and help her make a life for herself. Go partners in the catering business. That would provide a change of scenery, new friends, different situations. Maybe that was all both of them really needed.

"Let's get something to eat," Angie suggested.

"You sure we should go out?"

"No, but I can't stay in this room any longer." Angie went to the bathroom, instant hair color in hand. As she lathered the darker shade into the wig, she wondered what more she could do to find Nolan's killer. "Or maybe we could go to Nashua," she called.

"What for?"

Montez would be surprised to see them. What would they use as an excuse for going there? To buy a computer? The cops had confiscated both hers and Val's when they'd raided the place. These days, everyone needed a computer. What other reason could they have, that wouldn't make him instantly suspicious?

"What for?" Val repeated.

"I was trying to think of a reason to question Montez again. I'm sure he knows a lot more than he said."

Val's head poked around the bathroom door. "Besides, he makes you hot," she said before ducking out.

"He does not!"

Val laughed. "Maybe he's part of the reason you're reluctant to go back to Will."

"What the hell are you talking about?" Angie protested, instantly remembering the scorch of his hands on her flesh as he'd removed her clothes.

"Don't go all defensive, you're probably not even aware of it. But there's something going on between you."

A familiar and unrequited sensation surged through her. As she rinsed the long flowing wig, she clenched her thighs tight, but it did little to squelch the urges that were increasing to near-emergency status. Sex. An undeniable attraction. Truth be told, Montez's touch sparked a yearning she hadn't felt in years. When Montez was around, her flesh tingled and her insides burned—cliché yes, but true nonetheless. Thoughts of his smooth skin, glossy with a sheen of sweat, his strong tight shoulders and thick sensuous lips sent her scurrying into the shower. He hadn't tried to hide his attraction to her. He'd just had more willpower. His ego would accept her returning for satisfaction.

Finally, the wig dried and she settled it on her head. Uncomfortable, but she had to admire the way she looked with dark hair. When this was all over, maybe she'd grow out her own and darken the color. Angie donned a set of the clothes she'd bought at the thrift shop and they walked to Shipley's to try out their disguises.

The storm clouds still hovered, blocking out the moon and stars. They took a booth near the middle of the restaurant, watching for signs of recognition from anyone. The waiter, who'd served her many times in the past, showed no reaction at all. Angie and Val each ordered a chocolate martini and a steak. Halfway through the meal, the disguises had real tests when Wallace came in. What was he doing here? Angie had never known him to go to a restaurant. Anger flared. He probably spent her and Will's money. She wanted to fling herself at him and gouge out his eyes for the havoc he'd wreaked on her life.

"What's the matter?" Val whispered.

"Don't turn around but Wallace just came in."

He blinked a few times, getting used to the change in lighting. Angie clamped her suddenly-tense knuckles around the stem of the glass. In his normal attire—Will's jeans and blue Izod shirt—Wallace stepped closer.

She took a breath and glanced at her hands, still folded around the glass, almost forgetting her resolve to test her disguise. She'd never get to the bottom of this if she couldn't face a simple obstacle like Wallace Deacon. She forced her fingers loose. As he reached the table, Angie lifted her face and gazed directly into his eyes, willing him to know her, welcoming the forthcoming confrontation.

Her toes curled in her shoes as he passed without reacting. At first she felt satisfied. Then she realized: he'd followed her here, just like he'd followed her to the supermarket.

Stop it! He wasn't following her. Just like Tyson wasn't a member of the Black Bag Gang. Wallace was a thief and a no-good listless slob who'd driven her and Will into potential bankruptcy, but nothing more sinister than that.

Angie and Val left the restaurant, intending to pick up her car for the trip to Nashua. She found a note pinned to the door. *Message at office.* Angie handed Val the key. "I'll be right back." Val went inside. Angie had taken four steps toward the office when a large hand clamped on her shoulder. In a reflexive reaction, the free hand shaped into a fist. She spun around, pushing the fist upward, making contact with a face. Angie jammed her elbow into the ribcage and drove her body backward. The attacker reeled, his hands dropped away.

Angie dug her feet into the unyielding sidewalk at the front of the long row of motel rooms and ran. Right behind her, his shoes slapping, hands fumbling, almost snagging her shirt. The fingers did make contact with the wig and jerked it out of place. She flew into the motel office.

The clerk looked up and smiled, as though disheveled women appeared in his place every day. "Good evening."

"Call the police!"

The clerk just sat there as though she spoke some foreign language. The door flung open and slammed off the wall. Angie shrieked. The clerk picked up the receiver.

Montez's bulk blocked out the light for a second before he crossed the room and wrenched the phone from the man's hand. "We don't need the police. I just want to talk to the lady." He replaced the phone in the cradle and patted it with a giant paw as if telling it to stay put.

Angie's urge to see him had faded as she backed against the wall, clutching her room key in both hands like a cross to ward off vampires. Montez took her arm and led her to a pair of chairs in the miniscule waiting area, his dark eyes on the clerk. "I just want to talk to her."

She nodded to the clerk and allowed Montez to seat her in the chair nearest the door.

The man's eyes flashed toward the phone but he didn't touch it. He did sit and keep his eyes on them. Even when the phone rang, he groped at it without moving his gaze from Montez, and spoke to the person on the other end in monotones—telling them sure they could reserve a room for two nights.

Montez dragged the other chair and sat so close his arm touched hers, making the little hairs all stand on end. She resisted the urge to rub them down and moved her elbow to the back of the chair arm, as far away as she could get. She stared down at the key in her hand, running her index finger along the rough ridges. Montez reached over and tried to take it but she shoved it in her pocket.

"What's with the disguise?"

"How did you see through it?"

He laughed. "You cannot disguise that body." He moved his arm along hers again. "Now tell me what's going on."

She looked at him for the first time. His brows furrowed with concern. He put his hand on hers, hiding it from view. Her fingers tightened involuntarily around the chair arm. Montez laughed, low and sensuous. In the too-small seat, he stretched his legs in front of him; long, lean legs clad in tan Levis. No socks. Penny loafers without pennies. There came that all-too-familiar twitch in her groin.

She gripped her buttocks together and pulled her feet tight under the chair. The motion didn't begin to quench the thirst that continued to build inside her. She felt his knowing gaze and went back to looking at her knotted fingers. "You could tell me what you're doing here."

"So, you want to play it that way, huh?" He dropped his hand to his lap and crossed his legs. Long powerful legs that could wrap around a person and— "I had to deliver some computers to the marina. I was on my way into the restaurant when I saw you come out." He chuckled. "You aren't much of a detective. You should've seen me following."

"What are you doing in town?"

"What's got you so spooked you need a disguise?"

She shook her head, not trusting herself to speak. He laid the tips of two fingers on her arm. Juicy tremors went straight to the pit of her stomach. "Come on, let's go somewhere we can talk in private." He gave an exaggerated glance at the clerk, who still watched his every move.

Angie stood up and told the clerk, "We'll just be outside in the car. Please keep an eye out." Montez held the door for her to pass and shut it behind them. "I should tell Val where I am."

"You'll only be a minute."

At his car he helped her into the passenger seat. He shut the door but as he crossed in front of the vehicle, she opened it again, and left it that way. "Don't trust me?"

Angie ignored the humor and intentional innuendo in his words. The car sank under his weight when he lowered himself into the drivers' side and turned sideways on the seat. "Now tell me what's going on."

"I can't."

"Because?"

Angie didn't say anything.

"You're the woman they chased from WG's the other night."

Try as she might, she couldn't keep the surprise from her face. She put one foot out on the ground.

"Don't leave. I'm not going to hurt you. I want you to know I'm out of it. For good. When they killed Sonnie, I realized— Shit, yeah, even a big slob like me gets scared. I realized what was at stake."

"Why *did* they kill Sonnie?"

"Because we missed the shipment."

"They think you sold to the highest bidder, something like that?"

"Something like that."

"Are you going to tell me what's in the bags?"

"No. I'm in enough danger talking about 'em."

"Why not go to the police?"

He gave her a *you're kidding,* look. Angie shivered and clenched her arms around herself.

"You're right to be scared. Maybe it'll keep you from doing something else stupid."

Angie took a breath and asked the question to end them all. "Who killed Nolan?"

"Don't know. Wasn't me. We carried the bags, that's all. I

know you probably won't believe it, but I quit right after they killed him."

"They let you quit, just like that?"

Montez's laugh held all the scorn and pain of the past week. "No leaving once you're in. I been hiding out."

"What're you doing back here? Seems like you should be a million miles away by now."

"I have something to do first."

"Let me guess. You want to shut them down?"

Montez didn't reply, nor did he react to the question. He was beginning to remind her of that irritating Detective Jarvis. She pulled her leg back in the car and turned on the seat to point a finger at him. "You're Jarvis's mystery informant, aren't you?"

"He told you he had an informant?"

"He reacted the same way as you when I brought up the idea of one. Does he know you're in town?"

"He knows I'm around."

"Does he know WG's is the meeting place?" Montez couldn't disguise his shock. Angie shrugged as though it was all in a day's work. "The night of Nolan's murder, where did you and Sonnie go in that boat?"

He shook his head, surprised again. "Back to the island. Somebody dropped the bags overboard. How'd you find out about that?"

"A witness saw you sneaking down the dock." Maybe she wasn't such a bad detective after all.

He flexed his hands. "The bags were gone."

"So, what happens now?"

"I was in the middle of something when I spotted you. I'm going back to finish up."

"Need help?"

Montez shook his head. "Definitely not. It's too dangerous."

"Do they know what you're up to?" Montez didn't answer. Angie's fingers gave an involuntary twitch in her lap. "Well, do you want to tell me where you'll be in case you don't come back?"

He gave her arm a little nudge. "I'll be back in a few hours. I'll come for you and we'll have coffee or something, all right?"

"Okay." She couldn't help wondering what the or something might be.

"Will you do something for me? You and Valerie stay in that room, and no more detective work. Things are getting sticky out there, and I don't mean from the humidity."

"One more question. Why are you doing this?"

"Not sure what you mean."

"You aren't the altruistic type. There's a reason you're working with the cops."

Montez remained silent. Angie finally got out and went to the room. The television blared. Angie grinned, recognizing MTV. She twisted the knob and pushed the door open, intending to ask how the neighbors liked the show. The sight that greeted her made her knees turn to mush. She clutched at the doorframe. Before she reached the ground, Montez moved behind her, helping her up, guiding her to a chair.

On the floor, in front of the television lay Valerie Little. She sprawled partway on her side, legs and arms askew, like a rag doll someone had tossed in a corner. No blood in sight. Angie threw herself on the floor, moving one of Val's arms to make room. She laid the arm across Val's chest and touched two fingers to her carotid just as she'd done several days ago. She found a pulse, weak and thready but there nonetheless.

Montez's feet appeared beside her. He crouched. She saw the phone in his hand; he dialed 9-1-1. "I have an injured woman," he said to whomever answered. He gave the name of the motel and hung up.

Meanwhile, Angie probed the sides and back of Valerie's head and neck. No injury. Val's body arched slightly, and faced Angie. She got up and went around the other side, then lifted Val's clothing at the waist to peer underneath. Blood. Lots of it. Soaking into the carpet.

"Find something?" Montez asked.

She gave a grim nod and turned Val a bit more. Montez put out his hands to keep Val as motionless as possible. There it was, a filet knife, much like the one jammed into Nolan's chest. Tears rolled down Angie's cheeks.

How long she'd applied pressure around the knife, trying to staunch the flow of blood she had no idea. It was a long time though, her wrists ached. Val had lost a lot of blood; her skin now so pale it practically glowed in the rays from the EMT's spotlight. Ambulance attendants inserted IV's, attached tubes, spoke to the hospital. They loaded Val on the stretcher, on her side because the knife still protruded from the middle of her back.

The stretcher legs clicked into place. Her new friend, compatriot, and confidante was leaving. Hopefully it wouldn't be permanent. Tears pricked the backs of Angie's eyelids but none came. Her crying days had been replaced by anger and an equally compelling desire for revenge. Whoever did this would pay.

"How is she?" Angie asked.

"Can't say," the tech said, "We can't examine the wound with the knife in the way but from the location of the knife..." He shook his head and wheeled the stretcher out the door, into the glare of police lights and gawkers.

Angie stood up, her legs like jelly. "I'll go with her."

Jarvis shook his head. "I need to ask you some questions first. I'll drive you over afterward."

"You can ask me the questions over there," Angie argued.

"You're a material witness. I need you here."

"Val shouldn't be alone. And I didn't see anything. I wasn't there."

"I'll go with her," said a familiar voice. Someone stepped up beside her. Arms wrapped around her. She turned and wilted into Will's embrace. He eased her out the door and propped her against the building. "What happened?" She told him how there'd been a message on the door and when she'd come back, Val was lying there.

Will pulled her close and rubbed his hand in circles on her

back the way he always did when she was upset. Her rock. He unwound her arms and eased her back a couple of steps. "The ambulance is leaving. I'll see you at the hospital." Montez appeared at her side. "Buck up, everything will be all right," Will said and vanished around the side of the ambulance, probably headed for his car.

Angie stood there like a statue as the lights and siren came on, and the vehicle sped away. She said a prayer—she hadn't prayed in a very long time. She turned toward Montez and used words Val had said just a few days ago, "It's all my fault."

"It's not your fault." He reached into the room and dragged one of the chairs outside. He set it where the police lights didn't penetrate, between a box van and the building. Then he helped her into it. She bent forward burying her face in her cupped hands.

Montez's voice in her left ear was soft. "It's not your fault. Sometimes life is like this."

"Well, it stinks."

"No shit."

Someone stepped up beside him and he stood. Angie didn't look up. Then his voice came in her ear again. "I'll be right back, we're going to talk to the clerk."

She did look now, watching them walk the narrow paved area that looked like a tiny racetrack. When they disappeared into the red office door, Angie stood up and left. Nobody seemed to notice. Nobody called for her to come back.

She walked down the road and across to the promenade. Deserted, just like the street. She sat on the bench facing the water. Light from the full moon glimmered off the tranquil surface. Val would've commented on its beauty. And it was pretty—barely any clouds in a navy blue sky decorated with at least a zillion sparkling stars.

Angie dropped her face in her hands again. How many more murders would there be before this nightmare was over?

She didn't know how long she sat there. The moon moved far along in the sky, but she had no idea what that signified, and didn't care. Clouds now obliterated most of the sky, the water looked murky and sad. Angie stood up, took a breath and started back to the motel. A determination in her mood echoed in her gait. She would get the bastard who did this. Whether Val lived or died, they would pay—maybe with their own life. First on the agenda: retrieve her car and find another motel.

The parking lot at her old place was still jammed with police vehicles. Official people swarmed the area between the cabin and the vehicles. Most of the sightseers had left. She saw no sign of either Jarvis or Montez. She ducked behind a car to watch, to wait for a chance to get to her car, and the spare keys hidden underneath.

Angie's brain had time to register movement behind her. Before she could fully turn around, a blow to the back of the neck staggered her against the vehicle. The second blow struck her just above the left ear. She slid down the shiny surface and landed in a heap on damp pine needles.

Forty-Four

Montez rounded the motel parking lot again, knowing it was fruitless but having no idea what else to do. How the hell could Angie vanish into thin air—with a hundred people as possible witnesses?

Jarvis came out of her room holding a black garbage-sized bag that looked full. Montez waited till he'd locked it in his Jeep then approached the man. Jarvis started to speak, but the words became a wheeze of surprise when Montez took hold of his pajama lapels and lifted him off his feet. "Why aren't you out there looking for her?"

"I'm head of the Little investigation, it's my job to delegate. Believe me Clarke, there's someone on it." Montez set him on his feet. Jarvis moved quick to step away and issue a threat that it not happen again.

"What are they doing to find her?"

"They're following leads as we speak."

"Look asshole, I'm not one of the cops groupies. I'm not a reporter. I was here." Montez jammed a thumb in his chest for emphasis. "I know damn well there are no clues. So, I want you to tell me what they're doing. Where are they searching?" Montez dropped his hand. Why had he roughed up the cop like that? Probably there'd be an assault charge slapped on him now.

"I promise you, the bastard won't get away with this."

"Damn straight," Montez said, spun on a heel and left.

"Be in my office at nine a.m.," Jarvis called.

As Montez neared his car, he heard a male voice shout, "Jarvis, come here!"

Montez dropped his keys back in his pocket and followed Jarvis's trajectory to a spot under a huge pine beside a white cruiser with a blue stripe. He couldn't see what went on, the area was in deep shadow. Five heads ducked toward something on the ground.

Montez broke into a sprint then pushed through the gathering of officers to the driver's side of a white police cruiser. The spot lit up as an officer flicked on a high-powered flashlight. The beam's brilliance made Montez blink several times. The light trained on a bloody handprint on the driver's side door. The print, about three inches wide, and slender, definitely made by a woman. The palmprint was smudged as fingertips had dragged down through it. The person who made this had been falling, groping for something to hold onto. A desperation to the shape of the prints made him swallow hard. The five long slash marks started at the window edge and ended about a foot from the bottom of the door panel.

The single word "shit" was voiced by several people, Montez one of them.

So now Angie was not only missing, but also injured. How bad, or where was impossible to tell. Could be her hand or arm, but could also be more serious. Maybe she'd put up her hand to ward off a stabbing. Maybe she'd been shot—no, probably not, even with a silencer someone should've heard. There were literally hundreds of people around. The worst part of the whole thing, as they'd all been looking for clues to who'd stabbed Val, the perpetrator had been lurking in the bushes, probably knowing that he'd got the wrong woman, waiting for a chance to right his mistake. Or maybe, just maybe he intended to silence them both.

Montez walked back to his car, moving a lot slower than moments ago because as he stood there gaping at Angie's bloody handprint he suddenly knew exactly who'd done this. Trouble was, he didn't know where to find him. There were a million places to hide, to take a victim, to hide a body. More than a million.

Damn, why had he struck Jarvis? There were no clues, they both knew it. He couldn't send out a search squad, they didn't have clue-one where to search.

Except one place!

Forty-Five

Floating. Angie floated above the earth, looking down on fields of Queen Anne's Lace and newly hatched Monarch butterflies. Flower heads rippled like sheets on a clothesline. She heard the sharp crack as the breeze tried to tear them from the pins. On drying wings, the monarchs fluttered: orange and black snowflakes. Peaceful, carefree. Up ahead, a break in the stretch of Queen-Anne-white. A blot of green where the blossoms were pressed flat.

In the indentation, something pink, and something blue. Angie floated closer without actually moving. Someone reclining there; the sun illuminated them like a spotlight. Short blonde hair. Perky nose. A familiar face. Valerie! Angie wanted to scream out the name—opened her mouth, but no sound came to disturb the vaporous silence.

Was Val alive? As Angie focused, Val's pink shirt morphed to navy and white stripes, the jeans from light blue to navy, the blonde hair darkened and lengthened. The face melted; Val's suntanned softness dissolved in a mucky puddle leaving the body a plucked stem.

Again Angie wanted to scream, but before she could, Val's face re-formed, and became Angie's. Blood pooled around her head, caking her hair, dirtying her face. She put out a hand, wanting to touch her own lifeless cheek. An explosion of pain erupted up her arm and into her shoulder. Shards of agony rocketed into her head, blowing it apart. She heard brain matter splatter against a wall.

Wet newspapers, dirt, urine, the sick-sweet aroma of something long deceased, and the coppery scent of blood, pushed into her sinuses, wove into her senses. Like a well-worn pair of shoes it became part of her.

Angie opened her eyes. Or thought she did. Complete darkness, not a shadow showed anywhere. Not a shimmer of light. Even on the gloomiest of nights there was always some kind of light—if just the slimmest gray-yellow streak indicating the distant approach of dawn. But this darkness was intense, terrifying. This was what it felt like to be dead.

A light flicked on. Brilliant, blinding. Like a hundred suns against which closing the eyes was ineffectual. Angie threw up an arm to ward off its assault, and the pain came again, an arrow piercing her skull.

"Who's there?" Her voice came out as a croak.

"The devil," came a whisper so low she had to struggle to hear it. "You ignored the warnings."

A crack, like the sheet waving over the field of Queen Anne's lace, but closer, inches from her left ear, made her lurch to the side. Again, the pain came and she crumpled in a ball—the smallest possible target. Something moved behind the light source. A shuffle. Soft soles on concrete.

"Why don't you just kill me and get it over with?"

"Not yet."

The shuffle of feet again, and this time, a scent. Something familiar.

Angie's befuddled brain could almost focus on it. "What— are you waiting for ransom or something?"

A throaty laugh.

Who would he demand ransom from, Will? Lot of good that would do thanks to Wallace. Surely Will could amass some cash if he had to. Liquidate something. For one moment, she could feel his comforting arms around her.

The light went out. Darkness engulfed her again. She squinted into the incomprehensible blackness for any particle of light that remained. Nothing. Not a single solitary sliver.

The feet moved again, this time sounding a little further away. He was leaving. *Listen—for the location of the door. Look—for any tiny glimmer of light. Wait—for an opportunity.*

He took two gritty steps. Six feet to her left. Seven feet. Eight.

A thunk/whoosh, like a heavy door moving open. The merest flash of light as the door opened. Not light per se, just less dark, a tall rectangle of charcoal gray. No chance to glimpse anything beyond before the door clunked shut. Then, a lock sliding into place.

But the movement had rippled the air and sent that aroma back to her. Familiar but still elusive. She sniffed, but by now the scent had blended with the rest of the dreadful stench in her dungeon.

She wasn't bound or gagged, for that she was thankful. That meant her captor believed the fortress impervious and sound-proof. Guards. Perhaps a guard, or an army of men outside the door. He hadn't spoken, or acknowledged anyone when he left. Not a sound came through from outdoors, even though she strained her throbbing head to listen. No cars. No footsteps. No voices. Only rigid darkness.

Angie moved, testing her arms and wrists. She flexed her back. The pain raged everywhere, in her neck and left ankle, but mostly in her head. It didn't worsen with movement, just remained an echoing pulsation through her entire body. She sat on a mattress. Angie palmed her hand across its surface: no sheet, about six inches thick, twin bed size—and wet. She bent and sniffed, and gagged. Urine. Unmindful of the pain in her head, Angie leaped off the offensive item, bruising her knees on the cement floor.

More pain now. But, there'd been a sound. She tensed her senses, tried to hear it again. Nothing. Her knees hurt and she backed onto the merest edge of the mattress. Just enough to hold her off the floor. That sound again. A clink, sort of metallic, like a...

A chain!

She fumbled her fingers near her ankle. And found it. Large heavy links, maybe two inches each. Angie ran a hand along the length, trying to find either end. A rough surface, like one that might have held a ship's anchor, gouged from years in salt water. One link, two—she dragged it closer, counting to thirty-one before encountering resistance.

Then the tears came unchecked. For a long time Angie cried, her hands clenched around the icy cold chain. She'd been so damned caught up with her headache and her predicament that she hadn't even noticed the reason for the pain in her ankle, a shackle. An obscene ankle bracelet.

She punched at the mattress. Over and over she slammed her fist into it. While she'd thought herself unfettered, there had at least been a chance to get away, to outwit her captor, or even overpower him in some way.

She fingered the links again. It still reminded her of a ship's anchor chain. Was she on a boat? No. No lapping of water against hull. No motion at all. Like reading Braille, Angie examined each link with her fingertips, feeling not only for shape, but for imperfections, weaknesses. She had to get off the mattress and crawl to reach the other end of the chain. It was about six feet long. Through the last link was a large circular one, welded to a flat-headed thing that might be a railroad spike. The spike had recently been driven into the cement. Bits of mortar lay loose on the floor.

Perhaps she could dig the thing out.

First, examine the room. Maybe there was a chink somewhere, a boarded up window, something he missed when choosing this as a prison. It might also be wise to wait and see if he had a schedule, certain times when he'd feed her or take her to the bath—God, what is that? She put her hand on her inner thigh, then upward, to her crotch. Her pants were soaking wet. With an appalling gut-twist, she realized she'd wet herself. Sometime during that dreadful ordeal, Angelina Nadia Deacon had peed herself. She crawled back onto the mattress and wept again—for the present, for the past, for the lack of a future.

She didn't know how much time passed, if any. The dark didn't change at all. The only noise came from her rumbling stomach. Finally, that unrelenting voice in the back of her head broke through the self-pity.

Knock it off and find a way out. Pray for Val. Angie sat up, her cheeks itchy from drying tears, and she scrubbed at it with her palms. Get a grip. Stand up. Determine the size of the room.

She rose to her knees, unsteady, dizzy. Pain danced bullets down her spine and up into her head. She put a hand on the nape of her neck where the worst of it pulsed. Her fingers came away sticky with blood. Hers.

Angie felt again, probing with sensitive nurse's fingers. Two wounds. The worst on her neck: about two inches long and a half-inch wide. Not a gash. More of a dent. The blood was drying, which was good. The other wound was above her left ear, and had very little blood on it. For whatever it was worth, she'd live. For now.

Angie wobbled to her feet, stopping often, till the waves of lightheadedness and nausea abated. She put both hands in front of her, palms out, and inched her feet forward, feeling for irregularities in the floor, the wetness in her crotch a humiliating discomfort, the clanking chain a gloomy reminder.

Inch by tedious inch, Angie moved in what she thought to be a straight line, trying not to think of the possible vermin sharing her cell. This is what it must be like to be a blind person, always wondering what was around the next corner, afraid something was about to leap out at you. Frightening, so very frightening.

Finally, a wall. Cement. She feathered her fingers over the rough surface to an indentation, a gully about a half-inch wide and a foot long. Then a right angle that she followed the gully for another foot and a half or so. Cinder blocks. Her prison wasn't solid cement, it was built of sixteen inch cement blocks. Easier maybe, to gouge mortar from between them than to dig through solid wall. She'd think about that later too.

Groping to the right, always to the right, she determined the room to be about twelve by eight feet. Three walls were cinder block; no windows, either boarded up, or otherwise. The fourth wall was wood, plywood probably. She found the door, set about mid-way in the wall. The door was thick metal, like something from a walk-in cooler, with no knob or latch on her side. No blemishes in the floor except where the spike had been driven. Maybe she could get it out and use it as a weapon. What length were these things, generally?

She went back to the mattress, not caring about the wetness now. Somehow it was different being her own body fluid than that of some unknown prisoner before her. Angie's mind mulled over the possibility of other prisoners. Perhaps dozens had occupied this place before her. Perhaps none.

Her eyes had become used to the dark. She could see a little, discern walls and floor, just a bit. Or maybe it was just that her brain had registered the room's measurements and sent the image to her eyes. Where was that spotlight? It was still here, she'd listened closely and he hadn't taken it with him. While the beam bored into her eyes, it hadn't swayed or jiggled as it would if it had been hand-held or suspended on a wire. Therefore, it must be anchored, probably on the ceiling. How it was attached didn't matter, but the thought gave her something to focus on.

Angie got up again, more steady now. She felt above her in all directions, but was unable to reach the ceiling rafters or the light. She returned to the mattress and arranged herself in the same position she'd been in when the light had come on. Then she stood and moved toward where she imagined it to be. Still nothing. No break in the wall. Nowhere it might be. She raised up on tiptoes, but still couldn't reach high enough.

Of course, her estimation of its location could be off. So also could the memory of her position on the mattress. With no visual landmarks to go by, she just couldn't tell. By now, she could be all turned around. Tears threatened again, but this time she squeezed them back and went to sit on the opposite side of the mattress—to try again from that angle.

A sound, a soft rustle, like a footstep outside the cell. The latch slid back. Get him. Gouge out his eyes. But no time. She crouched on the farthest side of the room from the door.

She scurried to the mattress and lay down, trying to assume a pose that said she was upset, but resigned to her plight.

The door opened. This time, she could see, a little. For one infinitesimal second, the opening, blocked mostly by the bulk of her captor, lent a tiny glimpse—of a long room.

And, at the far side, another door. Just before the door shut, she saw something else. Shoes. Familiar shoes.

It couldn't be. Lots of people wear shoes like that. Sure, but lots of people weren't trying to kill her. Only a select few. How could she have been so foolish? So…blind?

The door closed. The latch didn't click in place. Was he getting lax already? No, it probably meant he trusted the enormous shackling chain would hold her.

The bright light flashed on. Angie didn't speak, just let her brain learn things like, the light's location—straight ahead and up—and that he'd moved a few feet into the room, and wasn't underneath the light. She needed to get him talking. Make him give something away.

Why? She'd never escape anyway.

As she fingered the thick, unyielding chain once more, a new resolve set in. Yes, she would escape. She'd hunt this animal down and—what? Kill him? Could she kill? She'd spent the last twenty-something years saving lives, helping people.

The glare of the enormous bulb made yellow spots in front of her eyes. It was then she knew—she could indeed kill him. He'd murdered three people, and he'd injured, or maybe killed Val.

For a long while, he didn't speak. Was he expecting her to beg? To humiliate herself—beyond pissing herself? That wouldn't happen. Ever. He could torture and starve her, even make her wet herself again but she wouldn't cower to him.

"How's the weather?" she asked.

There was a long hesitation before a whispered, "Dark."

Angie set her mental clock to nighttime. "Are you going to kill me?"

"Not yet."

"What are you waiting for?"

No answer.

"What I don't understand is why you're doing this."

"Tough."

Something landed on the mattress with a rustle and a thump that made her jump. "What was that?"

"Food."

Did he really think she'd eat anything he brought?

"You smell nasty. I wonder how sexy you feel now. Strutting around, flaunting yourself—like you're God's gift to the world."

Angie's fists clenched in her lap. How dare he say that? Think that? She moved her right foot a few inches. She flinched when her heel grated on the cement.

"Don't do it. I guarantee it'll hurt worse next time I hit you."

She heard him move. He was leaving. Don't go! Don't leave me alone. Stay. Talk. Give me a chance to get away. There was a tiny click and then a rumble of musical tones. It sounded like the intro for a news broadcast, but different somehow. The music stopped and a voice said, "Headline news today. Valerie Little, wife of the murdered tour boat owner in Alton Bay, died tonight."

Angie's ears stopped hearing. Anger flared like a gasoline fire. She lunged from the mattress. Flung herself at the spot she imagined his legs to be. Something, probably the radio, smashed down on her spine. Pain like a dozen rockets launched in her head.

Forty-Six

Knowing the killer's identity didn't make things any clearer. If anything, Angie was even further in the dark. She still didn't know why, but he'd murdered Nolan. Did he or Nolan have anything to do with the bags? Damn, maybe the murders weren't related to the bags at all; their presence on the boat a complete coincidence. Nero Wolfe always said *phooey* to coincidence, and once he knew the identity of the murderer, he always figured out the means and the opportunity. But that was in books, not real life.

If she thought hard enough, without outside interruptions—which wasn't a problem in here—she should be able to figure things out. Then again, what good would it do? All she'd have was the satisfaction of closing out one chapter of her life before the epilogue. Her hand touched the stuff he'd tossed on the bed: a paper bag containing what felt like a loaf of bread, and a bottle of liquid, probably water. Bread and water.

Her first inclination was to toss the stuff in the corner—show him what she thought of his alms. That would be dumb, she might be here a while and had better use her wits. Listening for the click of the security tabs, Angie unscrewed the cap and took a small sip even though she wanted to down the entire thing in one gulp.

She needed a plan. Her thoughts jumped to the spike, which tethered her chain in the cement. Loose mortar surrounded it, the spike obviously driven recently. Angie bent, the lightning bolts shot through her head and dizziness erupted, sending her back to her knees.

No bending over. How many times had she told abused women the same thing? Angie took hold of the head of the spike. About three inches across. She closed her fingers around the cap—this would make a great weapon. She wiggled it. It moved, only a little, but she was encouraged. Angie pulled up, putting the pressure into her back and thighs.

Nothing. She wiggled it again, back and forth. How long were these things usually? Two feet? Four? She continued pushing it back and forth but the hole in the cement wouldn't give. Her only chance was to yank straight up.

Slowly, Angie got to her feet and bent at the waist. The lightheaded feeling returned and she waited till it abated and she could stand without feeling like she would topple over.

She gripped the now-warm metal head in both hands, one atop the other, fingers of her left hand clenched around her right. She pulled, letting the backs of her thighs take the pressure, thankful for the diligence she'd put in at the gym.

Still nothing. She hauled up again, wiggled it from side to side, then gave an upward tug. Over and over, till back and leg muscles burned and her breath came in short urgent bursts. Between each burst of yanking and wiggling, she stopped to listen, to be sure no one was coming.

Another tug/jiggle/tug. Had the thing moved?

Angie couldn't be sure. She was so tired. To distract her brain from thoughts of exhaustion, she went back to thinking about the case, this time starting from the beginning.

Wiggle jiggle.

Seven people had gone on a fishing tour—two owners and five customers. Outside of the owners, and Montez and Sonnie, none of the others knew each other. It really did sound a lot like Gilligan's Island, except on Gilligan's Island the first mate got on everyone's nerves, not the owner.

Tug tug.

Nolan did nothing that Angie knew of, to incite something as insidious as murder, yet her captor had gone to the cockpit, picked up the knife from the tackle box and driven the blade through Nolan's heart. Just like that, no fuss, no argument. If he and Nolan had words, the other five would have heard.

Jiggle.

This time she was sure it moved. A half inch. With renewed vigor, she wiggled it again and again, this time stopping for a double sip of the room-temperature water. Put both feet beside the spike for leverage. Pull. Pull. Wiggle.

It definitely moved. The spike, which she could now tell was thick metal, about an inch across, was several inches out of the ground. More pulling. She didn't know how much time passed. There was still no glimmer of daylight in the room. Maybe there never would be.

Finally, the spike, which measured about a foot and a half in length, pulled out. It landed on the floor with a heavy thud. She flopped next to it, catching her breath, letting her muscles relax, and wondering what the hell to do next.

Angie must've fallen asleep. She woke with the smell of urine fresh in her nostrils. She flew into a sitting position, as far from the stench as she could get. And now, she really had to go. Things had reached emergency proportions. No putting it off any longer.

She listened, hoping her captor was returning. Maybe he'd take her to the bathroom. "Bah!" No he wouldn't. He was thrilled that she'd wet herself in the first place. He'd delight in seeing her grovel. That's when she'd swing the spike at his head and take herself to the bathroom. The thing must weigh ten pounds. It could put quite a dent in his head. Instinctively a hand wrapped around the head of the spike. The other went to the nape of her neck. It was sticky with fresh blood.

Angie went to her knees and urged the spike back in the hole. Then she brushed the bits of dirt and mortar that had come up with it under the edge of the mattress.

Unable to delay the inevitable any longer, she crept to the

furthest corner. She'd pulled down her still-damp pants and squatted before an idea popped into her head. It probably wouldn't work, but what did she have to lose? She crawled to the mattress, picked up the bottle of water and downed the contents. Then she peed in the bottle, a makeshift home test kit. Angie dried her hands on the rough paper bag and went back to sit on the mattress, setting the bottle on the floor beside it, hoping—praying she hadn't just made a colossal error.

What if Nolan's murder had been premeditated and not spur-of-the-moment as she'd been thinking? The killer pretended to fish, waiting for the right opportunity. She let her mind replay those few hours on the boat, blocking out the mortifying vomit scene, trying to figure how her captor fit in. Nolan abused Val verbally right from the outset. At individual times during the morning, Sonnie, Montez *and* Tyson confronted him. Will was the only one who'd held his tongue.

Nolan confronted Sonnie about smoking on the boat.

Tyson and Montez went to fish at the bow.

Nolan and Montez argued; Angie didn't know what started it, but Montez ended up striking Nolan when he called him the 'n' word. Nolan marched to the bow to "pout" as Will called it.

Valerie served lunch, shuttling dishes from the galley to the table on the galley wall. Will at the stern baiting his line. Montez and Sonnie at the stern too, whispering about something. Tyson... Where was he? Angie reran the mental video.

Tyson was fishing—at the bow! She remembered because he returned from there when Val announced lunch. How soon after that did she discover Nolan's body? Surely it wasn't more than a few minutes.

She heard a scratching sound outside the door, like soft soles on cement. Next came the raspy scrape of the hasp sliding back. She sat up straight, fighting off the dizziness that accompanied the sudden motion. The spike! Had she shoved it all the way back in the hole? Brushed away all the dirt?

The door opened. The patch of gray behind him held...

daylight. Dawn actually, which meant he'd left the outside door open. The knowledge produced a gush of adrenaline, and hope. Before the door swung shut she picked up the water bottle and leapt to her feet. Stifling the bite of guilt, she squeezed the contents in his face.

He dropped to his knees, howling. Angie tore the spike from the ground and flew past the whimpering man. Freedom!

Three steps and her feet were jerked backward. She crashed on her face. An explosion of agony ripped through her head and left elbow. He dragged her toward him; her nose and mouth scoured the cement. Her left hand clawed the mortar finding no handhold, not a single thing to slow the horrifying progress. Angie kicked out with both legs, her heels made contact with something fleshy.

He growled and his grip loosened, but he kept pulling. "You bitch." Fingernails dug her ankle, then her calf, her thigh. Closer and closer, every inch of her grated on that cement. "I should kill you right now." His breath seared her right arm.

In one movement she turned, sat up and swung the heavy spike. "This is for Valerie, you bastard!" The metal hit his skull with a hollow thump that made her stomach lurch.

His rigid hold loosened. She wrenched herself from his grasp and scrambled to her feet. Angie sprinted out the door and up three steps. Her foot caught on the rim of metal bulkhead. Again she crashed on her face. The earth was soft grass, yet the pain was intense. She scurried to her feet, draping the heavy chain around her left forearm. Angie fought the slime of her captor's blood on the spike and held on. Dawn shone on the horizon; to her light-starved eyes, it glowed like the noonday sun. She ran fifteen or twenty feet from the house before her eyes adjusted to the light. A few hundred yards east was a row of trees that looked like woods. The chain clanked, but no matter, the trees would hide her.

No thud of footsteps, no angry shouts followed. Still, she didn't look back or slow the pace. She stopped at the tree-line, crouching deep into the shadows to catch her breath. The chain was heavy and she set it down, in the silent layer of pine needles and wet leaves. Damp, stringy hair hung in her eyes. She pushed at it, but it fell back, heavy with thick, drying blood. The scent made her turn and face into the breeze coming up the hill. From here the house looked perfectly ordinary. A place any family with a dog and 2.7 children might live. A shudder rippled through her. Damn, why did all this have to happen?

In spite of the pain shooting through every molecule of her body, Angie got to her feet. She wrapped the chain around her arm. Prohibitively heavy, it cut the circulation, but this way wouldn't jangle so much. Besides, the road was only a hundred feet away. Someone must be out this time of morning, heading to work or walking a dog.

She took one last peek up the hill. Nothing moved. Where was he? Surely she didn't hit him that hard. A flash of guilt struck; first because she'd harmed someone, second because it was someone she knew.

He tried to kill you, her little voice said.

He's a human being.

No, he's an animal.

Angie skirted the edge of the woods at a lope, staying in shadows, moving toward the driveway, an easier route to the main road. The familiar neighborhood should have felt like home. This day every shadow held monsters and bogeymen.

At the top of the driveway, a motor started, a pair of headlights flicked on. They moved toward her. She pushed the lope into a sprint, ducking close to the trees. From here the driveway was less than fifty feet away. Any moment, the light might burst between the trees and illuminate her like a beacon.

The car moved at a crawl. She knew his eyes combed the property. How far could she have gotten? A woman carrying such a preposterous load would surely be slow. She stopped and lay on the ground as the vehicle crept near. The window down, she heard the broadcaster announced today's weather: sunny and in the high 90s with a dew point near 70.

The car passed. The announcer's voice faded. The taillights shrunk. Angie realized she'd been holding her breath. She took a couple of deep ones, feeling the contraction of muscles, and a painful reminder of the past hours. Angie stumbled back to her feet, faced downhill and began walking, still staying near the woods in case he returned.

The main road lay less than two hundred feet away. A left hand turn, then twenty feet later, another left led to the police station. Trouble was, between the first and second turns, there was a sizeable area of wide-open space; a veritable no-man's-land.

No choice. Angie went left. Her arm was numb, the chain preventing blood from getting to her fingers. Compared to the pain in the rest of her body, it was inconsequential. Her feet felt like stones. Each step jolted her teeth, some of which had to be loose from the pounding her face took on the cement. The back of her neck must look like a war zone. She stumbled in the open now. The second left, Main Street in sight. Twenty feet to go.

Headlights appeared. Someone going to work. She raised her right arm, intending to flag him down. The arm dropped a millisecond later. It wasn't so much the shape and size of the approaching twin beacons, but the slow speed at which they moved. He was back.

The nearest thing to provide shelter for a bloody and beaten woman was a dark-color pickup truck at the lower edge of Shipley's Restaurant. It had been there all night; dew encased the vehicle in a silvery cloud. She dug in her sneakers and ran toward it.

He started to go past. And stopped. She dove behind the truck.

He gunned the engine and swung toward it. A tremendous crash as he hit the pickup broadside. It lurched sideways, then plowed into her. The momentum knocked her to the ground. For the second time in a few days, Angie found herself under a car.

"Help!" she screamed, her voice sounding hollow and unfamiliar. The warm trickle down her cheek had to be the head wound, open again. "Help!"

Two options—why was there always a limit of two? Run. Or stay. Running would result in a chase and possible death by squishing in the road. If she stayed, he'd drag her out and beat the life from her.

Brake lights lit the area. A thump said the attack vehicle's transmission shifted. The lights dimmed. A thunk as a door opened. A dome light flashed on. And off. A foot scuffed on the tar.

Angie rolled from under the pickup and staggered to her feet. Every step pounding her brain to mush, she ran. She stayed on the shoulder because it was flat and unobstructed, and soft. Surely someone would be along any moment.

"Help!" The sound remained compressed inside her head ricocheting furiously off each corner of her brain. None of the sound managed to get out. It couldn't have or someone would have come by now.

Didn't anyone hear the crash? The slamming car door and roaring engine behind her were garbled as though underwater, but had to be his. He was leaving—running away. Too much risk of being caught. He would go back and wallow in his dungeon, trying to figure out where his plan went wrong. Forgetting about her.

Rubber screamed on pavement—toward her. In all her life Angie had never run so hard or fast; not even when she was six and the neighbor's dog bit her. Breath came in ragged lurches. Feet moved mechanically. She knew it because her brain stopped functioning when she started around the pickup truck.

The car screeched closer. She veered left and raced up an embankment, still shouting for help. No lights came on. No rescue came. Surely someone had to work at the crack of dawn. The butcher, the baker—not the candlestick maker, but what about the mailman or the milkman? Someone. Anyone.

Angie ran. Across a lawn. Up a driveway. The car followed, wheels slipping in the gravel. She ducked into the shadow of a tree.

Movement a few feet to the left. A growl, then the sensation of something moving. The clank of a chain and Angie leaped, crashing into the rough, hard trunk. The action jolted her whole body and turned her aching brain to mush. The dog lunged frantically against the length of chain.

A door opened. A voice yelled, "Shep, shut up."

Angie toppled to the wet grass. "Help," her brain screamed, but she knew words never came out.

The door slammed shut. The dog yipped on. Shep, quiet. Please stop barking. You're giving me away.

Brake lights glimmered in the driveway. A car door opened. The dome light came on.

Angie staggered to her knees. A car door shut.

Dog, please stop barking.

A silhouette stood outside the vehicle. She sensed him getting his bearings in the gloom. His head turned to the left and scanned slowly to the right. It came to rest on her—well, on the spot where she stood. Angie didn't think he couldn't actually see her. He started moving.

Angie crawled. "Help!" This time the word came out loud and clear. A spotlight came on. Angie howled in pain. Her knees gave way and she toppled to the very hard ground. "Help!"

Mercifully Shep quieted.

Something tickled her right ear, then the sound of sniffing. "Shep, back!"

Angie found the energy to lift her head. Shep's master towered above her, a vision in his bagging pajamas. His thoughtful expression showed his indecision. He probably wondered who he should call: police, ambulance or loony bin.

Angie tried to turn over. Shep started yipping again. He sprang and jerked against the chain. For one second she wondered if he was anchored by a railroad spike.

Finally the pajama-clad man moved. "Shep, shut...up." The dog obeyed. The man crouched. His fingers whispered across her face as they moved her hair from the back of her neck. "I'll call an ambulance."

"No," she managed to croak. "Police. Help me up."

"I don't think we should move you."

"Somebody...kill...me." Each word a challenge to utter.

He reacted by dropping to his knees and peering down the driveway. "I'll go inside for my phone and keys," he whispered.

"Stay where you are, I don't think he can see you." She lost sight of him as he ducked into the shadows outside the spotlight's circle. He reappeared fifteen feet from the back porch, out of sight of the attacker. In seconds he was out again, a cell phone held to his ear. He knelt beside Angie. "The cops want to know if he's got a gun."

"I don't think so."

He relayed the information into the phone. "Okay." He closed the phone and put it into the pocket of the robe he now wore. "They're on the way."

Something else she hadn't noticed; he carried a blanket, which he unfolded and wrapped around Angie's shoulders. Together they sat on the cold ground with Shep's nose pushed between their shoulders. The dog's even breathing barely audible over her hammering heart. Until he stopped, and tensed. Her heart stopped beating because, down the driveway, the dome light came back on. The hulking silhouette climbed from the vehicle. Shep stood. A growl began deep inside him. Angie felt more than heard it against her left shoulder as it rumbled into his throat like a tidal wave. Before it exited his mouth, his owner said, "Hush." The dog sat, but remained tense.

The silhouette started toward them. Forty-five feet away. Shep's owner reached up and unhooked Shep's chain. The dog stood up. "Stay." Shep obeyed, but remained watchful, waiting for the one word that would send him shooting down the driveway toward the second uninvited guest of the morning.

Thirty-five.

Thirty.

On the main road, the sound of a fast-moving car alerted

Angie's assailant. He stopped and tilted his head. She knew it was the cops. And he knew too. Indecision marred his profile. She knew he gauged time—did he have enough to kill her and escape before authorities arrived? Apparently he decided no because he whirled and sprinted back to the car. Shep's owner's arm tightened on her shoulder. The motion brought intense pain but she wouldn't allow herself to so much as wince. This man had saved her life. Angie collapsed against him. Her chain rattled, but her savior didn't seem to notice. She almost laughed. He probably thought it belonged to his dog.

Blue lights flashed into sight, lighting his car in nauseating clarity. If there'd been any doubt as to her captors' identity, all doubt disappeared in the glow of those blinking strobes. The police vehicle stopped and the scene played out below, just like on television: crouching officers, none of them Jarvis, a shadow running, two successive shouts: "Stop, police!" and "Don't shoot", then mere seconds later, the shadowy figure locked in the back of the squad car.

Two state police vehicles screamed onto the scene as one of the officers hurried up the hill. Shep wagged his tail. How did he know the cop was the good guy? The officer took one look at her and put a hand to his radio.

"No ambulance," Angie said.

"You really should go," Shep's owner said.

She would, but not till Valerie's death was totally vindicated.

They helped her into the back of a cruiser. A jackhammer played in her head, but the car cocooned her in warmth and safety and... A blast of cold air and a bright light startled her. For an instant she envisioned the attacker's spotlight in her eyes and lashed out with both fists. A soft voice told her everything would be all right. Shep's owner. Was Shep here too?

Someone took hold of her chain and spike. Two other someones helped her into the building, holding her so high her feet didn't touch the floor. Good thing because she didn't think they would've held her up. They assisted Angie down a long hallway, to a room where an enormous bolt cutter sliced off Angie's chains. She didn't watch. Nor did she look at the shackle they'd left lying on the floor.

Only three words were aimed at her, "Were you raped?"

Angie shook her head, and then a woman in street clothes escorted her to a bathroom. She remained close by watching Angie view her assailant's handiwork in the mirror. Then she helped Angie wash herself. Using many wads of rough brown paper towels, she made herself as presentable as possible, except for her urine-scented clothing, which nothing could help.

With more help, Angie shuffled to a small windowless room where the only furniture was a metal table and three chairs. In the center of the table sat a box of tissues. As she settled into a chair a huge mug of hot coffee appeared before her. Steam wafted, the aroma of hazelnut filled the air. She drank gratefully. Too sweet and too much milk, but the best thing she'd ever tasted.

Safe, warm and dry; three simple comforts she'd taken for granted. Things Angie had thought she might never have again. The door opened, making her jump, Detective Jarvis entered. The door swung shut and the automatic lock engaged. He walked forward, stopped and squinted at her. "Woman, you look like hell." He spoke into his collar-mic asking for an ambulance.

Forty-Seven

While they waited for the ambulance, Angie told her story to Jarvis and his tape recorder. "You were all busy taking Val. I went for a walk—to think." Jarvis opened his mouth. She knew he wanted to chastise her for leaving, so she spoke fast. "My life over the past week has been a complete disaster. Val's ac-accident just heaped one more thing on the pile of crap. I was feeling...I couldn't help thinking they meant to get me instead." She took a sip of the coffee. "And after what happened, I guess I was right, wasn't I?"

"We'll have to make that determination after we learn his motive. Continue."

"I came back to the motel, getting ready to go inside when I was knocked on the head. I came to. I was in a dark place. It smelled like—" Angie shivered.

The door opened and the woman officer poked her head in. "The ambulance is here."

"I really don't need an ambulance," Angie started to say when by a wave of wooziness sucked her under. The next thing she saw was the stark whiteness of the hospital ceiling. A nurse hovered over her.

"Well, well," cried Zoë Pappas, Angie's head nurse. "How do we feel this morning?"

Morning? It was still morning?

As if reading Angie's mind, Zoë said, "It's Tuesday, you've been asleep two days."

"What's wrong?"

"Outside of multiple contusions, a concussion, seventeen stitches in your head, twelve in your neck and a hundred twenty-seven in your ankle, you're just fine."

Angie laughed, surprised it didn't hurt. "What did you give me?"

"Plenty, but if you hurt I can up the dosage a bit more."

"I'm okay."

Zoë patted her arm. "In that case, are you up to a visitor?"

Angie's first thought was Will, but Zoë said, "It's a police detective." She leaned down and whispered slyly, "There something between you two? He hasn't left your side except when we threw him out."

Angie wanted to ask if Will had been there, but instead sighed. "I guess you can tell him to come in."

Jarvis stepped in the room, walking as though manure or something covered the floor. He pulled up the chair he'd obviously been sleeping in—there was a blanket tossed over the arm—and grinned at her.

"You look like you were hit by a dump truck."

"You oughta see the other guy." She managed a small smile.

"I did. What'd you hit him with?"

"The spike."

Jarvis nodded. "Good choice. So, how are you really feeling?"

"I'll live."

"I'm not being funny. I really want to know."

"Aw shucks, I didn't know you cared."

"How many times do I have to tell you? I do care."

"I thought you were being funny those times." Angie reached for the button to raise the bed a little, but he got to it first. The motor whirred, her head lifted. When she felt comfortably able to see him, she held up a hand. And got a look at her nails. Stifling a groan, she made a fist and buried it in the bedding.

"Do you feel up to talking about the other night?"

Might as well get it over with.

He took out his notebook. Compassionate Jarvis left. Cop Jarvis returned. "When did you realize Wallace was the kidnapper?"

"I recognized Will's shoes. At first...." She couldn't say any more.

"You thought it was Will."

"Right, but it didn't make sense. He was a cheater but I couldn't see him as a murderer." She hadn't seen him as a cheater either. Jarvis kindly didn't remind her of this. "I feel like such a fool for not knowing."

"Did you recognize where you were being held?"

"Not till I got away. Do you have any idea where his wife is? Marty and the kids never go anywhere."

"He says they're at his mother's. We're checking. So, he put you in his cellar."

"He came and flashed a light in my eyes. He played a...a radio where the announcer talked about Val's death."

Emotion welled up. For a long time she couldn't speak. Val was dead, all Angie's fault. How did a person live with knowledge like that? How did someone wake up in the morning and *not* think that the other person wasn't going to wake up ever again?

Angie opened her fingers and laid her palms flat on the bed. She wouldn't think about that now. If she did, she'd get out of this bed and, damn the consequences, kill Wallace herself.

"I don't get one thing. Well, there's a lot I don't get but, let's start with, what's Wallace's relationship to Nolan? I'm assuming he killed him?"

Jarvis reached into an inner pocket and withdrew the small black tape recorder from the other night. He switched it on. Wallace's angry voice filled the room, alternating with that of an interrogating officer.

"Yeah, I killed the guy."

"Why?"

"My brother paid me. He wanted the wife, what's her name—Valerie—to himself. He gave me $15,000."

A strangled sound came from Angie's throat before she could stop it. Jarvis punched the off button and leaned forward.

"Why didn't you tell me he was cheating with Val?" Angie couldn't stop the tone of accusation.

"At first, I thought you knew. Then, when I realized you didn't, I had to let things play out."

"The woman scorned."

Jarvis plucked a tissue from the box on the table and wiped her face.

"He cheated with his assistant too." She didn't—couldn't—mention the little boy.

Jarvis shook his head. "Will wasn't seeing Ms. Ferguson."

That's what Will said too. Okay, so he wasn't seeing Cassie. The momentary feeling of guilt at her accusation got squelched by the new realization. He'd been sleeping with Val! The woman Angie'd befriended. And almost got killed finding her husband's murderer. She put her palms to her face, her thumb touched a line of stitches on her throat. She explored the ragged row for a minute before daring to look Jarvis in the eye.

He turned the recorder back on. Wallace said, "to get the husband out of the way. He said we could frame Angie for it and get rid of her at the same time."

On the tape, there was a sound of a chair scraping on the floor, a door opening and Jarvis' voice saying, "Go pick up the husband."

How could Will do this? Were things so bad between them he wanted her dead? He could have just come to her and said he'd had enough. She'd have walked away—wouldn't she?

Angie suddenly felt like throwing up. She wrenched herself into a sitting position, one hand over her mouth. Jarvis gazed at her with undisguised concern. He reached out both hands as though to catch her. She swallowed several times, head bent forward, eyes squeezed tight. Jarvis didn't speak but his anxiety emanated through his hand lying on her thigh.

"I'm all right. Turn it back on."

"What about the grand theft charges against you?" the tape-recorded officer asked Wallace.

"I was just spending the money Will promised me."

"He never actually paid you?"

"He said he hadn't had time to get to the bank."

There was a stretch of silence on the tape. Jarvis flicked it off. "That's all till we talked to your husband."

Jarvis popped the tape out and slid in a second. "In this one, the brothers are together in the room." Will's voice rang clear and steady as the officer explained the situation to him and asked him to state his name. They played the Wallace tape for him. The sound of a chair being pushed back, then the sound of a struggle, and someone telling Will to please sit down and be calm.

"You expect me to be calm in the face of this—these lies?" Next Will obviously addressed his brother. "After all I've done for you! I protected you. I made excuses for you. I jeopardized my relationship with Angie because of you."

"She did all the jeopardizing herself," Wallace shouted. "Primping and cleaning..."

"If it didn't bother me, what business was it of yours?"

"She was driving you away. She wanted me out of the house."

"She was right, you should have been with your family."

"It wasn't up to her to tell me."

"How could I tell you? You had me over a barrel. The day you found out about me and Valerie, it was the beginning of the end."

Wallace made a sound like, "Pah!"

"Blackmail is bad enough, but to do it to your only brother." The sound of a chair moving again, and feet walking. Three steps, a shuffle and three more. Will must have been pacing. "I can't believe I let you do this to me."

The pacing feet stopped. "Tell me why, just tell me why you

killed Nolan. What possible reason could you have?"

The silence stretched out so long Angie thought the tape had run out. She knew Will tried to stare Wallace into submission. Finally Wallace answered, his voice quieter now, as though he'd finally realized defeat. "With him out of the way, you and Valerie could be together."

"What did you plan to do about Angie?" Will asked.

"She'd be arrested."

Footsteps sounded as Will rushed away and slammed out of the room. The officers didn't try to stop him. Angie's stomach rumbled; and not from hunger, although she couldn't remember her last meal. No doubt, Wallace planned to kill her down in that horrible dungeon.

Angie leaned back against the hard headboard. The pillows had slipped down, creating a lump behind her back, but she didn't care. Neither of them spoke. Angie watched people in the hospital parking lot—a tall woman in a green jacket, an elderly woman pushing a walker, a man battling a pair of crutches.

Jarvis's recorded voice asked. "Why did you kill Sonnie Phelps?"

"Didn't."

"What about the diver?"

"He saw me taking the bags."

"Did you kidnap Valerie?"

"No."

"Did you hire someone to do it?"

"Yeah. She woulda recognized me."

"Is he the same one who struck Mrs. Deacon?"

"Yeah."

"What's the guy's name?"

Wallace just laughed.

When Jarvis asked, "Why kill Valerie?" Angie tried not to listen. She hummed a ditty her grandmother used to sing. It didn't help block out when Wallace said, "She wouldn't stop. I warned her and she wouldn't stop. Besides, she saw me."

"When?"

"At the restaurant."

"She didn't see him," Angie said.

Jarvis patted her thigh. "I'll go and let you rest now." He put away the tape recorder and started to rise.

"No!" She wanted to holler, not to leave her alone, that she never wanted to be alone again.

He sat back down.

"Talk to me, just talk to me."

He pulled the chair closer. "How about if you talk to me, my venerable detective wannabe. Tell me how you think the murder was perpetrated?"

"Do you know?"

Jarvis' smile said he did indeed know. He got up, poured two cup of water from the pitcher on the table and handed her one.

She took a fortifying sip and handed the cup back to him. "I think Wallace borrowed a small motorboat and followed us out to Rattlesnake Island. I think he anchored out of sight and swam underwater to *Little One*. He and Will were always champion swimmers. I think he slipped on board during that last altercation between Nolan and Montez. He hid in the life jacket cabinet—it's big enough for a man to fit inside—and waited for just the right opportunity."

"What about the murder weapon? He used Nolan's filet knife. Wouldn't you think he'd bring a murder weapon with him?"

"Probably he did, but what better than to use the guy's own knife?" Angie said. "While waiting for an opportunity to kill Nolan, Wallace probably spotted the tackle box, and the knife. It was his footprint in the blood—in Will's shoes."

Jarvis nodded again. The little crinkles beside his eyes said he was impressed. He stood up. "You need to rest now. I'll come back later. I'll bring you a milkshake."

"Chocolate."

"Is there any other kind?"

When Angie awoke, Will was sitting in the chair. He gave

her a wan smile and touched her hand. "Hi."

She edged it out of his reach. "I know about you and Val."

His hands disappeared into his lap. "Oh."

"That's it? Just *oh*? Why the hell didn't you tell me when I was making a fool of myself over Cassie?"

Will lowered his eyes. "I tried. God, Ange. Cassie's mother died. I was just comforting her. Oh, what difference does it make? How many times can I say I'm sorry? I tried that day, to tell you it was Val and I, but you left. Angie, I swear Val and I broke up weeks ago. I know it's no excuse, but when I saw you becoming friends, I thought, what difference does it make who I was seeing? I fucked up, that's the main thing. I thought it might be best to let the whole thing blow over. It didn't make my culpability any less. For what it's worth, I'm really sorry."

Anger flared down her arms and into her hands. On their own, they made fists on the sheet on either side of her. "Stop telling me how fucking sorry you are!" Her voice echoed in her brain making it feel swollen and tight inside her skull. She unclenched her fists and clapped her hands to her temples.

She looked at him. "Tell me why were you acting so weird on the boat. If you and Val had broken up, what was bothering you?"

"Nothing."

"Don't give me that, Will. I might have been blind to your infidelity but I wasn't blind to that. Even...even Val noticed something was wrong." Angie swallowed. She hated saying the betraying woman's name. God she was surrounded by betrayal.

Will pounded his fists on the bed. "Dammit, I knew he was going to—"

She frowned. "You knew Wallace planned to kill Nolan? And you let it happen? God Will, I don't even know you any more."

"No. No. I didn't know what he planned. But I knew something was up. The night before, Wallace said, 'A lot of things are going to change in the next few weeks.' I pressured him a little and he finally said he'd decided to get his life back on track. He was getting off the beer and making another go with Marty. He got all teary-eyed and said he wished the two of them had as good a relationship as we had. At the time, I accepted what he said. I mean, it was something we both hoped for. I didn't tell you but right after his arrest, Marty took the kids and went to her mother's. She told him it was over, she'd had enough of his laziness and inconsideration. So, when he said that stuff, I believed him. Wouldn't you?"

No, she almost said, I wouldn't have believed him if he'd said the sky was blue.

"If only I'd pushed him harder, maybe things would've been different."

"If you'd pushed him—"

"I know if I'd pushed him years ago none of this would've happened. It's going to be hard to live with—knowing I caused all this."

Part of her wanted to tell him he wasn't all to blame. Part of her wanted to kiss him and never stop. Part of her wanted to punch him in the face.

Forty-€ight

Damn the bitch! Damn them both! He punched the brick cell wall. Once. Twice. Damn them all! He should've killed them when he had the chance. That's what he got for going all sentimental.

So what if it was his brother—his twin brother, god damn it—both women went gaga over? They were wrong for Will and he was too stupid to realize it. Weren't identical twins supposed to be alike, inside and out? Well, he'd never seen two people less alike. Where he let logic and sensibility guide him, Will was ruled by his crotch. It had always been that way. All through school he'd had to bail Will out with his parents, even going so far as to impersonate the fool so he could screw whatever bitch he was with. And he'd never once said thank you. Never fucking once.

Damn women! None of them could be trusted. Especially the disloyal bitch he married. The first sign of trouble and she left, lock stock and smoking barrel. After all he'd done to protect her, hanging out at Will's day after day just so she wouldn't worry about him being out of work again.

It just proved what he'd always believed: you should never do anything for anybody. You always got screwed. Upstairs, the heavy metal door opened. The air pressure changed. The rotten ass smell stirred up. He wanted to vomit. The door clanked shut. Footsteps started down the stairs. He wiped the blood from his knuckles on the sheets and stood up.

That kiss-ass Sergeant Wilson stood there big as you please. "Turn around," Wilson said, holding out the handcuffs. The things clicked shut, cutting off the circulation to his hands. The cell door opened.

Damn them all! Damn them to hell!

Forty-Nine

Nearing dusk the next day Jarvis dropped off Angelina at the motel. He'd moved her belongings to another room. "Are you sure you'll be all right?"

"Yes. Thanks. I just need a hot bath and some sleep." She waited in the motel door till he'd driven away.

She padded to the bathroom, Will's confession rang in her ears along with his subsequent request that she come home with him, let him make things up to her. He had to think her completely weak and without scruples if she'd just climb in the car and act like nothing ever happened. Besides, she needed time to think about the Will/Valerie thing.

She took off the clothes Jarvis brought for her to wear home, and slipped into her soft, fluffy robe. She pulled it tight around her, savoring the feel of the fleece fabric. The face that looked back from the bathroom mirror couldn't be hers. Her hair stuck out in all directions. Her nose swollen to twice its size. Both eyes were black and her right cheek scraped raw. The wounds on her neck and the back of her head had thick crusty scabs. Angie laughed out loud. This was the person Jarvis "cared about"? The man must have no taste at all.

She'd just crouched to turn on the water when a knock came at the door. It had to be Will, come to apologize again. Then she remembered, Jarvis said nobody knew where she was.

Tyson's voice called, "Angie, can I come in?" She tightened

her robe and opened the door. "Wow, Jarvis said you looked like hell. Can I come in a minute?"

He drew a piece of paper from his back pocket, unfolded it and handed her a check in the amount of $112,000. Was this shut-up money from the Black Bag Gang? Maybe it was payment to keep her mouth closed about the spreadsheet. Should she tell him Jarvis already knew?

Tyson sat uninvited in the chair near the table. Angie remained standing. She waved the check at him. "What's this?"

"Remember I told you I'm good with money? And remember Valerie said she'd have $50,000 from Nolan's insurance?"

"Yes."

"Well, I took an imaginary $50,000 and invested it. Since Valerie's gone, I think you should have it."

"Her sons should have it."

"I have another check for them."

"Holy shit, Tyson. How much—no, never mind, I don't want to know." She laid the check on the table. "I can't take this."

He shoved the check aside with his elbow.

"You made that much money in just a few days?"

"In a few hours, actually. But you have to promise not to tell my father because if he knew I could do this, he'd drag me into business with him."

"Why not when you have such a talent for it?"

"Because I hate it."

"What do you want to do with your life?"

"Well, I thought I could make good money fixing businesses for people. You know, showing them how to improve their bottom line. I tried with Nolan and look where it got me, practically accused of murder."

"That was your spreadsheet Jarvis found on Nolan's boat?"

"Yeah, I met with him the day before and gave it to him. He turned me down flat, saying he'd deal with his own finances. I went on the boat hoping to convince him to change his mind."

"What are you going to do now?"

"What I would like is for you two to invite me into business with you."

"Business?"

"You said you'd wanted to open a neighborhood theater. I can act. I'm stronger than I look; I can move scenery and—I also know a lot of people and can get backing from big investors."

She stopped listening. Her own business. What about it? She'd always wanted a theater, but had never seriously considered it—especially after Wallace ran off with their money.

"Well?"

"Give me a few days to think about it."

"Fair enough." Tyson stood up. "Hey, you won't believe what happened to me the other day. Remember when we were having lunch at WG's and my car alarm went off? Turns out I was robbed. Somebody took my gym bag. And my favorite sneakers."

"Is that right? How odd."

The phone rang just then. Tyson went to the door. "I'll call you tomorrow."

"You said a couple of days."

"I'll call you tomorrow."

Angie shut the door and answered the phone. "Hi Jarvis."

"How're you feeling?"

"I'm fine, why? You did just leave, you know."

"Get dressed, I'll be around to pick you up."

"I'm really tired."

"It'll only take a while. There's something I want you to see."

"Okay."

Jarvis arrived twelve minutes later. At the police station, he led her to the same little room as the day before. Montez overflowed one chair. He smiled at her and her insides puddled in her toes. In the middle of the table sat a black duffel bag. Mesmerized, she approached it.

Jarvis shut the door and came to stand at the head of the table. "I'm sure you remember Mr. Clarke. He was instrumental in bringing your Black Bag Gang to an end."

"You really did it?" she asked Montez.

Jarvis groaned. "And I thought this was going to be a surprise."

"That you've closed up the gang is a surprise, if it makes you feel any better."

"How did you know Mr. Clarke was working with us?"

"He told me."

"I did not. She guessed."

Jarvis rolled his eyes and tweaked his mustache. "Just once, I'd like to know something she doesn't already know."

"I don't know what's in the bags," Angie suggested.

"Guns," Montez said.

"The back room of the restaurant was the distribution center," Jarvis explained.

"The gang smuggled the guns from South Jersey. Alton Bay was their final stop before Canada. They brought them here by couriers, like Sonnie and me."

"Then, depending on where they were being shipped. Mr. Clarke and his partner delivered them. When they used the fishing tour, they lowered the bags over the edge, then telephoned the next couriers who picked them up and took them out through Canada."

"Wow." Nothing else she could say.

"There's more." Jarvis cleared his throat. "Your brother-in-law was involved up to his scruffy little eyebrows. He was the Canadian courier. His job was to pick up the bags from the drop-off point—"

"In the lake?"

Jarvis nodded. "Then he took them to the next drop-off spot in Quebec. As we speak, authorities are wrapping up things from that end. Penalties for gunrunning in Canada are strict. Wallace won't be bothering you for a very long time."

God, Will would be a basket case. "That explains why he was in Meredith that day."

"Just coming back from a drop," Jarvis said.

"That's why you were there too."

"Right."

"But why did he kill Nolan?"

Montez and Jarvis looked at each other. Jarvis nodded. Montez leaned ahead, spilling much of his weight onto the table. "Nolan was the ringleader—for this district."

"What! Did Valerie know?"

"No," Jarvis said.

"Okay, here's how it went. Sonnie's mother was killed when he was five. His father dumped him on the street and ran off. Nolan, whose real name is Victor, found him and took him in."

"Wait!" Angie called, wincing. "Victor—Vic. I found a picture in Sonnie's apartment. A white guy and a young Sonnie. One of the names on the back of the picture was Vic."

"Where's that picture now?" Jarvis asked.

"In my suitcase."

He shook his head, disbelieving.

Montez continued, "Sonnie and Nolan's home was the gang's headquarters. Anyway, the gang got into gunrunning. After a while, they expanded the business northward. Six years ago, Nolan came to Alton Bay and set up the fishing tour business. Nolan spotted Valerie one day, and thought marriage would make a good cover. He introduced himself and months later they got married. As for WG's involvement. Nolan either knew, or hired their bartender, who arranged for a back room to be used as a meeting place. By the way, there's no indication that either Tyson or his father knew of the deception."

"I don't understand why Nolan treated Val so bad," Angie said. "If he was trying to keep everything quiet and calm."

"Here's what I think," Jarvis interjected. "He grew to really care for her. His work, the deception preyed on him. The guilt grew. His treatment of her worsened. Perhaps, deep inside, he was trying to make her leave him."

"In one small way," Montez said, "it's good she's dead

because this would kill her."

"There is one other good thing that came of this. Our research found a safe deposit box in Nolan's name. It held several hundred thousand dollars. I'm going to do my best to see Valerie's sons get it."

Angie didn't want to hear any more about the two-faced Valerie. One of those faces she'd liked very much.

"Do you mind if I ask how you got involved?" Angie said to Montez.

There was that smile again. He sobered and leaned forward, his elbows bracketing a cup of coffee. "My sister Shanda was playing outside one day. She got caught in some gang crossfire. Shot in the spine. It was touch and go for months. She had to have six surgeries." Montez sucked his lungs full of air and let it out as he spoke. "Anyway, the bills started coming in; over a hundred thousand, right off the bat. Our parents worked but we were barely getting by. I was eighteen. She was six." He shrugged. "Sonnie convinced me to go to work for them. I could get the bills paid in a couple of years." He shrugged again.

"The bills got paid, but they wouldn't let you out," Angie said.

"When Jarvis pulled me in for questioning it seemed like a good time to come clean."

"What will happen now?"

"I'll go to court with him," Jarvis said, "see if I can convince the judge of the extenuating circumstances."

"How is your sister?"

"She's in a wheelchair, but her attitude has improved since I opened the computer shop. She practially runs the place. Besides, she's my biggest fan."

"I'd like to meet her sometime."

"She wants to meet you too."

Oh boy, he'd told his sister about her! Angie stood up to go, but stopped. "One more question, Jarvis: that spreadsheet of Tyson's. Did you figure out what it was doing on the boat?"

"Apparently, it's how he earned his spending money. He'd poke around small businesses looking for ways things could be improved, then he'd outline these things and get the owner to hire him to implement the changes."

"So he was telling the truth."

"You know about that too?"

"He approached Nolan, but Nolan turned him down. When Tyson and Paula ended their date on the dock that morning, he saw *Little One* going out and figured maybe he could convince Nolan to hire him."

So, Tyson really was legit. The check wasn't shut-up money or Black Bag Gang money. She pulled open the door.

"Needless to say, this is all hush hush," Jarvis said, getting up and coming around the table. Montez remained in his chair, grinning that Chiclet smile.

Jarvis stepped into the hall with her. "Angelina, I'll be done here in an hour, want to have dinner?"

"If we can eat someplace dark."

He touched her bruised cheek with a forefinger. "I'll get Wilson to drive you back."

Seated in a hot bath ten minutes later, she leaned a very weary head against the wall. So many things to think about: husbands, lovers, neighborhood theaters and checks for $112,000. "Yes, sometimes a decision really does come back to bite you in the ass."

The End

Angie gets into more trouble in the sequel

PLAY WITH FIRE

Excerpt:

Tyson's voice rang out in the theater announcing the start of Act Four. As the buzz of voices in the auditorium died Jarvis straightened his spine, drew the pillowcase bag from his pocket and stepped on stage. He crossed, almost on tiptoes, to the mantle and picked up the crystal figurine. As the curtain started to rise, he prepared to drop the statuette in the bag.

John and his little blonde daughter entered the living room from the left. "Okay, let's get your milk and get you back to bed." As they reached center stage, he spotted Jarvis. He thrust the girl behind him and held her there. "Who the hell are you?"

Jarvis reached into his pocket and pulled out the gun. He shook it at John. "Get over there."

John, keeping the child behind him, moved. "What do you want with us?"

"Kind of stupid question since I'm loading your stuff in this sack, dontcha think?"

John shoved the girl. "Get behind the sofa. Stay there." To Jarvis he said, "Take what you want. Just hurry up and get out."

From off stage, Brianna called, "Roman, can you come here, I've fallen."

John made a step toward the bedroom. "My wife has fallen out of her wheelchair. She might be hurt."

"If she was hurt she woulda said so."

"I'm going to her. You can shoot me in the back if you want."

Jarvis ran at him, clubbing John above the right ear with the butt of the gun. John dropped to his knees then sprang back to his feet. Jarvis raised the gun. John head-butted him in the chest. Jarvis lurched backward, but caught himself on the back of a chair. It looked so real Angie almost cheered. The gun swung downward. It went off.

John dropped to the floor. Jarvis looked at him, at his bag, and back at John. Then he sprinted for the door. Angie wanted to applaud. Jarvis had played the part to perfection. But why wasn't John getting up? He lay on the green print area rug, feet splayed the way he'd fallen, arms clutching his chest. There was a circle of blood on the rug—and his tan cotton shirt.

"Drop the curtain!" Angie screamed.

Play With Fire Coming SOON!

About Author Cindy Davis

Cindy Davis, editor, dressed in baggy sweats and floppy slippers is tied to her desk in southern New Hampshire for twelve hours a day. When she's finally set loose, she appears as a writer researching new and different venues and plot ideas for her mysteries. Chances are she's probably wearing jeans and t-shirt, unless it's snowing—again.

She's edited over 150 books, more than three quarters of which have been published.

Cindy is the author of five novels and three non-fiction books. Be sure to check out Cindy's new release *A Page from the Past*. And watch for the sequel to this Angie Deacon novel, *Play with Fire*.

Visit Cindy on her websites:
www.cdavisnh.com
www.fiction-doctor.com

Printed in the United States
150400LV00004B/92/P